THE END OF ENLIGHTENMENT

Other great stories from Warhammer Age of Sigmar

DIRECHASM
Various authors
An anthology of short stories

THUNDERSTRIKE & OTHER STORIES
Various authors
An anthology of short stories

HARROWDEEP
Various authors
An anthology of novellas

COVENS OF BLOOD
A novel by Anna Stephens, Liane Merciel and Jamie Crisalli

DOMINION
A novel by Darius Hinks

A DYNASTY OF MONSTERS
A novel by David Annandale

CURSED CITY
A novel by C L Werner

THE END OF ENLIGHTENMENT
A novel by Richard Strachan

STORMVAULT
A novel by Andy Clark

BEASTGRAVE
A novel by C L Werner

REALM-LORDS
A novel by Dale Lucas

GHOULSLAYER
A novel by Darius Hinks

GITSLAYER
A novel by Darius Hinks

HALLOWED GROUND
A novel by Richard Strachan

• HALLOWED KNIGHTS •
Josh Reynolds

BOOK ONE: PLAGUE GARDEN
BOOK TWO: Black Pyramid

• KHARADRON OVERLORDS •
C L Werner

BOOK ONE: Overlords of the Iron Dragon
BOOK TWO: Profit's Ruin

THE END OF ENLIGHTENMENT

RICHARD STRACHAN

BLACK LIBRARY

A BLACK LIBRARY PUBLICATION

First published in 2021.
This edition published in Great Britain in 2021 by
Black Library, Games Workshop Ltd., Willow Road,
Nottingham, NG7 2WS, UK.

Represented by: Games Workshop Limited – Irish branch,
Unit 3, Lower Liffey Street, Dublin 1,
D01 K199, Ireland.

10 9 8 7 6 5 4 3 2 1

Produced by Games Workshop in Nottingham.
Cover illustration by Alexander Mokhov.

The End of Enlightenment © Copyright Games Workshop Limited 2021. The End of Enlightenment, GW, Games Workshop, Black Library, Warhammer, Warhammer Age of Sigmar, Stormcast Eternals, and all associated logos, illustrations, images, names, creatures, races, vehicles, locations, weapons, characters, and the distinctive likenesses thereof, are either ® or TM, and/or © Games Workshop Limited, variably registered around the world.
All Rights Reserved.

A CIP record for this book is available from the British Library.

ISBN 13: 978-1-78999-958-7

No part of this publication may be reproduced, stored in a retrieval system, or transmitted in any form or by any means, electronic, mechanical, photocopying, recording or otherwise, without the prior permission of the publishers.

This is a work of fiction. All the characters and events portrayed in this book are fictional, and any resemblance to real people or incidents is purely coincidental.

See Black Library on the internet at

blacklibrary.com

Find out more about Games Workshop
and the worlds of Warhammer at

games-workshop.com

Printed and bound by CPI Group (UK) Ltd, Croydon, CR0 4YY

The Mortal Realms have been despoiled. Ravaged by the followers of the Chaos Gods, they stand on the brink of utter destruction.

The fortress-cities of Sigmar are islands of light in a sea of darkness. Constantly besieged, their walls are assailed by maniacal hordes and monstrous beasts. The bones of good men are littered thick outside the gates. These bulwarks of Order are embattled within as well as without, for the lure of Chaos beguiles the citizens with promises of power.

Still the champions of Order fight on. At the break of dawn, the Crusader's Bell rings and a new expedition departs. Storm-forged knights march shoulder to shoulder with resolute militia, stoic duardin and slender aelves. Bedecked in the splendour of war, the Dawnbringer Crusades venture out to found civilisations anew. These grim pioneers take with them the fires of hope. Yet they go forth into a hellish wasteland.

Out in the wilds, hardy colonists restore order to a crumbling world. Haunted eyes scan the horizon for tyrannical reavers as they build upon the bones of ancient empires, eking out a meagre existence from cursed soil and ice-cold seas. By their valour, the fate of the Mortal Realms will be decided.

The ravening terrors that prey upon these settlers take a thousand forms. Cannibal barbarians and deranged murderers crawl from hidden lairs. Martial hosts clad in black steel march from skull-strewn castles. The savage hordes of Destruction batter the frontier towns until no stone stands atop another. In the dead of night come howling throngs of the undead, hungry to feast upon the living.

Against such foes, courage is the truest defence and the most effective weapon. It is something that Sigmar's chosen do not lack. But they are not always strong enough to prevail, and even in victory, each new battle saps their souls a little more.

This is the time of turmoil. This is the era of war.

This is the Age of Sigmar.

PART ONE

PROLOGUE

THE DEAD MARCH

The light in the distance seemed to buckle and contract, a pale amethyst that deepened to a purple shade. The ground, grey and desolate, began to rise on a slight incline. As the army marched it left in its wake a great ribbon of dust that billowed out and rose up towards a blackened sky. Ahead, the steppes of Shyish rolled on only into a deepening shadow, the dead lands of the Equuis Main. There were no hills, no forests, no settlements, no life. There was only dust and desert, and a breeze that blew a cold melody across the flags and pennants of the marching host.

Tuareth Y'gethin reached again for the brooch on the tassel at her wrist, but of course it wasn't there. Her brother Carreth had it, back in Ymetrica. She had wrought it herself, spending many a moon of craft and artistry to get it right. She had given it to him as a small token to heal the rift that had grown between them. He had taken it from her with a look in those proud grey eyes that was for a moment almost like regret, but then the stern and unyielding mask had come down once more and he had coldly bid her goodbye.

The scholar's mask, Tuareth thought with sadness. *But he had been a warrior once...*

She turned her mind from these lost thoughts, looking out instead over the serried ranks of her Vanari wardens. One hundred and fifty strong, they marched in immaculate lockstep, their pikes levelled and their cloaks ruffling in the breeze. What light there was in this benighted realm dazzled on the tips of their sunmetal spears. The pale cream of their armour was unmarred by dirt or dust. They were the colours of the morning, after the brash announcement of the dawn had faded into something cleaner and purer.

The Luminous Host...

For a moment she almost pitied the foe they had been sent here to face. But pity was another emotion the aelves of the Lumineth Realm-lords had long been taught to master. Pity was a weakness, as were anger and rage. As Tuareth raised her sword and issued the command to close the gap with the regiments on either side, she knew with cold certainty that their enemies would show them no pity in return.

As she glanced beyond her own regiment, she saw the next in line marching in similar precision, and the next beyond that, and the next, and all the other Vanari regiments on either side, a sea of clear blue and white and gold. Behind the wardens marched the Vanari Auralan sentinels, their bows held lightly, their arrows nestled in their quivers. On either flank, a mile apart, rode the great surging tides of the Dawnrider cavalry, their stallions snorting and scuffing the ground in distaste at this slow, unseemly pace. Onwards the host marched, inviolable, thousands of troops in blocks of infantry, archers and horse. And yet as the army strode on, the sound of its progress was barely more than a mutter in the dead air of Shyish, a faint scuffle swallowed by the endless plains. Dead grass crunched underfoot. Old, wind-dried bones shattered under marching boots. The grey sand mingled with the dust to rise above them as a vast ensign announcing their presence – the Lumineth Realm-lords had come at last.

Tuareth raised her hand to touch her breastplate, where *Senlui*, the rune of swiftness, gleamed in gilded light. On either side, her warriors bore whichever runes they had dedicated themselves to, representing each branch of the Hysha-Mhensa. *Senthoi*, firm and yet welcoming; *Ydriliqi*, the force of the flowing river; intricate *Ylvan*, the sign of pride and honour, and the honesty of imperfection. Tuareth tried to calm her impatience as she touched the rune. War had come to Shyish, and if one thing was certain, it was that Nagash of all beings would not meekly submit. The necroquake, his great working, had been unleashed. Reality itself had been assaulted, and the thin places of the realms had to be sealed before his foul death magic destroyed them all. It was inevitable. Tuareth thought of her brother again, turning his face from her arguments.

Nothing is inevitable, Carreth had said. *If you unleash war, you unleash emotions that cannot be contained... You make a choice, my sister. Ensure it is the right one.*

It could not fail to be the right one, Tuareth thought with a grimace. *For how can anyone live in peace with a sword hanging over their head? And Nagash holds the very realms at ransom.*

A boom of thunder reached out across the plains, rhythmic and precise. As the army drew closer, Tuareth saw high black shapes rising from the mist ahead. The peaks of distant mountains, she thought at first, but then as they crossed the empty steppe the mists drew apart like a sundered veil. Beneath their gauzy wrapping, still a mile distant, were revealed the spires of three great towers, harsh and disturbingly precise in every cut and facet. They gleamed like oiled obsidian, a morbid crackle of green lightning playing around them. Between each tower was a curved curtain wall, with here and there a gatehouse or a lower keep built into the sweep of the fortifications. Spaced regularly along the curtain walls were strange pyramidal braziers, which sputtered a green fume into the air, wreathing the fortress – if such it was – in a pallid shroud of smoke. The boom of thunder came again, clashing like a hammer blow in some almighty forge.

A ripple passed through the aelven army as the fortress came into sight. Not fear, Tuareth knew, not unease or disquiet, but something more like certainty.

'The long march is at an end, high warden,' Dae'annis said at her side. He gripped his pike tightly, his mouth a grim line. A lock of yellow hair had come untethered from his helmet and danced in the breeze around his face. He looked at her and offered a thin smile. 'I confess – all of our months of training, and I'm still nervous.'

'Training is one thing,' Tuareth said. 'But now the real work begins.'

Calls rang out further down the Lumineth line, although in truth the orders were redundant. The arts of war were studied with as much dedication and seriousness in Lumineth society as the arts of peace, and each regiment knew as if part of some intricately wrought mechanism when to halt. All across the front of the army, marching feet stopped with utter precision. With a clatter of arms, pikes were brought to bear and bows strung with the first nocked arrows. The wind whispered across the sand. The only other sound was the flapping of cloth from the Realm-lords' ensigns.

Tuareth looked out across the span of empty ground towards the fortress, silent and mysterious, abhorrent in its dark majesty. The towers and the curtain walls, she realised, were not made of obsidian at all. Rather, they had been constructed from some kind of oiled black bone, moulded into new shapes and retaining in some places a hint of its previous form – skulls, femurs, ribcages, spines. As she looked down at her feet, and as the breeze erratically scraped a layer of dust away, Tuareth realised that the very ground they were marching across had given way to bone. The army was standing in the middle of a colossal avenue, which stretched on across the plains towards the fortress, and reached out behind them towards the limits of the Equuis Main. The avenue was covered with traceries and fissures like the plates of a skull.

More orders were given, the aelven voices ringing like the peal of a silver bell from unit to unit. As each order was given, so the soldiers of the Lumineth Realm-lords obeyed.

'Triple line!'

'Wardens to the front!'

'Nock arrows!'

'Form up!' Tuareth shouted. 'Triple line!'

She held up her sword, and around her the wardens, as fluid as a mountain stream, refashioned themselves into a block three deep and fifty wide. She saw another regiment sprinting to form up on their left flank, and then two more units to form the flank beyond them. To her right, the bulk of the army swung slightly in one unbroken line to match the frontage of the black fortress ahead of them, thousands of troops moving with perfect symmetry, not a step out of place. Reserve units dressed their ranks, and behind them the Vanari sentinels plunged spare arrows into the dead earth. The twang of tested bow strings quivered in the air like the notes of some strange instrument. Thrumming through the lines of the Lumineth host came the fierce, static charge of woven magic. Their weapons gleamed like the first bold blaze of sunrise.

Tuareth stilled her mind, felt her breath settle. She reached out and touched her thoughts against the sunmetal of her wardens' pikes. She felt the elements inside the metal contract and expand, combine and fall away. She felt the essence of the dust around her, the structure of the air, the energies that flowed and surged between each element of life. Although a high warden's magical skills were nowhere near the level of the Alarith Temples, it was the easiest thing in the world for her to take a strand of that energy and weave it into new shapes, and to charge those shapes with all the force of light itself. Right across the army, the Lumineth's weapons glowed with a golden heat.

That you should miss this, Carreth, my brother. The light of Hysh has come down to the underworlds, down to the darkest places in the realms...

She looked at Dae'annis and smiled. And then the gates of the fortress opened.

'Close ranks! Close ranks!' she screamed. 'Form square!' A haze of dust smothered her as the cavalry came on again. Blood gushed down her face from the cut in her scalp. Her helmet was a shattered ruin somewhere on the ground at her feet. She heard Dae'annis grunt as he swung his pike to her left, stabbing out with it and plucking one of the dead riders from its stinking steed. The skeletal figure came slipping down the shaft, gnashing its mismatched teeth, a mad glow in its green eyes. Tuareth snapped out with her sword and beheaded it, and Dae'annis flung the carcass away. Shadows and flame, the flash of blood. The dead riders charged in again, like a landslide sweeping all before them, hacking down with their scimitars, flinging bone-barbed spears deep into the Vanari lines. The horses – if they were horses – barged into the front rank, trampling aelves under their hooves, their riders stabbing in and out with their short swords.

In moments, the two armies had gone from wary appraisal into the hellish maelstrom of combat. The enemy had formed up in front of their fortress with all the calm precision of a parade: massive blocks of infantry, fifty deep at least; squadrons of skeletal horses; catapults that shimmered across the plain on creeping feet. Units of gigantic warriors with four arms and huge, gleaming falchions stood on their flanks. Their mages floated across the length of the field on waves of necromantic energy or picked their way between the ranks on bizarre walking platforms that scratched the ground with clawed feet. The two armies had stood there watching each other, appraising, judging, no more than five hundred yards apart. Then, as the Lumineth host readied itself to advance, the gates yawned wide once more and a great flood of cavalry came boiling out onto the plain, tearing off to the left, flocking like some dread murmuration into a lance of thundering armoured horse. It had crashed into the Lumineth flank like a thunderstorm, a billowing cloud of dust sweeping up in its wake, blinding the entire front as the enemy war machines began hurling their ammunition deep into the aelven host. Then all had been madness and death, the brutal press of hand-to-hand combat, the insane confusion of war.

The enemy horses now moved off, flowing around the aelves' left flank and disappearing into the haze, just the terrible thunder of their hooves shaking the air around them. Tuareth risked a glance to her right and saw through the dust and sand that the Vanari square had collapsed. There were riders behind them and the enemy's infantry were now crashing into their front.

'Reform!' she cried. 'The line's broken! Reverse wheel on the right flank!'

Leering skulls rose from the mist before her, grinning, hacking, pushing forward with their shields. She stabbed out with her sword, parried, cut, shearing off splinters of bone, hewing arms and skulls. They were being pushed back and her feet crunched dead bone underfoot, dead flesh from the aelves who had fallen in the first assault. She tripped, landed badly, her ankle twisting under her, raising her sword in a wild block as a spear point came stabbing down. She felt it plunge into her shoulder and screamed, her vision black – and then Dae'annis was there, sweeping his pike in a great arc over her, like bright lightning shattering the skeletons as they swamped over the front rank.

'The whole regiment has fallen!' he shouted as he pulled her to her feet.

'Move back,' she cried. 'Link up with the regiments on our right. If we let ourselves get surrounded, we're dead!'

How has it come to this? she thought. *How have we misjudged them so badly?*

Her left arm hung uselessly at her side, blood pouring from her shoulder. She pointed with her sword, screamed for the remaining soldiers to fall back and reform, but whether they heard her or not she couldn't tell. She could barely see any survivors, just here and there the flash of sunmetal, the crackling blue stab of magic surging through the dust. For a moment it just seemed to be her and Dae'annis, huddled together in a sea of corpses – dead aelves, dismembered skeletons. Except, she realised, they weren't skeletons, not really. She had seen the servants of Nagash before, the resurrected dead, but these warriors were different somehow. They were like weird constructs, things that from sheer habit may have taken the shape of men but were instead a grim assemblage of disparate bone-stuff. She had even heard them talking, their captains issuing orders in a harsh, clashing language just as the Lumineth officers issued their orders in turn.

'What are these things?' she muttered. 'What have we done?'

Doubt crept along the borders of her thought, hungering in the darkness. She turned her mind against it. She touched her breastplate, where *Senlui* still glowed, untarnished.

Be swift as the wind, swift as light. Let light splinter the darkness and cast it aside.

More joined them, other wardens leaping the corpses and taking up position next to her, the great blue crests of their helmets tattered or streaked with blood. A dozen more came staggering through the dust, and then another ten. They presented arms, pikes bristling like the spines of some vicious beast. Tuareth intoned her spells, weaving her magics, charging the sunmetal with all the blazing light of Hysh. She could hear aelven voices far off to her right, where the centre of the host had taken up position. Some of them were still alive, it seemed. There was a sound in the air, high above the clash of steel and the thunder of hoofbeats, that reminded her of breaking glass. It was bone, she realised. Bone shattering under forceful blows, rendered into pieces by the interlocking fields of charged magic. The Realm-lords were still fighting, somewhere in that sea of dust.

'We are all that remains of the left flank,' Tuareth called out to her troops, her voice breaking with pain. 'We are the last light in the darkness, and we need to hold this position, come what may. Sell your lives as dearly as you can, in the name of Teclis himself. For if we fall now, the entire host will be rolled up and destroyed. Do I need to remind you of your duty?'

'No!' two dozen voices cried back.

'Will you let the light of Hysh die in this benighted place!'

'No!'

Despite everything, despite the blood pouring down her face, her arm now numb beyond all repair, Tuareth smiled. She heard the tramp of marching feet, the rumble of hooves clashing over the plains, and she gripped her sword tight.

'Here they come!' Dae'annis shouted. He bared his teeth, crouched to receive the charge, the bright metal of his flared shoulder guards catching what light remained to gleam with purity and grace. Tuareth peered into the dust and saw the Bonereapers' cavalry careering onwards, dark shapes looming in the haze. At their head rode an ornately armoured figure on a tusked steed, his skull capped with a crested helmet of gleaming bone, a tattered cloak snapping out from his skeletal shoulders. He shrieked something incomprehensible in a voice like the dry crackle of flames and lowered his scimitar. He pointed directly at Tuareth, the troop of dead steeds leaping the bodies that littered the ground ahead of their position, the sound of their hooves drowning out the world.

'Hold!' Tuareth screamed. 'Hold the line!'

She tried to snatch the moonfire flask from her belt, but with her ruined arm she could merely scrabble at the clasp – and then the dead were on them, and the wardens were swept aside in a furious tangle of spears and shields, blood and dust and buckled armour.

Tuareth leapt right, thrusting with her sword, a jolt up to her elbow snatching the blade from her grip. She crashed to the ground, spat, rolled over, slithered down a pile of dead. Her forehead struck rock, sparking a white light behind her eyes. She heard a surge of water and realised it was the blood rushing in her ears. She saw a pike on the ground, spun it around without looking and tangled it in the legs of one of the dead horses as it crashed past, riderless, the great heap of bone thundering to the ground and cleaving the skull from its neck. She saw Dae'annis drifting through the mist, two other wardens with him, shouting something that she couldn't hear. She tried to stand, fell, looked down to see a shard of bone stabbing out of her broken thigh. She tried to scream but the breath had died in her lungs.

A shadow fell across her.

The leader of the cavalry, the Bonereapers' general, jewels throbbing with unlight in his crested helm, armour oily with a sick green glow. As if seeing it all in a dream, Tuareth watched him rear back on his steed, scimitar raised. The jaws of his skull stretched wide – as if the dead could laugh and found in the living only the simple stuff of cruel amusement.

The blade came down. Tuareth took the moonfire flask from her belt with her good hand. She whispered a prayer and threw it to the ground in front of her, and before the flames claimed her she seemed to see the light of Hysh expanding over the dead lands, washing her with its healing balm, reaching out and sweeping the corpse-things away and leaving in their place only this good, clean light – the last blessed glimpse she would ever have of her home realm, now gone from her for good.

Carreth... she thought – and then she thought no more.

CHAPTER ONE

ALAITHI

In the depths of the Temple of Ultharadon, Carreth Y'gethin wallowed in the pain and squalor of the past.

Standing on a slight rise in the shadow of Ultharadon, the temple was orderly and clean, a space reflecting the austere beauty and elemental holiness of the mountain that had given it its name. A large rotunda three storeys high was capped with a dome of vibrant, polished silver, and the arches above the pedimented windows complemented the soaring peaks of the mountain as it rose from the valley behind. Flowing from the rear of the rotunda was a long hall built in roughened stone, with two large quadrangles on either side. It was a complex of dark sandstone and polished marble, of shadowed cloisters and cool peristyles that stretched along the borders of cultivated gardens and courtyards. The soft chant of prayers and the sandalled scuff of passing feet blended with the gentle breeze. Birds fluttered in crimson plumage from tree to tree, their simple melodies spilling across the temple grounds in perfect mimicry of the waters that bubbled in the ornamental streams.

It was a place of peace and comfort, of art and beauty, but as Carreth plunged deeper into his studies the temple was none of these things. It receded from him the more he read. The world revealed in the pages of his books became more real than the world that surrounded him, and in his mind peace and comfort were replaced by bloodshed and cruelty, art and beauty with savagery and pride.

The Ocari Dara, the Spirefall... the line we walk across every day. On one side is order and balance and equilibrium. On the other side is possession and slaughter, and the very gates of damnation...

Although he was an Alarith Stonemage and the sacred head of the temple, Carreth's private chambers were modest and functional. The only decoration on the otherwise unadorned marble of his walls was a simple framed sketch of *Alaithi*, the rune of mountain, which Carreth had drawn in the earliest days of his magical training. His bed was a simple pallet in the corner of the room, and on a washstand beside it sat a plain clay bowl and a water jug. His desk was placed underneath a window that gave a clear, unobstructed view of the holy mountain's higher slopes, the mountain rising up from a mist-shrouded valley in sweeping, jagged peaks, vast and dominant, frosted with a dusting of snow. Across his desk were strewn volumes and scrolls he had taken from the temple library. As he read, Carreth paused to note down salient details, his quill scratching frantically against the parchment.

The Duel of Hexes, he wrote, *when the mages Maey've and Corah fought for six days, each unravelling six hexes against the other, the lands around them melting and reforming into what we now know of as the Crystal Caverns, in southern Ymetrica. Six, of course, is the number of the Thirsting God, Cursed Slaanesh, now bound and chained, and in the rift torn open by those hexes came pouring the daemons of its unholy order, in dread spectacles repeated countless times across the bleeding lands of Hysh...*

He turned a page and read on, noting further details down.

The Slight of the Broken Shards, when the great land bridge between Ymetrica and the Yntril Coast was swept away by a cascade of boiling warpflame, a host of Tzeentchian Flamers descending from the inverted portal that Uribalar of Iliatha hoped would banish her arch-rival Aranalei to the outer darkness beyond the realms...

He sighed and threw down his pen in disgust, stretching the crick from his neck and rubbing the heels of his hands against his pale grey eyes. How could they have been so blind, so selfish! Aelves driven to madness in their lust for power and fame, that they would come so close to destroying an entire civilisation. Everything he had read about those times made Carreth shiver in fear. All Hysh had teetered on the edge of the abyss and so many aelves of that awful age had felt no compunction about leaping over. He had read everything there was to know about the Spirefall, but still, buried deep in the temple archives, there were stories that remained new to him. Civil war between the continents, epic bloodshed that peeled open the veneer of reality and gained admittance to the daemonic hordes of Chaos. He well remembered the aftermath of those dreadful days, the battles he had fought as a young warrior to rebuild the realm, in the years after the Mage God Teclis had brought the teachings of the aelementiri to Hysh. A time of madness and despair, and the first faint glimmerings of hope...

The light was fading. The last of the sunset fell across the shoulder of the mountain like a cloak – red and ochre, fire and gold. It streamed from the mountainside to strike his chambers and bathe his desk in light. The pale moons of Hysh were drifting into being above the slanted peak. There was no true darkness in Hysh, but soon those moons would reach down with their silver fingers and craft the mountain into a cold and mysterious thing, and no less beautiful for that. Carreth smiled. He held the image of Ultharadon in his mind and closed his eyes. He saw the shape of it, that familiar silhouette, but he felt it too – the majesty of stone, the strength of its patience, its durability. He used the image of the mountain to draw his mind back up the paths of horror and despair to a pinnacle of purity and grace, and before long the brutality of the Ocari Dara was no more than words on parchment once more. It was ancient history, a lesson from dusty books.

Carreth sighed and stood up from the desk. He stretched his back, leaned for a moment against the open window as he stared out at the sunset. The temple grounds were spread out before him, sultry and peaceful. As the sun faded, they released the rich, dormant scents of the calcimine flowers and the stargazer jasmine in the eaves. Below him in the gardens was the simple juxtaposition of rock and water, where a moon bridge passed over a trickling brook. Trees murmured in the breeze. He could hear the Stoneguard being put through their paces, Alithis drilling them in the courtyard on the other side of the Avenue of Mages. Her voice rose and fell like a melody, moving swiftly between the martial forms.

He gathered up his books and scrolls and stacked them neatly on his desk, and something in him recoiled from the touch of the parchment. He closed his notebook and returned it to the drawer.

What is it I am looking for in these ancient accounts? What secrets can be revealed that have not been revealed already? Is enlightenment its own reward? The past must ever be a living flame, casting its light on the present and banishing the shadows of ignorance.

As he turned away from the window, Carreth's eyes fell on the brooch his sister had left him, which she had placed on the table by his bedside. It glowed softly in the declining light, a spark of flame crafted in such a way that it reminded him of Tuareth's passion, her determination. He saw her face in his mind's eye, the firm set of her jaw as she passed it to him, their fingers meeting. Aelven siblings most often shared a strict family resemblance, but

Tuareth could have come from a different family altogether. She was lithe and compact where Carreth was tall and refined, her hair flame-red where Carreth's was the silver of new-fallen snow. Most strikingly, her eyes blazed with a fierce green in fervid contrast to the pale grey of her brother's. She had the spirit of *Senlui*, the rune of swiftness and action, and as Carreth picked up the brooch and turned it over in his hands he saw the bold and flashing lines of the rune carved with delicate precision into the facets of the aetherquartz jewel. The stone gleamed, first red and then green, and as he held it to the light he saw the deeply embedded gold move sinuously through the crystal. It was perfect, he thought. A feat of great craft, a testament to Tuareth's ability to temper her passions into the refined work of true artistry.

Tuareth... he thought, and the thought pained him with all the words he had left unsaid. *My young sister, so bold, so free. What darkness do you move through now, and to what end? Come home, if you can. Come home.*

She had barged into the temple with all the respect of a mere human, as if stumbling into a mystery she didn't understand. But whereas Carreth could perhaps forgive a human its natural ignorance, his sister's boorishness could have no such excuse.

'Carreth!' she had shouted, her voice booming through the hall and falling back from the high, domed ceiling. She stood in the cool and open central chamber in full armour, barely glancing at the marble statue of the archmage Teclis, or the mosaic on the floor that depicted in gleaming artistry the meeting of Teclis and Celennar, the Mage God communing with the masked essence of the true moon. Her boots were dusty from the road but her armour shone with a pale, diamond light. Carreth had turned from his ritual of dedicating the new altar, a simple slab of stone quarried from Ultharadon's lower slopes, the weavings of his spell unravelling as he felt her impatient presence. Some of the younger votaries fluttered nervously about the chamber, clutching their robes, unsure how to react to this bold warrior in their midst.

'Ultharadon save me,' Carreth whispered as he turned towards her, 'from the demands of *sisters*.'

'Carreth, we must talk,' she said sternly. She removed her helmet, her red hair flowing to her shoulders and reflecting the glow of the torchlight like beaten copper. Carreth approached her in the full regalia of an Alarith Stonemage, the great horned helmet on his head, his pale blue cloak flowing in a graceful sweep across the marble floor, his staff towering above his head with its golden rune of *Alaithi*. The embedded jewels pulsed to the beat of his emotion. Tuareth held her helmet under her arm. Light glinted from the aetherquartz jewel on her sword hilt as it hung from her hip.

'You bring weapons into this holy place?' Carreth demanded.

'You think the mountain minds? This holy place is in the shadow of Ultharadon, and my sword moves like the swift winds in its highest peaks. I mean no disrespect.'

Carreth stared down at her and their eyes met, grey to green, the spark of her boldness quenched by the stillness of his elevated sight. She looked away, her face troubled, but Carreth masked his emotions.

Ever have I tried to protect you, Tuareth. Always have you made your own choices, good or bad.

He reached up and removed his own helmet. He noticed his apprentice, Aelthuwi, standing near, and he passed him the helmet as one of the votaries began to help him unhook his cloak. Carreth turned to them, young aelves in the early days of their dedication to the temple, who stood there nervous in their simple blue robes, and who looked on Carreth as if they stood in the presence of Teclis himself. Aelthuwi swallowed, his blue eyes bright, his thin, sallow face drawn in tight concentration.

'We will consecrate the altar another time,' Carreth said, dismissing them. 'Make sure the others practise their spiritual exercises before the Ritual of Symmetry this evening.'

'Yes, my lord,' Aelthuwi said. He took Carreth's staff in his other hand and bowed, showing Carreth the crown of his head, the cropped black hair.

'For the last time, Aelthuwi, I am a mage, not a lord...'

'Yes, my... yes, master,' the young apprentice stuttered, eyes wide. He bowed again as he retreated, scuffing backwards towards the door that led to the lecture hall, and the votaries' dormitory beyond it.

'Not grand enough to be a lord then?' Tuareth said.

'Too grand, perhaps.' Carreth allowed himself a smile. 'After all, "mage" sounds so much more impressive than "lord", don't you think?'

Tuareth laughed, and for a moment the tension between them slackened. Carreth took her hand.

'Come then,' he said. 'If we must talk let's do it in private. I have the dignity of my office to consider, after all...'

They crossed the marble floor, taking care not to tread on the mosaic of Teclis and Celennar. The walls around them, the high, domed ceiling above, were all of simple carved stone, the better to reflect the stark beauty of Ultharadon. Passing the altar with its plain decoration of alpine flowers that had been gathered in the moonlight from the mountain's higher slopes, Carreth was pleased to see his sister bow her head in reverence. She was a warrior, a high warden of the Vanari, but far more than that she was a Lumineth aelf. The modes of the Teclamentari were as sacred to her as they were to Carreth, even if they did each see the ladder of enlightenment from a different side.

As they headed to Carreth's chambers along the echoing corridors, their feet scuffing softly on the marble floors, the priests and votaries that they passed paused and bowed their heads. Carreth nodded at each of them in turn, muttering the words of a prayer.

'You have certainly earned their respect,' Tuareth said.

'The respect is due to my position in the temple as much as anything,' Carreth replied. 'I am an Alarith Stonemage and I have communed with Ultharadon directly, but I make no great claims for myself.'

'You should,' his sister said. She was a head shorter than her brother and looked up at him seriously as they walked. 'They know who you are, what you have done. You are more than a Stonemage, my brother. You were a warrior once, a great war hero...'

Carreth winced. They came to the doors of his chambers and he opened them for her, ushering her in.

'That is what you have come here to talk about, is it? War, and the making of heroes?'

'War is upon us,' Tuareth said, 'whether you like it or not.'

Carreth closed the door behind them and poured two glasses of amber wine from the temple's own vineyards.

'Anyone who speeds eagerly to battle is a fool,' he said. 'No one with the least modicum of sense *likes* war.'

'That's not what I mean, and you know it.'

Tuareth took the glass he offered her and looked around for somewhere to sit, eventually settling on the edge of his bed. Carreth remained standing, his back to the bare room as he looked out of his study window towards the mountain. Grim it seemed to him, suddenly. Grey clouds had stained the sky above its eastern flank, and a torrent of rain fell upon its base, darkening the girdle of forest that Ultharadon wore in spring. Carreth turned and looked at his sister, so incongruous in this austere chamber, sitting there in her polished war-plate, her ceremonial cloak, the sunmetal sword at her hip. She met his gaze, unflinching.

Whatever narrow space had briefly opened between them in the central hall, it had now slammed shut once more.

'My days of war and warfare are years behind me, Tuareth, you know that. I am the guardian of this mountain now, nothing more. And nothing less.'

'Nagash has struck a mortal blow across the realms – you know *that*, surely? Millions dead, millions driven mad, or snatched from their graves and pressed into his fell legions... Even here in Hysh, the dead have risen. His gheists have sacked cities, his deadwalkers have choked our holy rivers with their corpses...'

'And all have been destroyed in turn,' Carreth snapped. 'What happens in the realms outside is not our concern. Let the barbarians deal with their own problems. All that matters is that we keep Hysh safe, and we will keep it safe through vigilance, prayer, the dedication to the Teclamentari. Not through ill-judged military adventures like–'

'The God of the Dead will come to us in Hysh,' Tuareth shouted at him. She dashed the wine down her throat and cast the glass aside, shattering it on the stone floor. 'Do you think Nagash will give a damn about your vigilance and prayer then?'

Carreth turned away from her in fury, his heart racing, seeking out the sight of Ultharadon to calm himself again.

'I come to ask for your help,' she said, more gently. 'Hosts are being raised across Ymetrica, and across the other continents too – Iliatha, Zaitrec, Syar. All Hysh goes to strike back at the legions of the dead, to punish Nagash for what he has done. You have a famous name, Carreth Y'gethin, and you have powers many orders of magnitude beyond my own. You are wasted here while war rages beyond our border.'

'A war of aggression, a war of choice,' Carreth said softly, 'leads to nothing but disaster, Tuareth. History is littered with the failures of those who thought they could remake the world in their own image, or bend reality to their will. I will have no part of this. I'm sorry.'

She was silent. Even with his back to her, Carreth could sense her disappointment. No... it was not disappointment, he thought, not anger or rage. It was almost like shame.

She came near and laid her hand on his shoulder, gently drawing him around. Her eyes, he was shocked to see, were wet with tears.

'I know what it is you fear,' she said. 'I see the books you read, the studies you make of our darkest hours. You let the lessons of the Teclamentari hold you back, I think, because you cannot risk falling from the ladder. You think the drop would be endless, but I do not think it is. I have more faith in you, perhaps, than you do in yourself.'

'War unleashes passions which you cannot begin to imagine,' Carreth said. He raised his hand to cup her cheek, but at the last moment let it drop to his side. He remembered those passions well – the hatred, the savagery, the disgust. The Slighting of Aillianis, trampling those fleeing soldiers beneath his horse... the suicidal assaults against the Slaaneshi cults dug in around the Fractal Fjords... He shook his head. 'I will not risk that, you're right. And I would urge you to do the same.'

She smiled and shook her head. Carreth kept his face impassive, fixed into a mask that he would not remove even for his only sister.

'Then I wish you the best, my brother,' Tuareth said. 'Here with your books and your mountain. And I will love you for it, no matter where the fight takes me.'

She reached up to kiss his cheek and pressed something into his hand. Carreth looked down to see a jewel set in a bed of woven gold, an aetherquartz cut and polished to a dazzling shine. It caught the sunlight and seemed to melt it deep in its ever-shifting facets.

'I made this as a dedication to the journey,' she said, 'but now I want you to have it instead.'

'It is beautiful,' Carreth said quietly. 'I cannot take it.' He tried to give it back, but Tuareth raised her hands as if in surrender.

'It is mine to give. And now it's yours to look after. I will come to claim it when I'm back, I promise. When the war is won.'

'A token, then?' Carreth said. 'A promise – that you will return?'

'Of course.'

He nodded curtly and turned back to the view from his window, the brooch pressed tightly in his palm. He heard the rattle of Tuareth's armour as she left the chamber, and when she was gone, he placed the jewel on the table at the side of his bed. He sat there for a while, staring into the aetherquartz, the rune of *Senlui* first soft and then precise within it, as if revealed and subsumed by a leisurely tide.

Senlui, the swift wind, the call to action... But that is the curse of the wind. In the end, it can only blow itself out.

He looked down at the jewel now, losing himself in its ever-shifting facets. When the knock came at the door, he shook himself and slipped the stone into his pocket.

'Enter.'

A tall aelf, thin with advanced age, slipped into the chamber, the deep indigo of his robes indicating his high station within the temple's votary order.

'Forgive me, mage, but the seneschal is ready for you to review the Stoneguard before the Ritual of Symmetry.'

Carreth blanched. How long had he been wallowing in his studies here? And worse – indulging himself in nothing but self-pity at his sister's decision to leave.

'It is I who should be begging your forgiveness, Ilmarrin,' Carreth said. He tucked his helmet under his arm, and the tasselled horns reached almost from one side of the narrow chamber to the other. 'I was caught up in my work and the time escaped me. Please, lead the way.'

The Stoneguard were ranked up on the parade ground at the rear of the temple complex, a wide, flat square of flawless stone that had been beaten smooth by generations of soldiers' feet. A hundred warriors stood there in perfect stillness, rank upon rank, their eyes glinting through their horned helmets' eye slits. Their armour, more baroque than the plate Tuareth had worn as a Vanari warden, was like bleached ceramic, and their soft grey robes hung loosely to the ground. Carreth looked out across the parade ground to the barracks beyond it, a long, low chamber ringed by a plain colonnade, where the night guard would be waiting to march out. The woe trees were singing their soft dirge in the rough ground beyond the barracks, their branches rippling gently in the breeze. It was a sad sound, Carreth thought, appropriate to a solemn moment, when the light of Hysh dimmed and gave the Lumineth a hint of the dark. Ultharadon soared up from the valley on the other side of the barracks, no more than a mile distant – a vast shard of the sublime reaching to the heavens, trailing streams of vaporous cloud from its tallest spire.

Alithis tilted her head as Carreth approached. He was sure he saw an eyebrow raise a fraction of an inch on the Truestone Seneschal's face. The corner of her mouth turned up very slightly into a wry smile at his lateness, although when she saw the grim cast of Carreth's face she inclined her head instead and spoke the ritual words.

'Stonemage Y'gethin, guardian of the Temple of Ultharadon, bid me free to change the guard as the sun goes down and the true moon rises.'

'As Teclis and Celennar will it, so shall it be done,' Carreth replied. He raised his staff. 'The Light falls, and the Light rises.'

Alithis held out her twin stratum hammers, gesturing with them to the right. At this signal, the block of Stoneguard shouldered their weapons and came to attention. Alithis held one hammer high and lowered the other to her side, and the Stoneguard wheeled and marched crisply across the parade ground. As they did so, the doors of the barracks opened and the night guard marched out, ready to take up their positions at the four corners of the temple complex, to guard it through the half-light of the Hyshian evening until the day watch marched out to relieve them. Carreth listened to the sound of the soldiers' feet, the clatter of weapons, the stirring sense of unity from observing a well-drilled force. For a moment he dwelled in the past again, in his own days of strife and conflict. The serried ranks, the screams, the stench of blood and fire. He thought of Tuareth…

Alithis came and stood beside him on the cusp of the parade ground. The falling sun had moved now behind the summit of Ultharadon, and the evening was well advanced. The light fell like purple velvet, the stars beginning to spark into life above.

'Nothing the matter, mage?' Alithis asked. 'It's not like you to be late for the changing of the guard.'

She kept her voice low. Carreth could barely hear it over the sound of marching feet. Unlike the soldiers under her command, Alithis, as Truestone Seneschal, kept her head bare. Her black hair was scraped back from her face and tied in a tight topknot, and there was a white scar reaching from her forehead to the edge of her mouth on the right-hand side of her face. She was stern and implacable at the best of times, but there was a wryness to her as well, a sense of irony available only to someone who had seen much and done more, that Carreth had always warmed to.

'I lost track of the time, that's all,' Carreth said.

'Those books are a deadly snare, to be sure,' Alithis said. 'Words, I've never trusted them. Now, music – I could forgive you if you'd lost yourself in that art.'

'I know what you call music, Alithis. I'd rather listen to the woe trees.'

'I've been working on a melody,' she said, ignoring him as she warmed to her subject. 'The pitch rises and falls like the peaks of Ultharadon, and the – Carreth? *Carreth!*'

He seemed to see her as if she were standing at the end of a long tunnel, with the walls on either side closing in. Her face faded, and he was looking then on a blasted plain sheeted with green lightning, choked with dust. Screams lanced through the black air, the clash of metal, the feverish corposant of magic.

'Alithis…?' he said.

He couldn't breathe. The palm of his hand ached, his fingers locked and rigid. He looked down and saw that he was clutching Tuareth's jewel, the aetherquartz brooch she had left in his safekeeping. The jewel was cracked, a jagged line split straight through it, and pouring from the crack came a weeping trace of light that stung his eyes. Carreth looked up and saw her – his sister, screaming. Her helmet had been cleaved from her head, and she crawled painfully over a mound of bodies, blood pouring down her face. And yet, as he looked, the scene smeared out and became more indistinct, and leering through the mist came a foul skeletal face, the eye sockets hazed with quivering green, the teeth blanched bone, the jaw champing madly in some disgusting facsimile of speech.

'Tuareth!' he tried to call, but the words died in his mouth. He was choking, falling. He could hear Alithis crying his name, and as he hit the ground – although whether here by the temple or there on the blasted, corpse-strewn plain, he couldn't say – he saw Tuareth again, rolling onto her back, raising her sword. He saw the skeleton drop smoothly from the saddle of some desiccated beast, a grotesque amalgam of bone, and clack towards her. And then it raised its sword, and Tuareth screamed, and Carreth was lying there by the parade ground once more, his sister's jewel in his hand and tears streaming down his face. The Stoneguard of the night watch had sprung into action, forming a cordon around him. At his side Alithis knelt and cradled his head.

'Carreth! What is it, what's happened?' Her face was wild, her eyes searching his own for answers.

'Tuareth,' he said, and he couldn't disguise the crack in his voice. He held up the brooch. 'My sister... She's dead!'

CHAPTER TWO

THE STUFF OF SOULS

The corridors echoed with the clacking of bone, the dry tap of footsteps, the clatter of arms, the distant hammer blows of the Mortisan order rendering new weapons for conquest. Deep in the bowels of the necropolis, Liege-Kavalos Akridos added his own footsteps to the tumult. He passed into the great hall of the central keep, walking between the vast, serried ranks of Mortek Guard as they marched out through the High Gates towards the muster ground. Huge black columns of bone reached from the obsidian floor to the towering ceiling two hundred feet above him, the fan vaults marked out in ribs and femurs, where dark jewels and black glass brooded in the murk. As he passed beyond the confines of the Great Hall, the sound of marching soon faded away and was replaced only with an eerie silence.

He passed into a long corridor, lit by guttering flames on ragged torches. He passed doors made of bone, each a strange, fused marriage of different types – scapulae and femurs, ribcages and vertebrae. Onwards he clacked, precise, unhurried, a vague limp showing in his uneven stride. He came to an iron door that was studded with skulls, the eye sockets of each shining with an eldritch light. Their jaws champed together, unleashing a weird, discordant clicking sound, and as Akridos stood silently before them they seemed to nod in their iron prison. Slowly the door swung open. Ahead of him, another empty corridor stretched on like an enclosed avenue, as straight as an arrow. Akridos stepped through, and behind him the iron door swung shut.

The floor of this corridor was of polished basalt, the surface streaked like marble with emerald veins. Whereas the floor was smooth and unadorned, the ceiling high above was a ridged vault, a lacunar space where the natural curves of human ribcages had been fused to the rock. Akridos marched briskly on, his great curved scimitar at his hip, the green-tinged plate of his armour reflecting the torchlight in a sickly gleam. He was walking deep inside the curtain wall of the necropolis, a structure more than forty feet thick, an obsidian core reinforced and embellished with reformed bone. As he walked, his thoughts twisted around the chaos of the day before, skimming over each moment of the battle, trying to comprehend it in the whole. He saw the encircling move of his cavalry wings, the Mortek Guard stolid and immovable in the centre of the line, the Crawlers flinging their weights with desultory ease. He saw the aelf-kind unfold from column to line, their battle array moving with flawless precision to match the position of his own forces, their spear tips glowing white-hot and the crackle of aetheric energy imbuing them all with a radiance that, even for the Ossiarch Bonereapers, was difficult to look upon. He clutched a skeletal hand tightly on the hilt of his blade. The green light in his empty eyes glowed furiously, and all the facets of his thought flared up in bitter rage.

The battle had been a defeat, there was no escaping the fact. A commander has no choice but accept reality as it is, not as he would like it to be. Each part of the Ossiarch army had deployed perfectly, the infantry pouring out of the gates in an endless tide, the cavalry swarming out from the necropolis in a whirlwind of charge and counter-charge. They had thrown everything at the aelves, and yet their line had held. They had not broken, and as the Ossiarch force shattered itself against their defences, the aelves had somehow rallied and struck back. Their cavalry, sparkling like a swatch of diamonds, whipping along the Bonereapers' flanks… their infantry as immovable as a mountain range… Soon, the only option was retreat, or destruction. And so Akridos had retreated, seeking the shelter of his walls, the sanctuary of his fortress.

He ground his jaw together, feeling the disparate teeth scrape and crumble in his mouth. Bone dust trickled from his jaw.

Here and there as he passed them along the corridor, the arrow slits in the wall on his right gave a partial view down onto the great plains beyond. Akridos ignored them. He headed on, clacking his way down the silent corridor, aiming for a more comprehensive vista. Eventually he came to another door, flanked this time by two Mortek Guard with shouldered spears, their shields bearing the sigil of the Stalliarch Lords. They had been recently constructed, Akridos could see – the blended bone that formed their bodies still dripped with gore, and the bone itself was stained with a faintly pinkish hue. The guards stared with unseeing eyes. As Akridos approached, they grasped the handles of the door and pulled it open. He passed beyond, coming to a branching corridor that led off towards the Mortisan laboratories, and the libraries beyond them. He stood there for a moment, silent, reaching out with his mind to trace the shape of the soulmason, Kathanos, wherever he might be. Labouring in the fortress, no doubt, deep in the alchemical workshops where he plied his necromantic skills.

There… I feel him, refining in his laboratory the last souls captured from the field, blending them in his jars and vials, locking the apportioned soul-stuff to the jewelled phylacteries... I feel you, Kathanos... All are one in Nagash, but do not forget. On the battlefield my word is law.

Akridos felt the soul gem on his breastplate pulse and gleam as if in response, the brightness for a moment casting a pure white light into the dark corridor. Something lurched inside him, burning like fire. He snarled with an unfocused rage, clawing at the jewel as if he could rip it from his armour and stamp it to powder underfoot. Emotions were irrelevant to the hosts of the dead, but the elite of the Ossiarch Bonereapers were not as the other soulless automatons in Nagash's armies. They retained a shard of free will, a degree of whatever they had been before they were shaped by the arcane skills of the Mortisans. Akridos shuddered as he felt the mingled souls squirm inside him, each soul a mere fraction of the whole, a trace element carved off by Kathanos to best fit their new purpose. In battle, as the situation demanded, these mingled spirits had served him well. When defending against an overwhelming attack, Akridos could draw upon the righteous certainty of a Sigmarite priest and the gruff stoicism of a duardin engineer. While prosecuting a dashing advance, he tapped the vitality and reckless courage of a young Freeguild cavalry officer who had been killed and harvested decades ago after a lone charge against the advancing Ossiarch lines. In stamping his will on the legion entire, however, Akridos had brought to bear the deepest and most intrinsic part of his blended spirit – the soul of the king he had once been, the liege in ages past of a great swathe of the Equuis Main, from Sinda and the Zondtar Realmgate in the south to the Stalliarch Coast and Rook Nave in the north. That spirit was the originating spark. It traced its soul-stuff into every facet of his being, and it rebelled inside him at the parity he shared with Kathanos in the Ossiarch hierarchy. Soulmason and Liege-Kavalos, Emissarian and Panoptic castes respectively.

Priest, and king, and the priest has his fingers in my very lineaments... But the king commands, and his underlings should obey.

This new sensation burned in the very core of him, though. Akridos had never felt anything like it, and if he had had any real kind of physiognomy at all, he would have said that it made him feel sick.

Kathanos, what have you done to me? It burns like light, like life, and... and I cannot bear it.

Akridos mastered himself, squashing the sensation down, drowning it in the chattering soul-stuff inside him. He lowered his skeletal fingers from the facets of the soul gem and dragged his mind back into focus. The anger boiled inside him still, but at a lower heat. It was the aelf-kind that troubled him more than anything. The defeat they had inflicted on him the day before was near impossible to bear, and although the aelves had suffered grievously for their temerity, it was no real consolation. That they had inflicted this defeat in Shyish itself, in the very shadows of his own necropolis, was an insult too unutterable to accept. Akridos focused on that instead, allowing his rage to slip along a more profitable route. Already he could feel the will of Nagash unfurl across the dead lands of Shyish, drawing his armies together from every corner of the realm. He was mustering his forces, readying his response, and when it came, Akridos knew, it would be overwhelming. Akridos fully intended to be in the very spearhead of it.

Ahead of him was the beginnings of a spiral staircase that led up into the body of the Temenos Spire, forbidden to all but the senior elements of the ruling castes. Akridos took the first steps, climbing steadily and tirelessly, his feet clicking on the bone. Up the stairs led, twisting higher and higher in the core of the tower, the bone underfoot covered in a rime of dust, the black stone walls pitted with teeth. From the outside, the Temenos Spire was constructed in the form of a vast spear held in the grip of a gigantic skeletal hand. It loomed over the necropolis, mirrored in perfect symmetry on the other side of the central keep by the Anagos Spire, the twin spears reaching up to pierce the morbid sky as it rumbled and purled above the Equuis Main. Akridos passed the first knucklebone of the grasping hand, moving inside the shaft of the spear handle. Up he went, further and further, climbing without pause and without any sense of exertion, like a metronome ticking with inhuman precision as he mounted each step, higher and higher, past the second knuckle, the third, until eventually the staircase levelled into a narrow portico that led out onto a sheltered walkway. Ringed by a railing of crossed femurs, this walkway stretched around the sculpted cross guard of the spear, giving an unobstructed view of the wide and featureless plains below. Onwards they stretched, vast and terrible, reaching with a mild undulation towards the heart of the Equuis Main – a blasted land of grey dust and flat, forbidding steppes, where storms blew up from the Mausol Sound and swept across the Brass Mountains like a cavalry charge, and where traders' caravans now crossed only to reach the Zondtar Realmgate, if they did so at all. A black sun hovered in silent repose on the horizon, staining the clouds with its cold unlight. The sky unfurled above the plains, a rumpled, amaranthine sheet, and from far off to the south – impossibly far – came the queasy, subsonic hum of the Shyishian Nadir, the core of the realm, and the core of Nagash's plans for the realms at large.

Akridos could see, a thousand feet below, the shattered ruins of the equine statue that had dominated the entrance to the fortress. In bone and black obsidian, the statue had stood rampant on the wall above the gatehouse, a hundred feet of skeletal grace and fury, a riderless steed raised in glory to the Stalliarch Lords and the massed ranks of their Deathrider cavalry. As Akridos' battered host had withdrawn into the safety of the walls, they had watched in impotent rage as the aelves cast their magics and brought the statue down – a slight on their honour, a gesture that was meaningless in the grand scheme of victory and defeat, but one that Akridos had taken as an insult of overwhelming offence. He stared down at the shattered bone and the rage simmered in his skull.

As he watched, the empty plains below him began to fill. The troops he had passed as they filed out of the Great Hall were mustering now before the necropolis, the survivors of the battle and the replacements that had been formed and armed through the tireless efforts of the Mortisan order. Huge columns of Mortek Guard marched out, block by block, each formation a thousand strong – first ten thousand swords, then twenty thousand spears. The columns wheeled and reformed into line, each individual soldier no more than a pinprick in the grey earth far below. Their marching feet kicked up a billowing cloud of dust that soon rose and settled above the battlements of the fortress like a plume of smoke. Akridos gripped the railing as the banners of his cavalry emerged from the High Gates below him. He saw Takanos leading them at the front, the Kavalos Deathriders, core of the Stalliarch Lords legion and the finest heavy cavalry in the realms. Hammering the earth under their skeletal hooves, the horses moved out in two great wings that drew up in line on either side of the infantry. Even this far up above them the Liege-Kavalos could hear the clashing of their spears, the whipping of their tattered banners.

And this was not all. Following the cavalry came the legion's ponderous war machines, the Mortek Crawlers with their dread catapults, their sinuously writhing clawed feet. The Immortis Guard emerged next, four-armed giants sculpted from the most durable bone, then the Necropolis Stalkers, elite shock troops, each wielding vicious blades or falchions. On the troops came, all of them taking up their positions on the mustering ground, standing to attention and awaiting the command that would send them marching off to war. And if the command were not given, Akridos knew, they would wait there until time itself shuddered to a halt or they were ordered back inside, whichever came first.

In one day, the legion had almost made good its losses. As Akridos observed the silent array of his army, he noticed the Gothizzar Harvesters sorting methodically through the remains of the dead from the previous day's battle. Like vast, creeping beetles they picked through the refuse, the fused arms and the grinning automata on their chests reaching down and scouring the dirt, picking, sorting, flensing, shucking the flesh from the bone and casting it aside. Like a stinking, gory spoor, the Harvesters left piles of discarded meat in their wake. Their task was almost done – more would be added to the legion's ranks, until all the aelves' victory had availed would be to make their enemy stronger and more numerous than before.

Akridos looked on the legion far below him, choking the dead plains, without pride or delight, or any of the emotions a mortal general might have felt when reviewing his troops. Even the anger which had gripped him at the base of the tower seemed intangibly distant now. Up here in the Temenos Spire, where the view stretched far across the Equus Main towards the other brooding continents of Shyish, all his emotion had been subsumed by the will of Nagash. The army was the instrument of Nagash, first and foremost.

He was aware of the soul gem glowing again, that bright white light staining the blackened bone of the railing before him. He raised his fingers to it, his eyes drawn to the mumbling progress of the Harvesters on the far side of the plain. He felt his spirit respond as he looked on the bodies of the dead.

Of course, he thought. *An aelf soul to bolster my talents... Kathanos, you are ever keen to experiment with new discoveries...*

It sat there in the midst of his other spirits, blind and helpless.

He could feel it, as if listening to a muffled call on the other side of a thick partition. As he sank into himself, Akridos sifted through the souls, searching for the aelf-kind, the creature Kathanos had parsed and filleted while the boneshapers repaired the physical damage to his form.

What kind of thing are you, aelf? You are new to me, untried before the battle, untasted... There, I see you, I feel you... Light, burning, burning...

He sneered, felt the rage lurch inside him again, the burning light. As he draped the fringes of his consciousness against the aelf soul, he saw again the blood and madness of the battle – the charge of his Deathriders, the Mortek line beginning to crack, the butcher's work of swords and spears, the aelves' gleaming armour shining like the sunrise. Akridos saw his sword sweep down towards the aelf at the heart of her regiment on the right flank, the shock and agony on the narrow planes of her face, her streaming red hair thickened with blood, her green eyes flashing. Then all had become light and burning, an agony he had not experienced for an age, since he was a mortal man and the lands of the Equuis Main were his settled kingdom – a glowing flask of incandescent liquid that with her dying breath the aelf had unhooked from her belt and thrown at the ground with a whispered curse. A lightning flash, diamond bright... Akridos' steed had disintegrated with a scream, and then the light had spattered up to scour his arm to dust and melt half his face away. Physically, they were injuries that meant nothing, and that had been repaired within the day, but the light...

The light...

Akridos shuddered to recall it. He looked at his hands and realised he had torn the crossbar of the railing clean away. With a curse he threw it to the ground, reaching up with his new-grown arm to touch his new-grown face. Aelf bone, certainly, formed and reshaped to new purpose.

Kathanos...

He took one last look at his waiting army below him. Before he turned for the stairs once more, he glanced at the parched remains of the Shyishian steppes. Once this had all been grassland, he remembered. Fodder for the horses, the herds that his tribe had driven from one end of the Main to the other, from sea to sea. The smell of horseflesh and leather, of sweet grass and the hide tents they pitched as they moved from the grazing grounds onto the warpath. This had been the paradise of his people, their underworld, the promise at the other side of death.

He laughed – a dry, rustling sound. *The fools we were, when I was king.*

On the other side of death, there was only Nagash.

He found Kathanos in the necropolis library, deep in the heart of the fortress.

The doors to the library were of bleached bone, twice the height of a man and formed into the shape of a huge fanged maw. The fused teeth stabbed down from the arch of the upper mouth, swinging open on a creaking hinge as Akridos pushed them aside. He stepped into the shadowed space, the reading room stretching away from him for a thousand yards into the distant gloom, half a mile of shadows and flickering light. High above him the domed ceiling was lit with the eerie glow of candles mounted on human skulls, the candles' tallow rendered from the fat of the dead. The ribbed vault seemed to tremble in their green shimmer.

The room was filled with rows upon rows of dusty desks, each piled high with parchment and scroll, and at regular intervals along the length of the massive hall there were pillars of bone like monstrous spines supporting the mezzanine floor above. Up there, towering bookshelves processed like ranks of soldiers into the distant shadows, each filled from floor to ceiling with all the encyclopaedic material of the necropolis archives. Here, scholars of the Ossiarch Empire had collated information about the realms at large, noting down taxonomies of all the varied life that called the Mortal Realms home. There were histories of empires long since lost to the ravages of time, and mighty cultures that had degenerated into squabbling tribes thousands and thousands of years ago. There were collected works of literature and mathematics, poetry and song, plays written by dramatists whose bones were forgotten dust, in languages unlearned when the realm was young. Shelves were choked with treatises on the magic arts, with the ritual practices of obscure cults hidden in the depths of cities that were now no more than a scattering of shapeless stones in deserts long since abandoned by man. There were books bound in human skin, and scrolls made from the hides of orruks and duardin. There were texts written in inks distilled from the blood of entire civilisations that had once been put to the sword or absorbed into the ranks of the Ossiarch Empire. Strange skeletal birds flickered through the air between the shelves, bibliopomps darting down at the stacks and picking up volumes in their grooved proboscises.

In a fortress dominated by the silence of the dead, the necropolis library was a place where silence was at its most intense, qualified and enhanced by the boundless learning that surrounded it. It was a place, Akridos thought, where in time all things could be discovered, no matter how obscure.

Kathanos had settled himself at a desk halfway down the reading room, in an alcove underneath the mezzanine. As far as Akridos could tell, he was the only scholar availing himself of the books, although the library was so vast that any number of the legion's senior caste could have been deep in study, hidden in nooks and crannies that he couldn't see. A candle flickered on the desk by Kathanos' robed elbow, next to a pile of codices and scrolls. The soulmason scrawled careful notes into a vellum book with a quill made from human fingerbones. He dipped the quill into a pot of ink that was a rusty red colour, and as Akridos watched, the ink dried on the page in the colour of old blood.

'Liege-Kavalos,' the soulmason said, without looking up. 'It is rare to see you in the fields of study.'

'The fields of battle are my natural domain,' Akridos said. Their voices, dry and precise as the voices of all in the Ossiarch legions, rustled through the shadowed hall. Akridos stared down at the soulmason. He was not often seen without his Mortek throne, the bipedal contraption that conveyed him on the marching route or in the press of combat. His staff leaned up against the wall beside the desk. Without his ceremonial crown, his skull looked somehow brittle and weak, aged bone the shade of ancient teak.

'Indeed. Although I would not have thought that from the result of our clash with the aelven kind yesterday. They looked more at home there than we did, dare I suggest.'

Akridos was immune to personal insult, implied or otherwise, but Kathanos' words struck deep. The aelves had fought with rare skill, it was true, and despite the terrible losses they had suffered, in the clash of arms between them it had been the Bonereapers who had been forced back.

'We may have given up the field, but in the end their losses were unsustainable,' the Liege-Kavalos said. 'A setback for the legion was a devastating result for them. They will not be back.'

Kathanos deigned to look up from his work. Akridos stared down into the empty sockets of his eyes, the faint emerald trace of a malign and searching intelligence flaring out as the soulmason observed him.

'Will they not?' Kathanos said. 'Perhaps it is the case that while the aelves will not return, we will meet them on other ground instead? We would do well to study their methods further and forearm ourselves against that eventuality, do you not think?'

Akridos scorned the advice. He turned his back on Kathanos and strode from the alcove to stare down the endless, osseous rows of desks. Silence dwelled heavily in the room, broken only by the flitting of the bibliopomps as they crossed the air above him, the faint hiss of the candles as the wicks burned low.

'You give them too much credit,' he said. 'I have learned what I need to know from fighting them in battle. Next time, I will be better prepared. I know them well now. After all,' he sneered, turning to face the soulmason, 'you have made sure of that, haven't you?'

Immobile skulls cannot convey the range of emotions that mortal races take for granted, but Akridos was sure that he saw a trace of amusement cross the soulmason's face.

'You speak of the new addition to your soul gem? We of the Mortisan orders refine our methods depending on the materials to hand,' Kathanos said, inclining his head. 'A brave and determined foe, thus far unknown to us – it makes practical sense to draw upon that resource. I took the opportunity while you were being repaired by Morfilos.'

Akridos took the soulmason's word for it. He had no recollection of the moment he was dragged from the field and reconstructed by Morfilos, the head of the legion's boneshapers. 'I feel it fuming inside me like an ember,' he said, 'like… No, I lack the words to describe it. The experience is new to me. It burns, Kathanos. It leaks light, and… and something like life.'

'I assure you, Liege-Kavalos, that is not possible. I have taken from the aelf soul only those trace elements that will assist you, that will give you certain insights in combat, a tactical or strategic appreciation of their methods.'

'What would you know about tactics or strategy, soulmason?'

'I defer to your judgements on those matters, of course. Great Nagash places each of us in positions that best make use of our talents – or otherwise.'

'And to what end are you directing those talents now? I would have expected you in the Mortisan laboratories, preparing the host.'

'The host is near complete,' Kathanos said, inclining his skull. 'There is little left to be done. I thought I would make use of another resource available to us, the contents of our archives. Do you know what it was we faced yesterday?'

Akridos ground his teeth together, dwelling for a moment in the clash of arms, the thunder of the Deathriders as he led them like a breaking wave into the enemy flank.

'The aelven kind? We have met them before, the sea-dwellers, the tree folk, such as they are.'

'Ah,' Kathanos said, tapping his parchment. 'We have met variants of a kind, it is true. Twisted remnants of what once was, perverted by the weight of their failures, the depths of their despair. The aelven gods made many mistakes when they dragged the souls of their kind from the maw of the Thirsting God. No, Akridos, what we met on the field was not quite so malleable or broken a thing. This was the refined element, you could say.'

'Tell me then, soulmason – what enemy is this?'

Kathanos balanced his quill on the inkwell and turned the dusty pages of his book. His eyes blazed with a deeper green as he consulted his notes. The necropolises of the Ossiarch legions were fearsome military establishments, fortifications built over long ages to enforce the bone-tithe from outlying settlements, but they were also places of great learning and culture. Information and intelligence were as much a military resource as spears and shields and the warriors to wield them, and as Nagash's elite, the Ossiarch Bonereapers were designed to prosecute their master's will with every resource at their disposal. It was not unusual for the Mortisan order to delve into the archives for hidden records, searching for forgotten accounts of new adversaries to better defeat them in the field. But for Kathanos himself to have investigated their new foe was unusual. Despite himself, Akridos carefully attended the soulmason's words.

'That light you feel inside you is, I believe, the light of Hysh, their native realm. With truly astounding arrogance they refer to themselves as the "Lumineth Realm-lords". They are well versed in the magical arts – indeed, the records I have scoured suggest they are perhaps the greatest practitioners of magic in the Mortal Realms. Only the fell powers of Chaos can rival them, the sorcerers of Tzeentch perhaps.'

Akridos felt again the searing flame the aelf woman had thrown at his feet, saw the blinding glow of the aelves' pikes crashing into the Mortek line, their weapons charged or enhanced by the crackling vibrancy of magic.

'They are not as these other aelf races we have encountered, Liege-Kavalos. Those are degenerate things in comparison, while the Lumineth appear to be the purer strain, unsullied. Teclis and Tyrion are their gods, the archmage and the warlord, the wizard and the warrior. Both, it seems, have a lineage almost as old and as distinguished as our master, although the records are extremely scarce here, fragmented... Mere rumour and legend in the end. A world destroyed, a bargain undone, a betrayal...'

'The past interests me less than the present,' Akridos said, his patience wearing thin.

'As a race they are extremely cultured,' Kathanos continued. 'Great artists and poets gifted at crafts of all kind. By all accounts their civilisation is a refined and cultivated one, durable in a way that we have perhaps not encountered before.'

'I care not for their arts of peace,' Akridos hissed. 'Tell me of their arts of war!'

Kathanos turned the dry pages of his account, and in the silence of the library the sound was deafening. A bibliopomp perched on the corner of a desk clattered into the air in sudden alarm.

'In many ways, to understand one is to understand the other,' Kathanos said. 'Do you see? All citizens will come together to defend their civilisation, and military service seems obligatory. They fight to defend that culture, that sense of themselves as things apart from the common run. You must take account of them in the round, I believe. And yet, as the history of Keth'shala the Realm-walker indicates – and it is a most interesting account – the Lumineth are not–'

'You waste my time here, soulmason,' Akridos muttered, pacing away from the table. 'I have heard nothing from you that would give us an advantage on the field that I have not already determined for myself by actually fighting them.'

Kathanos held up a skeletal finger, stabbing it down again onto his notes.

'Even light must cast darkness somewhere, Liege-Kavalos,' he said. 'The Lumineth have in their history events of catastrophic bloodshed and slaughter. The Ocari Dara, they refer to it – the Spirefall, a moment when their innate corruptibility almost destroyed them. Chaos gained a foothold in their realm, through their own arrogance and depravity. That is what they fear now, I am sure. That is their weakness – that they cannot risk unleashing their full martial or magical potential for fear that it would destroy them. They defend a culture, a religion built on their worship of great avatars from the depths of their history – Teclis himself, the Light of Eltharion, their sacred groves and mountains... Threaten those aspects, force them to delve into the squalid soup of their emotions – and you will have them.'

Akridos stopped pacing and turned back to face him. Sitting there, Kathanos nodded his cracked and brittle visage, chattering with excitement – a scholar who had pinned down an elusive source, a weaver of souls, stitching spirits. Akridos seemed to feel the soulmason's fingers fluttering through the animus of his being, moulding him into spiritual shape.

It is... degrading, he thought. *In many ways I am at the mercy of one who should kneel before me. I, who was a king on the plains once...*

'Emotions...' Akridos said. 'Magic.' He pronounced the words as if they were distasteful to him, or concepts too alien for him to comprehend. 'I prefer to put my trust in superior tactics and troops who will not bend or break.'

'And of the two armies who met on the field yesterday,' Kathanos insidiously whispered, 'which demonstrated the superior tactics? Whose troops broke first?'

'It matters not! The legion is back at full strength and more. If we face them again on the battlefield then all the knowledge in this library of their art and poetry will avail us less than another five regiments of Deathriders and another ten thousand spears.'

'Deathriders you shall have, Akridos,' Kathanos said, slamming his notes closed with a scattering of dust. 'And spears. Spears so thick against the sky that they cannot be counted. Yes,' he said, the sockets of his eyes glittering. 'Soon... You feel it too, don't you, the drum beat of war? Our master calls us, and we are compelled to obey... Soon the legion will march again.'

Akridos paused. His hand dropped to the hilt of his sword. 'Compelled? I need no command to choose war, Kathanos. Ever will I reach for the sword rather than...' He looked at the stacked volumes on the desk, the dusty scrolls, the rows and rows of desks and the shelves on the mezzanine that soared up to the darkened ceilings. 'Rather than the book.'

'You "choose", do you?' Kathanos said, reaching for his staff. 'Haven't you ever wondered why Nagash gave the legions of the Ossiarch Empire a degree of free will? We are not as the others in his armies, that is clear. No mindless automatons, we, dug up from the graveyards of the realms, or slithering out of the shadows of ancient folktales and legends. What are we to do with this free will, I wonder? How far does it go?'

'He gave us the will to prosecute war,' Akridos said. 'And nothing less.'

He turned his back on the soulmason and stalked out of the library, his feet tapping harshly on the black marble floor, the bibliopomps scattering out of his way. He could hear Kathanos gathering up his notes, could feel the soulmason's sight on his back.

Nothing less, he thought. *But once it was so much more…*

CHAPTER THREE

THE MOURNING RITUAL

It was cold on the peaks of Ultharadon. The soft blue air of the lower slopes became harder the higher up you climbed – it cleared the lungs, cleared the mind of extraneous thought and made everything seem precise. Everything was sharper and more defined, and the petty concerns of day-to-day life fell away into inconsequence. Mountain flowers shivered by rumpled beds of soft lichen, their petals a range of pastel hues. The footpaths that led through the pine trees on the mountain's skirt gradually fell away to bare rock, the stone on either side lit like smooth purple velvet. The wind angled across the sharper planes, but it was an invigorating, unclouded air that smelled of pine and snow. It set the blood coursing through Carreth's veins.

He sat by a shallow cleft of rock above the timberline, his legs crossed on an apron of grass. Ultharadon's higher peaks soared above him on his right and fell away to the steep paths down the mountain on his left. Tough sedge grass quivered in the breeze around him. Far above, crossing over the tip of the mountain, beams of yellow-white light drew dazzling and silent traceries in the sky – concentrated magic, speeding across the realm of Hysh from the maelstrom at its very edge. To catch such light and harness its energy was to form the translucent prisms known as aetherquartz, the distilled essence of magic, a skill which had been taught to the Lumineth by Teclis himself.

Carreth leaned back and looked up, seeing the beams of light above the mountain even when he closed his eyes, their negative traceries like the secret pathways of the world, or the lines of glyphs and symbols that would unlock the secrets of reality itself. He felt the burning edge of magic prickling against his skin. He felt rather than saw its patterns and equations, the weave of time, the weft of life and death. He sighed deeply, breathing in that heady alpine air. A single tear, like lit crystal, dropped gently from his eye and fell onto the earth. He held Tuareth's brooch in his hand, the aetherquartz cracked across the centre and the encased light leaking like oil across his palm.

'Tuareth Y'gethin,' he said softly. 'Find peace in the underworlds of our people. Ultharadon, most holy of mountains, let your spirit guide her spirit. Give rest to the restless. Keep her safe.'

His face was daubed with ashes, and he wore only a simple gown of rough-spun cloth. His feet and head were bare, and the wind ruffled its cold fingers though his flaxen hair. Further back in the shallow cleft of rock was a small canvas bag with a few meagre supplies. Gone were the trappings of office, the ceremonial vestments of the temple's Alarith Stonemage. He wore instead the simple garb of a mourner, a pilgrim on the mountain path, who had journeyed up into Ultharadon's higher glades to mark the loss of his sister, to match his soul to the mountain's in order to share the burden of his grief.

Seven days he had been here, and the journey this far had taken seven more. At first, he had climbed the mountain paths with speed and vigour, but the higher he went the more his burdens pressed upon him, as if he were journeying deeper into his grief. The path had become more difficult, the pressed pine needles and packed dirt giving way to rough shale. He had found himself stopping more frequently to catch his breath or slake his thirst at the shatteringly cold streams that trickled down from the higher slopes. Passing through the treeline, stepping along a path that led under their dark canopies, he had felt trapped in his anguish. But this was the virtue of the mountain, he knew. Yard by yard it measured out the stages of grief. It brought the pilgrim through them one by one, until eventually he emerged from the struggle and the shadows into the clear and unobstructed morning once more, his head clear, his spirit balanced, the clean air preparing him for the proper term of mourning.

He could see the temple far down below on his left, raised on its mound and hazed by a drift of mist that spilled out of the shadowed valley below it. A long, grassy ridgeline connected the temple mound to the foothills of Ultharadon. On its right as Carreth looked at it, the ground sloped vertiginously down into the valley, which brewed with mists and shadows. That was a dark place, he knew, heavy with the legends of the time before the coming of the Lumineth. When the mountain was young, the valley had been there, waiting. Some said Ultharadon itself had grown from a seed planted deep in its forbidding soil. There were records in the temple archives written by his predecessors, stretching back centuries, and some spoke of the journeys they had taken to the depths of the valley in search of some final, ungraspable aspect of their souls, or, more recently, in an attempt to raise the avatar of Ultharadon to fight on their side – the spirit of the mountain, noble and uncontainable. The journey down, deep into the mire of the self, instead of the journey up into the clear, unfiltered air… Carreth shuddered, turned his eyes away from the valley and the secrets it held.

The temple looked no bigger than his thumb at this distance, the elegant porticoes and the marble dome indistinct, the square of the parade ground and the long, low hall of the Stoneguard barracks seeming like pebbles cast in the temple's shade. The fountain in the temple's forecourt glistened like a silver coin, the water sparkling as it cascaded from the pipes to the cupped marble bowl at its base. Carreth pictured the sculpted marble masks through which the water poured, each in the shape of a sacred ox head, the stubborn and resolute longhorns that were the symbol of the mountains, with which the Alarith temples decorated their wargear.

Looking forward, his gaze sliding down the mountain slopes in front of him, Carreth could see the long white road that led across the Ymetrican veldt, cutting through the ruffled grasslands and passing the Scintilla Realmgate in the far distance before it headed on towards the coast at Scholar's Gift. He saw the branching path that led towards the temple complex, each waymarker on the path distinguished by simple shrines to the grass and the trees, the open sky, the blended wind. As he shaded his eyes and stretched his sight, he could see a convoy of tiny figures moving slowly along it. A day's travel away, perhaps, pilgrims come to make obeisance to Ultharadon, to rest their weary souls in its enervating presence. He looked beyond them, staring out at the point where the horizon foamed into a wash of cadmium blue, where he knew the continent of Ymetrica dipped in crumbling shoals to the separating sea, and Zaitrec beyond it.

The day was falling now, dusk feathering across the sky behind the mountain. Carreth closed his eyes again and breathed deeply, aware of the birds cresting the higher peaks, the butterflies flitting to the mountain flowers around him. He had fasted these last seven days. His head was light but he felt unburdened, as if everything of consequence had risen up and floated away from him.

All that was left was the memory of his sister. He stilled himself and reached out with his soul, clutching the aetherquartz in one hand and pressing the other to the grass under him, the deep earth and the rock of Ultharadon. He drew shapes against the skein of reality, unpicking the weave of time and space, and into that sculpted breach he projected a searching spell – an element of his spirit cast into the aether, linked to Tuareth's sundered soul and anchored to his body as it sat in mute repose. As if feeling it in a dream, he was aware of the wind plucking at his hair and skating over his skin, and at the same time he felt his spirit move through the evanescent space between the realms, questing, searching, delving deeper into the blackness.

But there was nothing there, no spark of light he could focus on or draw towards him. There was only silence, and the endless pitch.

He raised the aetherquartz and stared deep into its glinting facets, watching the way the encased light swelled against the stone, flowing like a living thing.

Tuareth… where does your spirit hide? What has become of you?

It troubled him, but he pushed the concern aside. Standing up on stiff legs, he ducked into the cleft of rock and picked up his canvas bag, opening the drawstring and taking out the flint, the boxed shavings of his fire kit, a few sticks and twigs he had gathered further down the mountain. He collected a few loose rocks and made a circle of them on the grass, laying out the sticks in the centre and scattering the shavings around them. He knapped the flint to a rectangle of steel and watched the sparks ignite against the wood, and then with infinite care and patience he knelt and blew gently on the gathering flame, sheltering the fire from the wind with his hands as it grew and grew. He sat back and lost himself in its dancing, hypnotic glare. He could have started the fire with a simple spell, one even his apprentice could have managed, but the ritual of mourning emphasised simplicity. It was a way of dwelling in the self, relying on your base resources, connecting with your creaturely life.

When the fire had burned low, Carreth placed his offerings in the flames. There were flower petals from the temple gardens, the same green shade as Tuareth's eyes. There was a delicate cameo of his sister's face that he had carved from sardonyx, brought from the furthest shores of the Shimmersea. There was a poem he had composed, in words that had been wrought from his very soul in the days after he realised his sister was dead. He placed them all in the flames and watched the smoke rise, a pale ribbon writhing in the purple sky.

Last of all, Carreth held the aetherquartz above the fire. She would not be coming back for it now. The light in the cracked jewel was dark, smouldering in the dusk as the day came to a mournful close.

He felt the delicate gold traceries that framed the jewel, the spun silver, the metal clasp. He held here all that was left of his sister. He remembered her as a child, brought into life by his parents when he was already an aelf full grown – a warrior, a hero of the great conflicts in the centuries after the Spirefall, as they tried to bring peace and order back to Hysh. She had always looked up to him. She had worshipped him, and he had failed her.

Carreth slipped the jewel back into his bag. He watched the fire burn the offerings to nothing, sitting there on the little shelf of stone on the shoulder of Ultharadon where he had said goodbye.

'I name this place Tuareth,' he said, before he settled down to sleep. 'May all who rest here in the days to come find peace.'

Yet, he thought, *I do not have peace myself, as long as she does not have peace in turn. Her soul is out there somewhere, wandering the wild, untethered...*

* * *

He had been dimly aware of Alithis calling his name, the rushing of feet across the flagstones, the soft scent of the flowers in the clear evening. The vision had faded, and the present had intruded once more – the temple, the changing of the guard, the flank of Ultharadon soaring up above them.

'Tuareth...' he had muttered, falling back, weaker than he had ever felt before. They had carried him back to his chambers, Alithis directing four members of the Stoneguard to bear him up and take him through the echoing corridors from the parade ground at the rear of the temple. Carreth had hit his head on the ground as he fell, and he was reeling as they placed him on his bed. He scrabbled for the aetherquartz.

'Where is it?' he groaned. 'Where has it gone? Tuareth!'

Ilmarrin, who had picked it up from the ground where Carreth had dropped it, squeezed the jewel into his hand.

Alithis stood by the bed as Ilmarrin rushed away to fetch water and a cold compress, some healing herbs from the gardens. Carreth closed his eyes and forced down a swell of nausea. He felt as if he had been struck a mortal blow, a psychic assault that had channelled a lifetime of rage and sorrow through his system at once.

'What happened?' Alithis said. Her face was drawn, her brows knitted in concern. Carreth could hear the Stoneguard outside the temple, the officers shouting orders, the troops rushing to each cardinal point of the hill where the temple was raised, as if they expected imminent invasion.

Carreth stilled his breathing and tried to sit up. His head swam and he fell back against the pillow.

'I saw something,' he said. 'I felt it, and it...'

'You saw your sister?'

Carreth nodded. 'In Shyish,' he said. His voice cracked. 'I saw her fall, her regiment shattered. There was a face, leering at me out of the dust, skeletal, pitiless...'

Ilmarrin returned, moving unobtrusively into the room as if doing no more than restocking the incense in the braziers on the altar. He carried herbs with him, the leaves of the thasalla plant, and a basin of hot water. Carreth could smell the leaves' jasmine scent, and their refreshing odour cleared his head a little. The old aelf placed the bowl by Carreth's bedside and scattered the leaves across the water.

'When the temperature has cooled a little,' Ilmarrin said, 'try to drink. And you must rest,' he added, with as much sternness as he could muster. He placed his dry palm against Carreth's forehead, and his seamed face frowned.

'I will, old friend,' Carreth said.

'Rest is the best thing, mage. You are out of balance, I can see it. Your aura has been bruised with emotion, with very strong emotion indeed. Seek the first rungs of the Teclamentari, find your equilibrium once more.'

With a curt nod Ilmarrin shuffled out of the room, Carreth's thanks following him.

'He's like an old mother hen,' Alithis said, smiling. 'He cares deeply for you, and for the temple.'

'And I for him. I dread to think what would happen to the temple without Ilmarrin to run it for me.'

Alithis laughed softly and pulled up the simple wooden chair from Carreth's desk, but when she had settled herself her face was grave once more.

'So,' she said quietly, 'if what you saw is true, then the assault on Nagash has failed. Our armies have been broken.'

'I do not know. All I saw was my sister, her last moments…'

'Visions are often cryptic,' Alithis offered. She held out the hope like a lifeline to a drowning man. 'They show what might be, rather than what is.'

'No…' Carreth sighed. He held up the aetherquartz and showed her the broken jewel. 'I *felt* it, the moment my hand touched the stone. I had it in my pocket, my fingers brushed up against it... She crafted this jewel herself, and—'

'And it is a part of her,' Alithis said gently. She bowed her head and covered her eyes. In all the decades Carreth had known her, he had never once seen her express such emotion. He reached out his hand and took hers. Together they sat in silence, the Stonemage prostrate on his plain mattress, the seneschal on the chair beside him.

After a moment Carreth became aware of the Stoneguard again, their patrols around the perimeter of the complex. There were more of them than was necessary for the ceremonial processions of the night guard, and he could hear them muttering commands, shouldering their weapons, marching purposefully. Seeing the look on his face, Alithis stilled his concern.

'Some of us are still worried about the effects of the necroquake,' she explained. 'When you collapsed, I thought for a moment it presaged an attack, that you had been struck down by forces I didn't understand. The reach of Nagash is long, they say. Who knows what forms his malevolence can take?'

'You acted as you always have, and always will,' Carreth said, settling himself down again. 'Swiftly, and with unbreakable resolve. I thank you for it, but there was no attack.'

'Not yet,' she said. Their eyes met, and the knowledge passed between them. Carreth shook his head. 'If our assault has failed in Shyish, then I find it hard to imagine that the forces of the dead will not respond in kind,' Alithis continued.

'We don't know that yet. And in any case, we have met the dead before,' Carreth said. 'The foresight of the archmage protected the realm from the worst of the necroquake, but you know as well as I do that many a skirmish has been fought across Hysh with gheists and deadwalkers, all the tormented, enslaved serfs of Nagash's will.'

He closed his eyes again, feeling another wave of nausea crash over him. 'The dead are sad and lonely things, pressed into mindless service. I pity them more than I fear them.'

The room had become dark now. Alithis lit the lamp on Carreth's desk. Its limpid glow painted smooth shadows against the walls and made the simple chambers seem somehow even more austere. Alithis replaced the chair back by the desk and stood at the bedside.

'If it comes to war,' she said, looking down at him, 'there are those who could make a difference. Famous names, heroes… the saviour of Tor Glimris, perhaps…?'

Carreth laughed, without mirth. 'My fighting days are long behind me,' he said. 'And I don't crave glory as much as I used to. Tor Glimris was a long time ago. No,' he said wearily. 'What I crave now is rest, and the time to think of my sister.'

'Rest you shall have,' Alithis said, turning to leave. She stood at the door, looking back at him, her face strained with compassion. 'Time… well. We shall see how much time any of us get.'

Rest, he thought as Alithis left. *But I fear rest will ever be denied to me now. When I close my eyes there is only a leering skeletal face, and… and rage. Purest hatred, and the rage that ever drags along behind it.*

The dawn was cresting the temple's roof as he came down off the foothills onto the greensward. The marble of the rotunda glowed pink and gold. The longer stretch of the portico was angled out across the forecourt towards the fountain, which Carreth had seen from his perch high up on Ultharadon a few days before. He headed towards the fountain now, turning to look back at the hazy bulk of the mountain on the other side of the valley, the smooth stretch of ridged grassland that he had just crossed. The air was vaporous, soft, and the mountain seemed more like a painting than a bulk of solid rock. It had been sketched there in pastels and watercolours against the sky, and it lifted his heart to see it.

Ilmarrin was waiting for him beside the fountain. It would not have surprised Carreth in the least to learn that the old votary had been waiting there for the full fortnight he had been away, but his bearing was as dignified and impeccable as always. The breeze stuttered through the gardens and skimmed the water that streamed off the fountain spray, casting jewels of light against the grass and spotting Ilmarrin's indigo robes with dark drops. He bowed as low as he could manage. It was respect not just for the Stonemage but for the return of a pilgrim who had taken the mourning path up into the heights of Ultharadon.

'It is a great pleasure to see you back, mage,' Ilmarrin said. 'I hope you found the peace you sought.'

'Something like that, old friend,' Carreth said, smiling. He rested his hand on Ilmarrin's shoulder and passed on towards the fountain.

Carreth had communed deeply with Ultharadon for many years, and the paths he had taken up into the mountain had left his bare feet dirty but not bleeding. He climbed carefully into the bowl of the fountain as the spray cascaded into the air, reaching down to cup the water and splash it into his face. He washed the ashes away, washed the dirt from his feet, cleansed himself of the journey. The water was like ice, so sharp that it took his breath away. Ilmarrin, as he would have expected, produced a towel and held it out so he could dry himself.

'How has everything been here?' Carreth asked as he climbed out of the fountain. He took the towel and rubbed some life back into his feet. 'I hope my absence didn't disrupt the routines too much?'

'Everything has run as smoothly as would be expected,' Ilmarrin said in that dry, quavering voice. 'Aelthuwi has missed your guidance, it could perhaps be said...'

Carreth laughed, passing the towel back. Together they walked towards the portico of the temple building, where twin statues of Teclis and Tyrion, five times larger than life-sized, held up the entablature above the porch. They gazed down sightlessly upon the forecourt, both cast in shining bronze. Carreth lowered his head in respect as he approached.

'I often think Aelthuwi needs firm guidance to get out of bed in the morning,' Ilmarrin said dryly, 'let alone to properly attend to his studies.'

'I have perhaps been too soft on him thus far,' Carreth admitted. 'Yet the boy has the art – I see it – and he has the temperament to achieve great things with it.'

'A temperament he disguises well, clearly, behind a veneer of extreme arrogance. The gifted often mistake their natural faculties for hard-won achievement, I fear...'

Ilmarrin gave a mild cough and plucked gently at the sleeve of Carreth's robes to detain him as they passed under the roof of the temple portico.

'There is one other matter, mage, that you should be aware of...'
'Yes?'

Carreth looked at the votary, who couldn't quite meet his eyes.

'We have had many visitors in recent days,' Ilmarrin explained. 'Pilgrims to the temple, veterans of the battles in Shyish making offerings for lost comrades.'

Carreth remembered the figures he had seen as he sat amongst the peaks, many miles distant on the road across the Ymetrican veldt.

'I hope they were given all hospitality, in thanks for their service,' he said. He frowned as Ilmarrin looked away. His heart was beating faster, and the palms of his hands began to sweat.

'There is one here,' Ilmarrin said, 'who knows – who *knew* – your sister, mage. He waits for you inside. I thought it best to prepare you, before...'

Carreth nodded silently. He drew himself up.

'Thank you, Ilmarrin. I will retire to my chambers first and meet him in the sanctuary at noon.'

'As you wish, mage.'

'I'm sure we will have much to discuss,' Carreth said. He left the votary behind and passed into the cool shadows of the rotunda.

Much to discuss – and much I will not want to hear.

The sanctuary was a long, low room panelled in chestnut wood, with narrow windows and a great aetherquartz skylight in the ceiling. At one end was a stone altar, behind which was a vibrant fresco of Ultharadon that cast a penetrating light into the room. In that lustrous image the Spirit of Ultharadon strode like the mountain made flesh, a vast construct of stone and armour, its face a burnished mask that recalled the form of the longhorn ox. Sunlight fell in beams through the windows, like crossed spears in a ceremonial procession, and through the aetherquartz above came a wash of healing luminescence. There was a resinous smell in the air from lit incense, from the branches that some of the pilgrims had gathered from the pine trees on the mountain's skirt, and which they had laid in twin stacks on either side of the altar.

The young soldier rose from a prayer bench at the back of the room as Carreth entered the sanctuary. He was dressed in a simple pilgrim's tunic, but his military bearing was obvious as soon as he stood up. A Vanari warden, Carreth thought, from the core of the Lumineth armies. Carreth wore his robes of office, but not the high attire of official rituals, and his head was bare. He bowed to the soldier in simple respect, extending a hand to indicate he should sit down. For a moment they both sat there in contemplative silence. Further off in the room, Carreth could hear the muttered prayers of the other pilgrims as they placed stones on the altar, young men and women of the Auralan orders who had made the journey along the pilgrim's way, and who sat now on the low benches and lost themselves in thought.

'My name is Dae'annis Farren,' the young soldier said. 'I was with the Vanari host that marched across the Equuis Main, in Shyish, to slight the necropolis at Nykas on the Stalliarch Coast.'

'I understand you were in my sister's regiment,' Carreth said.

'I was, mage. Tuareth was the high warden, and a greater leader I could not have hoped for, I assure you. I hope you don't mind, but the name of Y'gethin means a great deal in Ymetrica, and Tuareth more than lived up to it.'

Carreth gave a thin smile – he supposed it cost nothing to humour the boy.

'She fought bravely, I'm sure,' he said. 'As did you all.'

'It was a fight harder than any of us could have imagined,' Dae'annis said, his face pale, 'against a foe more terrible than we could have known.'

'There is no shame in defeat,' Carreth reassured him, 'if the enemy outmatches you. War is a gamble, the greatest there is. Victory is not always assured.'

Dae'annis looked at him with something like affront.

'We were not defeated, mage. We had the field at the end, and we slighted their fortress, as much as we could manage. We won the battle, but our casualties...' He looked bitterly at the ground. 'But if that was victory, the archmage alone knows what defeat must look like...'

Carreth was confused. He reached out to grip the soldier's arm. 'Then the war is won? We defeated Nagash, and on his own ground?'

'I cannot say – I have no knowledge of such wider concerns. But rumour says that the Bonereapers made good their losses by the end of the next day, while our host will likely never recover.'

'Bonereapers?'

'The army of the dead, their elite. They are like nothing we have seen before, mage. Swifter, more aggressive. They... I would almost say they even *think* like mortal beings. They fight with skill and precision, and their armies are truly vast.'

'And what of Tuareth, my sister? You saw her fall?'

'No, mage, I–'

'What do you mean?' Carreth said quickly. His grip on Dae'annis' arm tightened. The soldier looked up into Carreth's eyes and then swiftly looked away.

'We became separated in the fight. The Bonereapers' cavalry came on in a terrible, sweeping scythe through our left flank – we didn't see them coming, only heard the thunder of hooves and there they were, eyes like corpse-light, cutting through us. We were on that flank, and Tuareth managed to reform the regiment to square before they reached us, but it was too late...'

'But what happened to her? Surely you must have seen!'

'The tide of combat, mage, it swept us both apart. I–'

'Don't tell me of the tides of combat!' Carreth shouted. His grip was like iron on the soldier's arm. 'Don't you know who you're talking to, boy? You ran, is that it? You ran like the coward you are and left her to die!'

He stood up from the bench and dragged Dae'annis with him, and from the fear in the boy's face his anger must have been terrible indeed. Carreth felt it boiling inside him, spiking through his limbs. The world around him became thin with inconsequence. The sanctuary faded, the fresco on the wall was drab and featureless, and the light that fell from the ceiling was just a wash of grey. All he could think about was this creature in front of him, and vengeance, bloody vengeance.

But then, percolating through the bedrock of his rage, came the first drops of hope. Dae'annis hadn't seen what had happened to her. He hadn't seen her die. Who was to say she *had* died, in the end? Did these Bonereapers, apparently more like mortal men than any of Nagash's troops, take prisoners? Was she even now languishing in the dungeons of Shyish, alone and afraid? He thought back to the mourning ritual, his groping search through the aether for the spark of Tuareth's soul. Perhaps…

He allowed himself to think it, and as he did so the light fell back into the room.

Perhaps she is still alive…

Carreth slowly unhooked his hand from the young soldier's arm. He was aware of the other pilgrims in the room looking at him with shock, and as he stared into Dae'annis' eyes he saw reflected there his own twisted visage, distorted by rage. It was like a blow to the heart.

'Dae'annis…' he muttered. 'Forgive me, I–'

'Mage,' a dry, respectful voice said. Ilmarrin was standing in the doorway, and behind him were Alithis and Aelthuwi, his apprentice. Carreth passed a hand over his devastated face. 'Perhaps a moment of reflection in your private quarters, mage,' Ilmarrin said. 'You're weak from the mourning ritual and should take the opportunity to rest.'

'Of course,' Carreth said. He looked at Dae'annis, tried to frame an apology that would be in any way commensurate to the insult he had inflicted on this young warrior, but Dae'annis merely nodded and stepped back, sitting once more on the prayer bench, his face creased with emotion, his hands wringing each other in distress. Carreth turned away. There was utter silence in the sanctuary – not the respectful silence of men and women at prayer, but the silence of sheer embarrassment and shock.

As he headed for the door, he could see the fresco of Ultharadon in the corner of his eye, but he was too ashamed to look on it directly.

The Ocari Dara, he thought. *The need for balance. But the line we walk along is thin indeed...*

CHAPTER FOUR

THE MUSIC OF THE SPHERES

He looked across the shroud of sky, and all the stars were black. He was walking amongst them, moving softly through blank fields of endless darkness, cold and silent. He was in the void, wandering far out in the space between space, the world between worlds. He stood and waited, his breath frosting as if it were the coldest day of winter. From far and wide came beams of light that crossed the darkness, shooting past him, as hard and bright as diamonds.

Then the dream shifted and he was a young warrior again, back from the wars as the Lumineth struggled to remake their realm, his armour stained with combat, his mouth a thin, hard line. His face was streaked with blood and dirt, and in the pause between battles he stood in his parents' house and held the new life they had made, a gesture towards a future that at that moment looked utterly precarious. Tuareth, which in the language of the Lumineth meant something like 'hope'...

'My sister,' he said to the child. She looked up at him with those sea-green eyes, her limbs wrapped in swaddling clothes. 'I will protect you,' he promised. 'Always.'

He leaned down to kiss her on the forehead but she was gone, and in her place was a rattle of bones, a skeletal face plastered with scraps of skin, screaming up at him, gnashing its jaws–

Then, twisting in its impossible logic, the dream shifted once more and Carreth was high on the slopes of Ultharadon, as high as he had ever been. The land was laid out like a rumpled sheet below him, dark and indistinct, as if a great hand had reached down and scrubbed it clean of light and life. The wind blew harshly, sharp as knives, cold as the grave. Carreth looked up and the very tip of the mountain was but an arm's length from him, piercing the firmament like a blade. No matter how hard he stretched he couldn't quite reach it...

And then he was in the darkness above, where the music of the spheres chimed and rang with unearthly melodies, and light and dark pirouetted in an endless dance together – Hysh and Ulgu, sun and shadow, life and death. He looked down and he was walking on dry earth, cracked and bone-white, covered with a layer of pale, undisturbed dust. His feet crunched through the dust as if he were walking on virgin snow. The bone-white field stretched off into the distance, bare and featureless apart from faint, cratered hollows in the ground. He looked up and saw only the endless night sky. Slowly, as he stared into the darkness, little pinpricks of light began to emerge, buds of white and silver that flowered into stars.

'Where am I?' he said into the silence. His voice boomed off and vanished in the aether.

You walk on Celennar, a voice said. *The true moon of Hysh.*

The voice emerged inside his head, unfolding there like a thought, an idea, a dream within a dream. If sound could be said to move with the properties of light, then Carreth would almost have said that it glowed inside him.

You do not dream, the voice said, as if reading his thoughts. *I have brought your astral body here, Carreth Y'gethin, to the place where the essence of Celennar took form and left only dead rock behind.*

Carreth was aware then of something moving behind him, prowling at the edge of his sight. He turned his head but it moved away, something wondrous and terrible, brighter than the sun yet casting no light on him. A powerful leonine body, a pair of unfurled wings, a masked face inscrutable and impassive, its tail lazily and sinuously whipping back and forth, lion's claws ripping trenches in the lunar dust. The wings, like those of some vast bird of prey, stretched out and blocked the stars. Carreth's heart was beating savagely with fear – with awe – but when he raised his hand to his chest, he realised it was not beating at all.

Celennar it was who showed me the ways of geomancy, and the true path of those who would dedicate themselves to the aelementiri.

'Teclis,' Carreth whispered. 'Archmage, I am not worthy…'

You have proved your worth to your people before, Carreth. The Wars of the Reinvention were a trial indeed, and one you bore without complaint. Many live now who would have died then, if not for your actions. But that was in an earlier age, was it not? You are not now as you were then, my servant. You turn from the fight and maintain your distance, your… equilibrium.

'Forgive me, lord,' Carreth said. He fell on his knees in the dust, head bowed in obeisance. He was aware of a light in the sky getting brighter and brighter, like a meteor drifting slowly towards the ground. Carreth stared at it until he felt his eyes would burn out of his head. As it came closer, he realised it was not light so much as the utter absence of darkness, and as it grew and reformed into the shape of a tall being in ornate armour, Carreth knew that he was looking on the Mage God himself. Too bright to look upon directly, Teclis floated by Celennar's side like a rising sun.

Shielding his eyes, Carreth could see the suggestion of his great horned crown with its flared cheek guards, the plume of his helmet drifting in the solar winds, his cape soaring out behind him.

You are torn inside, Carreth, riven by fear and hatred. I see it as clearly as I see your face now. You mourn your sister, but you fear your rage is stronger than your grief.

The light of Teclis seemed to expand then, and Carreth felt the heat searing his skin until he wanted to scream. He threw his arm across his face, but when he looked back, he was staring down instead at a grey, dead plain that shivered under an amethyst sky. Black clouds mustered in the distance, and a black sun hung oppressively on the horizon. Carreth looked closer, and he could see a great host marching across the plain, a forbidding fortress of ossified stone looming on the other side.

'The Luminous Host,' he whispered. 'Tuareth.'

Attend, Carreth. Look closely, and though it will pain you, do not turn your gaze away.

He saw the regiments of the Lumineth warhost drawn into their battle lines. He saw the gates of the fortress yawn open like a skeletal maw, vomiting out an endless parade of dead soldiers, unimaginable numbers marching in lockstep. He saw the two forces line up against each other on the dusty plain, the first clash of arms as they came together, the dust kicked up by their savage combat blocking out the sky. Then, as if thrown down into the very maelstrom, Carreth saw a regiment of Vanari wardens repulse the skeletal warriors who hacked at them with sword and shield, the sunmetal blades of the aelves' pikes gleaming like the dawn. He heard the savage cacophony of hoofbeats, felt the ground tremble, and then the Vanari regiment collapsed under the weight of cavalry that pounded into it – huge armoured horses, each a strange amalgam of bone from a dozen different creatures. He saw the aelves fight desperately, parrying and slashing with their pikes, and then his eye was drawn to the figure that led the skeletons – a warlord atop an ornate steed, his crested helmet dripping with black jewels, his scimitar rising and falling as he hacked his way to the front.

Then at last he saw Tuareth, her face covered in blood, thrown back by the warlord's blow. She scrambled backwards over the bodies of her comrades, unclipping a moonfire flask from her belt. Carreth saw her last desperate action as the undead warlord rose before her, his sword raised, his face an awful, screaming horror that chilled Carreth's blood. Tuareth threw the flask. There was light, as bright as the heart of a star. There was heat, like the depths of a volcano. The warlord screamed. The vision of Shyish went black.

'Tuareth...' he said, and the tears poured freely from his eyes.

That figure you saw is called Akridos, the Liege-Kavalos of the Ossiarch Bonereapers in the Equuis Main. A great king he was in days gone by, a warlord of renown, but a leader of little mercy. I fear his mercy has lessened in all the ages that have followed.

'Has?' Carreth said. Shielding his eyes, he again tried to look on the blistering form of the archmage. 'Tuareth killed him, didn't she? In the end? I saw it!'

Alas, Teclis said, and Carreth could hear the sorrow in his voice. *She did not. Your sister fought bravely, and with skill, but in the end she did not prevail. Though he was gravely injured, it is not so easy to kill the dead.*

'And my sister – what of her? I felt her die, I know it, but...'

Her body is broken, destroyed along with so many others in the battles of Shyish. Yet, I feel her soul remains...

'Then I will find it, I swear!'

Your sister's death is not why I have brought you here, Carreth. Many eventualities find their beginnings in this moment. Much of prophecy and foresight is woven about the figure of Akridos, and it seems he is destined to play a part that may lead to the destruction of us all. Hysh itself hangs in the balance.

'But... he is but one servant of Nagash. How can he hold such power?'

Across Hysh I have wandered, observing, and guiding the foresight of the greatest mages and seers, stealing into the dreams and visions of them all. Each of them agrees that Akridos will play some deep part in the wars to come, and that he threatens the existence of the Light of Eltharion itself.

Carreth felt a cold, sick sensation pooling in his stomach. Besides Teclis himself, the Light of Eltharion was the avatar of the Lumineth race, a being of purity and grace and a link to the sundered age of the world-that-was. It was a living legend that gave heart to all, an animate soul that in some intangible way represented the very best of them. It could not be destroyed, surely? To even think of it was to realise how much such an event would shatter Lumineth morale.

And although it is in ways that are shrouded even to my foresight, Teclis said, *Eltharion is the fulcrum around which the defence of Hysh, and the defeat of Nagash, turns. I am not sure how or when it will happen, but happen it must. Eltharion cannot be risked. Light must defeat dark. The shadow must be banished. Akridos must be destroyed.*

Carreth, his eyes burning, was aware of Celennar stretching out those vast wings, and he felt the solar winds blow over him like the chill blast of a winter's morning.

'Why tell me this, lord? What can I do?'

The fate of Akridos is woven around your own fate, Carreth Y'gethin. The great web of time and space is an intricate thing, but follow any thread from this moment and you will find Carreth and Akridos entwined as one. Trapped, one could say, but entwined all the same. You have your part to play in this, as do we all.

Carreth lowered his head, in fear as much as in awe. He could not believe he was going to contradict a god, but for too long he had explored the accounts of the Ocari Dara to turn away from the lessons he had learned there.

'It is a risk too great for me,' he said. He was almost pleading. 'I have delved deeper than most into the studies of our failures, and I am no stranger to the study of myself. I know what I would become if I took the path of war. It is why...' He swallowed and covered his face. 'It is why I turned away from the path of the warrior in the first place.'

You fear the emotions in you that yearn for release. The anger, the violence, the lust for war. Do not be ashamed to recognise it, Carreth. You have striven all these years in the shadow of Ultharadon to master your emotions, to find equilibrium and peace. But the risk must be taken – the sacrifice, if necessary, must be made. It is a great thing I ask of you, but it must be so.

Carreth wept. 'Do you command it, my lord?'

I do. The invasion of Hysh gathers pace, and before long the legions of Nagash will pollute our holy ground. Liege-Kavalos Akridos will bring his Stalliarch Lords to Ymetrica, and your paths will cross. You must raise your forces, prepare yourself for battle once more. It is a battle you cannot lose.

'Then as you command, I obey,' Carreth said. He got up from his knees. The light of Teclis burned through him like a spear cast out by the sun. Carreth cried out, and the music of the spheres became discordant and shrill, a violent knocking that hammered into his skull and threw him tumbling through the incandescent void...

Carreth woke. The knocking continued, shuddering at his door. He raised himself from his bed, groggy, his mind reeling.

'Mage!' a muffled voice called out on the other side of the door. 'Mage Y'gethin! Master, you were crying out – is anything wrong?'

Carreth, rubbing the afterimage of the vision from his eyes, the pinwheeling stars, the shattering light, pulled open the door. Aelthuwi stood there, his apprentice, and when he looked on Carreth his mouth fell open.

'M-master!' he stuttered in awe. He dropped to one knee.

'Aelthuwi, for goodness' sake, what is it?'

Carreth looked up, and he could see Ilmarrin in the corridor, the old votary's face wet with tears. Like Aelthuwi, he too dropped slowly to his knees.

'Mage Y'gethin!' he cried. 'By the Holy Light of Hysh... Teclis himself imbues you with his light!'

Aelthuwi reached out to touch the hem of Carreth's garment. He looked up with a joy that he was quick to master, controlling himself once more but unable to remove the look of reverence. Reflected in the boy's eyes, Carreth saw the light that was streaming from him. He held his arm up and saw his skin glowing with a faint illumination.

'The command of Teclis,' he whispered. He set his jaw and clenched his fist. 'Come, Ilmarrin, Aelthuwi, my friends. Rise up, and do not kneel before me.' He helped Ilmarrin to his feet, and as he looked at his old friend he saw, overlaying his sight, the strange planes and figures of his dream – the lunar crust of Celennar, where he had walked with gods. 'The age is set against us, it seems,' he said. 'Nagash prepares his response. It is time we prepared our own.'

CHAPTER FIVE

THE BONE-TITHE

A thousand would do it, Akridos thought. *No less, but certainly no more.*

He looked down the dusty valley at the human settlement below. The town had high walls, and it was flanked on one side by rough, broken ground that staggered upwards into a low tumble of jagged hills. On the left flank, the other side of the town abutted the shore of a great inland sea, with a strip of land between the water and the walls that was far too narrow for any army to deploy in force. The sea then curved away towards the north, so it was as if the town sat in the tip of a promontory, protected on all sides. The only possible approach was from the front, where the walls were thickest and where the ground was cramped and hard to navigate. This stretch of the coast had long been a refuge for bandit armies and petty warlords, human or otherwise, in all the ages that Akridos could remember. Strong walls, an impassable position – these were good things in war, regardless of the foe. Yes, they would surely feel themselves safe in such a place, as safe as anyone could be in the Realm of Death.

Akridos sat atop his steed and felt the cold wind course bitterly through his bones. He cast his thoughts back into the distant past. Had he led his warband here in days gone by, he wondered, demanding tribute, or just for the sheer pleasure of sacking a civilised place? Had he watered his horses on the shores of that sea, and had he led his retinue through those gates, broken and cast down by the force of his assault? He could not remember. Who he had been back then, and who he was now – they were just faded concepts squatting in his mind.

Akridos turned his steed aside and rode over towards Kathanos, hunched there in his Mortisan throne. It didn't matter where the humans had come from or how long they had been here. They would pay the bone-tithe, or they would die.

'Time presses,' Akridos said. 'If the tithe is to be gathered, it must be done soon.'

'It must,' Kathanos replied. 'Serendipity brings us along this path, where the tithe has not been paid in some decades. I will approach and remind them of their obligations.' His skeletal jaws champed together, as if in anticipation of the payment.

Akridos turned and looked back at the town's walls, no higher than three men, end on end. The gates were of solid wood, reinforced with iron bands. He could see heads peering over the crenellated battlements, militia or city guard bearing spears and crossbows. If it came to it, the Liege-Kavalos knew that he could take this place in moments. It would offer no obstacle if he should decide to send the merest finger of his army stretching towards it, let alone the entire fist. He glanced back up the valley, where some of his outriders were gathered with a regiment of Mortek Guard. The elders of the town no doubt thought them a fiendish enough foe, but beyond them, hidden from view on the other side of the ridge, was a wide plain covered in a layer of grey dust, a mile across, and on every square of that mile stood a warrior under Akridos' command. There was cavalry in their thousands, legionnaires in vast columns armed with sword and buckler, spears and shields. There were war machines, the beetled colossi of the Harvesters, the elite of his Immortis Guard. Yes, this miserable settlement could be taken in moments, he knew, but every moment they spent here was mere delay.

'The mustering is taking place as we speak,' Akridos told the soulmason, his voice crackling in the air like the rustle of dead leaves. 'Nagash calls all the legions to arms, and I would not tarry if it can be helped. If it is to be done, let it be done now.'

'The moment is ripe,' Kathanos said, inclining his head towards the town at the other end of the valley. With a gesture Kathanos directed the Mortisan throne forward and picked his way carefully down the scree towards the valley floor. 'Join me, then, and see how the tithe is enforced.'

Akridos spurred his steed and followed. *He cannot accept a command*, he thought, *but decides instead that the command and his intention were always the same.*

Mist lingered on the floor of the valley, curling over the dry ground. The only sounds were the muffled tread of Akridos' steed and the curious, scratching progress of the Mortisan throne. Above the settlement a pall of grey smoke rose from cookfires and forges, blending with the clouds that were thinly smeared across the sky. The air shuddered with wind, ruffling the cloak Kathanos had pulled around his crouching bones, as if he had flesh enough to feel the cold.

Akridos could see the defenders on the wall staring down at them now, pale, drawn faces, eyes wide under tarnished steel helmets. Spears trembled in uncertain hands.

What must we look like to them? The dead are numberless in the sands of Shyish, and familiar to all, but this... we must look like something else entirely.

They stopped a dozen strides from the gate. Away on the left of the town, beyond its walls, the turbid sea buckled and swayed. Akridos looked up at the walls, where the defenders gazed down in terror. Silence fell again across the valley, and even from the inside of the settlement there was no sound of voices or clanking weapons. Everyone waited. Then, at last, Kathanos moved forward on his Mortisan throne and spoke.

'Nine times nine medimnos of bone is the number of the tithe,' he called out. His voice, the creak of a dead branch in a desiccated forest, wailed across the dry land. 'Nine times nine medimnos. You will bring the bones to your city gates at dusk, where we will take them and consider the tithe paid. Not an ounce less. Nine times nine medimnos.'

The soulmason's voice trailed off into the dust. There was absolute silence. After a moment, Akridos could hear the scratching of a spear shaft against the stone above, a murmuring of hushed and frantic whispers.

'What if we have no bones to give?' a trembling voice called out. Akridos looked up, but he couldn't see the speaker. His steed scoured the ground with a hoof.

'Then we will return, in force,' Kathanos said. 'And take what bone you have. Whether you want to relinquish it to us or not...'

There was more muttered speech and harsh whispering.

'I don't see that you have much force to take it,' the voice said, more confidently. 'I see no more than a thousand troops.'

'A thousand troops are a fraction of what I command,' Akridos called towards the battlements. 'Beyond the rise there, ranked up on the plain, you will find thirty times that number, and ten times as many cavalry. You will see an army beyond your reckoning, and it will tear these walls down without the slightest exertion.'

'Nine times nine medimnos,' Kathanos said again. 'Not an ounce less. You have until dusk.'

They turned to go, Akridos leading his steed back along the valley, Kathanos directing the Mortisan throne to pick its way over the dry ground back to the encampment.

'Wait!' the voice shouted from the walls. 'Wait, please! What... How much is a "medimnos"?'

The lines of invasion had been laid down long ago, when Nagash first took back his realm and plotted the construction of his elite, the Ossiarch Bonereapers. The geomantic routes extended far and wide across Shyish, causeways of cracked bone that stretched arrow-straight across the plains or curved and swept along the lines of mountains and valleys, beneath churning seas, through spectral forests and ancient cities long since fallen down to dust. Lines of power and energy thrummed through the underworlds, guiding the legions of the dead, instilling them with renewed necromantic vigour. As Akridos had led his army onto this highway, marching it from the vast parade ground in front of the necropolis, he had felt the surety of purpose that came whenever the will of Nagash brushed up against his own. The route was immediately clear, etched into his mind without fear of deviation.

The legion had marched tirelessly day and night, pacing steadily through the grey steppes of the Equuis Main, heading towards the far coast on the continent's western side. They had left the necropolis empty behind them. The library, the Mortisan laboratories, the armoury and forge and the vast, echoing chamber of the Great Hall – everything was deserted once the journey had begun. Such was the scale of Nagash's displeasure, he would draw all of his forces towards him. They would return in time. Either they would be victorious in Nagash's war or they would be shattered to pieces on a distant shore. Riding at the head of his Kavalos Deathriders, at the very tip of the endless columns, Akridos looked on the coming battles with grim satisfaction. He felt the light uncoil in his soul gem, the aelven spirit flicker and pulse inside him. He squashed them both down. There was room only for Nagash.

As they marched on, the army passed through lands that he knew had once paid fealty to him. Rolling steppes of dry grassland where nomad tribes had, once a year, gathered in their thousands to give him tribute, low foothills of tumbled rock, where emissaries from distant cities had met to buy his favour and spare their settlements from his attention. A lord of the horse-herds, a king of the Main, Akridos had ruled his kingdom with relentless discipline and iron certainty, and he had been without mercy.

So much of those days was lost to him now. He tried to reflect on them as they marched, without sentiment, but he could recall no more than vague flashes of violence and conquest. He could not remember his own death, or the moment when his soul had been snatched from his underworld and pressed into service with the Ossiarch Empire. He looked down at his arm, holding the reins as he rode, the moulded core of aelf bone scavenged from the field after their defeat at the hands of the Lumineth. He reached up and touched his face, the sharp contours of his skull, and as his fingers brushed against the cheekbones and the sharply pointed chin, he saw a flash of light, the avenues and columns of a crystal city far away. He shook his head, snarled involuntarily.

'You are eager for the coming fight, Liege-Kavalos?' a voice said from the ground beside him. Akridos looked down from his steed to see Morfilos, one of the boneshapers who served the legion, the flared tendrils at the back of his skull twitching and undulating, as if feeling out the channels of energy along which they marched. 'I am a simple craftsman, but I, too, am keen for us to clash once more with our enemies. I have always found it a singular paradox that war is the most destructive business and yet, for the artisans of the Mortisan order, the most creative.'

He grinned, his sickly green eyes staring up at Akridos. The Liege-Kavalos turned away. The boneshapers were vital to the legion, more important than any armourer or commissariat, but Akridos had always found them strangely disquieting. No matter the strength of his will, he knew they could whip him apart with a gesture, strip him down to his constituent parts with no more than a thought.

'I am eager to serve Nagash,' he said.

'Indeed. And to serve the God of Death is to praise him,' Morfilos said. 'Nagash is all.'

'Nagash is all.'

Akridos spurred his steed onwards, breaking away from the columns of his marching troops and cutting up a slight rise to stare down at the desolate lands as they stretched away before him. Valleys and dead meadows, plains and heathland, all covered with the same dead layer of grey dust, dotted here and there with blackened rock. A troop of his Deathriders followed closely, fanning out behind him, ready to respond to any threat. Their tattered banner shivered in the breeze, the dead wind that coursed across the dead lands. Akridos looked out at the breadth of his former kingdom. He searched himself for... what? Regret? Nostalgia? The anger that all this was no longer his alone?

No. Kingdoms rise and fall, and kings with them. I am not as I was, and those days are gone down to the dust behind me.

He glanced back and saw Kathanos at the head of the column, the soulmason rocking gently back and forth on his bipedal throne, the jewels in his mitre catching at the dull light. Morfilos walked at the soulmason's side, and the two representatives of the priestly caste slowly turned their gaze upon him. Behind them, laid out in unbroken columns as far as the eye could see, the troops marched on. Skeletal feet and skeletal hooves trampled the earth, and the sound was like the distant boom of thunder. The Immortis Guard towered over the other soldiers. The great Mortek Crawlers trundled along far behind them, the arms of their catapults stowed for the journey. Akridos looked on it all with smouldering satisfaction.

But new kingdoms can rise, he thought. *New crowns can be won, in new lands ripe for conquest.*

'Onwards!' he called, gesturing with his sword towards the distant green line of the coast, far over on the other side of the Main. The light was just a feeble pulse inside him, a squirm of crushed resistance. 'Onwards, for Nagash, and victory!'

It was a pitiful offering, in the end. Akridos looked down from his steed at the nine baskets of dried cemetery bone, butcher's offcuts and street sweepings the townsfolk had gathered up and dumped in front of their gates. Brittle femurs and skulls were still dusted with dirt from where they had been dug out of the ground, and the butcher's bones were drizzled with gore. The gathering of the tithe was not his purview, but even Akridos could tell that this was an insult compared to what had been demanded.

The sun crested the battlements of the town, rising in a murky dawn. Akridos stared up into it, his sight unaffected. He could see silhouettes on the wall, the elders of the town nervously appraising the Bonereapers' response. The valley was cold and bleak behind him. Tendrils of fine sand uncoiled from the ground as the sea breeze shivered in from the coast beyond the settlement. The water lapped in an unsettled flurry at the shore. They would have to cross that sea to reach the muster point. It had been serendipity indeed that had brought them into the path of this place – although he was sure the townsfolk would not see it that way...

'Is it enough?' a voice called down. 'Damn you, we didn't know what a medimnos was, but it's all we could manage. We dug our own dead from the ground – you cannot ask for more! Take it! Take it and go, you monsters!'

Kathanos peered down from his Mortisan throne at the baskets. Akridos could feel his distaste. Slowly, he stared up at the waiting elders. Akridos saw them flinch back, could almost feel their held breath, their cold dread at the soulmason's response.

'It is…' Kathanos said, '…*not enough.*'

A spear came sailing over the wall and plunged into the ground at the feet of Kathanos' throne. He glanced down at it. Another spear struck the shoulder blade of Akridos' steed, chipping off a fragment of bone. Neither steed nor Liege-Kavalos flinched.

Akridos half-turned in the saddle and raised his sword, and a moment later, from the other side of the ridge at the end of the valley, came a low, vibrating snap. Akridos looked up, as he was sure the elders of the town were now doing. High in the sky, glowing with a weird fluorescence and getting gradually bigger, were half a dozen black specks. They made a low whistling sound in the silence as they fell, and as they got closer Akridos could see the screaming features of the necrotic skulls more clearly. Down they plunged, seeming to gain speed the closer they got to the walls of the town, until they crashed into the stone with a deafening explosion of bone and dust.

There was a scream, a puff of red mist from the battlements. One of the crenellations sheared off and yawed to the side, slowly toppling to fall in a cascade of stone in front of the gates. There was another low, vibrating snap, and then more missiles were falling – and then another, and more.

'Perhaps,' Kathanos said as he angled his throne backwards, a great chunk of masonry crashing to the ground before him, 'it would be prudent to rejoin the army further up the valley?'

'It would,' Akridos said. He didn't move.

'The Immortis Guard, at the very least, should be with us,' Kathanos grumbled.

'They should.'

Kathanos hissed with impatience, but Akridos ignored him. He could feel it then, through his steed's hooves, its skeletal legs – the rumble of a coming earthquake. He turned again and looked back up the valley. Slowly, a regiment of Mortek Guard drifted into view in a haze of dust as they reached the top of the rise. First their banners, fluttering and grim, the colour of old blood. Then their spear tips, then the warriors who bore them. Akridos watched them come on, the column marching at pace through the cramped ground, approaching the town walls with relentless discipline.

The Crawlers had switched their ammunition now, and with deadly precision were directing their cursed stelae onto the outer walls and the gate. Huge blocks of stone inscribed with foul death hexes, the stelae splintered the gate to kindling and crashed into the walls, forcing a breach. Other Crawlers threw cauldrons of torment high over the battlements and deep into the town, the trapped spirits within them howling with maddened grief as they tore through the air. Akridos could hear screaming from within the settlement, the groans of the wounded, the crazed shrieks of those who had nowhere to run.

The Mortek Guard passed him, row upon row, marching up the slope of debris and into the breach. In moments Akridos could hear the clash of steel. The column marched on, without pause, pouring like a tide into the broken town. Akridos spurred his steed and followed, scrambling up the scree, his sword low at his side.

'Liege-Kavalos,' Kathanos cried in his brittle voice. 'Is your presence really necessary?'

Akridos didn't answer. Necessary or not, it was what he wanted. He passed beyond the breach and entered a street that was littered with dead. It was a mean place, most of the buildings little more than wooden shacks raised high on grey stone foundations. The roads were narrow and the gutters were filled with churned mud and excrement, red now with the remnants of the town's dead. Some of the bodies had been crushed by the stelae or the necrotic skulls, their blood splashed liberally across the cobblestones or thrown up onto the walls of the tottering buildings around them. Others had been cut down by the Mortek Guard as they tried to defend themselves, each pierced in a dozen places by Mortek spears. Akridos saw the rear of the column advancing rapidly ahead, clearing the main street that seemed to run through the centre of the town. Another group had split up into smaller units to clear the miserable houses, most of which had been battered by the Crawlers' assault. Smoke and dust drifted like mist. Here and there, chunks of masonry or wood detached from stricken buildings and crashed to the ground. He saw fleet shadows running through the haze, the slap of feet, the huffed cries of those desperate for shelter. Akridos turned a corner and found another bundle of dead men, one impaled on a spear that was still clutched in a severed skeletal arm.

He glanced up as a scream pierced the air, cantering his steed to avoid the body of a young man who plunged to his death from a window three storeys up. Blood flashed up to paint itself against Akridos' leg. A desperate bellow spun him around in the saddle as one townsman came lurching out of the shadows on the other side of the street, stumbling from the shattered remnants of some tavern or gatehouse. He slipped, staggered, roared once more and came on, blood in his beard, madness in his eyes. He had a spear held awkwardly in both hands and he lunged forward with it. Akridos just had time to see the hammer of Sigmar hanging in a pendant from his neck before the spear was almost on him. He turned it aside with the flat of his blade. As the man stumbled forward, Akridos brought the sword back in a sharp forehand and hacked off the top of his skull. A fountain of dark blood pulsed from his head and a dribble of brains ran down his face. Akridos shook off the gore from his sword as the man collapsed.

He sat there for a moment, listening to the silence. There were no more cries, no more screams. A pall of smoke gathered in the streets. The town was dead.

He had been wrong, he thought.

A thousand troops had been far too many, in the end.

The sea slopped greasily against the shore beside the burning town, oily and black. The flames were reflected against its surface, a long streak of red and orange that rippled on the waves. Akridos looked across the expanse of water, which shuddered like a living thing. Far out, sea spray blurred the horizon.

Black smoke stabbed up into the sky from the settlement. Across the valley, the Gothizzar Harvesters trundled over the piles of dead that had been dragged from the burning streets. With manic frenzy, the fused torsos on the Harvesters' chests whipped up the body parts and peeled off the flesh, feeding the dripping bones into the Harvesters' maws. Behind them, boneshapers wove their necromantic magics, whipping the bone-stuff from the cages on their backs into huge osseous loops and reforming them piece by piece into new warriors for the Mortek Guard or the Deathriders. As the skeletal soldiers stood there, immobile, Kathanos moved between them, following the soulreapers who had shorn the souls from the dead. He muttered his prayers, taking the soul vials from the soulreapers and weaving those trapped spirits into new soul gems. Within the hour the army had grown by another hundred warriors.

Morfilos, who had finished overseeing the work of the boneshapers, joined Akridos by the shore of the bitter sea. Waves clinked the pebbles, ruffling up the grey sand.

'We must cross to Praetoris,' Akridos said. 'The muster takes place by the Nihilaus Realmgate.'

'The path of the invasion lines is clear,' Morfilos said. 'I do not know how deep the Saltcorpse Sea is, but it would not take too long to march across the ocean floor.'

'There are easier methods,' Akridos muttered.

'Indeed,' Morfilos said, nodding in agreement. 'Call forth your Guard, Liege-Kavalos, and I will make it so.'

Akridos turned and gestured at the regiment of Mortek Guard standing at attention nearby. They each took two paces forward and dropped their weapons in neat stacks. Morfilos raised his hands before them, light blazing in the caverns of his eyes. Waves of energy lanced from his palms, piercing the Mortek Guard, staggering them backwards. Slowly, shards of bone began to peel away from them, whipped off into a growing vortex that spun and drifted in the crackling air above. Arms and legs were shattered and sheared off; skulls were crumpled into fragments. Morfilos grinned and gestured, turning his hands as if moulding an invisible sphere, the green waves of energy pulsing with unlight. Whole ranks of Mortek disappeared into the wildly spinning vortex of bone. Morfilos turned and slowly guided the vortex towards the sea, a screaming whirlwind that whipped up the water into a fine mist. Akridos found himself retreating, hauling his steed backwards as the osseous matter began to stretch out and reform. The boneshaper moved his hands again, and great strips of bone began to mould together, piece by piece, and then, as these pieces combined into the shape of a vast, elongated bowl, Morfilos carefully lowered it to the water.

He moved again, snatching up another rank of Mortek Guard, jaw clenched with the effort. Slowly, in painstaking degrees, Morfilos pulverised the uncomplaining troops into the vortex, reforming and moulding them into the structure that floated beyond the shore – a monumental barge, its hull big enough to store half an army stacked like firewood, its deck wide enough for the Deathriders to stable their steeds.

Akridos watched with a feigned dispassion as Morfilos hauled another rank into the whirlwind of his art. Kathanos may see himself as the soul of the legion, the true representative of Nagash, but Akridos knew that Morfilos and his boneshapers wielded a power beyond comprehension. He clutched the hilt of his sword. What was steel against such force?

Hours passed, but eventually Morfilos drew down and dissipated the vortex. The troops were gone, just their stacked weapons to mark the place where the regiment had stood. The barge gently rocked at anchor on the black water before them, bigger almost than the town they had just destroyed. A thousand troops had made it, Akridos thought.

'We will need another,' he said. He called forward the next regiment of Guard. 'Proceed, Morfilos. Time is pressing.'

CHAPTER SIX

THE MUSTERING

They had long been a place of peace and silent repose, but the temple grounds now rang with the sounds of construction. The birds that sang their gentle melodies in the gardens had been frightened away. The soft play of water from the babbling streams had been drowned out by the rise and fall of hammers, the smack of wood striking wood, the barked instructions of aelves working from dawn till dusk. Each day, as the shadow of Ultharadon crept across the sward towards the temple rotunda, the work grew. More and more aelves arrived from the surrounding countryside and from the nearby towns and cities to help. The call had gone out and the citizens of Ymetrica had answered. The Temple of Ultharadon was slowly being transformed into a training camp for an army.

Alithis emerged from the Stoneguard barracks, dawn still staining the sky above the temple to her left. The sky burned with the colours of peach and cinnamon, but already the cool, clear light of morning was upon them. She stood in the doorway and fastened the straps of her armour. Over on the other side of the parade ground, she could see a new unit of Vanari wardens being put through their paces by Dae'annis, twenty citizens snapping their pikes to attention, lunging forward with all the force and vigour of regular soldiers. All aelves were by Teclis' decree committed to regular military training, but even so they were being stretched to the limit by Dae'annis' exacting standards.

'Acceptable,' he said in a tone that suggested it was anything but. Dae'annis walked down the line, clattering his sword against the pike tips, his face grave. 'But you are all too slow on the thrust. Again!' he cried. 'Stand to arms! Advance pikes! Charge pikes!'

The wardens snapped through the movements again, and even at this distance Alithis could see the satisfied smile on Dae'annis' face. He was proving himself a real leader, she thought. Tough when called for but encouraging when he needed to be too.

The young warrior had stayed, Alithis knew, out of some need for atonement. He blamed himself for Tuareth's death as much as Carreth did, and after the Stonemage's outburst in the sanctuary he was determined to redress the balance. He had seen war, she thought, and although it had clearly marked him, he felt it was his duty to continue fighting. That had to be worth something. It was strange what motivated some aelves to fight, though. Love of their people and their land, or hatred of the enemy, was one thing. But for some, like Dae'annis, what seemed to motivate them most was the sense of their own disgrace. He wouldn't be happy until he'd buried it in blood and bone.

Dae'annis saw her watching and raised his hand in a sharp salute. Alithis nodded, lifting one of her stratum hammers in acknowledgement. She would talk to him later about the new recruits, the stages of their training. There were so many coming in now that whatever schedule they drew up was soon overwhelmed. There just wasn't enough time, not nearly enough time to get everything ready...

She turned from the barracks, pausing for a moment to gaze up at the mountain as it rose from the valley, the soft velvet of its flanks, the crisp snows capping its peak. Thin clouds drifted across its shoulders, and she could see a flock of birds wheel slowly to alight in the treetops on its lower slopes. She closed her eyes, letting the afterlight of Ultharadon settle in her mind, bathing her soul with tranquillity. Seven days she had spent as an aspirant buried under the mountain's stones, seeking Ultharadon's favour so she could become one of the Alarith Stoneguard. Fasting and praying, and at the end relinquishing herself to its embrace, fully trusting that it would not kill her for failing in her sincerity. She remembered peering up through six feet of tumbled stone, breathing what little air seeped through the channels and cracks above her. How many years had she stood defending this temple, defending the mountain she loved and the Stonemage who ministered to it? And now everything was changing, and the pace of change felt too much for her to manage. Even Carreth was changing, blessed as he was by Teclis himself...

As long as I do not change. Like Ultharadon, I am the rock on which the Temple rests. No more, and no less.

The thought of the coming war fluttered in her breast, but she shook it away. She could tell no one and she could barely admit it to herself, but she was afraid. She remembered war, in those last battles of the Reinvention, and it wasn't something she was keen to experience again.

Alithis passed around the back of the Stoneguard barracks to see how work was progressing on the temporary accommodation. On the other side of a field of white tents, a dozen aelves were clambering about a wooden frame. Like a skeleton of the barracks behind her, it stretched out across a track of grassy, rough ground. Some aelves were hammering planks of wood to form the walls; others crawled across the slats of the ceiling to lay the slate against the roof. It would be a rough and ready structure when it was done, she thought, and an offence to any aelf who valued craft and artistry, but with any luck it should hold another two hundred recruits. Beyond the new barracks, on the rough ground that had long been left uncultivated, fifty Vanari sentinels trained their bows at the archery butts half a mile distant. Alithis strode over to watch, picking her way through the tents' guy ropes. Cook pots smoked over low fires outside the tents, and some of the recruits were only now sleepily rising from their camp beds. *How much did this align with their expectations of military glory?* she wondered. Cold nights, uncomfortable beds and not enough food – hardly the stuff of legends.

In the archery field, the sentinels nocked their arrows on command.

'Aim!' the high sentinel shouted, striding along the back of the line, hands behind her back. Fifty bowstrings were bent back, and the air thrummed with the tension.

'*Loose!*'

It sounded like the sky had been ripped open. The great Auralan bows all snapped out their missiles, and the arrows sailed on a searing trajectory towards the distant targets. Alithis shielded her eyes against the light and watched them rain down, plunging like meteors and peppering the targets with half a dozen shafts each. It was an impressive display. No more than a week of effort, and already Carreth's army was coming together.

She was heading back towards the Stoneguard barracks when she saw Aelthuwi remonstrating with the workers on the temporary hall. The young apprentice had a bundle of scrolls under one arm, and with the other he was gesticulating at the empty frame, the bare foundations still waiting for the floor to be laid.

'We have another five hundred coming in from Tor Prindis!' he was shouting. 'Due any day now, and nowhere to put them! *This* needs to be finished by the end of the day!'

The builders grumbled, as much at the lack of care being taken in these temporary constructions as in the speed with which they were expected to make them.

'The materials aren't coming in fast enough,' one of them complained, an older aelf with a deep scar carved down the line of his face. A veteran, Alithis thought. Come to help any way he could, and due more respect than this.

'Aelthuwi,' Alithis called as she approached. 'They're working as fast as they can – you know that. Some of these aelves have their military training to attend to once they've finished here. All of us are pulling together as much as we can.' Aelthuwi fumbled with his scrolls, dropping some onto the beaten grass. Alithis stooped to pick them up and pass them back. 'I'm sure Mage Y'gethin will understand.'

'I speak with the blessed voice of the Stonemage himself,' Aelthuwi said with a pious expression. 'Lord Y'gethin is deep in the weaving of a spell to scry out the movements of our enemies, and it falls to me to convey his demands. And at the moment, those demands are concerned with the army's logistics.'

'First of all,' Alithis said with a wry smile, 'Carreth isn't a lord. Secondly, military logistics are my purview. And thirdly...'

'Yes?'

'You're his apprentice, not his secretary. I've known Carreth for the best part of a hundred years, Aelthuwi, and he leads by example, not by demand.'

The apprentice looked at her with something like pity. He gave a sorrowful shake of his head.

'He is not as he was, seneschal. If only you could see it. The Stonemage is imbued with the light of Teclis. He has walked in dreams with the Mage God, and he has been tasked with a holy mission. And gods very much *do* make demands.'

Teclis save me from the righteous... Alithis thought. She wondered how pious the apprentice would look when she had pushed him over onto his backside in the mud. She had no time to find out though – from the other side of the temple complex there came a blast of trumpets and the rattle of hooves thundering along the pilgrim's way. Alithis instinctively reached for her hammers on her belt and saw Dae'annis sprinting towards her from the parade ground.

'Seneschal!' he shouted, waving his arm. 'We have visitors!'

They cut through the sunken gardens that ran along the side of the temple rotunda. When they reached the forecourt, Alithis saw a careering mob of horsemen clattering over the marble paving, some of them watering their steeds in the fountain's ornamental bowl. More were cantering up along the pilgrim's way. They moved so quickly that it was hard to judge their numbers, but Alithis guessed there were two dozen at least, Dawnriders on barded stallions as lithe and spirited as young colts. The riders were scarcely less exuberant, but their control over their mounts was absolute. A twitch of the reins, a whispered word, and each horse responded as if it was only too happy to please its master. Alithis stalked closer, her face grim, Dae'annis trailing at her side. Damn it, where were her Stoneguard? They had been stretched thin, but this was unacceptable. They were at war, and it shouldn't have been possible for anyone, friend or foe, to have breached the courtyard so easily.

'You nearly had me there, Ceffylis!' one of the riders shouted, reaching over from the saddle to slap a comrade on the back. 'That last stretch, I thought you were going to win by a head at least!'

'Aye, lord, and I would have done if it hadn't been for Gyfillim. That horse rides swift as the winds over the Xintilian plains, I swear.'

'Swifter, my friend!' the first aelf said, patting the horse's powerfully muscled neck. 'There are none on all the continents of Hysh that can match him.'

The riders noticed them at last. The winner of their race vaulted easily from the saddle and approached, his gloved hand extended. He was tall, taller than most aelves, and his pale cream armour was inlaid with gilded runes, beautifully worked. *Senlui*, Alithis noticed – the swift wind, Tuareth's favoured rune. The crest of his towering helmet was the colour of a clear sky in the early morning, and behind the Y-shaped slit of his face plate, his eyes glittered like the crystal waters of the Ymetrican shore. Despite his hard riding, his armour was spotless.

'You must be Alithis Stoneheart, the seneschal of Ultharadon?' he said. 'It is an honour to meet you.'

'I am,' she said. She did not take his proffered hand.

The rider withdrew the hand with a controlled smile and took off his helmet. Long dark hair fell in chestnut waves across the angular planes of his face, and his eyes, struck by the morning light, seemed to glitter with an even brighter blue. Behind the easy and affable manner, Alithis could see an intensity that he did his best to mask. Those eyes, she thought, so cold and clear, had seen the reality of war, as much as the aelf behind them still seemed to cleave to a dream of its glory.

'Truly though,' he said as he tucked the helmet under his arm and stared deep into her eyes, 'the tales I have heard do no justice to your beauty.' He bowed his head. 'Like the diamonds mined from the earth of the holy mountains, like a pass in the high places of Hysh, hard and unyielding, and sculpted with all the skill of an artist inspired by the stark beauty of the wind and the rain. Like–'

'And are you going to divulge your name, rider? Or do you have more poetry to recite first?'

'Poetry?' He laughed, teeth flashing. There was a chuckle and a groan from the assembled riders behind him. More of them had dismounted and were seeing to their horses' fodder. 'These bold riders know all about poetry!' He leaned towards her, as if sharing a conspiracy. 'I'm something of a dabbler in the art, you see, and many a midnight camp I've enlivened with a recitation or two... Perhaps, my lady,' he said in a husky voice as he took her hand, 'when our duties permit, you might indulge me and listen to my latest efforts...'

'I would prefer it if you would indulge me with your name and your business, horse master,' Alithis said through gritted teeth, pulling her hand back. The rider raised an eyebrow, a sardonic smile on his lips.

Before he could answer, Aelthuwi sprinted into the forecourt, having caught up with them at last.

'Don't you know, seneschal?' he panted. He leaned forward with his hands on his knees, regaining his breath. 'This is Lord Belfinnan, steedmaster of the Spears of Sariour! Belfinnan the Brave, they call him!'

Belfinnan demurred, raising his hands. 'Please, my young friend! Lord Belfinnan will be more than sufficient.'

'He led the charge at the battle of the Shadrian Crisis,' Aelthuwi went on. 'Split the Godseekers' army, then routed each half, one after the other, with no more than a hundred horse.'

'It's true, I was at that particular engagement.' Belfinnan laughed. 'And that was a hard day's work, let me tell you!'

'You're recently back from Shyish, lord, is that right? It's said you rode with the Mage God himself?'

Belfinnan's mirth died on his lips. His eyes went cold, then dark, and his carefree smile faded like the sun obscured by a drifting cloud. He looked away. Behind him his riders fell silent.

'Aye, we were there,' he said softly, and it was as if he was speaking to the wind. 'That was a hard march, and faint joy at the end of it. I didn't see the Mage God, but I too have heard he was there. Perhaps in a different host... I hear Mage Y'gethin's sister died in those battles?'

'She did,' Alithis said. 'As far as we know.'

'Then it is a sad tide that brings us here,' Belfinnan said. He turned back to Alithis, and as his eyes fell on her a little of his light returned. He pressed his hand to his breastplate. 'It is said that she bore *Senlui*, as I do. That makes her my sister, in heart if not in blood. I will compose a verse for her tonight and sing it in the dawn on the peaks of the holy mountain.' He closed his eyes.

'I was there as well,' Dae'annis said. As Belfinnan's dazzling blue eyes snapped open and fell on him, he nervously moved the pike to his shoulder. 'I was with her when she fell. Tuareth. She was a great leader.'

The steedmaster gave him a sober nod, and then, like a flash of lightning, he grinned widely and threw his arm around Dae'annis' shoulder.

'Then come, lad, show me where I can stable these horses and we'll swap tales of war and woe, and great deeds besides! We'll drink into the night and by morning we'll be comrades in arms – I hear the Temple of Ultharadon has the greatest cellar of zephyr-wine this side of the Shimmersea…'

Alithis watched them go, the riders leading their beautiful horses through the courtyard and around to the meadows at the rear of the temple, where the new barracks were being built, where the sentinels were practising their archery, where the hundreds of recruits to Carreth's army were slowly taking shape.

It is all changing, she thought. *It is all happening so fast… and not nearly fast enough.*

His chambers were dark, the thin muslin curtains closed against the dawn. He heard the clatter of the riders entering the courtyard but paid it no mind. He sat cross-legged on the bare stone floor, his desk pushed out of the way, his bed skewed over to the side. Carreth had been awake for hours, absorbed in the weaving of his spell, and it would take more than the faint gestures of the material world to disturb him or draw him from his path.

The words of Teclis burned in his mind, the Mage God's command. He should be out there in the courtyards of the temple, helping Alithis and Aelthuwi organise the new recruits. He should be overseeing the training or imbuing those citizens who had answered his call with the spirit of the holy mission that had been charged to him. The word had gone out, and as all Hysh prepared for war, Carreth had prepared himself for the role he had to play. As his cities and armies had been slighted in Shyish, so Nagash would strike back when the moment was ripe, and that moment felt very near. And so Carreth had gathered an army in turn, and waited for Akridos to reveal himself, the foul creature who had killed his sister.

He had seen her fall, in the visions of Teclis. The blood running down her face, the moonfire flask plucked from her belt and thrown to the ground as Akridos advanced – no one could have survived those injuries. He thought of the ritual up in the mountain though, the breath of his soul exhaled into the aether, reaching for her soul in turn and finding nothing. If she was dead, then where was she? If she lived, then where was she? He knew he should be focusing on nothing other than his preparations, but Tuareth's absence gnawed at him like a canker. He must know. There would be no peace in him until he did.

His hands deftly pulled at the weft and warp of space and time, gathering up in intricate gestures the invisible flow of aetheric energy. He saw the faint glow that seemed to pulse inside his skin. He uttered words in the secret languages, issued occult commands and felt his soul contract and then expand inside him. The room became dim, the sunlight faded. The breeze rippled the curtains and fell still. His heart beat once, twice, and then stopped. All the colours leaked away from the world, and the light of Hysh was just a faint white spark somewhere in the distance, on the edge of his mind. His soul made the leap from the material world into the astral plane and fell smoothly through the rippling void. In his physical hand he held Tuareth's brooch, and in the astral plane the aetherquartz jewel pulsed like a beacon on a distant coast, a light to warn of treacherous conditions. He steered himself by it, swooping over the jagged shoals of unreality, swimming through the dangerous waters of the void.

After a while, a moment that in the physical world could have been no more than a minute of sustained meditation, Carreth slipped from the void into the dead lands of Shyish, girded for war. The dead marched in limitless hordes, long lines of skeletons pounding the dust as they slowly stalked their way from ossuary to armoury. Corpses rose from the disturbed earth, overrunning settlements and towns long since used to the presence of the dead. Fell shapes flitted on the dark winds, and gheists screamed their horror in the night. The sky was like a bruise, livid and black, and the grey earth trembled under the weight of endless armies.

Carreth moved on, absorbing all he saw. Ruins emerging from the dust as it was blown by contrary winds. Inland seas of bitter salt waters, ringed by funeral barrows or the desiccated tombs of ancient kings. His soul flitted from underworld to underworld as he sought out his sister, quickening through the afterlives of countless civilisations, the bright light of the aetherquartz guiding him onwards. Shyish, strange and terrible, where the dreams of the dead found concrete form, and where the departed spirits from every civilisation in the Mortal Realms found peace for eternity… Carreth passed through underworlds that shimmered under the mantle of Nagash's will, wastelands where barbarian chieftains oversaw the endless feudal combats and feasting halls of their warriors, the tundra of nomadic tribes, the teeming libraries of obsessive scholars. He saw great wetlands where souls had been transmuted into migratory birds, herons and cranes building their nests in a strict hierarchy depending on the soul's social position in their former life. Through it all Carreth saw the aetherquartz sparkle in the distance. Like a miner panning for gold he sifted its glint from the dross that surrounded it.

He passed through a valley that was littered with torn cloth and scraps of mouldering flesh, where ragged birds descended from the sky to pick over the offal and screech their misery at each other. At the end of the valley he came to the smoking ruins of a small town by the sea. Its defensive walls had been smashed aside, its gate broken, and in the soot-stained streets he saw only the detritus of war – dried blood, carrion birds, discarded weapons. Doors hung off their hinges. Broken windows leered down into the shattered roads. Ruined houses spewed a drear smoke into the air, and the only signs of life were the scavenger dogs that clicked their way on nervous claws through the rubbish-choked alleyways. A sad and bleak little place, Carreth thought. He couldn't imagine what possessed living men to make their home in these grim lands, but even so this little settlement of no real consequence had been shown not an ounce of mercy. Everyone had been killed.

He passed on, his soul drifting through the smoke and skimming across the black waves of the ocean beyond the town. The water seemed depthless beneath him, a void, cold and unforgiving. The surface of the water was ruffled by the wind, stretching away from him in an endless grey sheet. He felt his soul shiver, squeezed by the weight of death that surrounded him in this awful realm, the infinite patience of those for whom time had utterly ceased to be an imperative – the endless dead, without number, without empathy or kindness or emotion, without the true sense of balance and the rightness of action that marks the living thing from the blind automaton. He girded himself, set the sights of his soul on the beacon of light that drew him ever onwards.

He raced across the surface of the water, and after miles and miles of blank, featureless space, he noticed a black speck on the horizon, bobbing in the sway of the waves. Closer and closer it grew. Although it was dwarfed by the breadth of the seas it crossed, Carreth knew that he was looking at a vessel of incredible scale. Its hull would have swallowed up the Temple of Ulltharadon itself, twice over. Hunkered on the deck was a long cabin, a mast raised above it trailing a vast banner that caught the wind like a sail. Following in its wake were three other ships, smaller but no less impressive, and as he got closer Carreth realised that these ships were all made of moulded bone. Here and there a skeletal face screamed out of the hull as the spray kicked up around it, or an embedded bony arm scrabbled ineffectually at the deck. Although he couldn't see them, he could feel the stacked weight of skeletal warriors packed into the hull of each vessel, silent and uncomplaining.

There were three figures standing on the deck of the larger ship, their feet fused to its surface, staring out towards the horizon. One was hunched and somehow more ancient than the others. It leaned on a tall staff, and its skull seemed filled with malice, the bare sockets of the eyes glowing with a fiendish green. The second figure was taller and thinner, its skull fringed with strange tendrils, like the tines of a mouldering crown. Carreth's soul recoiled to see the third figure, but he was drawn inescapably closer to it, drifting nearer and nearer. It was tall and powerful, its skull covered by a flared helmet that was studded with dark jewels, its armour polished to a bright, viridescent sheen. It had a curved scimitar at its hip, and Carreth knew that he was staring at the thing that had killed his sister – Akridos, Liege-Kavalos of the Stalliarch Lords, the Doom of Eltharion, the warlord that Carreth had been tasked to destroy. Rage simmered in his soul to see him, the lust for revenge, but Carreth mastered his emotions. That time would come.

He tried to move away, to leave his enemies behind and continue in his search for Tuareth's soul, but he found himself drawn back again to the figure of Akridos. There was something there that he couldn't move beyond. It gripped him, tried to draw him close, reeling him in like a fish on the end of a line, the hook piercing its throat. Carreth stared down at the Liege-Kavalos, the empty black pits of his eyes, the yellowing, mismatched teeth. Light rippled through his soul-sight, and the gem on the warlord's breastplate began to glow, piercing the Shyishian gloom. Buried in the heart of it was something as pure as starlight – trapped, squashed down and almost burned away, but as familiar to him as the cracked aetherquartz he held in his physical hand, back in his chambers in Hysh. Akridos directed his baleful gaze ahead to the distant shore as the undead army sailed on, but for the briefest and most horrifying moment Carreth saw through his twisted spirit to the truth. She was in there too, subsumed, drowning in the sea of his malice.

'Tuareth…' he sobbed.

The ancient skeleton hissed and snapped his head around, staring straight into Carreth's withering soul. The undead priest reached out with his staff, stabbing it past Akridos' shoulder. Carreth screamed, although whether his scream rang in his temple chambers or only here in the desolation of Shyish, he couldn't say. It felt as if all the aetheric sinews of his spirit were being shredded and torn apart, and it was only some desperate reflex that saved him from the priest's groping magic. Carreth uttered the words of a counter spell, a phrase that would join him with his corporeal form once more. He flicked out an aetheric hand and there was a diamond flash of light. He heard the priest howl with frustration, and then Carreth's spirit was winging its way across the waters, shrieking high above the sea, higher and higher, until he was looking down on the spinning ocean, the encircling lands, the invasion lines that glowed like corpse-light across the disc of Shyish. Each of those fell pathways was choked with the marching dead. From every corner of Shyish they came, Nagash's elite, the legions of the Ossiarch Bonereapers.

The invasion was about to begin.

CHAPTER SEVEN

THE LINES OF INVASION

Long they sailed across the Saltcorpse Sea, then down past the clashing rocks of Xanda into Taker's Reach. The black oceans, like spilled oil, sloughed and wavered in the coarse winds, but the bone ships pressed ever onwards. For days and days they journeyed. At every stage Akridos stood upon the prow, staring out into the spume of the waves, undaunted.

Near the Vitris Pillars the army steered their ships onto the bleak shore, beaching them on the rocks. The ships' hulls were torn apart by reefs and hidden sandbanks. Dozens of Mortek Guard spilled out and sank beneath the crashing waves, dragged down by their armour. The steeds of the Deathriders were shattered by falling spars, and the mast of one of the smaller ships pitched over and smashed the deck of the vessel that ran aground beside it. There were hundreds of casualties. For any mortal army it would have been a disaster, but within a day most of the damage to the troops had been repaired. Morfilos stood on a spur of land further down the rocky beach and gazed out at the stricken vessels. Once the army had disembarked, he wove his necromantic magic and stripped the hulls back down into a great loop of osseous matter, spinning like a necrotic gyre high above the shore. Before long, Akridos had his Guard back to full strength.

Kathanos moved between the ranks to ensure that they had been properly ensouled.

'Everything is as it should be, Liege-Kavalos,' the soulmason said. He glanced up into the lowering sky, his eyes flaring with light. 'Yes,' he whispered. 'You feel it too, don't you? The God of Death is calling us.'

Akridos did feel it, the presence of Nagash. It was like a pressure squeezing against the limits of his mind, a drumbeat hammering in the distance that was at the same time part of the contours of his thought. He tried to shift his mind around it, but wherever he turned, there it was.

Nagash… Nagash is all.

He gave the order to form up. The Mortek Guard and the war machines took up position in the centre, while Takanos led the Deathriders to cover their flank on the right, the coastline covering their left. There was no risk of attack here, not this close to the mustering point, but the habits of command were not easily shaken off. As always, Akridos rode at the head of the column, his personal guard of Deathriders fanned out behind him, the Immortis Guard following. The shadow lands of Praetoris fell away to their right, a mist-shrouded landscape of low hills and spectral trees, the hint of mountains in the distance. The coastline fanned out to their left, into the beginnings of a narrow promontory that stretched for a hundred miles into the ocean, but the invasion line extended onwards straight ahead. At the end of it, they would find the gathered hosts of Nagash's armies, and the Nihilaus Realmgate.

Akridos could see Kathanos hiking over the softly inclined

ground in his ponderous throne. A chill wind knifed across the shore to meet the breeze that curled in off the ocean, and as the army progressed they were caught in a buffeting gale that thrashed their banners and snatched Kathanos' voice away when he spoke.

'I have been thinking further on the spirit that tried to attack us as we crossed the ocean,' he said.

'A gheist of one sort or another, I should think,' Akridos said, although for the moment he kept his real suspicions to himself. 'The winds of Shyish are thick with them, the lost and the tormented too unstable for Nagash's purpose. No doubt it was the spirit of some drowned fisherman, cursed to haunt the surface of the waters that killed him.'

'There is that possibility...' Kathanos said. He tapped dry fingers against his chin. 'To manifest so suddenly like that, though, and then the speed with which it vanished... That was unusual, to say the least.'

Akridos remembered it, the spirit suddenly blazing in the air before them, its screech of agony and dismay, the blinding flash of light that sent it hurtling off across the seas. *White light, burning, burning...* 'Unusual' wasn't the word. Something had shuddered inside him, lurching with horror, and he seemed to feel again the savage pain of that blazing liquid the she-aelf had thrown at his feet in the battle before the necropolis. It had been no random spirit wandering lost over the unforgiving seas. It had come for him specifically. It knew who he was.

How much Kathanos suspected of this, Akridos wasn't sure. He wasn't sure either why he kept the suspicions to himself. Surely the soulmason knew already? He dealt in the stuff of souls every day. It had always been unclear to Akridos how much the priests of the Mortisan order knew of those they had ensouled. Did Kathanos even now peer into him like a physician staring into an open wound? Could he see that blend of cowed spirits roiling inside him – and could he pluck them out, one by one, on a whim?

'If you have something to say, soulmason, then come out and say it,' Akridos muttered.

'Indeed, I shall,' Kathanos laughed. It was a sound like the rattling of chains. He clacked his fingers against the arms of his throne as he thought. 'The spirit was not of Shyish, I am sure.'

'How so?'

'You could not perhaps see it with the same clarity, but to me it was obvious that it was not the soul of something that had died and that had passed into the underworlds here.'

'Then where did it come from?'

'It was a projection of some sort, a soul sent out from a living thing across the aether.'

'Is that possible?'

'Anything is possible,' Kathanos said slyly, 'if your skills in the magical arts are sufficiently developed. An aelven mage, say, would have little difficulty in such a conjuration.'

The spirit flared up inside him. 'The Lumineth,' Akridos said. 'They send spies to follow our progress.'

'Perhaps,' Kathanos mused. 'Gathering intelligence is one of the arts of war, after all.' He moved his throne away, falling back into the body of the army behind them. 'We must keep our wits about us. Perhaps it was not drawn to our progress at all, but to one of us in particular…'

The dry, flat ground began to rise ahead of them and then abruptly fell away, the long and featureless steppe revealing itself as just the bleak tip of a vast continental plateau. Beyond it was a truly huge depression, a sunken valley a hundred miles wide, like a massive crater beaten by a god into the ground of Shyish. It was ringed on all sides by the escarpments of Praetoris, and pathways led down into the depression from all sides, rough, grass-fringed tracks and wide avenues carved out of the stone and the earth, with here and there weathered waymarkers and shrines to forgotten gods. At various points down the pathways that led to the bottom, Akridos could see the black mouths of tunnels that delved into the earth of the escarpments – entrances to the underworlds of forgotten cultures and societies, the afterlives of dead races consigned to faded memory. Here was where death itself came to die.

But that was not what truly drew his gaze. Gathered in endless ranks along the bottom of the valley were the massed legions of the Ossiarch Empire – hundreds of thousands of troops, a sea of skulls and spears and swords, the infantry organised in colossal blocks, the cavalry parading in deathly silence. Dozens upon dozens of Crawlers were lined up at the rear of the gathering, and scores of Gothizzar Harvesters hunched there like immense armoured beasts from the wildest jungles of Ghyran. The armour of the Immortis Guard and the Necropolis Stalkers, unit after unit of the Ossiarch elite, shone with polished fire. There were even morghasts, Akridos could see, hovering on their skeletal wings, the will of Nagash himself rendered in pale bone. The colours of every legion were present – the smoky black of the Null Myriad, the burned bone of the Crematorians, the arterial red of the Petrifex Elite and the brooding purple of the Mortis Praetorians. Akridos took it in with a glance, stiffening in the saddle with mingled pride and shame – pride that the empire could field such staggering numbers, and shame at the thought of subsuming his ambitions within it.

A faint haze of grey dust rose up from the assembled multitudes. Akridos drew the army up along the line of the plateau, and then the hekatoi of each regiment issued the orders to descend. Akridos sat and watched, the troops marching under his commanding eye as if on review, all of them taking the long and winding pathways deep into the valley. The war machines took the wider avenues, trundling with care over the rocky surface, while the infantry and cavalry marched in near single file down the narrower tracks. When all had passed, Akridos followed. He watched Kathanos and Morfilos pick their way down the stony ground before him, and with a twitch of the reins he directed his steed to follow. Descending, hiking down into the vast, sunken valley, the Stalliarch Lords joined their numbers to the ranks of the dead. There they waited in silence for God to speak to them.

At first it was a change in the quality of the air that heralded his presence. High above the valley, the sky began to glow with a deepening purple shade, and the glittering, noctilucent cloud began to break apart and draw aside. The air became colder, duller somehow, as if the oxygen had been sucked from it. A thin and fibrous mist crept over the edge of the escarpment at the northern end of the valley. The silence, which had been absolute before, became if anything deeper still. Akridos clutched the reins of his steed. He was aware of Kathanos nearby, still hunched in his Mortisan throne, brittle skull tipped back in seeming ecstasy.

A ripple of sound, like the tearing of a mighty grave cloth, drew his eyes. Lightning flickered and strobed in the gathering darkness. In the sky high above the crater the clouds slowly formed together, and from the middle of that swirling cumulus a huge skeletal face gradually took shape. Transparent, blurred by the creeping gloom and the swirls of cloud that wreathed themselves around it, as big as the crater it loomed above, a hundred miles from brow to chin, the face of Nagash stared down.

Nagash…

Nagash spoke. It was as if the words already existed inside Akridos' mind and were only now being revealed to him. Whether those around him heard the same words, he wasn't sure. He suspected not. After all, couldn't they see that Nagash was looking directly at him, and at him alone? Couldn't they tell that his commands were solely for Akridos' attention, that the mission he gave him could be carried out by no one else?

The invasion of Hysh is upon us, the voice said in Akridos' mind. *The light of the aelves will diminish and die, and the Lumineth will be punished for their transgression.*

Akridos stared up into the sky, and the vast caverns of Nagash's eyes stared back at him, blacker than the void, pitiless as the deepest ocean, beyond such simple concepts as malice or mercy.

All will bow before me and place the offering of their souls on the altar of Death. All the petty magics of the Mortal Realms will be mine to do with as I will. Each here is an aspect of my will in bone and nadirite, and each has their appointed task.

As the voice rang out inside him, clanging like a distant bell, Akridos saw that task like a waking dream. An armoured figure stood before him, almost too bright to look upon. It was clad in white plate, and it bore in its hands two swords that glowed like the heavens themselves. The wings of its helmet fluttered like the wings of a bird in flight. The eye slits were dark and without substance, and yet the whole figure was wrapped in a dazzling nimbus of light. It radiated terror, and something Akridos was surprised to realise was almost like hope…

The Light of Eltharion, fell champion of the Lumineth Realm-lords, an avatar of the ancient days in the world-that-was, is come again to frustrate my designs. Destroy it, Akridos. Destroy the Light, and in so doing destroy the light that torments you, the little spirit that squirms in the lineaments of your soul. This task I assign to you, and you will carry it out without question. Take your legion through Nihilaus Realmgate to Hysh. Scorch the lands of Ymetrica, find the Light of Eltharion and destroy it.

Akridos found his voice, croaking, 'Yes, lord... I swear, Nagash... There is only Nagash!'

Across the huge depression, choked from end to end with the legions of the dead, the chant went up. From hundreds of thousands of skeletal mouths, screeching across the flat, dead air, the cry went out. *There is only Nagash...*

'*There is only Nagash! There is only Nagash!*'

Akridos had drawn his scimitar and raised it above his head, and around him the warriors of the dead followed. Swords and spears, axes and falchions, all lifted in grim salute to the phantom above them, the cruel visage of the God of the Dead – Nagash, who looked down on his will made manifest and slowly faded away into the gathering night.

They marched for Nihilaus, leaving the crater and heading further along the coast of Praetoris. Around them, other legions took different paths, heading for different conduits to disparate parts of Hysh, or to the wider Mortal Realms. Yet others set forth across Shyish, to scour away any remaining resistance to the rule of Nagash. The mustering had broken up, and as they marched, Akridos knew that this was only one mustering amongst many, and that at each Nagash had appeared to issue his commands.

And yet he spoke to me directly... He sees me for what I am, what I was – a king, who once commanded an empire, who will command an empire of his own again...

The Light of Eltharion would die – he had sworn it. He was commanded, and he would obey, but on the other side of this fulfilment he knew there would be something else. Victory would be followed with reward.

And if Nagash does not reward me, then I will take what I want for myself. The ripe lands of the aelves will be mine. Their plains will be the herding grounds of my horses, and their bones the sinews of my army. I will prosecute Nagash's will, and in time I will prosecute my own.

The Realmgate loomed out of the darkness ahead of them, crackling with green flares and shards of lightning. It had been carved into the basalt flank of a dormant volcano, the soaring residue of ancient lava that had once spewed across the Praetoris plains. Fifty yards high and half as wide, the Realmgate had been fashioned into the shape of a screaming skull. Aetheric energy rippled in the skull's mouth, and around the eye sockets were etched runes that glowed with emerald light. The portal stood there like a vertical tide, a slick pool of dark water, infinitely deep. Without pausing, Akridos rode towards it, his sword raised to guide his troops. He disappeared into the murk, swallowed up like a stone dropped into a well. Behind him came Kathanos, and Morfilos, and all the soul-workers of the Mortisan order. Behind them came the cataphracts of the Kavalos Deathriders, and then the endless ranks of the Mortek Guard. All stepped without pause into the oily portal of Nihilaus, swallowed by the screaming skull and ready to be vomited up an unguessable distance away, in a different plane of existence entirely. Akridos and his Stalliarch Lords passed on from the dismal lands of dead Shyish.

The invasion of Hysh had begun.

PART TWO

CHAPTER EIGHT

DARKNESS WITHIN

The stairs before him were dark, each step saddled by the weight of centuries of feet. They curved down into the darkness, a spiral staircase that twisted its way deep into the bowels of the temple. Shadows crept up the rough-hewn walls. Behind him, Aelthuwi tried to conjure a ball of light, muttering the arcane phrases and trying to cup the flickering flame in his palms. Carreth turned around and sighed.

'Your help organising the training and the accommodation has been invaluable, Aelthuwi,' he said. He held out his hand and visualised the rune of kindling, and there was a blaze of blue flame. Carreth passed the swirling ball of light to his apprentice, who carried it gingerly in his hands like a precious jewel. 'I worry though that with all this... *change* around us, your studies are being neglected.'

'I'm sorry, mage,' the apprentice said quickly. 'I don't mean to neglect them, it's just there's so much to be done. I felt the priority must be the war–'

'We're not at war yet,' Carreth snapped. 'Not openly, at least. These are only the opening moves. Much yet hangs in the balance.' He frowned and pressed his hand to his eyes. 'Forgive me,' he said. 'The fault is mine. I have not been there for you, to guide you in your development.' Carreth smiled up at him with regret, the ball of light crackling in the apprentice's hands, casting his face in leaping shadows. He remembered the bold young lad brought to the temple by his parents, their mixed expressions of pride and anxiety. All the aelves of Hysh demonstrated an element of magical skill, to a greater or lesser extent, but Aelthuwi was one of those who was clearly destined for mastery. Even at a young age he seemed to understand magic not as a tool to be used but as an art to be perfected. He was naturally gifted, but he had never seemed to follow the guidance that was given to him. Carreth sighed. 'I have not been a very good master, I fear.'

Aelthuwi's face was drawn with sincerity. He looked almost horrified that Carreth could hold such an opinion of himself.

'Master!' he whispered. 'None could have been greater!'

Carreth laughed and put his hand on Aelthuwi's shoulder. 'You do me great honour,' he said. 'Now, come – we have work ahead of us!'

The light flattened the shadows and tinged the stone with a hint of silver. As far as Carreth knew no one had been down here for some time. The archives of the library were a forbidden space to any but the head curator – and to the Stonemage himself. It was about time his apprentice had access to the deeper mysteries of the temple.

'Raise your light,' he said to Aelthuwi. 'And take care. The archives are not a place to be taken for granted. There is much down here that would be better off… forgotten.'

'Yes, master,' the apprentice said. Carreth saw the light tremble.

He clutched the key in his hand and descended, twisting around the tight stairwell, his footsteps muffled in the dark.

Is this right? he thought. *Am I doing what needs to be done, or what I want to be done instead? But I must know if it is possible... There is no peace in me until I know, and knowledge often lies at the end of dark paths.*

Halfway down they came to a rusted black gate. While Aelthuwi held up the conjured ball of flame, Carreth fitted the key to the lock. The gate screamed open before them. More stairs lay beyond it, twisting further down into the foundations of the temple.

The deeper they went, the colder it became. Another black gate met them, locked this time by a great iron bar and by warding symbols etched into its iron frame. Carreth leaned for a moment against the frame with his eyes closed. He drew the warding glyphs in his mind's eye, painting them within the astral plane in lines of fire and light. Subtly he altered their shapes, reconfiguring them, blending some to others, taking others apart. After a moment, the wards fell and their shapes faded away, leaving only an ancient door fused to the rock. Carreth pushed it open, the hinges shrieking with rust.

Ahead of them, a short corridor opened into a wide, low-roofed chamber, black with shadows. Aelthuwi stepped forward and gently cast the ball of light into the air, and as it drifted up towards the unworked stone ceiling, no more than an arm's length above them, the library archives were revealed in all their musty glory.

There were piles of bound books and scrolls on the flagstones, some warped with damp, all of them coated in a thick rime of dust. Others were piled up haphazardly on the listing shelves, the lines of bookcases stretching away into the darkness along the length of the chamber. Carreth couldn't see the end of it, it was so far. He hadn't been down here for years – the shelves of the library proper were more than sufficient for his studies. Cobwebs drifted down from the corners of the ceiling, and he was sure he could hear the papery scrabble of mice behind the bookshelves. Here, Carreth knew, amongst the pedantic accounts of archivists and librarians from the temple's earliest days, nestled between local histories and archaeological records of the nearby Ymetrican veldt, was where the most secret and dangerous texts in the library were kept. These were books of ancient magic that had survived the Ocari Dara, and some of them had in many ways been instrumental in turning Lumineth society from its proper path. These were the books he needed now.

'We must be underneath the forecourt, if I didn't get myself turned around,' Carreth said, looking up at the ceiling. 'It is many years since I was last down here – probably not since I was an apprentice, like yourself.'

Aelthuwi swallowed nervously. 'I don't know why, master, but I feel… strangely frightened. It's like…'

'Like the books themselves are listening to you?'

Aelthuwi glanced at the shadows with alarm and slowly nodded.

'It's more than understandable,' Carreth said quietly. 'There are volumes down here that are not to be taken lightly. In the wrong hands, or even in the right ones, they could be extremely dangerous.'

There was a desk and a group of chairs in the corner, ancient, mouldering things eaten with rot. The surface of the desk was covered in old parchment and boxes of paper. Carreth carefully placed them on the floor and found a brace of candles that he lit with an uttered word, fixing them into a candlestick. Their smoky glow crept out over the chamber. Aelthuwi cancelled the conjured light.

'See if you can find more candles,' Carreth said. He stood there with the candlestick raised high, the light falling in an amber pool around him. As Aelthuwi began rifling through the shelves, Carreth gazed down the narrow length of the archive, a long, low chamber of dormant energy, dark thoughts and dangerous magic. He wasn't even sure what he was looking for – he would just know it when he found it.

And when I find it, Tuareth, you will come back to me, I promise. I will save you.

She crossed the stone terrace at a fast clip, ashamed and slightly incredulous that she was late. The flowers in the ornamental gardens, a riot of purple and green and yellow, nodded their heads in her wake as if eagerly agreeing with her.

Alithis scolded herself under her breath, cutting across the moon bridge, a scattering of dead leaves lazily turning in the silver waters below. There was so much to do, so many demands on her time. Appointments came and went without her realising. The forges in the nearby town of Tor Caelthwys had been commandeered to make weapons for the army, but once all the material had been transported to the precinct it had become painfully clear that the temple didn't have sufficient armourers for the volume of weapons they needed. Accommodation was still an issue too. By decree, each Lumineth citizen was meant to keep some basic equipment on hand for their military service, but aelves were arriving at the temple without any usable supplies, let alone their weapons. They were short of tents, utensils, uniforms – all the dull logistics of an army that make it capable of fighting in the first place. In all the years since the Spirefall, and even after the horrifying conflagration of Nagash's necroquake, it seemed Lumineth society was getting complacent. They were a society on the permanent edge of open conflict, and yet some seemed content to let others think about the fighting for them, so secure in their confidence that Hysh was a realm apart, a place untouched by the squalid sufferings of the realms at large.

Like Carreth, she thought, and then cursed herself again for her disloyalty. She bit her lip and hurried on, passing over the moon bridge, half running, half marching through the fragrant gardens. The leaves on the shrubs and trees had grown dull as the afternoon passed. For weeks there had been no real plan or strategy, just this frantic organisation. And now this, a meeting of the council, the first step in thrashing out what exactly it was they were meant to be doing here.

It was unfair to blame Carreth, of course. He was devastated by his sister's loss. He had been more of a father to her than a brother, someone who had raised her after their parents' deaths in those last days of the Reinvention, as the realm was painfully put back together. But war makes mourners of us all, one way or another. At some point, a choice must be made, the right path chosen. Decisions cannot be put off forever.

'You seem in quite the hurry, my lady,' a mellifluous voice said from the sunken gardens. Alithis turned on her heel to see Belfinnan lounging on a stone bench, a flower raised to his nose. He breathed deeply of the flower's scent and closed his eyes in ecstasy. 'What assignation could possibly put the enigmatic Alithis Stoneheart in such a fluster, hmm?'

Briefly, and with some relish, she pictured what his saturnine, handsome face would look like if she were to plant one of her stratum hammers smartly in the middle of it, but then she hit upon a more perfect riposte. She smiled widely.

'I'm heading to the council meeting,' she said innocently. 'Where, I believe, you are meant to be too?'

Belfinnan leapt from the bench, flower cast aside. He masked his alarm by matching her smile and stepped forward to take her arm.

'Of course,' he said smoothly. 'I was… I was just waiting for you, of course.'

'Of course.'

'I couldn't bear to watch you walk into that room alone,' he said, sweeping his hand out. 'To see all those disapproving stares! Safety in numbers, wouldn't you say?'

'A sound military strategy,' Alithis said. She disengaged her arm and marched on, Belfinnan following in her wake with long strides.

'I agree entirely, of course. I'm sure you've heard of my victory on the fields of the Silent Meadow, where I crushed the Khornate warbands of the Blood-Steeped Hand?'

'It somehow passed me by.'

'I shadowed the barbarians for miles, picking off the stragglers one by one, and when the moment was ripe...' He smacked his fist into his palm. 'Overwhelming force, with overwhelming numbers. An extraordinary assault, even if I do say so myself. Not one of them made it off the field.'

They passed into the shadowed cloisters and followed them along the side of the portico until they came to a door barred by two Stoneguard in full armour, with crossed diamondpick hammers – huge two-handed mauls that they raised as Alithis and Belfinnan approached. Alithis almost willed the two warriors to use those mauls on the steedmaster, but she tempered her irritation.

'Alithis Stoneheart, for the council.' She sighed. 'And Belfinnan.'

'Lord Belfinnan, but you know me already, lads, don't you?' He slapped them both on the shoulder. 'Honestly, seneschal, you should see these two put away the wine when they're off duty – they almost matched me drink for drink!'

The Stoneguard warily glanced at their seneschal, but Alithis only nodded. The hammers came down and the door was opened to them.

The council chamber was no more than a simple meeting place for the votaries of the temple to pray and reflect, but it had been hastily converted into a command post for the coming campaign.

A large square table was covered with an unrolled map of lower Ymetrica, centred on the Scintilla Realmgate. Alithis could see that the temple, in its commanding position on the edge of the veldt, had been clearly marked, as had Ultharadon, which dominated the surrounding countryside. Possible lines of attack and defence had been sketched onto the surface of the map, but everything else felt in flux to the seneschal, uncertain, without focus.

Carreth leaned over the table, his weight on his hands. His skin was pale and there were dark rings under his eyes. His face was tight with fatigue, and although he was looking down at the spread map before him, it was as if his attention were being wrenched elsewhere, to distant vistas no one else could see. Alithis stood next to him. She apologised for being late, but no one seemed to notice. Ilmarrin was there too, bearing a tray of iced zephyrwine in crystal glasses. Dae'annis stood guardedly near the door, as if he wanted to bolt as soon as possible, unused to such elevated company. Only Belfinnan seemed at home – he snatched up a glass from Ilmarrin's tray and engaged Dae'annis in conversation. Alithis couldn't hear what they were saying, but no doubt it had something to do with epic cavalry charges, or games of cards, or drinking. Or possibly all three at once.

She turned to Carreth, who still gazed down at the map.

'Is everything all right?' she asked. 'Ilmarrin says you've spent much of the last few days in the library. You have that *look* about you.'

Carreth roused himself. He stood straighter, stared at her as if he had only just noticed her presence or as if he wasn't quite sure where he was. Alithis met his gaze. His face was blank, but then something clicked and the expression flooded back into it. He looked pained suddenly, and rubbed two fingers against his temple.

'What look?'

'You know,' she said. 'Like a mushroom hidden away in the dark, pasty and cold.'

He smiled then, but she was perturbed to see the pain that flashed across his eyes.

'Research,' he said. 'They never tell you about that when you become an apprentice. So much of magic is study. Old scrolls, dusty books and dead ink, and not the flashy fireworks you might expect.'

'Speaking of flashy fireworks...' Alithis muttered.

Belfinnan came around the table and stood next to them, his glass drained. He stood with his hands on his hips and a smirk on his face. 'Now then,' he said. 'Dae'annis over there tells me he's going to be leading the warden contingent, and before the young hothead wins the war single-handed, we'd better come up with some plans of our own.'

'Charge madly at the enemy and hope it all works out?' Alithis offered.

'Remind me,' Belfinnan said, staring up at the ceiling and stroking his chin. 'How do the Stoneguard fight again? You basically just... *stand still*, don't you, and hope the enemy stumbles somewhere near your hammers, am I right? Not terribly glamorous, is it?'

'Not *quite* as glamorous as having your entire command killed in a glorious headlong assault, I agree–'

'And what happens if the foe is just that little bit too far away? Are you allowed to move then?'

'Enough!' Carreth said. His voice cut across the room. 'All this frivolous talk of war blinds us to the reality before us. We don't know when or even if the forces of the dead will start their attack, and if they were to move against us now, we have no ready means of response.'

'More recruits come in every day,' Alithis said, pointing to the map. 'From the Emerald Fens and from Paerthalann, from

Cathillys, from all the outlying settlements, people are taking up arms in your name. We will have the numbers, and the means to use them, if we wait and hold our nerve.'

'They say you are the will of Teclis made flesh,' Belfinnan added sombrely. 'His light flows through you, and there is not one amongst us who would not risk all to be in the presence of that light. You inspire them, mage, and inspiration is worth more than any number of spears.'

Carreth laughed then, a harsh, flat bark, without humour. The will of Teclis or not, Alithis could see that he was conflicted by all of this. If you turn from a path and make a decisive break, it's hard to force yourself back onto it no matter how urgent the need, and he had turned from violence a long time ago. She remembered that warlord of earlier days, the warrior she had followed without question in the last days of the Reinvention. His cold fury, his blazing eyes, the decisiveness, the energy that crackled around him. Where had he gone?

'A leader must always make a decision, you once told me,' she said. 'Even if it's the wrong one.'

He glanced at her, mouth twitching with irritation. There was more to this, she thought, than his unwillingness to send aelves to their deaths. A great weight hung heavy on his mind, more than questions of tactics and strategy, or even the simple apprehension of battle. Research, he had said. But what exactly had he been researching, down there in the archives, for so many days?

'Regardless,' Carreth went on, sweeping his arm across the chart, 'we need more information. The Mage God told me that the forces of Nagash will mount their invasion at any moment, and it would be reasonable to assume that they are on their way, if they are not here already.'

'We should send out scouts,' Belfinnan added. 'Reconnaissance, a screen to mask our own preparations.'

'Agreed. But reconnaissance only – do not engage with the enemy until we have a better idea of his dispositions.'

'You need only ask, mage, and my Dawnriders will obey, without question.'

Alithis saw the softening in Carreth's attitude then, the weary smile that crept across his face. 'I don't need blind obedience, steedmaster. Just your riders' skill at arms.'

'Skill at arms you shall have,' Belfinnan laughed. 'Bright lances, and brighter hearts, and woe betide those who stand in their way! Ilmarrin, come – bring over that jug of zephyrwine. I have a great thirst on me.'

As the old retainer carried over the tray, Alithis frowned with irritation. 'This isn't a parade ground, or an opportunity for glory. This is serious business – don't let yourself get carried away.'

'Serious business?' Belfinnan scorned. 'You think I don't know that?' His face turned hard, and for a moment Alithis regretted her words – but only for a moment. 'I saw these Bonereapers in Shyish, and Teclis knows I cut down enough of them. They're tough, aye, you won't get any disagreement from me there. But we can't afford to give them the upper hand. They will overwhelm us, without pity. Once they show their face, we need to strike hard and fast, shatter those bones before they've got a chance to reform.'

'And risk everything on a roll of the dice so you can feel the wind in your hair? We have no idea of their numbers, their objectives, their strategy. We need to be cautious, and we need to fight defensively. If we assume that they'll enter Hysh through the Scintilla Realmgate, then Ultharadon is clearly going to be in their path. We need to guard the mountain, not expend our forces piecemeal in futile gestures. We don't even know if the Realmgate is properly defended!'

Even Belfinnan's obvious annoyance couldn't shake the disquiet she felt about this. As they spoke, Carreth seemed to drift further away, the goblet of wine at his side untouched, the chart before him no more than blank parchment.

His mind is not on this at all, she thought. *He's wandering different pathways, and we're not helping by pulling in two different directions.*

'Dae'annis?' Alithis said. 'I'd be interested in your thoughts. You've fought this enemy, and your wardens will be the centre of our line regardless.'

The young warrior started, as if shocked to have been asked anything. He moved closer from the door and looked down at the map, and Alithis felt he was expecting the answer to leap out at him. Carreth gave him a measured look.

'I have no real head for grand strategy,' Dae'annis admitted. 'I have long looked to others to lead me…'

'Speak freely,' Carreth said gently. 'You are amongst friends here.'

Dae'annis swallowed, nodded curtly. Alithis saw the flush of pride in his face, that the Stonemage would consider him a friend, especially after his outburst in the sanctuary.

'I know what the Ossiarch armies can do,' he said, 'and my inclination would be to fight defensively.'

'What about Akridos, their liege?' Carreth asked. 'Where is he likely to be in their battle array?' He was staring at the young warden with what Alithis thought was an almost hostile intensity. Dae'annis became flustered.

'Their warlord was in the thick of the fighting in Shyish,' he said. The pain of the recollection was visible in his face. 'He led the charge that rolled up our flank, where… where Tuareth fell.'

Carreth's hands were bunched into fists as he rested them on the table, and the muscles in his jaw were tight. 'To lure him in,' he said, so softly that Alithis strained to hear him, even though she was by his side. 'Yes, that might work…'

Dae'annis spread his hands. 'If you're asking my opinion about strategy, though, I have to admit that we don't have the numbers. Not now, and not likely in the near future. We're going to be outnumbered, and if we want to win, I believe we need to play to our strengths.'

'Which are?' Carreth asked, half smiling. Alithis could tell that he already knew the answer.

'Our faith,' Dae'annis said simply. 'Our trust. In each other, in the purity of our cause. In the light that guides us to the right path.'

As Carreth slowly nodded, his eyes downcast, Belfinnan snorted and tossed back another goblet of wine.

'Noble sentiments,' he said. 'And I agree with them. Beautiful sentiments, even, that genuinely move me.'

'Do you feel another poem coming on?' Alithis asked. Belfinnan ignored her.

'But to think I've lived so long to see Lumineth aelves become so cautious...' Wearily, he shook his head. 'We should have sweeping patrols, in force, ready to respond at a moment's notice. A mobile reserve ready to plug the gaps and reinforce once we know where the dead are massing.'

Alithis struck the table in frustration. 'We're going around in circles here!'

'Better than going backwards, surely?' the steedmaster said. He raised an eyebrow and, on finding his glass empty, reached for the jug.

'The Mage God spoke to you, Carreth,' Alithis said quietly, as if they were the only two people in the room. 'Did he give any guidance on this?'

'He did not.'

There was silence in the chamber. A shaft of light fell softly through the wide, high windows to touch the outspread map on the table between them. From elsewhere in the temple, Alithis could hear the chanted prayers that marked the turning of the day, the Dusk Descending on the Slope of the Mountain. Ultharadon's spirit would be invoked, offerings would be placed on the greensward, and in the ornamental gardens the votaries would contemplate the marriage of the elements – water, earth and wind, and the light that illuminates all of them and holds them in perfect balance. The thought that all this could be lost, torn down by the blind malignancy of the undead, clawed at her guts and made her feel sick with rage. They were like children, frightened of the dark, and here Carreth dawdled uncertainly between them, bewildered somehow, diverted by whatever it was that gripped his thoughts and was more important than a danger so imminent it was almost reaching out to touch them.

This is how the dead win, she thought. *They have one purpose, only one, and they march towards it without a moment's hesitation. They cannot be bargained with; they cannot be turned aside by anything except force.*

Rumours abounded across the land – whispers on the breeze, fell winds that stank of death. Terrible nightmares, visions, prophecies, curses. She had heard that there were refugees beginning to choke the pristine roads, although no one could say what they were running from. All Ymetrica felt poised on the edge of calamity. So many had died in Shyish, in a victory that felt more like a defeat, and the dead would be here any day now. Alithis had felt the tension dogging her steps, resting its hand on her shoulders, whispering in her ear as she tried to sleep. She saw it behind Belfinnan's bluster, in Dae'annis' hollowed-out fear. She saw it now in Carreth's face, etched there in the lines on either side of his mouth, in the dark shadows under his eyes. War was coming. It would almost be a relief when it finally arrived.

She looked at the aelves gathered there, all of them now silent and nursing their private doubts. The Stonemage riven with solitary fears. The steedmaster as brash as he was brave. The high warden untested by command, who doubted himself above all. And herself, the high seneschal, whose tenacity was as much paralysis as steadfastness. Only Ilmarrin seemed utterly unperturbed. He moved around the table, collecting glasses, as if not a single note of discord had played in the room before him.

'And what about you, Ilmarrin?' Alithis said, breaking the silence. 'What would your advice be?'

'I'm not sure if one as old and untried as myself would have any advice to give, seneschal,' the old votary said. He held up the tray of glasses, the empty jug, and made to leave the room. He paused at the door, looking back at her, at Carreth, his old eyes glittering with craft. 'But perhaps balance cannot be found here because the proportions are not equally weighted?'

'Meaning?' Carreth said.

'Something is missing, mage.' He nodded at the company in the room, each in turn. 'You have the rock, the wind, the earth. You lack, perhaps, the spirit?'

The door clicked shut behind him. The light fell from the window. As the dusk advanced it slowly broke away, leaving the map on the table in darkness.

After he had dismissed the council, Carreth returned to his chambers, fatigue dragging like a sodden cloak against his shoulders. He walked through the cloisters outside, hoping the fresh evening air would invigorate him, but the weight of expectation was too much for him to bear. It seemed like every other step brought a respectful greeting from one of the temple votaries, or an awed genuflection from one of the new recruits in the ornamental gardens. The moment he was through the door into the cool silence of his chambers, he stumbled. He grabbed for the back of the chair by his desk, misjudging his weight, the chair tipping backwards, and it was all he could do not to crash to the ground.

He collapsed onto his bed, the hard straw mattress feeling as soft and welcome as a bed of clouds. He pressed his fingers to the bridge of his nose. A thin, wheedling pain was stabbing through his head and his eyes felt like they were burning. For four days he had secluded himself in the archives, hunting through the dust for the remnants of ancient days, searching for that which he knew would be better off buried and forgotten. He had spent hours delving into magical systems that made his skin crawl, and that made the shadows in the archive creep nearer, as if they were peering over his shoulder at his transgression. The Flensing of Souls, the Spirit Trap, Elements of Grave Sand... It was all death magic by any other name. At one desperate point in Lumineth history, the deluded aelves of Hysh had dabbled in this filth, and in their arrogance thought that they could contain it. Carreth knew perfectly well that there was only one being in the Mortal Realms who could – and he would not share his secrets.

Nagash...

Carreth shook himself, the taste of ashes and dust in his mouth. He poured himself a goblet of water from the carafe at his bedside, and as he did so his eyes lit on the cracked gem of Tuareth's aetherquartz brooch. He had found her, in the end. Now all he had to do was save her. And while he tarried in this task, the aelves of his army looked to him for guidance, and he had none to give them.

There was a knock at the chamber door.

'Enter.'

Alithis stood there, fully armoured in preparation for the evening guard. Under the circumstances, Carreth's presence wasn't required for the ritual – much had been simplified and stripped down in the temple's schedule since the threat from Shyish had become known – but Carreth could think of no other reason for her presence at this time.

'Seneschal,' he said. 'The Ritual of Symmetry is suspended – I thought you had been told?'

'I know,' Alithis said. She came into the room and closed the door behind her. She was in many ways a slight figure, and certainly not as tall as Carreth, but there was a martial presence to the seneschal that crowded out the room. Carreth had always felt the lesser aelf next to her, but nothing made him feel as secure as knowing that she was on his side. She was as immovable as the mountain she had dedicated herself to, as reassuring in the right mood and as forbidding in the wrong. 'I wanted to speak to you about the council earlier.'

'A dazzling display of strategic decisiveness, I'm sure you'll agree,' Carreth said wearily. He took up his goblet and drained the water, but the taste of dust was still there in his mouth. The residue of all those mouldering scrolls, weeping their decay into the archive's air. 'Belfinnan wants glory in a headlong charge, you want to dig us in here, and Dae'annis just desperately wishes someone else would take the responsibility out of his hands. I keep thinking that if only we gather everyone together then the right course of action will present itself by osmosis, but of course that's not the case. As you said, eventually a decision has to be made, even if it is the wrong one.'

Alithis stood by him at the open window, and together they stared out at the night. The smell of the evening flowers, heady and sweet, the sounds of the new wardens coming back from a night march, the whicker of the Dawnriders' steeds in their temporary stables.

'You're afraid of making the wrong one, though, aren't you?' Alithis said.

'Who wouldn't be?'

'I would, that's certainly true. But I remember you in older times, when you would have not hesitated for a moment when there was an enemy to fight.'

'And what did that get me?' Carreth said bitterly. 'Deaths unnumbered, blood on my hands that will never wash off. An ache in my mind that has never really healed...'

'You saved lives unnumbered. You spared so many aelves from staining their own hands with blood, and you made sure our whole society came through its hardest trial in something like one piece. You sacrificed much, Carreth, and no one will ever forget it.'

'Least of all myself,' he whispered.

'And now Teclis himself commands you.' Alithis took his arm and turned him around to look at her. Carreth couldn't meet her eyes. He tried to step back, but she held him fast. He felt like the foul depths of his researches were smeared across his skin, that he was rank with their odour. Alithis stared at him, piercing and intense. 'Remember what Ilmarrin said,' she told him. 'We have all the elements we need for war, but we still lack something.'

Carreth thought back to the last moments of the council. He had been so distracted by his tiredness, his work, that he had swum through most of it in a daze, but he remembered the old votary clearing up the glasses, looking at each of them in turn.

'Spirit,' Carreth said.

'*Spirit*. Don't you see? There is one who has not answered your call. Anyone can tell that your indecision is more than just a reluctance to send aelves into battle, to issue the order and see them die. And some of them *will* die, you know that. But there's something else gnawing at you, Carreth, and your soul is sick with it. Grief for Tuareth, the weight of the Mage God's command, your fear of that part of yourself that revels in war...'

Her words cut into his heart. 'I never revelled in it,' he hissed. 'I despised it more than you can know!'

'Let *her* find the answers for you. Assuage your guilt, your fear. You know who I mean.'

He did, perfectly well, and the realisation stabbed through him. 'It's been years,' he whispered, '*years* since I saw her last. I cannot–'

'You *must*!' Alithis urged. 'The army is not complete without her, and you will not be complete until you have properly confronted yourself. Admit this to yourself, Carreth, and you will conquer whatever it is that is holding you back.'

He nodded, trembling, as sick with apprehension as an untried recruit waiting in the line to receive an enemy charge.

'I will,' he breathed, and it was like a weight lifted from him. 'Thaerannan the Desolate… I will seek her out.'

CHAPTER NINE

THE VALLEY OF DESOLATION

The water was like ice as he cupped it in his palm, and when he raised it to his mouth it made his teeth sing. Carreth wondered if the stream had trickled down from the springs on Ultharadon, gathering pace until it surged and bubbled through the moorland ahead of him. He lay on the bank and filled his canteen. The bank on the other side of the stream was bearded with moss and studded with white flowers. Gladebells, he thought. He could smell their bitter scent in the air, and it refreshed him as much as the water. Further on, the stream curled away to the left and dropped slowly through the declining moorland, a strip of glinting silver that twisted off towards the distant sea. Carreth's path did not lie in that direction, though. He turned and looked off to his right, where the fresh grass and meadow flowers began to fade, where the landscape fell away into a maze of hollows and depressions, sparsely marked here and there by the twisted branches of dying trees. Clouds were gathering. He could see a sheet of rain draw down like a veil across the land a few miles off. He sighed, shouldered his pack, lowered his head and continued on. After a few steps he glanced back to see Ultharadon in the distance, its isolated peak no bigger than his palm. Light struck its purple summit, a froth of cloud falling against it like a crest. The light of Hysh fell in its purest form there, wholesome, inspiring. Ahead there was only gloom – rain, and rough country. He felt the weight of the journey pressing against him.

'Holy mountain,' he whispered. 'Guide my way.' He looked ahead to where the sheet of rain had lifted, where bleak beams of light now fell weakly against the valleys and the sunken moors.

'Remember the writings of Athaer'alis,' he exhorted himself. '*The Book of Meditations*. "The intellect is the armour against despair, and nothing ill can defend against the application of reason."'

For long years he had kept that sentiment to heart, but what seemed profound in the abstract often had the shakiest foundations when properly tested. What was reason against grief? He touched his sister's brooch, hanging from a chain around his neck. What use was the rational against the irrational tides of horror?

Carreth felt the gloom settle on him again as he walked across the rough country, leaving the stream behind. Three days he had been walking now, camping out under the stars in glades and dells, hunched by his campfire, cooking his simple provisions. Belfinnan had offered one of his Dawnriders' steeds to speed the journey, but the ground ahead would be boggy and treacherous. In many ways, Carreth had told him, the journey was the point. When you sought out Thaerannan the Desolate, you moved from the clean vigour of the lands around Ultharadon to the wilder places in the heart of Ymetrica. You moved from light to shadow, and as you moved your heart settled into a darker space inside. The Scinari Cathallar was not someone to be approached lightly, or in an unprepared frame of mind.

Belfinnan had seen the length of the journey as an indulgence, though. 'A week away!' he had shouted. 'If time really is as pressing as it seems, then surely we can't afford for you to be absent so long!'

'It needs to be done,' Alithis had countered. Steedmaster and seneschal confronted each other in the council room as Carreth told them of his decision. 'If we are to win this fight, then we need to draw on all of our resources, spiritual as well as military.'

Belfinnan had touched the rune on his breastplate, *Senlui* embossed in yellow gold. Reverently he closed his eyes.

'I am a simple aelf, and deeply spiritual as you know,' he had said, to Alithis' raised eyebrow. 'But blades win wars. Bright spears and bright hearts.'

'A Cathallar will lighten the load of even the darkest heart,' she said. 'She will lift our fears and turn them against our enemy. We need her.'

Indeed, Carreth thought now as the pack lay heavy on his back. *We need her. But will she need me? How many years has it been since I last saw her, since my heart was last in her care?*

He brushed the thought away and trudged on. The afternoon declined around him. The grass was wet underfoot, the air grey. The breeze, whispering across the moor, brought only the rumours of bird calls. He looked up into an empty sky.

When night began to fall and the light of Hysh was dimmed, leaving only the scattered jewels of stars and the celestial orbs wheeling high above him, Carreth decided to stop and set up his camp. The ground was too rough and uneven to continue in these shadows. He peered into the gloom and saw a pale finger of stone rising out of the darkness ahead, no more than a quarter mile distant. He found that he was standing on the beginning of a tangled track, a pathway of cracked paving that dipped down and headed off towards it. The moorland on either side of the path was dark and indistinct. Carreth followed the pathway, one hand lightly resting on the hilt of his knife, the other gripping his staff. He was not afraid of attack on his own behalf, but in his stained travelling clothes he could easily be mistaken for a simple wanderer in the wild. He would be loath to reveal his power if he didn't have to…

He came to an overgrown courtyard that was clotted with weeds. The finger of stone on the other side of the courtyard was a broken tower, long since fallen into ruin. It was a narrow structure, thin as a needle, no more than four storeys tall. The pointed roof was of beaten copper, green with age and exposure. The pale marble of the walls, threaded with silver veins, was crumbling, and the thin arrow-slit windows were dark and empty. A great section of wall had fallen away on one side, revealing a circular room on the ground floor and two narrow chambers above it. The main door, a solid slab of reinforced oak, listed into the courtyard on one hinge.

It was a sad, abandoned place, wreathed in sorrowful memories. A ruin of the past, from the days before Ocari Dara. The realm was littered with the faded glories of yesterday – great mansions and palaces, cities and towers, utterly destroyed by the madness of the Spirefall and leaving only these faint traces in the earth, hints of what had once been achieved by the Lumineth and what had been squandered in the fires of their madness. Carreth thought it probably a mage's tower or a scholar's retreat, a bleak shard staring out at the moors, in perfect isolation. Who had built it, or where they had gone, was a mystery.

Inside, a circular stone staircase was wrapped around the tower's wall. Steps were missing, the stone slabs loosened by time and sent crashing down to the ground below, but it was easy enough for Carreth to climb. At the top of the tower, underneath the copper spire, he found an empty chamber. Half of the stone floor had collapsed, the mortar rotted by the rain that came through the gap in the wall, but the other half, on the near side, was still sturdy, and he was sheltered from the wind by the angle of the tower. He set to work preparing a small fire, ringing it with stones that had crumbled from the walls. The pointed ceiling stretched up above him, cold and austere. When the fire was lit Carreth crumbled some oats into a pot, softening them with water he had taken from the stream. He added a few herbs and spices, and the heady scent brought him back to the airy precincts of the temple, lightening his heart. Once he had eaten, he lay back on the blanket and stared up at the night sky, the spinning procession of the cosmos. He could see Celennar wheel slowly into place. The true moon of the Lumineth, its spirit now joined to the spirit of the Mage God, the boon companion of Teclis himself. Carreth gazed at that rocky orb. His meeting with Teclis seemed like a dream, and already much of it was indistinct. The dazzling light, the awed terror of Celennar prowling the shadows just outside his sight. Carreth raised his hand and looked at his skin, where the glow was fading. The will of the Mage God made manifest, they said. He gave a bitter laugh. He was too fearful to move forward, too consumed by rage to turn away. He had buried himself in arcane researches instead, weaving the lineaments of a spell that had not been seen in Hysh for centuries and that he was too terrified to use.

He rolled over on his blanket and tried to sleep. Before he drifted off, he seemed to see the grinning skull of Akridos laughing at him from the shadows, where the campfire's flames did not fall.

He travelled on in the morning. The tower lost some of its mystery in the light of day, even in a light as subdued as this. It stood there grey and crumbling, a solitary gesture of civilisation in the depths of the wilderness around him. He wondered who had built it, who had lived here in the midst of this bleak moorland. One day, would he find himself in such a place? Self-exiled, rushing to embrace isolation, weary at the weight of his failures…

Rain fell in a fine mist as Carreth left the tower behind, heading back up the broken track. He pulled up the hood of his cloak. The land had dipped down so much that the peak of Ultharadon was invisible now, and he doubted he could have seen it in this bleak weather in any case. Soon, only a few yards further on across the heath, the tower had been swallowed up in the mist.

He pressed on for much of the day, head lowered, mind turned only towards the ground in front of him. There was no track to follow, just the humped tussocks of the grass threatening to turn his ankles. Midday came and went. He didn't bother to stop. There was no shelter in the landscape around him, and it would be pointless to light a fire. He trudged on instead, yard after yard, his hands tucked into his cloak, the straps of his pack chafing against his shoulders, rain dripping down his face from the lip of his hood.

A few hours further on, Carreth looked up through the smirr to see that he was approaching the sloping edge of a narrow valley. The land drifted away into further moorland off to the right and left, smeared out in the mist, but ahead he could see the dip in the ground, the withered branches of blackthorn trees marking the hollow's sides. He approached the edge of the slope and looked down. The valley was no more than a hundred yards across, and the bottom of the depression glistened with drizzle, unrevealed. He couldn't say how far it stretched on. There was darkness down there. Something bleak and frightened tugged at his heart, a feeling of strange sorrow. His blood felt cold in his veins. He noticed an outcrop of rock further along the valley's edge, and as he approached it, he saw that it was a weathered shrine, greasy with rain and blanketed in moss. Spikes of sedge grass stabbed up to smother its base. He ran his hands over the aelven letters carved into its side. They had been blurred by the elements into mere suggestion.

Here lies the Valley of Desolation, his fingers read. *Sick is the heart that yearns for peace. Enter, and find it.*

He swallowed. His fingers were cold and the stone felt like ice. On top of the shrine someone had left a scattering of pebbles, a twist of hair threaded around a bone, a leaf. Offerings to the Cathallar…

Carreth unsheathed his knife and laid it down with the other items. He tightened the straps of his pack and gripped his staff. There were rough-cut stone steps, he saw, leading down into the mist. Down, where desolation lived… He touched the brooch at his throat again and took heart from its presence. He took the steps. He didn't look back.

The whispering of the breeze died away as he descended. The air was flat and still, and the mist beaded against his skin. The steps twisted down, a short flight of no more than twenty feet, he guessed. Before long he was standing at the bottom of the depression, silent in its dank and oppressive atmosphere. The ground was a tangle of weeds and broken stones, and there was a smell drifting through the air of woodsmoke or stale incense. He saw a rough path snaking through the hollow. On either side there were lank gorse bushes, thorn trees, coiled lengths of bramble. The grey sky above was like a lid tightly fastened on the valley. Carreth felt the gloom settle heavier on him. As he walked, a squall of fear built up inside him, like a stormfront. The walls of the valley were lost in the haze on either side; there was only the path ahead. He held his staff tighter and pressed on, leaning into his fear as if forcing himself through a hurricane.

He came into a small glade bounded by thorn trees, the ground covered in glistening grass. Emerging from the mist on the other side of the glade was a black space framed by grey, the jagged, narrow entrance to a cave, a fissure in the rockface. The light, such as it was, did not reach inside the cave mouth, but emanating from this fissure was a sense of utter, cloying despair. He could almost taste it, and as he felt it crawling over his skin he saw flashes of past regrets across his mind's eye – Tuareth turning from him as she left the temple, the pleading look in a cultist's eye as Carreth vengefully swung his blade in some old, half-forgotten skirmish, the bodies of old friends and comrades, stricken on the field of battle. He shuddered, bared his teeth against this motionless gale of dread and sorrow. Tears leaked from his eyes. His throat was thick with sadness. The smell of incense was overpowering now, a choking fug that hazed the air even further. Carreth dropped his staff and fell to his knees in the grass, covering his face with his hands.

'Thaerannan!' he shouted, his voice muffled by his fingers. He dropped his hands, raised his face to the frigid sky. 'Thaerannan the Desolate! Carreth Y'gethin calls on you. The Stonemage of Ultharadon calls on you! Answer me!' He dropped his head, whispered, 'Answer me, please, and let this sorrow end.'

The voice was like a whispered hymn, chanted across the glade.

'Carreth Y'gethin… a name I have not heard for many years… a face I have not seen for time out of mind… and the face you wear now is not one that I recognise, Stonemage. What brings you to the Valley of Desolation?'

She emerged like a ribbon of smoke from the mouth of the cave, a tall, lissom figure pacing on bare feet into the glade. Her black robes fluttered in a breeze that seemed to come from nowhere, a diaphanous veil of near-transparent silk whispering across her face. Her headdress, gleaming with silver and gold, decorated with droplet gems of the richest aetherquartz, hung like an inverted crescent moon above her head. She held a censer in one hand, an elongated goblet of white ceramic, and from the bowl black smoke fell, pooling like water on the ground. Her skin was so pale it was almost translucent, and Carreth could see the deep blue traceries of her veins through it. The fragrance of incense was almost suffocating. As she came closer towards him, Carreth felt the desperate need to turn around and run. The weight of sorrow that she seemed to bring with her was intolerable.

He forced himself to look into her eyes, half hidden by the drifting silk of her veil. They shone like polished jet, and he could only hold their impassive gaze for a moment.

'I need your help,' he said, his voice breaking. 'We need your help.'

'And who is "we", Stonemage? The votaries of your temple? The followers of the mountain path?'

She stood before him, and as the breeze moved through the hollow, her robes brushed up against his face. Carreth, still kneeling, recoiled. The smoke from her censer dripped down around him, radiating guilt and anger, an unbearable sadness.

'All of us,' he said, gritting his teeth. 'All aelves who call Hysh home. The war against death has come to our borders at last.'

'You fear death, do you?' Thaerannan said in that hushed, chanting voice. 'I sense the death you carry in your soul.'

'My sister. Tuareth, killed by the Ossiarch Bonereapers in Shyish.'

There was a rustling in the breeze, like the jagged whisper of dead leaves brushing against each other. Carreth was horrified to realise that it was Thaerannan laughing. She paced off towards the edge of the glade, brushing her fingers against the barbs of the thorn trees.

'That is but one of the many deaths you carry within you, Stonemage. Deaths that you blame yourself for. Hundreds live in you, don't they? I see them… I feel them, killed by your blade, or by your magics, or by your… indifference.'

Carreth clenched his fists. 'If I could live a thousand years, I would kill no more! Nor see others killed on my orders or by my actions. I swear it!'

'And yet you are drawn to death as the answer to your sorrows... I see it wreathed around you, an amethyst flame, darkening by the hour. You dabble in forbidden magics, ancient magics that once cursed our lands.'

Carreth stilled his thoughts. He calmed himself, reaching for the equilibrium that he had so long trained himself to feel. 'I must make the attempt,' he said. 'Tuareth's soul is trapped in the foul confines of the creature that leads the Ossiarch army. I must free her, if I can.'

'Beware, then, Stonemage, that your methods do not destroy both you and her instead. It is a dark path that you follow, the darkest...'

'Nevertheless, it is one I *must* follow.'

She smiled behind the veil, a twitch of her dark lips, and then she turned away. The wind blew a mournful melody across the valley. Carreth stood up.

'I have come for your help, if you will give it,' he said. His voice was measured, certain, as if reason alone would be able to persuade this dark figure before him. 'A Scinari Cathallar is the heart of the Lumineth. Only a Cathallar can siphon off our fears and doubts, can leach the anguish from our aetherquartz and burn it away. Without you...'

'Yes?' she said, turning to face him once more. Carreth swallowed, crushing down his dread.

'Without you, we will not have the heart to go on. We will lose, and we will die. All of us.'

She came closer, the smoke from her bowl billowing around her. Her veil hung loose as the breeze died away. Through its shimmering weave he could see her dark eyes interrogating his own, peering deep inside him, paring away his soul. Carreth held her gaze.

'You are lost, Carreth,' she said softly. She reached up to touch his face, her hand as cold as stone. 'You wander in a maze of your emotions, and you do not know the way out. I see the Ocari Dara gleaming like a beacon in your mind... Take heed of it. Remember it, as you remember the days of sadness and horror that followed it. Do not stray from the path you have made for yourself, for it is a path of great honour and value. You have lost the spirit of Ultharadon. Only when you find it can you be whole again. Remember this.'

Through the veil her breath brushed against his face. He closed his eyes, reaching up to take her hand.

'I remember you,' he whispered. 'Help us now, for all that we meant to each other once.'

'Carreth...' she said, and he could hear the sadness in her voice. 'We chose our paths long ago, and they led us in different directions. We left each other behind.' She rested her palm against his chest. 'And yet I was never far away, in truth.'

'Will you help?'

She shook her head, her eyes downcast. 'I cannot, Stonemage. The time will come when I am needed, but it is not this time, not yet.'

Carreth closed his eyes again, in bitter regret.

'But do not despair,' Thaerannan said. She touched his brooch, hanging from its chain. 'There is one thing I can do to ease your troubles.'

Slowly, Carreth took it from around his neck and passed it to the Cathallar. She wrapped the chain around her fingers, gently running her thumb across the cracked jewel. It glowed in her hand, a rich, smouldering amber. The crack across the jewel sealed itself, but as the aetherquartz glowed brighter and brighter, Carreth could see a darkness blooming deep in its heart, unfurling until the amber glow was subsumed in shadow. The smoke from Thaerannan's censer swelled out of the bowl, black and flecked with embers, and Carreth found that tears were pouring down his cheeks. He looked into Thaerannan's eyes, but they were closed. A lance of pain shot across her face. Still the smoke billowed out, and then the jewel sputtered and died in her hand – the amber aetherquartz was no more than a blackened shard of coal.

Carreth took it from her in trembling hands. Despite everything, despite all the angst and sadness of this hidden glade, the grief that suffocated him like a grave shroud, he felt as if the burden of his sorrows had been lifted – not completely, but enough to have made a difference.

Carreth looped the chain around his neck again, tucking it under his shirt.

'Thank you,' he said. He reached for her hand, but Thaerannan turned and paced slowly back to the cave, the smoke from her censer following her like a wake.

'Go now,' she said over her shoulder, her voice rich with sorrow. 'If you will not heed my warning, then do what you must to save your sister's soul.'

'I will,' he said.

'Look for me in the days to come, Carreth. When I am most needed, I will be there.'

She stepped into the shadows of the cave and was gone.

He turned to leave, to retrace his steps along the valley to the flight of stone stairs that led up to the shrine. He glanced down. There, where Thaerannan had stood as she held Tuareth's aetherquartz, the grass was blackened and dead.

CHAPTER TEN

THE DREAM OF EMPIRE

It was the light, more than anything. He had not expected the light to be so rich, so penetrating. There was some relief in marching at night, but in many ways the quality of light seemed undimmed even in darkness. It emanated from the land itself as much as from the celestial orbs above. It was a presence saturating everything in Hysh, and although the Ossiarch troops were indifferent to light or shade, cold or heat, for Akridos the light seemed to lie on him like a weight he couldn't shift. It inhibited thought, made decisions that much more difficult. He twisted in the saddle and stared blankly up at the wash of blue above him, the clear sky unblemished for a thousand miles in every direction, the green orbs of his dead eyes flaring in the light.

Hysh, the Realm of Light... When we are done with it, all will be shrouded in the amethyst skies of Shyish. This light will not even be a distant memory.

A bright clash of metal, the remote cry from a living throat of orders being given and received, drew his attention. He looked off across the level ground, a spread of vibrant green grass dotted with yellow flowers, to where the town was mustering its troops. A mile distant, and yet from the rise where he stood on his steed he could clearly see the aelves' blue robes fluttering in the breeze, the glint of light reflecting on their spears and shields, the rippling crests of their tall, conical helmets. The town itself was laid out like a crystal garden behind them, the streets geometrically precise, the buildings progressing in a staggered line from the lower one- or two-storey structures at the edge of the settlement to the higher towers in the middle. The towers were capped with domes and turrets of gleaming silver-blue, and here and there reached the branches of tall, silver-barked trees, their leaves rustling in rich greens and burnished gold. Blue banners snapped in the wind from flagpoles mounted on the highest towers, each marked with the inscrutable runes of this inscrutable realm. From here, at this elevated position, Akridos could see the glint of running water inside the town – fountains, or ornamental gardens threaded with silver streams. White birds rose like flakes of ash from the dome of one tower, wheeling out across the greensward before gaining height and turning off towards the north-east. They cried with a sound that made Akridos shudder.

He looked again at the aelves as they formed their battle lines on the grass. There could not have been more than two thousand of them, mostly infantry, spears and shields with a scattering of archers. There was a small block of cavalry off on their right flank, slightly behind the line. A mobile reserve, perhaps. Akridos considered them, taking in the obvious strength and power of their horses, the vigour of their riders, the shining scale of their armour.

Kathanos, hunched as always in his walking throne, appeared at his side. Under this unforgiving light, his parched skull looked somehow more brittle than usual, brown as a nut, desiccated, flakes of scurf falling off to dust the shoulders of his robes. He held his staff lengthways across his knees and gestured with a tilt of his chin towards the town before them – its gleaming white stone, as bright as polished diamonds, its angles and planes arranged with a perfection so absolute it was almost repellent.

'It disturbs you, in some way,' Kathanos said, as if reading his mind. 'The shape, that sense of ideation inherent in their designs. Their architecture is truly most fascinating,' he mused.

Akridos was compelled to admit it – there was something of profound disquiet in the structure of the Lumineth settlement. The more he looked on it, the more its strange geometries unsettled him.

'I have devoted much thought to this since we first stepped onto the soil of Hysh,' Kathanos said.

'Your conclusions?' Akridos asked.

'It is to do with the aelves' central aesthetic, I believe. Their love of symmetry, of balance, one side equally weighted against the other. We,' he chattered, 'are not as they are. We are not symmetrical things, are we, Liege-Kavalos?'

'It is not a subject I have given much attention to,' he growled.

'Of course,' Kathanos said. 'You are in many ways a simple soldier, eager for combat. But taken philosophically, you must understand that we are amalgams, at heart. We are constructs, things made of many things, a variety of bones and souls crushed together. And variety does not tend towards symmetry. True symmetry is… alien, in many ways.'

Akridos felt that uneasy blend of spirits roiling inside him once more. The aelven soul, crushed down to its essence, sparked in his bones like a burning wire.

'Expedience seems to trump aesthetics,' he said. 'They do not make their dispositions on symmetrical lines.' He pointed at the aelven troops dressing ranks, the block of spearmen in the centre, the archers behind and now moving off to one side, the riders on their right. They had drawn themselves up perfectly, as far as Akridos could see. The horse would screen their foot on the right flank, and the infantry had been set up in two blocks, one slightly behind the other. If they drew the Bonereapers on, the second block of infantry could swing back like a closed door and guard their left, while the archers peppered any frontal assault. With such low numbers they would need to fight defensively, but their position was basically sound.

'You see their cavalry?' Kathanos asked.

'Of course.'

'It is said they are the finest horsemen in the Mortal Realms, their steeds as fast as any gryph-charger. The riders form spiritual bonds with their horses, and in battle they think as one.'

Akridos bristled. 'You seek to goad me, soulmason. We shall see if their reputation is well earned when battle comes. I would rate my Deathriders against them, without hesitation.'

'I confess, though,' Kathanos croaked, 'I don't understand why they are so eager for battle. Surely they realise the scale of the force that opposes them?'

'You see the town before you?' Akridos said.

'Of course?'

'Note that it has no defensive walls. They are compelled to fight, or to withdraw. And I suspect the aelves of this realm have had enough of withdrawals.'

'Ah,' Kathanos sighed, clattering his teeth together. 'Their warriors' shields are their walls. I see. Brave, but, given the circumstances, perhaps unwise.'

Akridos glanced over his shoulder at where the Ossiarch army had drawn up on the grassy plains behind him, rank after rank of Mortek Guard in two dozen regiments. Vast troops of his Stalliarch Lords cavalry. The Immortis Guard like towering giants, pitiless in combat. They could have outflanked this small Lumineth town easily, leaving only a scratch force to oppose it, but Akridos had felt that the example must be made. They had shattered the disparate forces that had met them on the other side of the Realmgate, taking them utterly by surprise, and as the army had marched on across the wide Ymetrican plains they had met only scattered resistance. They had passed small villages and isolated keeps, each abandoned as news of the Ossiarch advance had reached the inhabitants. Much of the Lumineth army, it seemed, had been whittled down in the battles of Shyish, leaving them spread thin in their home realm. The landscape they passed through was mountainous, harsh, a spread of grassy valleys and abyssal chasms. Between outcrops of rocky hills and towering mountain ranges, there were these wide greenswards, grasslands with small towns and settlements nestled in their midst, but this was the first they had reached where the aelves had decided to make a stand. And Akridos had always thought that if battle was offered, then it must be received.

'Brave or otherwise, the result will be the same,' Akridos said. 'We will not be delayed here long.'

'And then onwards,' Kathanos said. 'Onwards, as Nagash commands.'

'As I command,' Akridos snapped. 'Onwards, destroying everything in our wake, until we find the Lumineth champion at the end of it. I will destroy this Light of Eltharion and fulfil Nagash's will. I will have my reward,' he muttered. 'A kingdom of my own again, carved out of these lands.'

'And held in Nagash's name?'

'Of course,' Akridos said, through gritted teeth.

Kathanos fell silent, shuffling on his throne. He placed his mitre on his skull, the facets of its jewels foaming with dark light. He seemed to grin at the Liege-Kavalos.

'Confidence is a virtue in a military commander, of course,' he said. 'But I would advise against arrogance in this instance. The Light of Eltharion is–'

'Is no more than some feeble aelven champion, I am certain. I will sow such destruction against its people, against its holy places, that it will be forced to respond. These Lumineth place their cowardly hopes in it, their superstitious beliefs, and when it is dead their resistance will crumble like the shore against the tide.'

'And yet, when the tide goes out, the shore remains.'

'What do you mean by that?' Akridos demanded. The presence of Kathanos at his side was increasingly irritating, and he found himself becoming more and more abrasive towards the soulmason. Questioning, 'advising', undermining – it was intolerable. He sat there hunched on his creeping throne, whispering always in that dry voice, and not a word he offered was of true value or insight. 'Speak in plain terms,' he snapped, 'so that a simple soldier such as myself may understand.'

Kathanos chattered his teeth again, a facsimile of laughter. 'The roots of this land are deep, and the Lumineth's roots with it. Do not underestimate their dedication, their sense of sacrifice when all they love and value is threatened.'

'Love? I hear it is something the mortal races experience,' Akridos scorned. 'Another weakness to exploit.'

'Do not underestimate this Light of Eltharion either, Liege-Kavalos. Nagash has given you the command, but the means to execute it still rely on your judgement and skill.'

'And you doubt both, I expect?'

'Not at all,' Kathanos said in an obsequious tone. 'But there are scattered legends, ancient tales, that I have come across in the necropolis archives concerning this champion, or some past version of him. It is said that in the world-that-was, it took the great mortarch Arkhan the Black himself to kill him. And if Eltharion lives now, it is because the Mage God, Teclis, has willed it so. A living avatar, imbued with the light of the Lumineth's own god… Swords alone may not conclude this tale, I fear.'

Akridos dragged his steed away, snarling over his shoulder.

'Then attend this lesson, soulmason.' He raised his blade and commanded the army to advance. To the thunderous rattle of tens of thousands of skeletal troops coming to attention, he said, 'There is not one thing living or dead that cannot be unmade by a sword in the right hand – or enough swords in enough hands. Mark my words, Kathanos. And let the Light of Eltharion mark them too.'

He turned to the troops as the Mortek Guard began their advance across the grass.

'Leave one alive!' he screamed. 'Destroy the rest!'

The aelves moved their pikes forward first. The leading block of infantry, perhaps a thousand strong, split with expert precision into two lines of five hundred each. Both moved forward, a narrow gap between them, and through this gap the cavalry funnelled with incredible speed. Like lightning the horses shot across the sward, lances down, sunlight gleaming off their metal tips. There was the charge of magic in the air, an ozone reek, and the lances fizzled with energy. On the other side of the Lumineth front, the second infantry block moved up to support the others, advancing in depth, pikes bristling and shields held in tight formation. Akridos dragged his steed back and galloped behind the Mortek line to join his Deathriders in the centre. Over the savage bluster of the wind, he could hear the tramp of the aelves' marching feet, the rattle of their arms brought to bear, the shocking progress of the cavalry.

Say one thing for this race, Akridos thought. *They are unpredictable.*

'Hold on the right flank!' he shouted. The Mortek Guard snapped to attention, utterly unperturbed. The hekatoi snapped out orders, the line bracing for impact as the Lumineth cavalry thundered closer and closer, great clods of earth torn up by their hooves, the aelven riders leaning into the charge, teeth bared, lances couched – a streak of silver and blue, hammering onwards, relentless, undaunted. Akridos reached the centre and reeled around, leaning up in the stirrups to see the Lumineth cavalry crash like a lightning bolt into his right flank, a wedge of armour and muscle and steel, fifty strong, crumpling the Mortek Guard like paper. Bones shattered, shields were broken. The aelves' eerie war cry shrieked above the tumult.

'Deathriders!' Akridos commanded. 'Form up! On me, now!'

He led them in a quick canter, weaving through the Mortek regiments in the centre, heading over to the left flank. Arrows began to drop around them from the Lumineth archers, flitting like hard rain to pierce skulls and ribcages, shattering bones, pinning warriors to the ground. The rate of fire was incredible. Akridos remembered them from the battle outside the necropolis, the archers' three-stringed bows inflicting staggering losses on his force before it had even engaged. He glanced around, saw the aelven cavalry break off, a few riders dragged from their horses and spitted with despairing screams on Mortek spears. The rest streaked off to loop around the advancing Lumineth infantry, reforming, charging again in that lightning-fast wedge to crash into another block of Mortek Guard in the centre, not a hundred yards from where Akridos sat. He saw shattered bones tossed into the air, shields caved in, skulls hacked from spinal cords. By this time, the aelven infantry had reached the Ossiarch lines far over on the right, and as their pikes glimmered with frosty light, shining silver and blue like oiled metal, they lowered them and charged, chanting in their convoluted aelven speech. The Ossiarch right flank was collapsing. The centre was under incredible pressure from their cavalry. Akridos felt a surge of mingled rage and exultation.

'*Yes...*' he whispered. 'Yes!'

This was war, this was the dread fury of battle, no quarter given or received. Spear to spear, shield to shield, both sides running in that desperate race for mastery. Akridos watched his infantry being rolled up on the right flank, hundreds of warriors cut to pieces as the Lumineth cavalry withdrew, reformed and charged again.

He saw it at once, their fatal mistake. The cavalry had moved off to charge the right flank again, to bolster the Lumineth infantry's progress and try to get to the Ossiarch rear. They fought, he saw, as rational beings who assumed they faced rational beings in turn. They would expect their opponent to draw his left flank back to avoid the risk of encirclement, to bolster his right with his reserves, but Akridos was not minded to play their game. There would be no withdrawal, and his reserves were already committed. He raised his sword instead, straining up in the saddle.

'Deathriders! Charge!'

He led them from the centre along the frontage of the army, wheeling left, reforming, lining up and cantering on, the skeletal horses rattling as they quickened their pace, the grass churned up under their hooves to a morass. Overhead, vast blocks of stone turned end over end, cursed stelae sent over by the Mortek Crawlers, lazily dropping towards the perfect symmetry of the Lumineth town on the other side of the sward. Akridos gave a dry chuckle to see those towers fall, their domes and spires shattered into pieces. He glanced back and saw the Lumineth cavalry struggling to disengage, their pikemen in danger of being swamped as Akridos' centre pressed into them. Still the arrows fell, kicking up the turf as his Deathriders charged, dropping into the Mortek Guard as they reformed the line. He saw Kathanos weaving a spell, a glister of purple magic imbuing the Mortek with new vigour. Hundreds of his own troops had been destroyed, but Akridos did not care. It had been a bold effort on the aelves' part, but in the war of attrition only numbers count – and the Ossiarch Bonereapers had numbers in abundance.

The second line of Lumineth infantry recognised the danger and began to withdraw, trying to link up with the archers. It was testament to their discipline that the archers didn't flee, and instead tried to blunt the Deathriders' charge. They knelt in the grass, faces grim, three-stringed bows sending out a near-horizontal rain of arrows. Akridos, juddering in the saddle, felt a bolt smack into his shoulder, another stab deep into his thigh. It made no difference. On they went, their horses' hooves hacking the grass, some with swords raised, others with spears couched. The tattered banners screamed in the wind of their charge, and then the aelves were trying to dart out of the way, some running back towards the town. The city was burning now, plumes of black smoke rising from the houses, streets shrieking with the maddened gheists released from the cauldrons of torment the Crawlers had thrown far over the battle line.

Akridos saw one aelf madly reach for arrows in an empty quiver, eyes wide, mouth open to scream. In a blur, he swung his sword down on the backswing and cleaved the aelf from shoulder to sternum, splattering his steed with blood. He tugged the reins, turned, parried a sword thrust with a clash of steel, leapt his steed forward and crushed another aelf under its hooves. He hacked left and right, staving in helmets, cracking breastplates, lopping off arms and heads, until the grass where the archers had stood was slick with blood, a greasy torrent. A few aelves sprinted towards the burning town, only to be ridden down with spears. Akridos watched them writhing in agony, the Deathriders calmly dismounting to end their torment with a swift blade to the back of the head.

Akridos looked to the battlefield behind him. The Lumineth infantry was surrounded in the middle of the right flank and was being whittled down without hope of escape. The cavalry had become hopelessly entangled with the Immortis Guard, the bone giants' spirit blades and falchions cutting down aelf and horse alike as the riders fought for their lives. All that was left was the remaining block of infantry, uncommitted, stranded in the middle of the field between the Bonereapers and the burning town. Already the Crawlers were directing their fire on them. Burning skulls fell amongst their ranks like cannonballs, sending up gouts of blood from severed heads and limbs.

'Reform!' Akridos shouted. 'Line! Advance!'

Two or three dozen riders had fallen on the charge across the sward, but Akridos still had near five hundred at his command. Effortlessly, as one, they reformed around him, and without hesitation began to charge.

As the undead cavalry drew closer, the aelves formed a square with their battered ranks. Akridos laughed to himself as he charged, the wind whipping through his bones.

They don't always do what is predicted, but sometimes, it seems, they do fall into the expected trap.

At the last minute he drew his cavalry aside, half of the troops plunging to the right while the other half cut left, both wheeling around the enemy square while the Crawlers continued to drop their dread ammunition into their packed ranks. Aelves died in dozens, crushed together with no escape, and marching on from the Ossiarch line came the regiments of Mortek Guard to finish them off. Hundreds of the Guard had been destroyed, but thousands remained.

Akridos took up position on his army's right flank again, where he had begun the battle. The surviving Lumineth cavalry had been cut down, the last of the infantry surrounded and slaughtered on all sides. All that remained now was the dwindling band of aelves in the middle of the field, their shields raised, their pikes outthrust.

They had fought bravely, with vigour and courage. They had gambled, and they had lost.

'Mortek Guard!' Akridos shouted across the field. 'Remember – leave me one alive.'

He looked up into the sky, the pale blue streaked with white cirrus. It was strange, he thought. The light didn't seem so powerful now.

They dragged the last aelf over and threw him to the ground. Smoke from the burning town bulged into the sky, and the proud white towers were now streaked wreckage, stained with fire. Dead littered the streets. More still covered the field of battle, across which the Harvesters now made their ponderous progress, scavenging the bones. Soulreapers and boneshapers, led by Morfilos, moved in their wake as they built new ranks for Akridos' army.

Akridos looked down from his steed at the aelf bleeding in the mud. His expression was fierce, proud, his thin face contorted with hatred, a streak of dried blood clogging one eye shut. He was all that remained.

'I salute your courage,' Akridos said. 'You, I choose to let live. Go, tell those abroad in Ymetrica that Akridos is coming. The Stalliarch Lords are coming. The Ossiarch Bonereapers are coming. Nagash is coming, and none who oppose him will live.'

The aelf grimaced, spat in the grass.

'I would rather die in the shadow of Paerthalann, my home,' he groaned. He struggled to his feet. At a gesture from Akridos, the Mortek Guard left him unmolested. 'But think on this, undead scum. Barely two thousand of our troops held up ten times that number – twenty times that number! When you meet us in our power, you will be utterly destroyed!'

'In your power?' Akridos scorned. 'I see no power here, aelf. Just arrogance, and failure.'

'Mage Y'gethin will stop you,' the aelf muttered. He dropped back down in the grass, the pain of his wounds overwhelming him.

Akridos started at the name. He felt his spirit shiver inside him, and he was gripped for a moment in a sickened frenzy.

'Who do you speak of? Tell me!'

The aelf glanced up, aware that his words had struck a nerve. He smiled, his teeth stained with blood.

'Mage Y'gethin, Stonemage of Ultharadon, the holy mountain.'

'*Ultharadon*, yes...' Akridos muttered. 'Y'gethin, a name that lives within me...'

'Your days are numbered, Bonereaper. The wrath of Teclis will sweep you and your unclean army away, and in time none shall even remember that you once profaned this sacred land. Now,' he said, baring his throat, 'I choose not to run.'

Ultharadon, the sacred mountain. Y'gethin, the mage of this place... I am drawn to both, linked in ways I do not yet understand. Connected by this spirit that pollutes me. To profane such a place would be unendurable to them... Eltharion would be compelled to respond.

Akridos, horrified and compelled in equal measure, drew his mind away from the name of Y'gethin. He felt the tug of strong emotion deep inside him. He looked down at the aelf, staring into eyes as blue as the deep sky above them, stained now with smoke. He nodded. Miszoios, the lead hekatos of his Mortek Guard, stepped forward, cutting down with his blade.

The aelf dropped, his head rolling away across the grass.

'Paerthalann, he called this place,' Akridos said, his voice coming as if from far away. 'A place of artists and philosophers, gem-crafters and musicians...'

He snapped back to himself, looking with pleasure on the burning town.

'Add its name to our banners,' he sneered. 'Add it with all the rest.'

CHAPTER ELEVEN

THE ADVANCE

The temple shone with the promise of home as he returned across the moors. For miles he had guided his path by the solid bulk of Ultharadon, like a barbed arrowhead lying flat against the horizon. Clouds trailed ribbons of white from its jagged peak, and as the sun rose and fell the mountain seemed to glow like cut diamond. He felt his spirits lift the closer he got to it, the temple glinting like a pearl in a riverbed at the mountain's base. Then he turned and looked back the way he had come, past the broken tower where he had spent the night, towards the dim valley cloaked in mist, where all the moorlands hunched under a persistent drizzle, dank and brooding. Where Thaerannan the Desolate held her brimming cup, the black smoke of sorrow spilling into the huddled dell…

But to look back on those dark lands was to think only of the war that still lay before him.

When I am most needed, I will be there, she had said. But how could she be needed any more than she was now?

He touched the brooch, felt the jewel like a rough stone embedded there, leached of colour and life – and yet its presence sustained him still. More so, even, now that Thaerannan had sapped the sadness from it. Like a surgeon letting blood, she had drained the poison from his system and left him cleansed, if not fully recovered.

Carreth adjusted the straps of his pack and hiked on, pressing his feet into the springing grass, the dew soaking through his boots. He was sore, tired, hungry, but he felt refreshed at the same time. There was work ahead, hard work, but for the first time since Tuareth had visited him at the temple, since Teclis himself had appeared in his dreams, he felt he had some inkling of how to achieve his purpose. But even as he thought this, and as his stride took him with more confidence across the grasslands and past rushing brooks and groves of gently swaying trees, Carreth heard the voice of Thaerannan as if she were whispering over his shoulder, deep in that shadowed valley where desolation lay.

You dabble in forbidden magics… Beware then, Stonemage, that your methods do not destroy both you and her instead. It is a dark path that you follow, the darkest…

'Dark,' he muttered to himself. 'But often it is only through darkness that we can find the light.'

There was a commotion over by the new stables as he approached the temple, hiking up from the wide grass fields into the new training grounds and barracks. He could see a dozen Dawnriders in cream and gold unhooking their armour, stable hands brushing the horses down. When he was still some distance away, he saw Alithis, immovable, standing with hands on hips and head bared, eyes boring into the riders. She didn't need to gesture for him to recognise how angry she was – and when she was that angry, Carreth was confident she could stare down Ultharadon itself.

He climbed the stile over the lower fence, feet squelching into the rough ground of the paddock where the Dawnriders exercised their horses. He could hear voices drifting over to him across the field, recognised one of the riders as Belfinnan. The steedmaster swept his helmet off, the lustre of his chestnut hair catching the light and glinting with red sparks. Aelthuwi was there too, thin and callow in his blue robes, hair still cropped close, his arms folded as if he were unsure which side in the argument he should take. He was trying to look composed, but his composure broke when he noticed Carreth walking across the field towards them. His arm snapped up to point, eyes wide.

'The Stonemage returns!' Carreth heard him shout.

Alithis turned, raising her hand in a laconic salute. Belfinnan tucked his helmet under his arm and stood as if at attention. Beyond them, the other riders were seeing to their weapons and armour. As he got closer, Carreth could see that one or two of them bore light wounds – a scratch against a forehead, a bloodied sleeve – and the horses were shivering with rough travel. Carreth increased his pace, dread uncoiling in his stomach.

'What's happened?' he called.

Alithis just stood there, face grim. She cocked her head at Belfinnan, while Aelthuwi darted forward to take Carreth's bag.

'I fear tensions are reaching a head, Stonemage,' the apprentice said in a low voice as he unhooked the strap from Carreth's shoulder. 'Things have been somewhat strained since you left.'

'Against your express orders,' Alithis said, 'Belfinnan decided he could win the war single-handed.'

'You exaggerate,' Belfinnan said, his voice clipped with anger. Carreth hadn't seen the steedmaster so exercised before. Normally a model of breezy irresponsibility, there was a coldness to his face that was just the right side of real rage. He gripped the pommel of the sword at his hip. Carreth could see the marks of hard riding on his armour, the dust on his boots.

'Explain yourself,' he said. 'Belfinnan?'

The steedmaster raised his chin and stared off into the middle distance. 'The day you left,' he said, 'I took out a scouting party, as we discussed.'

'You made contact with the enemy?'

'Aye,' Belfinnan said ruefully. He glanced at his riders as they milled about the stables, some tending their wounds. None looked seriously hurt, at least. 'Perhaps a day's ride to the west, we took a high path overlooking a narrow valley near the Paerthalann mountains. There was smoke in the distance, the town itself burning, perhaps. We tried to get closer along those damnable mountain paths to get a better look, but we were surprised.'

Carreth raised an eyebrow. Belfinnan saw it and shook his head, frowning.

'I know, I know,' he said. 'But they'd sent out scouts of their own. They came from the high ground and we didn't see them in time. Couldn't withdraw either, not without having to give an account of ourselves. Damn, but they've hard riders amongst their number, I'll admit that much.'

'Their horsemen?'

'If you can call them horses,' Belfinnan said with a grimace. 'And if you can call them men. Monstrosities both, I'd rather say.'

'There were no casualties though?' Carreth demanded.

'No,' Alithis leapt in. Her face was a mask of scorn. 'As luck would have it.'

'Luck!' Belfinnan shouted. His face was pale with anger, and his struggle to master it was clear. There was something cold and terrible about him, and well could Carreth believe that he *would* try to win the war single-handed. 'My Dawnriders' skill, more like! Indeed,' he said, turning again to Carreth, his eyes alight, 'hard riders or not, we turned them to piles of broken bones before we made our withdrawal!'

Carreth felt his own anger welling inside him and struggled to cap it. 'You were not supposed to fight, and you should not have got yourself into a position where fighting was inevitable.'

Belfinnan huffed with exasperation, his hands outspread. 'Then what am I here for, Stonemage, if not to fight?'

'A skirmish and a few scouts sent back to the dust won't win the war, steedmaster!' he shouted. 'If you want to fight, you will do it when we can achieve a victory a touch more comprehensive, perhaps!'

Belfinnan swallowed his anger, the muscles in his jaw working as hard as if he were chewing a stone. Alithis was shaking her head at his folly when Carreth rounded on her.

'And you!' he said as her eyes widened. 'When I am absent, the command devolves to you, seneschal. See that you impose proper discipline on those under you.'

'Under... *her*!' Belfinnan cried. 'My Dawnriders follow no one's command but my own, and certainly not this... this...' He waved his hand, looking her up and down.

'We fight as one, or we don't fight at all,' Alithis spat.

'Not fighting, that's something you seem used to, seneschal! Or are those hammers purely decorative!'

Alithis, a cold sneer on her lips, took a step forward and stared up at him, her head no higher than his chin. 'Maybe you'll see me fight a lot sooner than you expect?'

'My expectations are low, seneschal. I doubt very much you could raise them any higher.'

'Sort this out in your own time!' Carreth roared. 'For now, ready your commands, and make sure the best trained troops we have are ready to march at first light.'

Belfinnan's head snapped around. 'First light?' he said, a glint in his eye.

Alithis stared blankly at him. 'For... for what?'

'What do you think, seneschal?' Carreth asked. 'We have dallied long enough. It is time to strike.'

Carreth dismissed them both with a curt gesture, his jaw set. He strode off towards the temple, Aelthuwi scurrying to keep up, leaving them spluttering at each other on the edge of the paddock. The sky, as if mirroring his mood, began to darken and spot with rain. As the light changed the temple rotunda seemed to dim, the bright marble leached of life until it looked no more than dead grey stone. Ultharadon, the dark mass behind him, pressed its weight against his back.

'And what about Thaerannan?' Alithis called to him. 'Is she with us?'

'No.' He gritted his teeth. 'We're on our own.'

He pressed on through the gathered tents, across the churned ground, past the long barn of the new barracks with its sloped roof, the slate oily and dark. There was a sense of restlessness in the air, as if his words had already spread throughout the camp, conveyed by that strange alchemy of grumbling rumour that always rose up whenever soldiers were grouped together. He saw a unit of wardens marching back from the parade square after the dawn patrol, a new snap in their step, a gleam in their eyes as they shouldered their weapons. He saw a troop of Stoneguard, fresh vigour in their movements as they oversaw a weapontake, the replacement spear shafts and armoury equipment loaded onto a baggage cart by the side of the barracks. It was as if everyone was working against time, as if the deadline that had long hovered at some indeterminate point in the distance was now dangerously near. The closer and more visible it became, the more urgently did everyone strain to reach it.

But did they know what they were reaching for, Carreth thought, or even what they would do with it once it was in their grasp?

There were veterans amongst them, he knew, aelves who had

seen war stripped of all its supposed glory, but for every veteran there were a dozen untried fighters. Young aelves, male and female, who had only held a pike in the practice yards as part of their weekly training, or had shot a few arrows at a motionless target on the range. In number, and with all the benefits of their training and discipline, he would put even these green aelves against the worst the Mortal Realms could throw at them, but Carreth knew that the foe they faced was implacable beyond all reason, with a discipline and ruthlessness that could well outmatch their own. In the balance between quality and quantity he would always weigh more heavily towards the former, but when the two were combined the results could be deadly beyond description.

'And do we have the numbers?' he muttered to himself. 'Do we have enough to hold them without yielding?'

'Mage?' Aelthuwi said at his side. The young apprentice dogged his steps, still holding Carreth's travelling bag, his staff. Carreth had forgotten he was there, he was so absorbed in his own thoughts.

'Did you prepare the books?' he asked. 'And my chambers?'

'All is arranged as you instructed before you left, mage,' Aelthuwi said. 'Your bed and your desk have been removed, and the chamber cleansed with the sacred incantations. Your robes are ready.'

'Good. Thank you, Aelthuwi. Take my pack and staff and leave them in the sanctuary. I will collect them later.'

'As you wish, mage.' He cleared his throat. 'Will… Will my presence be required?'

'That will not be necessary,' Carreth told his apprentice, although he didn't add, *And I will not inflict this on you if I can.*

They had reached the rear entrance of the hall by the northern quadrangle, where usually the double doors of blue crystal were kept open as a symbol of the temple's welcome. With the exigencies of war, though, those doors were now kept closed. Two Stoneguard in full armour stood aside as the Stonemage approached, pulling the doors open. Carreth passed through and entered the cool central chamber with a sigh of relief, away from the sight of the new recruits and the officers he must soon lead into battle. The cold, clear stone stretched up around him, unadorned, and the tile floor echoed with his footsteps.

They passed through the hall, exiting through another set of crystal doors, and on to the cloisters on the other side. They skirted along the edge of the ornamental gardens. The paths through the gardens were empty, the gravel unraked, the flowers drooping in the rain as it quickened from the sky. They walked to the other side of the rotunda and into the southern quadrangle. When they reached his chambers, Carreth turned to dismiss Aelthuwi.

'Work on your geomancy while I'm gone,' he told the young apprentice. He stood with his fingers resting on the door handle, strangely reluctant to enter. 'Study the lineaments of the aelementiri, practise bonding your spirit with the earth and the stone. It's at the very heart of what we do here. And remember – you are as much inviting the earth to partake of your spirit as the other way around. Do not be too proud, for the bond goes both ways.'

'But...' Aelthuwi stuttered. 'Surely I'm going with you, master? You can't leave me here!'

'That's precisely what I intend.'

'But if the army marches then I should be at your side!'

'You are not ready,' Carreth said gently. 'The risk is too great. If I should fall, then all that I am, all that we have built here, will reside in you, Aelthuwi. The temple needs you, and I need you here.'

'What if...'

Carreth saw him swallow, afraid to voice the fear in case doing so made it real.

'What if we fail?' he said. 'Some of the Stoneguard will remain, a sizeable troop of the wardens and sentinels. I will not leave the Temple of Ultharadon undefended. You will be safe.'

Aelthuwi frowned and looked at his feet. 'That's not what I meant. My safety is nothing compared to the safety of the temple – and the mountain it guards.'

Carreth laid his hand on Aelthuwi's shoulder. 'If all things were well you would have many years of your apprenticeship left, many decades to learn and study. We would have peace in which to rebuild Ymetrica, and Hysh itself, and to find our places on the Teclamentari.' He stared down into Aelthuwi's eyes, holding his gaze. 'But we do not have peace. My generation was born into a red age, and it seems yours must suffer an age equally violent. Before we have peace and light again, I fear we must walk along many a dark path.' He glanced at the closed door. 'Along dark paths indeed.'

'Then the Cathallar counselled war?' Aelthuwi said.

Carreth gave him a grim smile. 'Thaerannan the Desolate has not grown less cryptic with age, and her counsels are rarely so straightforward. Say what you like about war, Aelthuwi – at least there is little ambiguity about it. You see the enemy,' he said, 'and you try to kill him.'

When Aelthuwi had turned to go, Carreth closed his eyes, his hand against the door. He could almost feel them in there, the volumes drawn up from the archives, the ancient scrolls and scribbled treatises. Dark magics lurked amongst their pages, sinuous and deadly, strange slivers of ancient souls.

For what is magic, Carreth thought, *but an art where aspects of the weaver's soul are gifted to the spell?*

A shadow of amethyst, Thaerannan had seen about him. The colour of Shyish. The colour of Nagash. The shade of death.

He shuddered as he turned the handle and stepped inside, into the blank chamber, where the spell waited for him to weave it.

Dawn broke like red ruin in the sky. Streaks of crimson spilled down the mountain like lava, and the bellies of the clouds were bloody. The clank of steel, of weapons and canteens and harnesses. The creak of baggage wheels, the muttering of soldiers tramping to their regiments. The grass slick underfoot, grey in the half-light, wet with dew. The stone of the fountain glistening as the light struck it, dawn rising faster now, the beams of light caressing its flank. The temple seemed to rise from the darkness, ancient and precise, immutable. More troops marched up from the barracks, heads bare, helmets held loose at their sides. The great stallions of the Dawnriders were led up from the paddocks and the stables, cantering quickly around the forecourt, hooves clattering on the stone. Their riders spoke to them in a soft mutter, soothing, calming, holding up handfuls of fodder or red apples plucked from the orchards in the wild ground to the south. The fountain trickled and burbled. As the breeze shifted, a faint haze rose up from the agitated water, a thin mist that caught the deepening light and seemed to both sharpen and diffuse it at the same time, throwing out shards and fractals of blue and red and green against the paving stone – indigo and violet, the searing white light of Hysh somehow refined by its passage through the water. Carreth, standing in the atrium at the front of the temple rotunda, stared into the depths of that light, unblinking, while his army mustered around him.

Bursting its bounds, the dawn grew wider, the bloody red softening to amber and gold. Amongst the soldiers there was less talk as the light rose, less grumbling, less reticence or confusion. Regiments came together, ranks were drawn up. The temple forecourt was wide, almost an acre in breadth and depth, and as the troops formed into their marching order they began to comfortably fill the space. This was not everyone, Carreth knew. He had ordered the newer recruits to stay behind and continue their training, and a sizeable complement of Stoneguard were staying with them to defend the temple. He had ordered Alithis to remain, but her refusal had not just skirted the line of insubordination – it had flown right over it. No drama, no wild emotion or remonstrance, just her flat rejection of what she had been commanded to do. Carreth smiled to recall it, that hard, unyielding face staring up at him, daring him to try and order her a second time. Belfinnan had laughed to see Carreth's exasperation.

Well, he thought. *You fight with what you have, not what you would like to have. Although in this case, I have what I want well enough.*

He looked out over their ranks as the sunlight struck gold in the sky above, clean day come at last, the drizzle having moved off to dust the flanks of the mountain behind them. Immaculate blue-and-white cloaks, light sparkling from the white plates of polished armour, from the bright lances and sword points, the arrowheads in packed quivers, the barding of the cavalry. All the runes of the mandala shone on the shields of the Vanari wardens, their pikes held at arms, on the robes and banners of the Stoneguard contingent, on the breastplates of the Vanari sentinels. He had called and they had answered. Ten thousand aelves, girded for war.

He saw Belfinnan leading half his cavalry from the forecourt onto the grasslands on the left, skirting the infantry to take up position in the vanguard. A screen of Dawnriders would cover the advance, the other half of the cavalry held at the back to cover the rear. He saw Alithis at the head of her Stoneguard in the centre, the elite warriors with their huge two-handed mallets outnumbered by the wardens around them. Alithis looked tense, fussing with the ranks, gesturing at the ground ahead of them that they had to cover. Carreth couldn't hear what she was saying at this distance, but he knew the seneschal did not approve of the action. There would be hard marching ahead, and the Stoneguard were ever designed to be a defensive force, as immovable as the mountains and as deadly as an avalanche. There was much ground to cover, though. Carreth's plan would only work if they could strike first and strike hardest.

If it is the right plan, he worried. *The right plan, and for the right reasons...*

He reached for the brooch, surprised as ever to find the stone shrivelled down to a blackened husk.

Dae'annis approached and joined him on the step. The young warrior looked at him with a grave expression. The mask of command was never an easy fit, but Carreth knew the warden was doing his best. He had risen to the challenge, and every doubt he felt was only a flail to whip him onwards to greater effort.

'The wardens are in position, mage,' he said. 'We're ready to march.'

'And are you ready to fight?' Carreth asked. He turned to look at him, watched him flinch at the recollection of combat.

'Without hesitation,' he said. 'Without... without failure.'

There was no performance in it, no bravado. Carreth held out his hand. Surprised, Dae'annis took it – the warrior's grip, wrist to wrist.

'There was no failure then, my friend,' Carreth said. 'I'm proud to have you with me, and I've no doubt I'll be calling on your expertise by the time this is done.'

'You call on me?' Dae'annis laughed. 'I should think it'll be the other way around!'

'You've fought these monsters before, though – I haven't. Experience is a deadly weapon in the right hands.'

'I'm not sure mine are,' the high warden said, looking down at his spread palms in their battered leather gloves.

'I have faith in you,' Carreth said, gripping his shoulder. 'What was it you said at the council? We must play to our strengths. Our faith. Our trust in each other, and in the purity of our cause. In the light that guides us to the right path...'

'You remembered?'

Carreth looked down at his own hand. The light of Teclis had faded now, and in its place crept the nagging doubts that always seemed to dog him these days. *The light that guides us to the right path... an amethyst flame*, she had said, *darkening by the hour...*

'No matter,' he mumbled.

'Mage?'

He glanced up, saw Dae'annis staring at him with something like concern. Carreth thrust his hand into a glove and took up his staff, forcing a smile onto his lips.

'No matter,' he said again, more forcefully. 'I owe you an apology, Dae'annis, and it is the most heartfelt one I have ever made. I doubted your courage, your skill as a warrior, your sense of honour. What is worse, I doubted your friendship with my sister, and for that I will ever be in your debt. I do not ask forgiveness–'

'And yet you have it,' Dae'annis said, without hesitation. His voice cracked as he spoke. 'There is no question that you have it, mage. My life is yours, in honour of Tuareth. I will earn back her death in the numbers of Bonereapers I will skewer on my spear, you have my word. I will not let you down.'

Carreth looked away, nodding furiously. He told himself it was just the breeze that conjured the tears from his eyes.

'There is only one thing more I need from you,' he said after a moment.

'Anything.'

'In Shyish, you said that this Akridos, this Bonereapers general, personally led the charge that broke up your left flank?'

'Indeed, mage – I will never forget it.'

'A bold leader, then, you would say. One who leads from the front, who is in the thick of the action?' Carreth tapped his fingers on the hilt of his staff.

'Aye,' Dae'annis said, frowning. 'As far as I can tell from one engagement, in any case. Is there some key to your strategy here that you're not telling me?'

'Perhaps...' Carreth smiled and clapped his hand to Dae'annis' shoulder. 'All I ask is that you hold the line when I need you to, and that you do not break. If I can personally destroy the monster that leads them, then perhaps we have a chance.'

Dae'annis grinned, gripping his spear. 'You have my word on that count. For Tuareth,' he said. 'Make him suffer.'

'For Tuareth.'

'Are we going then, Stonemage?' Belfinnan called across the forecourt. He held up his sword. 'These dead scum don't stop to eat, you know, so I doubt we'll be spoiling their breakfast if we go now!'

Aelthuwi appeared at Carreth's side. He draped the Stonemage's cloak over his shoulders, passing him the ceremonial helmet and the Staff of the High Peaks. Fully adorned, Carreth walked between the waiting ranks to the front of the army.

But are there enough? Do we have the numbers for what I need to do?

He stood before them, staring into the eyes of the wardens and the sentinels, glancing over at the Dawnriders who had taken up positions on the army's left flank. Speeches were a good thing at a time like this. Inspiring words, something to stir the blood and quieten the fear. These aelves, he saw, had no need of fine words. They were ready. They would follow him no matter what he said.

He turned and faced the Ymetrican veldt, the great green plains rolling off like a blanket of emerald, the pilgrims' path that led to the Scintilla Realmgate perhaps a week's march away, the mountain ranges of Paerthalann Pass in the distance, where the land had been rucked out of shape. There they would find the enemy, and this would be decided one way or another.

Carreth raised his hands. He closed his eyes and fell into the deep and welcoming embrace of stone and earth, the weave of magic that tied them both together. He plucked a string of that weave, reaching out with his aethersight to mould and form the ground beneath him. There was a low, bass rumble and the earth began to shudder. Pebbles and stones trembled at his feet, flicking up into the air. The ground started to split under him, as if carved open by a savage axe strike, buried stones and great chunks of rock rising and reforming, smoothing out into a moulded seat that he settled himself into as if dropping easily into his chair back in his chambers. He sat cross-legged, the staff resting lengthways in his lap, and as his stone platform floated onwards at the head of his army he heard a rousing cheer break out behind him – the clash of arms, the beating of shields, the exultation of aelves now marching off to war. He felt it beat in his own breast, that wild joy for combat that he hadn't experienced for decades, and it was almost strong enough to still the fear that he was leading them all to war on the promise of a lie. He looked at his hand, where the light of Teclis had faded from his skin. He felt the death magic coil inside him, the contours of the spell he had created from the forbidden texts in the library archives.

He marched not to destroy his enemies but to save his sister's soul.

CHAPTER TWELVE

THE BATTLE OF PAERTHALANN PASS

Dawnrider scouts reported them first, refugees from the west, fleeing the Bonereapers' advance and staggering in miserable groups along the trackless paths. No more than five days' march from the temple and here were the young and the old, children, the infirm, those too badly wounded to fight – shuffling along, picking over the stones, turning haunted eyes on the army as it filed through the gorge. Some held out their hands for food or water, beseeching them for help. There were hundreds of them, Alithis realised, and the wretched trail stretched back for a mile at least. It was a pitiful sight, but she hardened her heart against it. The mountains soared up on either side of them, craggy and black, and the only sure pathway was through this narrow defile. If nothing else, the refugees were blocking the way and making it more difficult for the army to pass.

Belfinnan rode up in a clatter of hooves, scattering dust from the grainy soil. He looked down from his horse at the passing refugees, pressed into the side of the gorge by the progress of the army. Some clutched bloody bandages to their wounds and looked back at them with defiance, while others stared only at the ground. Belfinnan shook his head sadly.

'This is desperate stuff,' he said. 'I've never seen the like. Some of these poor souls have been fleeing for weeks, and every refuge they think they find is just another brief halt in the Bonereapers' advance.'

'We should send them on to the temple,' Alithis said. She unhooked a flask from her belt and passed it to a young mother who bore a crying child. The aelf took the flask with weeping gratitude, wetting her baby's lips and drinking deeply herself. 'There's no shelter between here and there, apart from the mountains and the plains.'

'No!' Carreth snapped, his voice cold and firm. Even above the sound of marching, it rang against the walls of the gorge. He stepped from the rock that bore him, striding over to her. 'The temple will be the next line of defence if we fail here. You would be putting them in greater danger.'

'Then where?' Alithis protested. She swept her hand out, gesturing at the pitiful procession. 'These people have nothing, they're at the end of their strength.'

'They can find what provisions we can spare when they reach Ultharadon, but they must keep going until this is done. Belfinnan?'

'Aye, mage?'

'Send one of your scouts back to the temple, let them know the refugees are coming. But they must not stay.'

The steedmaster nodded and called for one of his riders. Alithis bit her tongue. The longer they had marched, the more Carreth's old face seemed to be showing, and it was one she hadn't seen for years. Hard, merciless, glad of war. It was small comfort that there were fewer virtues better suited to battle.

As Belfinnan's scout rode hard up the defile, heading back the way they had come, another came haring down the pass in a great scattering of stones. Ceffylis, his name was, she remembered. His face was grave, eyes dark behind the slit of his helmet.

'You've the look of an aelf with urgent news, my friend,' Belfinnan said. 'Let's have it.'

'Contact, my lord,' Ceffylis panted. 'The Ossiarch army is near, moving through the eastern end of the Vale of Paerthalann.'

Carreth looked up the defile, almost as if he expected the Bonereapers to come pouring down it at any moment. The Lumineth army stretched away up the narrow channel, a snake of blue cloaks and white armour, steel glinting on their shouldered arms. A crooked slice of sky shone above them, a hint of blue amidst this dank and clammy gloom. Alithis found that her hammers were in her hands, and she couldn't remember having drawn them.

'Then we need to move quickly,' Carreth said. 'The defile widens about half a mile ahead, where the pass cuts through the mountains.'

'A decent chokepoint,' Alithis said. She knew the ground, although she hadn't passed this way in years. She pictured it, an oval of grass bordered by the slopes of the mountains on one side and the sheer drop to the cliffs below on the other. To be caught in that space would be murder, and a few score troops could hold up an army there.

Carreth strode off towards the head of the column. 'Belfinnan, screen our movements with your horses. Alithis?'

'Yes, mage?'

'See if you can extricate your Stoneguard from this mess and have them move up to the front. I need you in the centre, around me.'

Belfinnan whooped and charged up the defile. Alithis nodded, saying nothing, forcing herself to move. Her hands were shaking. She was surprised again at how difficult it was to stride eagerly towards the threat of death. How long had it been since she had last fought? She caught Dae'annis' eye as the high warden stepped back from his troops, issuing his orders, encouraging them to pick up the pace. He turned, saw her, offered a strained smile. She did the same. And then there was nothing to do but follow the orders she had been given.

'Stoneguard,' she bellowed. 'On me! And get ready to fight!'

The pass was no more than half a mile wide at its broadest point, a vaguely concave lawn of yellowing grass that led upwards on a slight incline to sweep through the mountains and descend once more to the level plains beyond. On the left-hand side as Akridos looked at it, there was a rough acre of stony ground where gnarled buckthorns and bramble choked the edge of a steep escarpment. Beyond was a drop of a thousand feet or more to the rocks at the mountains' base. On the right, steep buttresses of stone studded with gorse reached up into the mountains' flank. The stone was a deep grey, and here and there great sheets of slate had detached from the flank to crash down into the pass below, their wreckage littering the grass. There were some narrow paths up there that led back into a slender defile, but nothing suitable for an army to use. The only sure route to the Ymetrican veldt was through this pass. To detour around this vast range would take weeks. To follow the twisting tracks would put the army at unacceptable risk, not to mention the impossibility of getting the Crawlers and Harvesters through. There was no other option. And the aelves knew it.

'It's quite a shame that they managed to get here first,' Kathanos hissed at his side.

Akridos sat immobile, his steed under him. Rain flecked down from a pale sky, and the shadow of a cloud was briefly chased across the grass. He looked up. Here and there were patches of blue trying to break through the cloud cover, the dense coherence of light from the celestial orbs. He looked back to the horizon. The Lumineth army was taking up position on the high ground about a mile away. They had anchored their line by the escarpment and had set some of their archers to climb the rocks over on the right. Akridos could see a wedge of cavalry held well back, waiting to exploit any gaps in the Ossiarch line. The infantry was lined up in regiments, no more than a stride between each block. Their shields glowed white even in this half-light, their pikes resting on the notch at the top of their shield rims. He could see the crests of their helmets shivering in the breeze.

'They have the high ground,' Akridos admitted. 'A narrow frontage, what looks like a decent number of spears. They cannot be more than ten thousand, though.' He cast an appraising eye over their deployment. 'The ground is unambiguous, at least.'

'Meaning?'

'Flat, little in the way of terrain, relatively narrow.'

The soulmason hunched over and chuckled in his seat. 'We have the numbers, though. Can we not force our way through?'

They were over on the right, positioned in front of the Ossiarch army on a small hummock of grass. Kathanos swept his bony arm back to indicate the Ossiarch column behind them, an endless parade of troops that stretched out of sight down the length of the pass and back to the burning town of Paerthalann five miles away. Blocks and blocks of infantry had churned the grass to mud. They had stopped by the Liege-Kavalos' position and were slowly forming into their battle lines, the Mortek Guard clattering from column to line, five regiments covering the frontage of the pass.

Akridos sneered his derision. He pointed with his scimitar at each flank of the Lumineth army. The faint cries of command came floating down the pass towards him.

'On ground like this, the numbers favour them. We would need ten times as many troops to prise them out of this position and still have a viable army at the end of it.'

There was a pause as the soulmason made his calculations. 'And what do we have?'

'Not ten times their number. Not quite.' He gave a dry laugh. 'Still, there are ways and means for every situation.' He summoned over a hekatos from the Mortek Guard. 'Where are the Crawlers?' he demanded.

'At the rear of the column, lord,' the hekatos said in a crackling, grinding voice. 'It was not certain whether we could bring them through here.'

'Bring them up, now,' Akridos commanded. 'Disassemble them and bring them in pieces if you have to. Have them deploy at the base of the pass, well out of arrow range.' He turned to Kathanos. 'If the aelf scum want to present me with an easy target, I see no reason not to oblige.'

'No reason,' Kathanos said, starting back. 'But I do not think they will oblige you for long. See, Liege-Kavalos – the aelves are marching! Perhaps you should explain your strategy to them!'

They ran the last hundred yards, scrambling up to take the high ground before the Bonereapers could seize it for themselves and trap the Lumineth army in the defile. Alithis sprinted forward, ahead of her troops, her chest heaving and her limbs flooded with adrenaline. The Stoneguard assembled around her, locking into position, hammers raised. The wardens flowed around them and ranked up in a solid line across the frontage of the pass. The ground sloped off in front, running into a thin, leaf-shaped spread of grass that was studded with rock and the occasional crooked spray of gorse. The stone of the mountainside gleamed wet and dark off to the left. High winds drifted up from the sides of the cliff on the right, where the escarpment fell away into the jagged foothills of the range.

If this pass is leaf-shaped, she thought, *then we're embedded in the stem when we should really be in the tip...*

Carreth paced the ground behind the Stoneguard, looking out to where the first ranks of the Ossiarch army could be seen marching into position. The great horns of his helmet flared out on either side, the tassels fluttering in the breeze. Alithis watched the Bonereapers as they formed up – the front-line units in solid columns, behind them a vast and disorienting jumble of troops and cavalry jostling for position, stretching off down the opposite slope towards the Vale of Paerthalann. A column of black smoke rose up from the direction of the town, staining the clouds above it.

'We've missed our chance,' Alithis said, pointing at the Bonereapers. 'We should have pressed forward, caught them in the narrower part of the pass on the other side.'

'Any further in,' Carreth said, 'and we'd be at risk of letting them outflank us. Take my word, if we were going to make a stand, here is the best place for it.'

'"If",' Alithis said. 'Why do I have the horrible feeling you have something else in mind?' She looked over her shoulder at the Stonemage. Carreth's face was as hard as steel, and there was something unpleasantly satisfied in his eyes.

'The smaller army can only dominate through aggression,' he said. 'Offensive action, perfectly timed, always compensates for being outnumbered.'

'And if they don't see it that way?' Alithis said.

The moment hovered there in the breeze, as if daring either side to snatch it first. Who would act, and who would react? And whose decisions would end up being the correct ones?

Dae'annis came jogging over from the blocks of wardens in the centre line, just before and beneath the Stoneguard.

'My units are in position, mage,' he said. 'The sentinels have taken position on the slopes and are ready to rain fire on the Bonereapers.'

'Then get ready to move, and move fast,' Carreth said. 'Alithis?' He pointed with his staff. 'The wardens will clear a space and engage the Bonereapers in the centre. Your Stoneguard must be the rock on which the wave will break if the wardens are pushed back. I *must* have time to complete my spell. Nothing else takes precedence, do you understand?'

'Aye, mage.' She felt herself stiffen as if on the parade ground at the temple, leading the changing of the guard at the Ritual of Symmetry. Blood fired up in her veins, and despite the anxiety, the apprehension, all the dead hours marching with the weight of approaching battle heavy on her mind, Alithis found that there was a hard smile on her lips. When the moment came, she would not be found wanting. She hoped.

'You seem to have left me out of your equations, Stonemage?' Belfinnan called over from the rear. His Dawnriders were spread out across the width of the pass, here at its narrowest point. 'Keeping all the fun for yourselves?'

'Hit the flanks as and when you see fit,' Carreth commanded. 'Keep them from overwhelming us, push them back if you can, but do not get bogged down. If everything goes wrong, steedmaster, I'll be relying on your Dawnriders to get us out of this.'

Belfinnan crowed with laughter. 'Don't worry, seneschal,' he shouted. 'I'll come and rescue you if need be!'

'Just think about your own duties,' Alithis said with a scowl. *You damned fool...* 'Otherwise I'll be forced to rescue you myself.'

'Ah! I feel that there's an ode for the ages in all this,' he called. 'Two great warriors on the battlefield, fell of temperament, breaking each other's hearts through their shared sacrifice...'

'I would dearly love to break more than your heart, steedmaster,'

Alithis muttered. Dae'annis grinned, and then he turned and sprinted back to the line of wardens.

'Charge your pikes!' he shouted as he ran. 'Prepare to advance!'

Alithis brushed a lock of hair out of her eyes as the wind spilled down from the cold peaks. She clutched her hammers, feeling the Stoneguard behind her gird themselves for combat. Banners fluttered around her, and for a moment all she could hear was the keening of the wind, like the echo of an ancient grief.

They came on in one broad wave, spears levelled, the crests of their helmets trembling in the wind. There was the clash of metal striking metal as greaves knocked against shield rims, as swords rattled from scabbards. Orders were bellowed across the advancing line, the answering shout of the warriors shifting position – as smooth as water flowing across marble, as the sun rising in the morning sky. Akridos gnashed his brittle teeth, spitting shards of bone, leaning up in his stirrups to hack his sword against the buffeting air. He gave a calcareous grin.

'Move up the right flank!' he screamed, his voice crackling like breaking glass. 'Mortek Guard, to arms!'

He rode fast to the centre of the battle line, hooves hammering the grass. The Mortek Guard smoothly unhinged to let him pass. He was aware of Kathanos quickly scrabbling to hide himself in the bulk of the troops, urging his throne onwards. Akridos croaked with an almost savage glee. The Mortek Guard reformed after he passed through them, and as Akridos cantered his steed towards the rear the first arrows began to fall. He turned, caught a glancing blow as one bolt skipped across his helmet, saw the Mortek Guard peppered with shot from the aelf archers on the slope of the mountain on the right. Nimble as goats, they moved up and forward, seeming to skim over the sharp incline and find ever more deadly positions from which to rain down their luminous fire. Mortek troops staggered and fell apart under the rain of shots, raising shields which did little to protect them. A few desultory spears were thrown up from the Ossiarch ranks, to no effect. Akridos turned, hauling his steed to face the front, saw the aelf infantry, those deadly pikemen, come charging across the sward with terrible, flashing eyes, their weapons glowing like the risen sun. A hundred yards, then eighty, then no more than a dozen strides... They were advancing all along the line, the grass behind them churned into mud by the speed of their charge, the light, that terrible light, blasting across the bleak afternoon towards him.

'Ultharadon!' they screamed as they ran. 'Ultharadon and Y'gethin!'

'Brace for the charge!' Akridos howled at the Guard in the centre. The whole flank seemed to stiffen, even as the Lumineth on the mountain slope shifted their aim to fleck the Ossiarch right with shot.

There was nothing he could do with his Deathriders now. The pass was too narrow, too choked with his own troops. He hauled on the reins, tried to force his way through the Mortek Guard that were still spilling into the pass, packed in as tight as they had been on the bone ships that took them across the Saltcorpse Sea. Skeletal warriors fell uncomplaining under his steed's hooves as he barrelled them out of the way. The Lumineth were almost on the centre, charging across the grass, their reserves moving up to exploit any gap.

How had they been caught like this? Trapped by the weight of their own numbers, unable to respond, to manoeuvre, to strike back even! Akridos raised his sword again to call the left flank into a wheel so they could try to envelop the aelves as they made contact. But then the wrath of the Lumineth was on them, the last few feet of the sward covered in an instant, and all thoughts of manoeuvre or tactics were no more than classroom exercises, base theory quickly cast aside by the practical needs of the devastating moment. Akridos watched, craning over his steed's neck, gazing out across a dozen serried ranks of Mortek Guard as the Lumineth spearmen crashed into the Ossiarch centre.

'*Ultharadon!*' came the keening cry. '*Ultharadon and Y'gethin!*'

Their pikes shone like starlight fallen on the earth, so blinding he couldn't even see the aelves who wielded them. The whole pass was a surge of white, like a blazing tide smothering everything before it.

'No...' Akridos whispered. And then the entire front rank of the Mortek Guard burst apart.

Shards of bone rained down on the Ossiarch army, buckled shields, broken swords, spears. Skulls rattled to the ground, ribcages and spines went sailing through the air, and a great buffeting wave sent Akridos staggering backwards. He tightened his legs against his steed, gripped the stirrups with his feet. A cloud of dust ballooned into the sky, swept away after a moment by the quickening wind.

He had seen this in Shyish, aelf magic charged into their weapons, making every stab and thrust like a knife slipping into water. Through the dust he saw a glowing spear blade rend Mortek bodies apart like they were paper. As it cleared, he saw that the whole front rank was now no more than debris and ashes, and the centre had buckled into a great salient, with the aelves frantically pushing their way forward as if trying to burst out of the pass itself. Behind them, more units rushed in to exploit the advance, and still the arrows fell – unerring in their aim, relentless.

Akridos threw the next line of Mortek Guard forward, smashing the head from one warrior with the tip of his blade as he wildly gesticulated.

'Onto them!' he screamed. 'Choke their spears with your bones!'

He saw the blue flash of magic somewhere off to his left, near where the rough ground fell away into a scattering of rocks and boulders to the drop of the escarpment. His Deathriders milled about behind the left flank, a hundred yards from the fighting, hemmed in by the three regiments of Guard that were still trying to wheel into position. Akridos spurred himself forward, crunching more of his troops underfoot. The pass was like a vast parade ground, the Ossiarch troops packed shoulder to shoulder, utterly unable to move as the aelves pressed them back. A handful of troops from the left flank went tumbling over the edge of the escarpment as they tried to wheel through the tussocks and rocks. Troops jostled at his side. Akridos lashed out with his sword to right and left, clearing space, lurching forward a foot at a time.

Kathanos, eyes glowing pale with anger, cantered over on his throne, the end of his staff scorched and smoking.

'This is a disaster!' he screamed. His voice was no more than the whispering of the wind in the mountains. 'What is being done, Akridos? We will be cut to pieces here!'

'Silence your whining, soulmason,' Akridos shot back. 'If you fear for your own bones, take them elsewhere.' He barrelled forward again, as close as he was going to get to his cavalry without personally cutting down half his army.

Kathanos hissed at him, eyes blazing. Akridos ignored him, turned, saw the Mortek ahead of him evaporating under the Lumineth assault, no more than four or five spear lengths away.

'Deathriders!' he howled. 'On me!'

It was like crouching behind a barrier as a storm raged – shielding your eyes, ducking your head, girding yourself to press on through it. Alithis bared her teeth behind the backs of the Vanari wardens, shards of bone splintering up into the air before them, her Stoneguard poised in two units to break either right or left and shore up the wardens' defences. Not that they needed much shoring up, she thought. They were forcing the Ossiarch troops back step by step in front of her, closing ranks wherever gaps appeared, stepping forward in one unbroken phalanx and thrusting out with the boiling sunmetal blades of their pikes. Aetherquartz jewels glowed white-hot all along the line, bolstering the channelled magic into their weapons, and each time the spear tips met Ossiarch armour or bone they melted through it like butter, or burst it apart in a searing blast. The grass underfoot was a crunching carpet of shattered bone. Rain whipped from the blackened sky, spattering in her face. Weapons gleamed wetly. The slopes of the mountains loomed up on her left, and on her right, on the other side of the pass, the wind crackled up from the long drop to the plains far below.

'On the right!' Alithis called. The Bonereapers were funnelling a fresh unit into the grinder, coming in at a diagonal from their left flank. She tapped her hand down on the shoulder of the warden in front of her, three ranks back from the front line. He nodded, his crest quivering, and called out to his fellows.

'Dress right!' he cried. 'Spears of the Veldt, quarter turn!'

Like oiled water, they smoothly wheeled a fraction to their right, lancing out to immolate another rank of dead warriors. All was chaos and confusion, but here, Alithis thought, in the very centre of the maelstrom, everything seemed at least clear. They pressed on.

There was shouting from a thousand ragged throats – cries for help, screams of the wounded, screams of rage. On the other side came the creaking commands of the Bonereapers' captains, the clatter of teeth, the stench of mouldering bone. Above it all, the clash of swords and spears, the snap of broken wood as a pike staff was cut down, the percussive crunch of dead skulls being caved in, the harsh, gasping breath of the aelves who were reaching the limits of their endurance – face to face with the dead, the leering skulls, the sheer mind-bending *wrongness* of these awful things, not even crying out as they were cut to pieces. In the bloody, dusty scrum, Alithis pressed herself onwards, roving her eye around to make sure the Bonereapers hadn't outflanked them, watching her Stoneguard and just *waiting* for the moment when she would have to strike. She stumbled, feet tangling in a patch of boggy ground – then she looked down in horror at the pulverised body of a dead aelf beneath her, his face wrenched apart by a sword thrust, mangled by trampling feet as the army pressed forward. Looking over her shoulder, she saw Carreth striding in their wake with his staff at his side, the great horned helmet like the head of some colossal beast, his eyes raging with a purple fire. He looked terrifying, she thought, like the Lumineth's vengeance made manifest. Although the aelves were outnumbered near ten to one, for the first time she felt that they would not just win here but annihilate their enemy completely.

'Keep near,' she heard Carreth call. 'Alithis, the moment is almost on us.'

With a cold smile, he held out his arms. Waves of amethyst energy flickered across his hands.

She heard Dae'annis shouting orders. She strained up and saw him in the front rank, stabbing and shearing with his pike, conjuring the light of Hysh to charge his regiment's weapons with magical force. She glanced at the rain-flecked faces around her, the set jaws, the eyes grim behind the slits of their helmets, hammers held up against chests.

The moment is almost upon us…

But how could anyone judge the right moment in the middle of this madness? It had been too long for her, too long since she had spilled blood in the press of battle – she had forgotten how awful it was.

There was a shift in the air, a shock that seemed to pause the Lumineth advance just for an instant. She felt it rather than saw it, rippling down the line. Someone had fallen and the gap hadn't been closed quickly enough. Or perhaps the purple gouts of magic vomiting up from somewhere far back in the Bonereapers' ranks had stalled a crucial unit, and the line was beginning to break up? Whatever it was, suddenly the pressure seemed to be coming from the other side, as if at last the Bonereapers had realised how much weight they could really bring to bear. Alithis saw it on Dae'annis' face, ahead and to her left, twisted with strain as if he were trying to wrestle the entire Ossiarch army to a standstill with his hands alone.

'I don't know if we can hold!' he called back towards her. 'Seneschal, we need you here now!'

'Hold, Alithis!' Carreth cried. 'Hold fast!'

Something made her glance right, a change in pressure maybe, a shift in the wind, the bent tone of steel striking steel. She saw the right-hand block of the Spears of the Veldt shudder and crumple inwards, the whole unit like a sheet of thin metal struck with a hammer. Aelves fell, pikes cast aside, helmets caved in. She heard screams, before the screams were cut into a bloody gurgle. She strained to see, hauling herself up on the shoulders of her lieutenants, craning her neck–

'This is it!' Carreth yelled. 'Stoneguard, on me! Akridos is upon us!'

'Mortek Guard!' the Liege-Kavalos cried, holding his sword level above their heads. The marching ranks paused and came to attention, whole regiments of them trapped in a jostling block between the advancing Lumineth and the Deathriders trapped at their rear. Arrows slammed down here and there amongst them, piercing a skull, tearing a shield from a broken arm. Akridos chopped his sword down. 'Flat!' he called. 'Lay yourselves down!'

Without a moment's hesitation, two thousand troops prostrated themselves on the churned grass, lying on their shields, skulls pressed into the mud. From Akridos' advantage, high up on his steed, it was as if the whole front rank had just been swept away by a petulant hand.

'Deathriders! Now!'

He wheeled around, saw the front rank of the aelven infantry stagger forward as the Mortek Guard fell down, pulled out of formation as the barrier they had been heaving against suddenly collapsed. He felt rather than heard the charge of his Deathriders, their armoured warhorses sweeping like a vast plough over the bones of the dead. Mortek Guard were crushed to pieces under their stampeding hooves. Then they were sweeping past him, furious as an avalanche, swords and lances levelled, crashing over the bony ground to slam into the Lumineth's front rank. Akridos spurred himself forward, howling his deathless croak. He saw riders snatched from the saddle by the sweep of a pike, saw dead horses smashed to pieces by the swinging hammers of the Lumineth reserve – fierce-looking fighters who scrambled to fill the gap in the line, their horned helmets dazzling with bright reflected fire, their hammers and picks as hard as diamonds. Rain was lancing down now on a steel diagonal, hard and merciless. It made not a single difference to his troops.

He pushed forward through the mass of aelves, cutting down to sweep the head from one warrior, parrying against a pikestaff that came lurching out of the press, stabbing the point of his blade into a screaming face with a hot burst of blood. Rain pattered against his helmet. To his left, the first wedge of his Deathriders had cut a swathe into the Lumineth infantry, distorting that seemingly inviolable block so it was in danger of being split in two. Another spearhead of his cavalry came through on his right, a great column five abreast, trying to push back the Lumineth centre. He could feel the moment, sense it, savour it like the memory of a taste in the far-gone days when he still had a tongue. They were close now, very close...

'Press on!' he croaked, waving his sword above his head. 'Mortek Guard, up, advance!'

Behind him, with a clash of arms, the surviving Guard lurched to their feet and staggered forward, shuddering on through the mud to hack their way into the gap the Deathriders had carved in the Lumineth line. Aelves died in dozens, their pikes caught up against the bolstering cavalry, not enough room left for them to swing around and face this resurgent threat. Their bodies fell to the mud, trampled underfoot as the Guard clashed their shields and forced themselves on.

But still... the hinge of battle could swing both ways. This foe was as deadly and unpredictable as any he had ever faced, and they had already bested him once. Akridos leaned up in the saddle and waved his sword as another troop of Deathriders came hacking past him. He could see the Necropolis Stalkers striding towards the centre, pushing Mortek troops out of the way, falchions already unsheathed, the Immortis Guard behind them. Akridos jabbed his sword wildly towards the Lumineth line. The charge of the Deathriders had come to a halt, bogged down by the rallying aelven troops in front and the surging Mortek Guard behind. The aelven cavalry, those swift and deadly fighters, were now launching hammer blows at his flanks, their warhorses crashing into his infantry before withdrawing for another assault.

'Deathriders! Pull back, reform!' Akridos howled. 'Strike to their rear!'

But the riders were now just standing there, immobile, hacking left and right. The whole battlefield, the most constricted space Akridos had ever fought in, was just one huge, jostling mob of warriors, each fighting on a field that extended no further than the point of their blades. It was a quagmire a mile long and half a mile wide of struggling fighters packed shoulder to shoulder. The only question now was which side could funnel its troops fastest into the gaps.

He saw the Immortis Guard stalk forward, halberds already swinging to add their tremendous weight to the press in the centre. He saw the aelven horses wheel around the rear of the Lumineth line to launch another lance strike wherever the Mortek Guard looked like they were going to break through. More of the Guard were funnelling up the pass from the rear ranks, and another spearhead of cavalry was preparing to charge from the now open spaces on the left against the Lumineth's crumbling right. The aelves were in danger of being surrounded and overwhelmed. It was almost over, the tide was turning...

Then he saw him.

Akridos' blended soul shrieked out in horrified recognition, cringing and yearning at the same time. He gripped his sword and spurred his steed onwards, oblivious to the aelven pikes that scraped up towards him, the skeletal soldiers he crushed underfoot.

'Y'gethin...'

The mage was wrapped in a nimbus of amethyst light, his eyes like shards of black slate, the huge, branching horns of his helmet like the skull of some vengeful daemon. He stood there on the churned grass, in the centre of a group of grim warriors, all of them swinging their devastating hammers at any Ossiarch soldier who came within range. The sky above seemed to flicker with purple lightning. Sparkling black motes of magic swirled around him like the smuts cast out by a bonfire. He was muttering inaudibly, his arms spread wide, calm and unhurried as the aelven army struggled like fury around him. The grass was a ring of black slime beneath his feet. As if in a dream, Akridos approached, cutting and parrying with his sword, forcing himself closer and closer, the crushed aelven soul inside him weeping with distress...

Then the mage turned his terrible black eyes on him, and Akridos screamed.

It was now, and only now, as the army teetered on the brink. Carreth felt the spell uncoil inside him, like a rank snake slithering from its hole. The maelstrom raged around him, aelves and skeletons, Lumineth and Bonereapers, pike and lance and sword, all swirling in that deadly dance of blood and thunder. Aelves died with screams on their lips. Bonereaper constructs were smashed to pieces in a spray of dust. Some of them, newer recruits, Carreth assumed, still had scraps of flesh hanging from their bones, dried blood in the plates of their skulls.

Aelf blood, he thought. *Aelf bones. Aelf souls.*

He saw Akridos lead the charge of his cavalry, their steeds barrelling through the Lumineth lines like bulls, scattering wardens aside as if they were dolls. But the line held – Alithis wielded her Stoneguard like she wielded her stratum hammers, with unerring precision. The Stoneguard barely seemed to move, as immobile as rock, but the reach of their hammers was long and the Bonereaper cavalry paid the price for their boldness. Horses burst apart, riders were dragged from their saddles and bludgeoned to pieces. Still the rain fell, but Carreth did not feel it. The sky was like a sheet of steel. Flickering here and there as he muttered the words of his spell came shards of lightning, purple and dark.

'*Akridos*...'

It was now. It *had* to be now. He glanced right, saw Akridos heaving himself closer, saw the mad green gleam in his eyes, the grinning teeth like stained ivory. The closer he got, the more he could feel Tuareth buried there – a light that shone in the darkness, trapped, strung out and twisted beneath the chains of Akridos' evil.

He muttered the words as a tear leaked from his eye. The grass died under his feet. He raised his hands and in the corners of his eyes they seemed like shards of bone. He took the sick lessons he had learned from the books in the archive and blended them with his art, weaving a grave shroud of magic in the air between himself and the Bonereapers' general. Everything was overlaid with a pale purple light. The rain seemed to fall like drops of blood, cold and clammy against his skin.

'Tuareth,' he said. 'I call you out.'

He looked at Akridos, turning the full measure of his art against him. Carreth unwove the lattice of dead spells from around his foul corpse, and it was like reaching into a tangled hole choked with dead roots. He felt the light, the light of Hysh, his sister. He reached for it. The skeleton warlord screamed, his eyes blazing like comets, his sword falling from his grip. His steed reared and sent him tumbling from the saddle, crashing into the mud. Lumineth blades flicked out to pierce him, but then the Bonereaper cavalry, as if maddened by the sight of their liege so vulnerable, spurred themselves onwards and forced the aelves back. They were no more than a spear's length away now, but still Carreth wouldn't move. He reached out again, a savage pain creeping across his face, tearing through his body as he strove to pluck the soul from the Liege-Kavalos, who shuddered in the mud, screaming in a voice like the crackle of old paper – like the scrolls Carreth had dug up from the pit of the library archive, dead things that should have never seen the light.

The pain was eclipsing, like being bathed in cold fire. Carreth groaned, but the more he strove, the more he felt Tuareth's soul slipping through his fingers. Anchored deep in the Bonereaper warlord, threaded through every line and lineament of his form, it was impossible to grip. Like oil, like mist, it slid away. The light was dimming, the light of Hysh. He felt a howl of pain tearing across the void, the unhinged agony of his sister torn between two contrary wills.

He was killing her.

To tear her free would be to spin her into mist, to cast her into no more than inchoate soul-stuff that would dissipate on the merciless breeze.

'Tuareth!' he cried. 'Come back to me, please!'

The grip of his magic began to slacken. The dead spell shimmered and began to fall apart. Dae'annis was at his side suddenly, face caked in blood, his armour notched and battered. *Senlui* was a scarred ruin on his breastplate – Tuareth's rune, her symbol of swiftness and vigour. The high warden grabbed his arm, shouting, but to Carreth his words came as if from underwater.

'You cannot give up now!' he cried. 'You have him, and you almost have her! Please, Carreth, or it will all have been for nothing!'

Dae'annis, he thought. *You have guessed my purpose in this, but I have failed you too. I have failed all of you...*

The spell broke apart, a sundered web of amethyst. He saw Akridos helped to his feet by his warriors, ushered back through the surging Bonereapers' line, and then Carreth was falling back onto the muddy grass. He wrenched his helmet off, feeling the cool rain spatter onto his face, the broad flank of the mountain off to his left looming dark and wet, the Pass of Paerthalann like a charnel house around him. Dae'annis looked down with grief in his eyes.

Carreth hauled himself to his knees. Alithis stumbled back in front of him, wrestling against the weight of the dead warriors before her, the Stoneguard tirelessly swinging their hammers and picks, the wardens stumbling backwards on the left as they desperately tried to hold the line. It was almost over. He had lost.

'I would have killed her,' he cried to Dae'annis. 'She is buried too deep. Plucking her out would have been like pulling a worm from the earth – I would have torn her in half.'

Dae'annis, his face wet with tears or rain, silently nodded. He reached out a hand.

'You have done all you could,' he said. 'No one could have asked for more, my friend.'

He gave a sad smile, full of forgiveness. Carreth reached for his hand. And then a blade burst from the high warden's chest in a spray of blood.

Alithis screamed. She saw the grinning Bonereaper rip its sword from Dae'annis' back, the aelf collapsing into Carreth's arms. She darted forward, both hammers in a savage backswing that obliterated the Ossiarch warrior in a burst of bone. More stepped in to fill the gap – more, and then more, the whole pass clogged with the dead.

'Stoneguard, reform on the mage... Now!'

Her warriors stepped back, two ranks exchanging places, the second holding back the tide while the first took up their new position. Even in the midst of this mayhem it was perfect, like the smoothly interlocking parts of a mechanical clock she had once seen a duardin artificer display in the streets of Settler's Gain. The Stoneguard formed a crescent around Carreth, who knelt there holding Dae'annis with a look of utter shock on his face.

'He's gone!' Alithis called to him. 'Carreth, we need to fall back now or the army is lost.' She looked at Dae'annis, felt the lump in her throat as it threatened to choke her. 'He's gone...'

The giants of bone were getting closer, towering over the Bonereaper infantry, each swinging their four arms and their dread blades, cutting a swathe through the line of wardens. Some of them were studded with arrows from the sentinels who still unleashed their fire from the mountain slope. The centre was about to break, and once it did everything was over. The battle, the whole damned war, Ultharadon itself… everything would be gone.

She looked at Carreth, broken in the mud. She stared at the body of Dae'annis, sprawled in Carreth's lap, his life's blood pooling in the rain. She looked up to see the tide of the dead pressing on, unstoppable, relentless, clambering over the bones of their comrades and the bodies of aelves who had already fallen. The wardens were falling back, trying to reform the line a few yards further up the pass. The archers were scrambling from the mountain slope, back to the narrow tracks and defiles before they were cut off completely. She saw all this and she set her jaw to it, teeth bared, hammers raised.

Let us fight then, backs to the wall. Let us fight as true aelves of Hysh, until the light is dimmed at last.

She swung out, snapped the jaw from one skeleton, caving in its skull on the backswing. By her side, Stoneguard thrust out their hammers with emotionless precision, battering shields aside, shattering ribcages. In a crescent around the Stonemage they fought and died, without complaint. Fifty of her warriors, her honour guard, cut down to forty, then no more than two dozen, but the toll they took of the Bonereapers was immense. A carpet of bones covered the grass, as high as their knees. Alithis kicked her way through it to strike the legs from under one of the bone giants, throwing herself back to parry the blow of its falchions as it fell groaning to the earth.

'Carreth, run back to the wardens now, before it's too late!' she cried. 'Where the hell is Belfinnan–'

An explosion of light behind her eyes, red pain across her face. She fell back, breath knocked from her lungs. Blood blinded her. She scrabbled around for her hammers with one hand, scraping the blood from her eyes with the other. One of the bone giants loomed over her, twice her height, blades raised to strike a second time. It stank of death, of ancient tombs and buried grave shrouds. She lifted her arm, as if flesh alone could block the blow, flinching as two of her Stoneguard battered into the creature's side, hacking at its legs with their diamondpick hammers. The bone giant reared back, toppling, carving one Stoneguard in two with a great swing of its blade as it fell, buckling as the other Stoneguard smashed its skull in with her hammer. But where one had fallen, three more took its place – and the great blocks of Bonereaper infantry were marching forward all the time, relentless.

Alithis staggered to her feet, scooped up the hammer of a fallen comrade. Her face was numb down one side, sticky with blood. *Another damned scar,* she thought with a grimace.

There were only a dozen of them left, and the dead were swarming around. The wardens were about to collapse.

'Alithis,' Carreth called softly. 'I'm sorry that I've brought you to this. I thought I could save her...'

'We're not done yet,' she spat, clutching her hammer. 'You know, I really think we've got them on the run now...'

He smiled weakly. His hair was white. His face looked like it had weathered another hundred years. He still held his staff.

'Here we die then,' he said, putting his shoulders back, raising the staff to his chest. 'But we'll make an end fit for the songs of aelves, for a thousand years or more.' He glanced down at Dae'annis. 'A song fit for heroes.'

There was a roll of thunder across the sky, a shake in the ground beneath their feet. Alithis gritted her teeth, hands squeezing the shafts of her hammers. No, not thunder, she realised. It was the sound of charging horses. Let them come, then, the dead riders. She would crush their skulls and break their bones, and she would not falter.

'Mountain stance!' she cried. 'Make them pay for every inch of ground!'

It was not the dead cavalry but the Dawnriders who came on then, speeding past like an arrow in flight, deadly accurate, unswerving. Belfinnan was at their head, his lieutenants paired behind him, four more riders leading the column behind them, a spearhead formation that sliced through the Ossiarch ranks. Skeletal warriors collapsed under the heavy barding of their warhorses or were immolated by their gleaming lances. One of the four-armed bone giants tried to swing around to block their path, but Belfinnan ducked down in the saddle and brought his lance up to pierce its chest, flinging the giant back even as the lance was torn from his grasp. He drew his sword, a blur of silver as he hewed the press around him, never pausing for a moment. He ducked right, the whole column of horse following him as he drew them across the frontage of what remained of the Lumineth army, protecting the troops as they fell back. His horse came level with Alithis. She saw the grime and sweat on his face, the rends in his armour, the blood that leaked from Gyfillim's trembling flank. They had had some hard fighting too, no doubt.

'You're wounded, seneschal!' Belfinnan cried. He tugged the reins, drew himself closer, distraught, reaching out for her. 'Are you all right? I doubt any sight could make me more furious, but seeing the blood on your face is a wound I can hardly bear.'

'I'll live,' she said. She paused, then took his hand – the warrior's grip, wrist to wrist. Belfinnan grinned wildly.

'Your beauty is undimmed, seneschal – indeed, I'd say it is more luminous than ever. Damn, but this is dry work,' he said. 'All bone dust and mud. What I wouldn't give for a flask of Ultharadon's zephyrwine right now, let me tell you…'

His eyes flicked to the ground, where Dae'annis lay in a pool of his own blood, his eyes closed, his dead face a mask of pain. A look of sorrow flashed across Belfinnan's face.

'The price has been too high,' he muttered, 'if brave aelves like this have been the coin we had to pay.'

'Draw back, Alithis,' Carreth said, raising his staff. His eyes were like flint, his face drained and worn. 'Let us save who we can, while we still have the time. Let me make amends for what I have done.'

He closed his eyes, drawing on the deepest wells of his power. The earth trembled beneath them, the churned mud flicking up in droplets from the ground. Alithis staggered, and Belfinnan calmed his horse as his riders still laid about them with lance and sword. A great wave of energy seemed to burst out of the ground, flinging rocks and debris high into the air, raining them down onto the Bonereapers' ranks as the skeletal horde was thrown back. Carreth's voice came high and piercing over the boom of sundered rock, and then a vast pinnacle lanced out of the ground before them, tearing upwards into the sodden sky – bows and buttresses of rock, a great flank of stone that grew wider and wider the higher it reached, splitting the warring armies in two and shielding the Lumineth from their foes. The Dawnriders' horses shied and whinnied, but in moments they were under control. Alithis lowered the arm she had flung in front of her face as the vast wall of rock reached higher into the sky, a hundred feet of shielding stone that sliced across the pass from cliff edge to mountain slope. Its flank was scored with a huge, stylised letter 'Y', thirty feet tall, overlaid against an inverted 'V' – the carved sigil of *Alaithi*, the rune of the mountain.

'That will do it, Stonemage!' Belfinnan gasped. 'You wield the very elements themselves to protect us!'

The Bonereapers were trapped on the other side, only a few stragglers falling into the Lumineth lines. Wardens and Dawnriders were quick to cut these warriors down, scattering their bones to the mud.

Carreth collapsed, his face grey, his staff lying in the grass at his feet. He was utterly spent. Alithis pulled him up, his arm across her shoulders.

'Belfinnan! Get the mage back to Ultharadon.'

'Aye, seneschal.' Together they hauled him up behind the saddle of Belfinnan's horse. 'Gyfillim will not let him fall, don't worry.'

'Ride, then – make all haste, and do not stop until you get there. We have to withdraw and regroup. That wall won't hold them forever.'

She glanced around the shambles of the field, the suppurating mud, the scattered bodies. Aelves and Bonereapers, like so much refuse littering the churned ground. Proud warriors, husbands, wives, sisters and brothers. She looked at the scattered units of the Lumineth army – what remained of it. Warden regiments had been broken apart and numbered only handfuls of survivors. Half the Dawnriders were dead. Her Stoneguard were down to a dozen warriors, and only the Vanari sentinels had been left untouched. Despite this, she was already thinking of Ultharadon's defence. The sentinels would be key. The sentinels, the Stoneguard she had left behind, the few wardens still being trained, others they could recruit from the margins of Ymetrica…

She swallowed, but the challenges of defence were for the future. Right now, they had to save who they could.

Belfinnan kicked his heels to Gyfillim's flanks and raced off towards the far end of the pass, mud splattering from the horse's hooves as it bore Carreth back to the temple. Alithis stood before the wall of rock, the rain stippling its flank with black spots. The sky was grey, unmoved, as if what had just happened beneath it were no more than the usual business of the realm, and not a calamity such as she had never seen before.

The blood dried against her face. Her arms hung loose at her sides, muscles aching. She watched the battered Lumineth forces march off in dribs and drabs towards the end of the pass, there to take the tracks and paths back down to the Ymetrican veldt and the long journey home. She waited, and when there was no one left but the bodies of their dead, Alithis turned to go. Before she left, standing where they had started the day, she stooped and gathered up a handful of dirt. She looked back at the bloody ground. The Pass of Paerthalann – where the Lumineth Realm-lords had offered battle and had gained only defeat.

PART THREE

CHAPTER THIRTEEN

THE BONEWAY

Higher the tendrils of bone went, creeping like a virulent weed up the towering flank of rock. In the shade of the Lumineth's barrier, Morfilos and his boneshapers whipped up a storm of osseous matter, sending it lashing out in wavering coils against the stone, desperately trying to tear it down. Each strand of bone was still bloody and wet from the bodies of the butchered aelves, sparkling with a sick red glint as the clouds broke apart. Light filtered through the strands of cirrus high above the pass, watery and trembling, and then harder and brighter as the afternoon drew on. The tendrils of bone crept onwards, feeling their way up the vast spur of stone as Morfilos guided them, twisting his necromantic energies, his jaw strained wide with the effort, eyes glinting like emerald shards. Splitting the pass in half, the huge barrier of rock seemed to cast down a filtered light from the monumental rune that had been carved into its side.

As hard as Morfilos worked to smother it, the Bonereapers' army could barely stand to be near its presence. It seemed to radiate the same cursed light as the realm itself, but condensed somehow, distilled and more potent. The troops pulled back to the lower end of the pass, a hundred yards from the stone. Akridos felt the presence of that rune-shadow like a terrible weight against his soul, and he willed Morfilos on as the boneshaper howled with effort. The glistening mass of bone matter whipped further up the rock like a vertical avenue, a boneway they could use to bypass the terrible force of its geomantic magic, but as each tendril touched the lower elements of the Lumineth sigil it reared back like a living thing in agony, melting away to reform once more in the concretion of bone beneath it.

Akridos trembled with rage. He stood far over on the left, on the edge of the long drop to the mountain range's lower slopes, where the rough ground and the clumps of gorse had been spared the worst of the battle. The tall grass shivered beneath him, and the yellow flowers of the gorse relinquished their petals in the quickening wind. Far below, the foothills rolled away in slumped barrows and jagged peaks, a corrugated plain of purple heather and bitter sedge, of impassable grey rock and shale. Petulantly, he kicked a pebble into the abyss, watching it tumble end over end, disappearing from sight. To retreat back down the pass and onto the plains would take days, and to bypass the mountains altogether would take weeks. No, there was only one way through now if the campaign was to successfully proceed. He looked again at Morfilos and his boneshapers, sagging with the effort of guiding that great sludge of bone up the sides of the Lumineth's conjured barrier, a slab of rock splitting from the earth, as tall as a castle wall and far more difficult to break down. Three days they had been here now, trying to batter their way through this aelven magic.

The ground before the barrier was littered with discarded equipment, broken in the grass. Spears and pikes, shields and helmets and breastplates, split and battered and dented. The sundered

Ossiarch troops had been collected from the field and fed once more into the blender of the boneshapers' art, their weapons stacked to one side, ready for them to collect once Kathanos and his cadre of soulmasons had imbued them with life essence once more. Akridos watched the Harvesters, who had finally made it to the field, go about their business, trundling in their coleopteran way across the mounds of dead aelves. The fused sorters on their chest-pieces ripped great chunks of flesh from the corpses and tossed the scraps to one side. Some of the aelves, despite their terrible wounds, were not even dead when the Harvesters went to work. Their howls of horrified agony as the meat was torn from their bones were like a jangling, discordant music that rang out across the pass. In time, the Bonereapers' foes learned to burn their dead, but when they were forced to flee the field that was not always possible.

And the Lumineth had certainly fled. If he had had lips to smile, Akridos would have stretched them now to think of his victory.

It had been close, though, closer than he ever would have admitted. Three times now he had faced the Lumineth Realmlords in open battle, and still their spirit and vigour shocked him. A great commander did not underestimate his foe, and Akridos felt a grudging respect for their abilities in the art of war. There was a singularity of purpose to them, a tactical flexibility and a sheer martial strength that made them unlike any opponent he had encountered before. It galled him to admit it, but Kathanos had been right back in the necropolis library – the Lumineth were an enemy apart, masters of war and magic alike. For barely ten thousand aelves to come so close to besting him…

He grinned his skeletal grin again. He gazed out over the bloody field of battle, the carnage and detritus of war.

He had won.

With a howl of rage, Morfilos let slip his concentration and the huge bow wave of bone fell apart and collapsed to the base of the rock. The aelf mage's magic was too strong for him, the enchanted rock burning off his efforts. He screamed at his fellow boneshapers, no doubt aware of both Kathanos and Akridos watching him, waiting for him to make some kind of progress. Kathanos was some distance back from the barrier, his bipedal throne motionless in the mud as the soulmason slumped in his seat, his staff across his knees. Akridos glanced away as Kathanos turned his gaze on him.

Curse him for a defeatist, a politician quicker to assign blame when the battle seemed to be against us than to work on a strategy for victory. Well, Kathanos, defeat did not come! Victory was mine, and mine alone.

Akridos kicked another scattering of stone over the edge of the escarpment, watching it trickle off into the buffeting winds. Beyond the foothills at the mountain's base the wide plains stretched on towards a distant line of sea, impossibly far, no more than a faint glint of silver light against the blurred horizon. This land was truly vast, wide and airy and strewn with wealth, from the great grasslands and the endless plains to the cities and towns scattered like a swatch of jewels along the coasts. Beams of magic in fantastic array sped like spears of light across the firmament, and there was a cool, tempered precision to everything he saw, from the blades of grass under his feet to the plump symmetry of the clouds unfolding across the infinite blue.

And it will all be mine… Every repellent beam of light will be in my grasp and twisted into suitable forms, made to serve my empire. I will be a king again, an emperor of Death's new outpost in the Mortal Realms, and every aelf under my dominion will be stripped of their flesh and blood and squeezed into shapes more pleasing to me. All this I decree.

He felt cold suddenly, chilled by a ripple through his bones.

He remembered the aelf mage, his terrible black eyes, the twisting forms of the spell he had woven as Akridos drew near. Death magic, unmistakably, as shocking to him as a bath of fire. He shuddered to recall it, the moment the mage had reached out with aetheric energy, a grotesque inversion of the process by which Akridos was first ensouled. He had felt the deep wells of his entire being poisoned by the aelf's will, felt the ropes and sinews of his soul gripped and twisted in those probing fingers. The aelf had dabbled greedily in the very stuff of his being, and the pain had been so intense it had eclipsed the entire battle around him – pain, a sensation that was now utterly alien to him, and all the more powerful for that. His vision had gone dark, he had collapsed to the ground, the clash of steel fading to a distant buzz, the falling rain no more than a faint blur in the air. His Deathriders had dragged him from the field, and when he came to the battle was over and the mage was gone.

Y'gethin...

The Stonemage of Ultharadon, linked in some way to the aelf soul that cringed inside him, as he was now linked to the Stonemage in turn. Akridos could almost feel his presence across the wide plains of Ymetrica, a pulse of light that blinked weakly in the distance and drew him ever on. They would face each other again, he knew. It was fated, compelled. He would destroy this Y'gethin and sever at last the link with this pollution inside him, and once the mage was dead the aelf soul's last faint hope would be scoured clean away, and it would sink into the roiling sea of his blended spirit and be gone. He would march on this cursed mountain and slight its sacred slopes, corrupt it so absolutely that the Light of Eltharion would be drawn out onto the field of battle – and destroyed.

Across the trampled grass, Morfilos summoned his energy again and whipped the bone matter into another swirling loop, augmented this time by the additional materials scavenged from the field by the Harvesters. Twenty feet high it churned in the air, like a spinning wheel turning faster and faster, casting off a spray of blood and flesh from the newly harvested bones. Akridos saw the bone-wheel stretching and smoothing out like an arrowhead, a vast spear that Morfilos plunged into the stone barrier with an audible crack. The boneshaper cackled in triumph, the fringes on his skull pulsating. Akridos vaulted up onto his steed and cantered across the pass towards Kathanos, who still sat brooding on his throne. Akridos could see where the legs of the throne had been notched in the battle, struck with sword and spear, although Kathanos himself was unmarked.

More's the pity…

'Liege-Kavalos,' the soulmason spat as Akridos came near. 'You are recovered from your ordeal, I see. I pray it wasn't too traumatic for you?'

'The discomfort disappeared with the aelves when they fled this pass,' he said. He fixed the soulmason with an impassive stare. Kathanos, agitated, squirmed in his throne.

'Days have been wasted on this effort,' he complained. 'Morfilos and his cabal of fools have barely made a dent in this wretched barrier. Why are we not bypassing it, or trying to find another route through?'

'There are no other routes through,' Akridos said. He nodded down the pass, where the Ossiarch army stood at patient attention – regiments of foot, troops of horse, the war machines and elite of the Immortis Guard, block upon block ranked up on the grass. They had taken horrendous casualties, far more than Akridos would have thought possible, but already the numbers were being rebuilt. 'To take an entire army up into these mountains is one thing. To take it all the way back down again would seem… bad strategy.'

'Bad strategy!' Kathanos hissed. 'It was your strategy that nearly lost us this fight, Akridos!'

'And my strategy that won it.'

'Ha! From what I could see, luck played as much a part as tactics.' The soulmason jabbed his staff towards the Lumineth's geomantic barrier, pointing to where the massive slab of rock crashed into the mountain slopes on the right. 'Luck that the aelves didn't crush us beneath tons of stone torn from the hide of this mountain!' His eyes glittered and his creaking voice dropped. 'Luck that their mage seemed so unduly fixated on *you* in particular...'

Akridos flinched. He kept his jaw set, staring off at Morfilos as he wrenched the tide of bone from side to side with aetheric force, shards of stone crumbling from the barrier. Still the sigil burned high above him, the dread rune of the Lumineth.

'Yes, you didn't think I had noticed that, did you?' Kathanos went on. He jabbed now at Akridos with his staff. 'Compelled, I would say. Fixated... The aelf soul that writhes inside you, I wonder if it is connected in some way to the leader of these aelves, this Mage Y'gethin?'

'The aelf soul that *you* forced inside me, soulmason,' Akridos said through gritted teeth.

Kathanos laughed, a dreadful, crackling sound. 'I thought it would give you an insight into our enemy, should we meet them again. I confess, I didn't think for a moment it might have worked the other way around.'

'It worked better than you think, I suspect,' Akridos said. He gazed down at the bloody scraps of flesh that were scattered around the battlefield after the Harvesters had done their work, the piles of wrecked equipment, the discarded weapons. He spoke as if recounting a dream, the edges of which were already beginning to blur in the cold light of day. 'I can feel this Mage Y'gethin, even now... I know his fears, I feel his rage...'

'And what was his purpose then?' Kathanos probed. If nothing else, Akridos seemed to have snared his professional attention. The Liege-Kavalos tapped a bony finger to the contours of his soul gem, embedded in his scarred breastplate.

'I have inside me someone dear to him, I think. He tried to tear the trapped soul from inside me.' *And he nearly succeeded...*

'Most interesting,' Kathanos mused. 'I felt the contours of death magic on the field, in forms I have never experienced before.'

'Do you believe the aelves have mastered our own arcane disciplines?'

'I cannot say...' Kathanos tapped his teeth with his fingertips. He stared off towards Morfilos again, fifty yards across the sward, hunched in the shadow of the aelves' impossible barrier. The boneshaper groaned as he forced the osseous matter into the gap he had created – it was like threading a needle with a sponge. The other boneshapers leaned in with their support, reforming the bone matter wherever it spilled over, surging it back into the main body of the mass. 'Truly they are more skilled in the arts of magic than even I had anticipated, if that were so. And yet, I do not believe this Y'gethin's spell came naturally to him. I felt great *resistance* in the aetheric web, an unresolved tension that threatened to snap if he had pushed it any further.'

'He could not remove the soul inside me without destroying it,' Akridos said. 'That was why he stopped. It is yet another insight that I have gained, another tactic I can use against him. My life,' he laughed, 'is too precious for him to risk.'

Kathanos dismissed the idea. 'It doesn't matter, in any case. The aelf mage and his cobbled-together army have been fatally weakened, and we need not concern ourselves with them again.'

Akridos kept his voice level, although the anger was surging inside him. 'Meaning?'

'Meaning, Nagash has given the legion its orders. The Stalliarch

Lords are to draw out and destroy this aelven champion, the Light of Eltharion. Everything else is subordinate to this aim. You know this.'

Akridos spoke his next words carefully, not out of fear of offending the soulmason but because he could not trust himself to vent his true opinions. 'Matters of strategy and tactics are my preserve,' he said. 'I will not leave so dangerous an enemy with the opportunity to regroup his forces. We will proceed to this holy mountain, Ultharadon, and destroy it. And we will destroy the aelven army at the same time.'

'You would waste our time on these petty vendettas?' Kathanos said in disbelief. 'Surely they pose no more threat to us? I must protest at this strategy!'

Akridos turned his steed to face the soulmason. He glared at him, their eyes level – one on his horse, the other on his throne. 'Do not pretend you understand enough of my strategy to disagree with it,' he said. 'This Ultharadon is holy to them, a site of purity and grace. Destroying Y'gethin and slighting his mountain will draw out Eltharion. For what champion of the aelves could possibly stand by as their sacred places were profaned? Eltharion will be compelled to intervene, and we will destroy it.' *And, you cringing fool, when this land is mine I will suffer no remnants of the aelves' feeble religion to remain. I will scour them and their memory from the contours of the earth itself!* 'I would ask if that meets with your approval, soulmason, but your approval is of no importance to me. I command, and you will obey.'

Kathanos hissed his rage, the clawed feet of his monstrous throne scouring at the dirt.

'You go too far, Liege-Kavalos! You seek to wrest this army as an instrument of your own will, but let me remind you whose will we truly serve! Nagash! Nagash is all!'

'Surely I have no true will,' Akridos said coldly. 'Is it not the case then that my decisions reflect the will of Nagash alone?'

'Such sophistry will not save you, Akridos. Be assured that I will remind he who has given us this dread unlife that there are some among his ranks who feel it is a privilege they can claim for their own! What Nagash gives, Nagash can easily take away.'

The soulmason stalked off across the grass, cursing, heading back to the main body of the army as it waited in its silent ranks. Akridos watched him go. Inside he felt a spark of satisfaction kindle to a flame. He laughed, and in that moment the decision was made.

Nurse your righteous anger well, Kathanos. Your days are now numbered, and before I take this land as my own fiefdom, I will see that flaking skull shattered into a thousand pieces, your bones scattered to the indifferent wind.

At that moment Morfilos cackled as the bone matter finally split the Lumineth's barrier from top to bottom, a huge, ragged crack snapping through the carved sigil, loud as a thunderclap. Spears were clattered against shields, swords were rattled in scabbards, and the dense blocks of troops began to march. Akridos sat atop his steed as he had so many times before, watching the regiments of his legion parade victorious from another battlefield. The light fell down from a clearer sky, and the high banks of slate-grey stone on the border of the pass gleamed dully in the deepening day. The two great halves of the Lumineth barrier fell back with a shattering roar, shaking the pass underfoot, the apotropaic magic of its warding sigil cast into the mud. Revealed at last, the farther end of the pass was open. The route to Ultharadon lay ahead.

CHAPTER FOURTEEN

AVALANCHE

The temple smouldered in the dusk. Built from the quarried stone of Ultharadon, marbled with veins and bright minerals, it gleamed like a patch of sunlight in the depths of a dark forest. As the last brave beams of daylight curved around the flank of the holy mountain, it seemed to kindle with a fiery glow. Alithis could almost feel the heat of that light as she looked back across the grassy ridge, the steep slopes on either side dropping down into the shrouded valley at the mountain's base. It was like staring across a bridge after a long journey and seeing the home fires burning, promising good food and warmth and the company of old friends. But their journey did not lie in that direction. She raised her lit torch and turned back to the darkness, towards the long stretch of the greensward as it lifted up into the foothills of Ultharadon.

The ground ahead was a slope of rough scrub patched with sedge grass and thick foliage that undulated gently upwards. She heard the breeze roughening the branches of the pine trees on

Ultharadon's lower slopes, the trickle of a stream hidden somewhere in the coarser ground towards the west, where the flank of the mountain tumbled off in a carpet of boulders and rock. An owl sobbed mournfully in the evening air, flitting through the trees like a restless spirit. Alithis sighed. Beside her, Belfinnan reached out a comforting hand and laid it on her shoulder.

'Come,' he said softly. 'It's a sad task, and relished by neither of us, but it has to be done.'

'It does,' Alithis said. She looked at the steedmaster, his face hidden in the shadows of the torchlight. 'And I would have no one else at my side while we did it.' She clasped his hand with her own, briefly. Breaking off, she strode purposefully into the darkness, the torch throwing a shivering oval of light at her feet.

She heard Belfinnan following her. With his long strides he could easily have overtaken her, but he kept a respectful few feet back.

Absurd, in a way, she thought. *Neither of us really knew him, and I had no particular claim on his friendship. But comrades become something more than comrades when they die – they become our brothers, our sisters. Dae'annis is no longer just a friend or a fellow soldier. He is my brother now, and he has earned this honour through his sacrifice.*

They walked on, pacing slowly, sweeping through the dry grass. When they reached the other side of the greensward, the mountain rising vertiginously above them, Alithis swapped the torch to her left hand and brushed the branches of the pine trees away from her face. They found the needle-strewn path and followed it as it curved up the slope, the torchlight casting the trees on either side in a wavering, spectral light. For the proper mourning ritual, both should have been dressed in the simple garb of a pilgrim, but instead they wore full armour – the exigencies of war could make pragmatists of the most pious. Alithis had her stratum hammers strapped to her belt, and Belfinnan carried his short sword at his hip. Befitting her status as seneschal, Alithis had her head bare, but in the torchlight Belfinnan's towering crested helmet made him seem like a knight stepped out of the pages of legend.

Like Eltharion himself, Alithis thought. She smiled as she heard the zephyrwine slosh in the steedmaster's flask. *Although I can't imagine Eltharion took a bottle with him when mourning a comrade...*

On they went, passing through the trees and coming out onto a gentle series of sloping humps that rose in tiers to the steeper shoulders of the mountain. The ground here, she knew, was mostly loose shale and grey slate, threaded with strips of tough yellow grass. Under the flames of the torch, it looked no more than a vast patch of shadow, although the pale light of Celennar was slowly making its presence felt above them, a blanket of silver that gently fell against the ground and unmasked its contours. They crunched across the shale. It was rare for any but the most ardent disciple of Ultharadon to be so honoured, but Alithis had made the suggestion to Carreth and he had agreed at once. Dae'annis had fought with bravery and skill, with uncomplaining sacrifice, and his memorial here would link him to the mountain forever. He had earned it.

'How much further?' Belfinnan asked. 'I confess, I haven't spent as much time on Ultharadon as I should. I'm an aelf of the Xintilian plains, and although I can feel the power of this place, there's much about it that...'

'What?' Alithis asked, breathing hard as the incline steepened.

'That intimidates me,' Belfinnan admitted. Alithis glanced at him and he looked away. 'Its strength, its endurance. I'm not ashamed to admit it,' he said quickly. 'Hysh is a web of holy places, and I feel them more deeply than you would imagine.'

'Of course,' Alithis said, not unkindly. 'I keep forgetting you're a poet.'

'I am. I would have written a verse for Dae'annis, but the grief is too near.' She could hear him swallow in the dark, could feel the thickness in his voice. 'In time, maybe, when grief can be tempered with hope.'

Alithis nodded, not trusting her voice.

'I always meant to ask, my lady, what is your art? Dae'annis was a skilled engraver when the mood took him. He showed me some of his work before we marched out. He was working on a mandala combining *Senlui* and *Alaithi*, on a bed of polished crystal, with *Senthoi* overlaying them both. It was beautiful.'

'*Senthoi*?' she said. She pictured the rune. 'Yes... unity and loyalty.'

Belfinnan cleared his throat, clearly searching for the words. 'But in certain contexts, it can also mean "broken promise". I think he...'

Alithis sighed again. 'Of course. He blamed himself to the end.'

'I expect it's gone now,' Belfinnan went on. He stumbled slightly on the loose ground, cursed, righted himself. 'Left with the rest of him in Paerthalann Pass.'

'Left with so many others.'

With their bones and their souls, and Teclis alone knows how much of each has been scavenged into the ranks of those foul creatures. Perhaps even now Dae'annis' soul screams in agony, chained inside the husk of some dead warrior.

The thought was too appalling. She pushed it away. There was no comfort in such thoughts, no utility. The only thing they could do was keep going, maintain as much of their equilibrium as possible while the realm collapsed into violence and hopelessness around them. The implacable enemy would not let himself be derailed by regrets or griefs. They owed it to all who had died that their grief be no more than the whetstone to their blades.

* * *

The journey back from Paerthalann Pass had been dreadful. Limping from the field, what remained of the army had marched in a shocked procession, still trying to maintain a semblance of regimental unity. Ten thousand had gone out; barely four thousand came back. The Dawnriders screened the retreat, but as soon as Belfinnan passed out of sight with Carreth on his steed, a mood of fatalism seemed to settle like a black fog on the troops. Tirelessly, Alithis had moved up and down the column, encouraging, exhorting, even threatening where she had to. The command had passed to her, and she had felt its crushing weight every step of the way. After two days of marching, the rise of Ultharadon in the distance had put new vigour into their step, but as the survivors trooped into the field before the temple, Alithis had dreaded to think what effect they might have on the newer recruits, those who had stayed behind to complete their training or those who had flocked to Carreth's banner in the days since they set out. Wounded, stained with battle, bitter at the loss of friends and comrades, they were not the most inspiring sight.

What was done, was done, though. A moment's rest was all that could be permitted before attention had to turn to the defence. Alithis had set everyone who could hold a spade to dig trenches and cavalry pits all around the temple grounds. Carpenters who had spent weeks crafting barracks now turned their hands to hammering palisades or spiked barriers together. There was no time to lose on any of this, and no knowing when the Bonereapers would break through the wall Carreth had thrown up in the pass. There was no knowing when Carreth himself would be able to rejoin them, to drag himself out of the despondency that had gripped him since his return...

They came to a saddle in the ground where it dipped into a gentle depression, bordered on three sides by sharp, outthrust blades of rock. For the most part the ground was hidden in the shadows, but when Alithis lifted her torch she could see the trickling progress of a stream at the bottom, a few scattered shrubs of laburnum and broom. She could smell the faint scent of their flowers in the night air. She didn't know why, but immediately she knew this was the right place. It felt peaceful, detached somehow from the rest of the mountain – a place apart, where the memory of a friend could be celebrated and laid to rest. Alithis set the torch against the rocks, and in its shivering light she laid out the offerings they had brought – some nightbloom flowers from the temple gardens, the soil she had scooped up from the ground at Paerthalann Pass. There was little else. Dae'annis had left none of his effects behind in the barracks.

They prayed over his memory, chanting his deeds in the sacred aelvish tongue. Alithis bowed her head while Belfinnan uncorked his flask and poured the wine against the grass, spattering the flowers and the soil.

'I knew him briefly,' he said, 'but the day we first met we shared this wine and laughed into the night. Laughed, aye – and wept at the griefs we had known, the friends we had lost. I count you among them now, Dae'annis. Drink well in the underworlds, if you can.'

He tipped the flask back and took a long gulp. When he passed it to Alithis she paused a moment, trying to think of the words. She was not one for words. Fine words were a secret speech to her, a sharp blade when she had always favoured the hammer.

'You blamed yourself for Tuareth's death,' she said at last. 'But no one else did. Judge an aelf for what he admits, not for what he blames in others or excuses in himself. You were my friend, Dae'annis.'

She drained the flask and passed it back to Belfinnan.

'I never answered your question,' she said. 'My art. I play music.'

She thought of the cithara back in her chambers, locked in its case, untouched now for weeks. She looked at her hands and couldn't believe those fingers would ever pluck the strings again. 'I tried to find the melodies for light,' she went on. 'A way to represent the properties of light in music, its evanescence, its...' She looked up into the dim sky, flecked with starlight, with the brooding black bulk of the mountain. 'But light has no sound. It just is, or it isn't.'

She looked again, and there, creeping up the flank of the mountain, glinted a speck of fiery gold. Carreth, ascending with torch in hand, seeking atonement from Ultharadon.

I hope you find it, she thought as they turned to go. *For all our sakes.*

The night of Hysh had fallen, a strained, dusky light that in the shadow of the mountainside was almost dark. The air was sharp, carrying with it the hint of the turning season. Carreth shivered in his robes, the torch casting out a smear of red against the dun grass and loose stone on either side of the track. Up it climbed, twisting around boulders, through tangled copses of barbed thorn. Beyond it, on his left, the ground fell sharply to a rolling series of slumped barrows where pines grew at strange angles from clefts in the rock. He sighed and pressed on, feet slipping on the treacherous ground. He was heading for Tuareth, the small apron of ground where he had mourned his sister's passing. Maybe there he would find peace and forgiveness, a signal of how to continue. It had soothed his soul before – before he had made that fateful, misguided decision to try to save her soul in turn. Before he condemned them all to ruin and defeat.

He scrambled along the steeper paths, hauling himself up by exposed roots and tough clumps of grass, skinning his knuckles and knees on the coarse stones that erupted from the ground like molars from a jaw, but the closer he got, the more the mountain seemed to shrug and try to shake him off. Paths he had known and followed for years had been smothered by a loose avalanche of shale or drowned in the overflow of the freezing mountain streams as they broke their banks. He climbed on, his torch held high, his bare feet bleeding on the sharp stones that seemed deliberately strewn in his path.

In all his time here as guardian of Ultharadon, he had never feared the mountain. He had respected it, he had loved and cherished it, but not for a moment had he thought it would ever do him harm. Now, he wasn't so sure. He had felt it the minute he crossed the ridge from the temple, the instant he stepped into the mountain's shadow. The bond that had always existed between them felt immediately strained, and as he crossed the grass it was as if he were pushing against some invisible force, a sense of weird transgression that made him nervous and afraid. Ashamed, he would almost have said, as if some rancid little crime had at last been exposed.

He had tried to ignore it, but now, as Carreth scrabbled for purchase on the long, winding track that snaked around a bulging flank of stone, he couldn't deny that Ultharadon had turned its spirit from him. He held the torch in his left hand, the rock bulging out on his right, the path curving around it and narrowing to a needle-fine path no thicker than his foot. He hugged the rock as he slithered around, inching his feet forward, the torch flame crackling in the breeze. It almost felt like the stone was pushing against him, heaving itself out from the bulk of the mountain to brush him from the track and send him plummeting down the slope.

In the end he had to drop the torch so he could hold on more securely. He watched it flutter down into the shadows at the mountain's base like a falling star, until it hit the ground far below him and sputtered into nothing. Carreth gritted his teeth and hooked his fingers into a dimple in the stone, edging around, creeping another inch or two. The pale night was leaden and dull around him, untroubled by the pinpricks of stars above. He tried to conjure a flame to guide him on, but although the forms of the equation were sitting there clear in his mind, it felt almost impossible to weave them together. A simple spell that even the lowliest apprentice could manage was suddenly beyond him. He shook his head, trying to clear his thoughts, his fingers aching where he gripped the stone.

Ultharadon, why do you fight me so? I had to try, don't you see? I couldn't leave her there, I can't–

He reached for the conjuration again, to weave light from the darkness, but the ache in his fingers seemed to blur the forms of magic in his mind. He was going to fall – he felt his feet slipping on the narrow track, a trickle of stones dislodging to tumble down the steep slope below him, fifty feet or more to the level ground of loose feldspar and tough grass.

'Ultharadon! Forgive me!' he shouted.

He tried to throw himself around the rock another few inches, leaping out with his arm straining for another handhold. His foot brushed the ground on the edge of the path, but the dirt crumbled and fell away. Carreth gasped, sucking in a breath, eyes wide. He ripped his fingernails on the stone, his foot paddling in empty air before his toes scrabbled for a grip. Sweat beaded against his forehead as he clung on with all his strength, his eyes screwed shut with effort. The flank of the rock was cool under his burning face. Through it he could almost feel the mountain's disquiet, its revulsion at him for what he had done. Death magic, the corrupt sorcery of those who would break the natural order. Those who had let grief unbalance them. He had stained his art with the foulest colours. He had turned from everything he knew to be good and true. The right path was ever the hardest. He had turned instead for the easy way, and now he was condemned to wait here until his strength gave out, stuck on either side of the track, suspended above the void.

Thaerannan had warned him. Death corrupts. It is the essence of corruption, and all who touch it die a little in return.

'Teclis,' he whispered, lips brushing against the rock. 'Give me another chance, I beg you...'

He heard a trickle of stone, a light dashing of pebbles as they fell from the upper slopes. Two or three of them struck the rock, pinging off into the shadows beneath him, falling onto the loose ground far below. One smacked into his jaw, not enough to truly hurt but more than enough to draw his attention. He glanced up, arms shivering with strain, and saw more stones beginning to fall – smaller and larger, some dropping like a rain of dust, others clattering down the slope as big as his fist. He ducked his head, tucking his face under his arm as the stonefall became worse. In moments it had turned from a trickle into an avalanche, the thudding rumble of a rockslide.

A stone dashed against his shoulder, loosening his grip. Carreth gasped in pain, grasping on with one hand as he swung out into the emptiness. His foot slipped and he felt himself start to fall as more stones and boulders tore past him, hissing through the air, and then the great outcrop of stone he had been trying to clamber around began to shift and unsettle. It thudded forward with a crunch, and the narrow path it had been leaning against began to collapse. There was a sickening lurch in his stomach, a sensation of falling, and then the huge boulder was leaning far out into the empty air. He clutched desperately at the sides, but he couldn't hold on anymore. His fingernails tore at the dimpled stone; he clutched at it with his legs, but then the rock was falling forward and Carreth was falling with it.

He had only moments to act. Kicking off with his feet, Carreth tried to throw himself backwards and to the side, the great boulder flinging its way past him as he tumbled and stretched, twisting around to fall forward, his legs braced, his arms tucked into his sides. The cold air whistled in his ears, but then he saw only bright light, felt the crash of thunder, a red lance of pain that cut across the back of his head. He didn't even have the breath to cry out before he hit the ground, slamming into it on his side, tumbling end over end as he fell down the slope of the mountain. The loose shale cut his face and the stalks of grass slashed against his palms as he tried to clutch on to them. Stones were still falling from the avalanche, outliers that skipped across the ground and smacked into his ribs, others pattering around him like a hard rain. The back of his head was wet with blood. He rolled on, skidding to a halt only as he crashed up against the leaning trunk of a pine tree that reached out into the abyss from the side of the mountain. A fine rain of needles fell about him as he scrambled for breath, his lungs burning, his ribs on fire. He collapsed face down on the rough grass, the trunk supporting his weight and preventing him rolling any further. Blood trickled from his head, from a hundred cuts and scratches across his face. He moved his arms, stretched his legs – his ribs were bruised, but there was nothing broken as far as he could tell.

Gradually the sound of the avalanche died away, the great rockslide crashing down the sides of Ultharadon deep into the valley below. If he had not managed to throw himself to one side at the last moment, he would have been crushed to death in the middle of that violent storm. Slowly, in agony, Carreth rolled over onto his back, feeling the rough bark of the tree trunk scratch his skin beneath his robes. He had come up here to meditate, to seek answers and find guidance after all of his failures, but the mountain had only given him one response. It had tried to kill him.

Carreth passed a hand over his eyes as the tears welled up and broke. He sobbed, covering his face, adrift on a tide of shame.

His cries echoed down the mountain slope, the sorrowful call of a creature hunted to its limit and ready only for death.

Ultharadon had rejected him. He was nothing now. Death had won.

Night, the louring, twilit night of Hysh. Alithis had dozed fitfully, but then something had woken her and sent her creeping from her bed to stand at the window. Her night-robe gleamed in the dim light. The temple gardens outside her quarters were laced with moonlight, but the other side of the quadrangle was flattened in shadows. The trees were glistening silhouettes. She stared at the flank of Ultharadon as it rose up above the temple walls on the other side of the ridge. It was monumental, a spear point lancing up from the mist-shrouded valley. She had heard a cry, a scream, but as she shook off the cobwebs of sleep, she thought it was no more than the sound of a hunting bird. A raptor, maybe, riding the thermals and skimming down for its prey on the lower slopes. They were still safe, for now.

Alithis was about to get back into bed when she saw the glint of light under her door. A flame, she thought, flickering and unsteady. She crept over and opened the door, but there was no one there. All she could hear was the soft tread of marching feet as the Stoneguard patrolled the perimeter of the temple grounds – vastly reduced, no more than sixty of them left from the hundred she had commanded before. The others had died in Paerthalann Pass.

She was closing the door when the light caught her eye again. There on the doorstep, tucked off to the side, a candle burned in a brass stick. Beside it were a bottle of zephyrwine, a glass and a small scroll of paper.

Alithis looked up, scanning the gardens, but there was no one there. Cautiously she picked up the scroll, unfurling the blue ribbon that kept it closed. It was a poem, she saw, signed at the bottom with Belfinnan's bold flourish:

> *No great deeds inoculate the heart*
> *From grief, and even when all griefs*
> *Are rendered down by time,*
> *The memory of those we lost*
> *Will make of an untroubled moment*
> *An ocean of remembered pain.*
>
> *But now the day is near us still,*
> *And all we carry from the field is loss,*
> *The loss of comrades and of friends,*
> *And hope the greater loss.*
> *All seems cast down to ruin,*
> *Nothing gained but sorrow's coin.*
>
> *Yet stone hearts do not gladly falter,*
> *And hope is yet a coin to spend.*
> *Take up your courage once again*
> *And stand beside me, friend.*

She rolled the scroll back up and held it for a moment at her breast. The gardens were still empty. The night was still cool, and the moonlight still fell in pale stripes against the grass, but Alithis felt something she had not experienced for some time – a sense of peace.

She collected the bottle of wine and the glass from the doorstep and went back inside. She left the candle burning.

CHAPTER FIFTEEN

THE WILL OF THE DEAD

Of course, they were not the only army to invade Hysh. Nagash, in his infinite wisdom, would not have risked the scale of his plans to the efforts of one legion alone. In divisions great or small, the Ossiarch Bonereapers had been unleashed across the realm, on several different fronts, with a myriad different objectives. Akridos knew this, and occasionally reports had reached him from his scouts of other Bonereaper armies across the vast continent of Ymetrica, laying siege to vital nexus points, razing cities to the ground to draw attention from thrusts elsewhere, drawing out and destroying in the field the aelves' scattered forces. The realm was burning.

We are not the only instrument in Nagash's hand, he thought. *But we are the one on which it all depends. I know this. Nagash has spoken to me. Nagash wills it, and I will it in turn. Eltharion will die. Y'gethin will die, and it will be my hand at their throats, my victory...*

He looked down from the jutting bluff on which he had called his council, a spear of rock that rose above the plains, the last blunt extrusion of the mountain ranges they had just passed through. A hundred feet beyond him, past the gently sloping ground as it fell in barrows and hillocks from the foothills, the plains of Ymetrica were wide open. They stretched off in great fields of emerald grass, smeared with drifts of purple heather. Here and there he could see the bones of ancient ruins, the sad remnants of the aelves' civilisation before they tore it all to pieces in the maelstrom of their Ocari Dara. The Spirefall, Kathanos had called it. The secret shame at the heart of all they do.

On the plains swept, vast and featureless, and making a virtue of that featurelessness in their simple, austere beauty. It was a sight, Akridos supposed, almost designed to broaden the mind. With the right temperament, you would look on this landscape and feel your thoughts unburdening themselves of any extraneous detail, finding freedom in simplicity. And like the focal point towards which you would guide your thoughts, there in the far distance, a hundred miles or more, rose the sharp pinnacle of Ultharadon – a spear blade lancing up from the unbroken ground, vaster by far than the mountain ranges the Ossiarch army had just crossed.

Ultharadon, the holy mountain, towards which the weary pilgrim would turn her feet, refreshed. Ultharadon, where the temple lay on a slight rise to the mountain's side, guided and guarded by Stonemage Y'gethin.

Yes, Akridos thought, *if you were of the right temperament indeed, this would be an inspiring view. It is a pity in some ways that I am not – but the view will be mine all the same, when I am king again. When Ultharadon is no more.*

His most trusted lieutenants stood to attention beside him. Takanos, second-in-command of his Deathriders, Miszoios, the lead hekatos of his Mortek Guard, even Morfilos, leader of the boneshapers cadre. Ten Immortis Guard stood in a crescent beyond them, the traditional accompaniment for the gathering of the army's lead elements. Akridos was not ignorant of the vague threat they posed to his underlings, standing there twice their height, their halberds held at a cross guard in front of their massive shields. The Immortis Guard were sworn to the Liege-Kavalos alone, and they would obey no other.

'Where is Kathanos?' Morfilos croaked. 'Surely he should join the discussion of our strategy?'

'You mistake me,' Akridos said, his back to them all. He stared out at the open plains, the blade of the mountain in the distance. The air was fresh and cool, laced with the hint of the changing season. 'We meet not to discuss strategy, but only for me to impart what I have already decided. The strategy is mine alone.'

'Of course, Liege-Kavalos,' the boneshaper said in an obsequious voice. Akridos could easily picture the depth of his bow, the tendrils on his skull wavering in the breeze. 'I meant no other implication.'

'Kathanos is only another instrument I wield,' Akridos said. 'He is a tool I use when I see fit, as are you all. And I fear his use has now come to an end.'

He turned and looked boldly at them. Miszoios and Takanos were utterly impassive, and Akridos knew he had nothing to fear there. They were beyond loyal, and their wills were practically enmeshed with his own. Despite the frozen width of his grin, though, Morfilos had a haunted look on the planes of his skull. The green necromantic light in his eye sockets purled for a moment, shuddering left and right. Akridos, imperceptibly, prepared himself to strike. The Immortis Guard would cut Morfilos down in an instant if he gave the word, but then the light in the boneshaper's eyes settled to a steadier glow. Morfilos was not stupid – he had a ruthless cunning and he had clearly read the shift in the army's hierarchy. Kathanos would find no allies here.

Again, the boneshaper bowed, and the frozen grin stretched a tooth wider.

'I await your instruction, my liege.'

Akridos turned back to the plains. He unsheathed his scimitar and pointed at the distant mountain.

'There lies Ultharadon. We will proceed in column across the veldt, following the pilgrim route. Once we reach the temple, we will surround and destroy it. Miszoios, you will take the vanguard. You will pin the remnants of the Lumineth forces in the temple complex. Takanos, you will lead half of the Deathriders to encircle the temple around the right flank. I will take the other half around the left, cutting off their retreat into the mountain. The Crawlers will slight the temple before the Necropolis Stalkers move in to destroy any survivors.'

'A masterful strategy,' Morfilos said. 'The aelves do not stand a chance.'

'These aelves always stand a chance,' he said bluntly. 'They are not to be underestimated, not while Mage Y'gethin lives. Once we have dealt with them, we will then turn the fire of the Crawlers on the mountain itself. Cursed stele, necrotic skulls, cauldrons of torment – we will drown every inch of it in torment and death.'

'And you are sure this "Light of Eltharion" will be forced to intervene?'

'He will have no choice. Concentrate on destroying Y'gethin and his wretched mountain,' Akridos said, 'and Eltharion will strike back. Honour compels it, and fate has willed it so. But Y'gethin must be destroyed, do you understand? He *must*.'

Akridos clutched the soul gem on his breastplate, feeling the pulse of light flash through his bones.

Y'gethin... so close are we now I can almost feel you. I yearn for your life under my blade as I have never yearned for anything before. Soon we will be joined, together in death at last...

Morfilos nodded his agreement and Akridos dismissed them. The Immortis Guard stepped aside, opening up like a hinge as the lieutenants stepped through, setting off to prepare their troops for the march. Akridos followed, vaulting up onto his steed where it had patiently waited for the conference to be over.

'Akridos!' a screeching voice called. He looked from the saddle across the rocky ground, where the Ossiarch army was defiling from the mountains and spreading out on the plain below, a mute parade of marching infantry and clanking horse, row after row. Kathanos was hobbling towards him with that strange, jerking motion of the throne, the clawed legs lashing at the grass. 'Akridos, you dare hold a conclave without my presence!'

The soulmason drew up short before Akridos' watching eye. He glanced at the Immortis Guard, who had now reformed into a phalanx at the Liege-Kavalos' side. His mitre quivered on his skull as he shook his head in rage, fingers scrabbling at his staff.

'Your presence,' Akridos said, 'would have been merely a profitless irritation. The strategy is decided – the army moves for Ultharadon at once.'

Kathanos screeched with anger. 'Has this not already been discussed? The war proceeds elsewhere in Hysh, and the forces of Mage Y'gethin are practically destroyed! I have heard disturbing reports that the great mortarch, Arkhan the Black himself, has been repulsed by the Lumineth far to the north. At Avalenor, our forces are massing for the final strike. *There* is where your so-called strategy should be taking us!' Kathanos sat there hunched on his throne, incandescent, gnashing his teeth. The gems at the head of his crosier pulsated with energy. He gave a dry, creaking cackle. 'You are an imbecile, Liege-Kavalos, too blind and ignorant to see the roots of your desire, yet I see it plain as day. You think you move to your own designs, but you are merely tugged on the string of the aelf soul inside you. *That* is what yearns for Y'gethin. *That* is what squirms and creeps inside you, desperate for release. I put it in there,' he hissed, 'and I could as easily pull it out.'

'My will is my own,' Akridos said. He was calm, precise, stating no more than a simple fact. 'I go where I choose, and I command who I see fit.'

'Let me remind you of the hierarchy that exists between us,' Kathanos said as the army continued its march behind him. 'The Emissarian caste of the Mortisan order occupies the exact same level as the Panoptic caste – no more, no less. We are of equal stature in this legion, and it is not yours to do with as you please.'

Akridos looked at him with a cold certainty. 'In an age gone by, I was a king of a great people. I was the head of an empire that lasted for a thousand years. I have come into my power again, soulmason, and when Y'gethin and his mountain are destroyed I will be a king once more.'

'A king! You fool – you stumble over memories that are no more than ghosts, whispers of an age so distant you can barely recall it! Your delusion would be amusing if it were not so pathetic. You think you are a man resurrected,' Kathanos spat, 'a king of old brought to new unlife? Let me assure you that you are not. You are no more than the echo of a man, blended with the echoes of a dozen others. You are nothing, Akridos, without my magic to prop you up. Nagash commands you. Your god commands you, and you will obey or face the consequences!'

'A king obeys his own commands,' Akridos whispered. 'And if I transgress the will of Nagash, then let him strike me down...'

In a silver blur he unsheathed his sword and swept the skull from the soulmason's neck.

A maddened shriek burst across the land, ringing back from the foothills of the mountains, tearing off across the flat ground of the plains. It was a wail like a hundred trapped souls screaming off into the void, free of their torment at last but too long tortured to find anything in their freedom but further wretchedness and sorrow. Kathanos' bones collapsed into a rattling jumble, wreathed with spectral light. As if awaiting this signal, the Immortis Guard stepped forward as one, their halberds raised, and hacked the Mortisan throne to pieces. Akridos turned his back on the scene, standing again on the spur of rock and looking down at the plains as they rolled away from him, where his army, utterly impassive to the soulmason's destruction, formed up in their marching order.

'Leave me the skull,' Akridos said. 'Scatter the rest to the wind.'

In the distance, Ultharadon shone with a pale blue light, like a beacon calling him on. It was no more than two days' and two nights' march away.

Soon, Mage Y'gethin. Your time in this miserable realm draws short, and soon all you love and favour will be ashes and blood.

There is a strange comfort in failure, Carreth thought as he sat there in his tattered robes. *In many ways, when you have reached the bottom you are finally safe, because there is nowhere else to fall.*

Days had passed since he had been thrown from the mountain. How many days, he couldn't say. All that had passed since then had been subsumed into his distress, and his blind and agonised retreat from the slopes of Ultharadon was no more than a disfigured memory in his mind, laced with pain. As if moving by their own accord, his feet had carried him across the greensward towards the temple grounds, where he had collapsed on the grass and passed out.

He was sitting now on one of the stone benches in the ornamental gardens, in the temple's eastern quadrangle. He leaned forward and gathered up a handful of bleached white pebbles from the gravel path, absently skimming them into the pale green water of the pond. Silver fish made flitting darts for the safety of the shadows as each stone broke the surface, hiding themselves under the leaves of trailing weeds. The breeze lifted for a moment, cold with the coming autumn, and ruffled the petals of the flowers around him. They would die soon, he knew. The air would turn colder, the ground would harden with frost, and the first snows would carry the flowers off. Would they return in the spring? Would these be the last blooms in the gardens of Ultharadon, before death became a permanent guest?

He sighed, threw another stone, watched the ripples spread out across the water in concentric circles until they broke apart against the wall of the pond.

Our actions are little more than stones thrown into the water of time. A few ripples spreading outwards, dissipating into nothing, while the stone sinks into the numb, cold depths beneath.

The temple was quiet around him. Under Alithis' direction, all the work to prepare its defences had been finished. Now the temple was ringed with ditches and palisades, earthworks, chokepoints, barricades. More recruits had arrived while the army had been fighting in Paerthalann Pass, but still their numbers were pitifully low. Any defence, Carreth knew, could only be a bold gesture of defiance before they were swept away – the subject of a song for the bards to sing, if there were any bards left by the time the Bonereapers had finished. Scattered reports had reached Carreth from across Ymetrica, and it seemed the Lumineth forces were engaged on every front. It was only a matter of time now…

He threw another stone, watched it plop into the water. He held a last pebble in his hand, rolling it between his fingers, feeling its roughened surface in his palm. The stone of Ultharadon, gathered from its slopes, imbued with its holy presence… It almost burned his skin. He clutched it tightly, willing the pain to worsen and grimacing as it did.

I deserve nothing less. All the disgust and revulsion you are capable of, Ultharadon, pour it on me. Heap the rubble of your contempt on my unworthy head, bury me in it.

He gasped and dropped the stone, feeling sick inside. He looked down at his bare feet, still scabbed and cracked from the climb up the mountain. His side ached and his face was a mass of cuts and bruises. The back of his head was tender, his shoulder stiff where he had wrenched his arm. He was lucky to be alive, Ilmarrin had said. The old votary had run out from the temple to meet him as Carreth staggered across the ridge, catching him as he fell. He had helped him to his quarters, but Carreth, floating briefly into consciousness again, had dismissed him as soon as he was through the door.

'Leave me,' he had groaned. 'Don't even look at me, old friend, for I should be lower than the foulest daemon in your sight!'

Protesting, Ilmarrin had left, shocked by the vehemence of Carreth's distress. Before collapsing on the bed, Carreth had swept the scrolls and volumes of forbidden spells from his desk, snatching them up and flinging them at the walls, a hurricane of ancient paper, a futile gesture of self-disgust.

The spells are not to blame, he had thought. *They are only what they are, and nothing more. It is I, Carreth Y'gethin, who bears the sole responsibility. I am the one who has failed.*

He heard the crunch of approaching footsteps on the gravel path but made no effort to compose himself. Any new recruit, wide-eyed with tales of the legendary warrior Carreth Y'gethin, or the celebrated Stonemage of Holy Ultharadon, would have to make do with this pitiful sight and adjust their expectations accordingly. He stared down at the ground, his hands clasped as if in prayer.

'I imagine you feel even more pathetic than you look,' Alithis said. He felt her sit next to him on the bench. 'And I have to say, you look pretty wretched.'

He gave her a small smile. 'I am not, perhaps, at my best.'

'None of us are, my friend,' she said. She laid her hand on his shoulder, and her voice was tender. 'We all carry our regrets, our sorrows. It is how we manage that burden that counts, what we do with the pain that we feel.'

He touched her hand. 'Alas, this burden has overwhelmed me.'

'But it doesn't have to. Not when you have friends to share it.'

He shook his head, closed his eyes. He wanted to cover his face and weep, but some small spark of dignity remained to him and he turned away instead.

'I would not force this burden on anyone,' he said in a cracking voice. 'All my life I have studied the lessons of the Ocari Dara, the great tragedy of our race. I fought as a soldier in those awful wars when it was over, to bring peace to the realm. I thought I had learned my lessons well. Teclis was the exemplar, and with Celennar's help he showed us how we should live. Balance, study, equilibrium, peace. Each rung of the Teclamentari brought me to a greater understanding of my own failings, such that I would never risk the same degenerate fall into folly and ambition – or so I thought.'

'You never have,' Alithis insisted, gripping his arm. 'You have always been the exemplar to me, Carreth, the model I try to follow!'

'Then your idol has feet of clay,' he spat. 'For when I came to the ultimate test of my character, my failure was absolute. Ultharadon cast me off as a parasite, as an ox shaking off a tick, because I had so corrupted myself.'

'You made a mistake,' Alithis said, 'one motivated only by your grief. The magics you used were forbidden, but you wielded them only in the service of love.'

'Blind love falls on one side of the true path as much as blind hate falls on the other. It is no excuse. And in any case,' he said, 'I have no doubt that it is too late. The dead are marching, and they are nearly upon us.'

'What about the barrier in the mountains, the stone wall you conjured?'

'It will not hold them longer than a few days. And... I can *feel* them getting closer. I can feel him, Akridos, their warlord. He has Tuareth's soul embedded in him, and it's like a beacon calling to me. It won't be long now.'

Alithis stiffened at his side. He turned and looked at her, saw again that old defiance in her face, the grim fortitude as unshakeable as rock.

'Then we will meet them before the temple and die with weapons in our hands,' she said. 'If death is near, then all that matters is the manner in which we meet it.'

Carreth nodded, not trusting himself to speak. After a moment, composing himself, he said, 'You were always the best of this temple, Alithis. You were Ultharadon made flesh, the spirit of the mountain.'

He saw something flash behind her eyes, and then she was gripping his wrist tightly, her face flushed.

'The spirit of the mountain,' she whispered. 'Of course! Summon it, Carreth, the avatar of Ultharadon! Summon the spirit of the mountain and we will unleash such power on those undead scum that we'll knock them all the way back to Shyish!'

Carreth shook his head. 'You don't understand,' he said. 'It would be impossible for me now, inconceivable.'

'Nothing is impossible, not when our lives depend on it!' She stood up from the bench, dragging him with her, and despite her smaller stature it was as if she towered over him.

'It cannot be done!' he protested. Carreth shook, unable to meet her blazing eyes. 'The mountain has rejected me utterly. It has turned its spirit away from me!'

'Then I will go,' Alithis said. He looked at her, saw the determination etched on her face, as if she would stride off this minute and give the mountain a piece of her mind. 'Let me ascend and beg the spirit's forgiveness.'

'You would be destroyed,' he said simply. He collapsed to the bench again, leaning his elbows on his knees, staring over at the settled surface of the pond. The breeze shivered across the gardens, plucking the scent from the nodding flowers. 'Only the anointed Stonemage of the Temple has that authority. Ultharadon would kill you.'

'I will take that risk.'

'It would be no risk. It would be mere certainty. I would not lose you to my folly too, Alithis.'

'Then all is truly lost,' she said simply. She sat beside him again, her head bowed. 'All that remains is to wait, and to fight, and to die as well as we can.'

It was late in the afternoon, but the light was still fine – the bold, clear light of Hysh, like a balm of better days. Carreth raised his face to the light, trying to steer his mind from thoughts of Teclis, of Celennar and their meeting in the aetheric plane, of Dae'annis and Tuareth, and everyone he had failed. *Let the light cleanse you one last time*, he thought, *before it goes out forever.*

As he thought this, so the light seemed to fade. There was an edge to it suddenly, the gloom of a dusk that was still a few hours away. Carreth looked around the ornamental gardens, at the white gravel paths, the flagstones around the pond, the borders and beds of alpine flowers, the shaded corners over by the moon bridge, where the woe trees dipped their heads to the gentle waters of the stream. Everything seemed shaded with darkness, as if he looked on a painting, the surface of which had been coloured in a wash of subtle ink.

'Carreth?' Alithis said in a careful voice. 'What's happening? I feel…'

He glanced at her, saw a tear slip from the corner of her eye.

He felt it too, a bone-deep sorrow, as if the weight of a lifetime's griefs were slowly being lowered onto his shoulders.

They both stood up from the bench, Alithis with her hand on the hilt of her hammer, Carreth standing there in his plain and tattered robes, his feet bleeding on the stone. The garden paths were now ruffled with a trailing mist, and the gardens themselves had become opaque behind this drifting, sorrowful haze.

'Carreth Y'gethin,' that chanting voice said, like an elegy or a funeral oration. 'Stonemage of Ultharadon...'

'*Thaerannan*,' he whispered. He held out his hand. She stood a short way off, shrouded in mist further up the path. He hadn't seen her approach – it was as if the mist itself had carried her all the way from the Valley of Desolation. The veil drifted across her face, and the deep grey smoke of her censer spilled like a tide of sadness around her bare feet. At last, able to stand it no more, Carreth wept.

'Did I not say that I would return to you,' she said, 'when I was needed most? Now, Stonemage, old friend... time runs shorter than you think. And Ultharadon is waiting for you...'

CHAPTER SIXTEEN

THE ROOT OF THE MOUNTAIN

He stood and looked at the mountain rising high above him. He felt its weight the way you would feel a buried shame, some memory you have long suppressed. Its scale was so big it was in many ways easier to overlook it, rather than risk taking it in completely. Carreth shielded his eyes from the glare of the light as it crept around the mountain's flank, glinting off the minerals buried in the rock, calling up a hard reflection from the snows that dusted the higher peaks. The shadow of Ultharadon slid closer to him across the grassy ridge as the light rose higher, and it was as if its shadow had as much weight as the mountain itself. He turned away, still dressed in his ragged robes, his feet still cracked and bleeding. He would not attempt the heights of Ultharadon again. He was not worthy. This time, he would seek its depths instead.

The slope at the side of the ridge was steep and sheer, a shelf of thick, shaggy grass that petered out into bare earth and stone.

Carreth slid down with his feet angled to the side, his left hand thrown back on the sloped ground to keep his balance. The grass was wet with dew, and as he reached the lower slope his feet dislodged a trickle of dirt and stone. He stared down into the depths of the valley, but it was hidden in the mist. It reminded him forcefully of the Valley of Desolation, where he had found Thaerannan – that same dank and crawling atmosphere, the same tendrils of greasy fog lingering in dell and hollow.

He slid further down, grasping at the last twists of grass to keep himself from falling forward. The light began to slacken, blocked out by the shadow of the mountain. His skin prickled with cold. Far over to his right was the bare flank of the mountain, its roots plunging down into the depths of the valley beneath him, wet with mist, blackened, bare of life – a sublime construction of the natural world. More than ever before, Carreth felt like an ant in its shadow, utterly insignificant. The mist hung against the vast flank of stone like a layering of cloud, rolling out to smother the valley below. A sea of smoke, and Carreth the diver risking everything to plumb its hidden depths. He slid down another few feet, the mist reaching out its clammy fingers to smear its dew against his forehead, and then he was through and into the Vale of Ultharadon at last.

What you find in those depths, Thaerannan had said, *is what you bring with you. Your secret shames, the moments you regret most, the petty selfishness and the devious deceptions you have woven all your life. As the roof of the mountain helps you to discover your best self, so the root of the mountain disinters all that you most want to hide. There*, she said, with a sad smile just visible behind the gossamer veil, *is where you will find your worst self.*

And when I find him? Carreth had asked. What then?

Then… you must make peace with him. You know this, Stonemage. Only in reconciling our true natures are we finally free. Balance comes from weighting both sides equally. Ultharadon needs your power, as much as you need it in return. All of us need it now.

The mist was like smoke rising from the earth, buffeting out in wisps and plumes, a rank breath hissed across the ground. It crept over his bare ankles like the fingers of a chill hand.

Eventually the ground began to level out. He could see twisted clumps of weeds peering through the fog, the rippled black water of a stagnant pool. Here and there, huge, misshapen boulders were slumped across the ground, furred with grey moss – shed by Ultharadon, and tumbling all the way down to this forgotten dell. Carreth wasn't sure how long he had been descending, but his legs were shaking with effort by the time he reached the bottom. His head pounded and his robes were clammy with sweat. He began to shiver in the cold. The light of Hysh was eclipsed by the side of the mountain this far down beneath it, and the air shimmered with a strange, subaqueous tint. He stood there in the swaying gloom with his arms wrapped around himself, uncertain which way to go. The mist swirled thicker around him, and he could only see a few feet ahead at a time. Although he could no longer see it, obscured as it was, Carreth could feel the crushing weight of the mountain above him. The rumpled ground, the veins of rock pushing through the dirt, were the coils of its roots, the bones of its vast and overwhelming form.

In the temple library he had read the records of his predecessors, the Stonemages who had come before him, as well as the priests of the temple's earlier days before Teclis brought them the teachings of the aelementiri. Even in the dawn times, when Teclis and his brother Tyrion walked the Ten Paradises of Hysh, Ultharadon had been recognised as a holy place. Legends said that as the Twin Gods brought more aelf souls into being, and as the predecessors of the Lumineth Realm-lords spread across the lands, their priests had built the first humble temple in the lee of Ultharadon, that they might worship and pay homage in its shadow. The library held scattered fragments of those times, ancient accounts in long-dead dialects. Scattered infrequently throughout those accounts were dark hints of voyages taken down into the vale beneath the mountain – pilgrimages to seek Ultharadon's forgiveness for unspecified infractions, spirit-journeys to cleanse an afflicted soul, to scour it clean of corruption. During the Ocari Dara, as Carreth's researches had told him, one mage had sought refuge in the depths of the valley to prevent himself from succumbing to the factionalism that was raging across the realm. He had clambered down the same slope Carreth himself had just descended, and he had never been seen again.

The vale is a place apart, Thaerannan's voice seemed to whisper in his mind. *To descend into the chasm is to venture into the lowest despair, but only there can true knowledge be found.*

'And what if it can't?' Carreth mumbled. 'What if I'm condemned to stumble about here in the shadows, finding nothing but my own miserable death?'

Then that is the path Ultharadon has chosen for you, Stonemage. You must walk it and discover the truth. Only there can you reconnect with the spirit of the mountain.

'But which way?' he said. He looked around him at the rolling mist, the saturated ground that sucked at his feet, the rank weeds and dead water. 'I don't know where to go.'

Where you go, Carreth, is inside. It is not a destination, remember. It is a path.

He wandered for hours, his feet and the hem of his robes heavy with mud, his breath emerging in chill plumes. The only noise was the wet, sucking sounds of his footsteps – and sometimes the far-off, strangulated cry of a creature somewhere deep in the mist, screaming its distress.

He was exhausted and miserable, sickened at the time he was wasting when the hordes of the Ossiarch army could be on his very doorstep. Like his predecessor of old, had he really retreated down here to avoid the risk of violence? Like that ancient priest, would he ever be seen again? No, it was not so simple. Thaerannan's suggestion had filled him with dread, but he knew instinctively that it was the right thing to do. The mountain still had to be confronted, and although their chance of victory hung by the thinnest thread, it was a thread that was deeply entangled in the roots of Ultharadon. There was no other choice.

Despite this, his head thudded with exhaustion and his legs trembled with every step. He had barely recovered from his fall down the mountain's slope, and as much as it had bruised his body, it had battered his courage as well. Each step through the cloying mud, parting the veils of mist, seemed to claw at his nerves. He walked with his hands clenched at his sides, his teeth bared in an animal snarl of fear. Shrieks leapt out of the distorted air; rank pools bubbled like a stinking stew, releasing foul marsh odours. The feeling of the weeds and the mud under his feet repelled him. Still he staggered on, forcing himself against an adversary as forbidding as the Ossiarch Bonereapers themselves – his own terror.

He tried to clamber across a rotting log, grimacing at the feel of the fungus and moss under his hands, but the wood crumbled underneath him and pitched him off to the side. He stumbled, flung out an arm for balance, tried to grab on to the log as it disintegrated in his hand – and then he was falling, smashing face first into a squalid foot of marsh water that enveloped him like a dank sheet. Carreth gagged for breath as he hauled himself up, coughing out a lungful of slime, thrashing through the muck to try to drag himself out. Clambering up the slippery bank and throwing himself into the mud, he howled with disgust and rage, with all the rank self-pity of someone who has found himself cast down to the very lowest depths. This was it, he thought, this was the very bottom – there was nowhere else to go.

He lay like that for an hour, dropping into a fitful and dazed sleep and then being ripped out of it as another shriek tore across the stagnant air. Things slithered in the foetid undergrowth, and tattered moths as big as bats shambled through the fog. There was nothing here. There was only the gathered filth and detritus cast off by the mountain, the fecund rot that multiplied in the shadows at its base, where no light reached.

'Thaerannan,' he said as he lay there sprawled on the ground. 'If you can hear me, show me what to do? For I am lost as I have never been lost before.'

He raised his head. A light had kindled softly in the mist ahead of him, and as he stared at it the light seemed to grow. The mist on either side began to part, and in that pale, wavering flame he thought he could see a figure kneeling. He stared at it, a silhouette that gradually formed into shimmering detail.

'Tuareth?' he whispered.

It was his sister, as he had known her once – a child orphaned by their parents' sudden death, a young aelf who had been raised with love and kindness by her older brother.

He saw her kneeling in a blank and vacant space, a translucent image torn from his memories. She was playing with her toys, absorbed in her games. Suddenly she started with excitement and ran to a door that opened before her. She called, but Carreth could hear no words. All he could hear was the blood thrumming in his ears, his heart thudding in his chest. He gazed on the pale vision and saw Tuareth eagerly approaching a tall figure, an aelf of grim visage clad in battleplate who callously brushed off her attentions and swept from the room. As he turned, Carreth saw that the warrior bore his face. He watched Tuareth crying in silence, with all the vehemence of a child. His heart lurched inside him.

The image shifted, breaking apart like the ripple of a stone cast into still water. When it reformed, he saw her staring from an empty window, or crying at night with loneliness and sorrow – all of her sadness unnoticed by the driven young warrior who passed through her life like a blast of wind, indifferent to her pain. He saw himself deep in study, committed to the teachings of the aelementiri, apprenticed to Mage Ghryth'aenis at Ultharadon. He saw Tuareth pleading with him to teach her the ways of the Vanari, so that she could become a warrior as great as he was – but again, for the apprentice Stonemage this child was a mere distraction. His own study was all that mattered, his own achievements, his own drive for power and respect. She had taken the route of the Vanari anyway, practising her drill in the garden of their family home on the Ymetrican coast. The mist of the vision unfurled to new vistas, showing him Tuareth studying the tactical treatises of great generals and theorists, polishing her armour, sharpening her spear. He saw her rise through the ranks to high warden, but at each stage of her achievement there was an absence that deadened its significance – her brother, too busy to pay the slightest bit of attention to the sister he had virtually abandoned, and who had been forced to raise herself alone. Then the mist peeled back, and suddenly Carreth was looking down on a blasted, dead plain. In the distance rose a fearsome jagged fortress, composed entirely of black bone.

'No,' Carreth whispered, covering his face with his muddy hands. 'Please! Do not show me this!'

But he couldn't look away. He saw the Lumineth host march confidently across the plains. He saw the massed ranks of the Bonereapers come out to meet them. He saw horror and violence, mayhem and death – the breaking spears, the sundered shields, the bodies and bones trampled underfoot. And he saw Tuareth, bleeding, in agony, crawling over the bodies of her comrades. As Akridos drew near, her face was a mask of pain and terror.

'Not this!' Carreth cried. He hauled himself up from the mud and threw himself into the mist, tearing it apart with his hands. Woven in the tattered tendrils of the fog, he saw Akridos leer closer – and then Carreth had a sword in his hand, and his heart was hot with hate. He swung out. Sword met scimitar, warlord met mage, and in a burst of light Carreth cut him down, his brittle bones erupting into dust. In triumph he stooped down to lift the warlord's skull – but the face that grinned back at him, flensed and bloody, was his sister's.

Carreth screamed and threw the skull to the ground. Freezing fingers gripped his heart. The mist swirled about him like a web. He spun around, trying to retrace his steps, but the ground sucked at his feet, grasping at him, holding him back. He flailed out and screamed again, whipping the veil of mist from his face, throwing himself forward and scrabbling across the filthy ground, the cold slime of dead weeds thick in his hands, the stench of stagnant water in his nose, vomit pooling at the back of his throat. On he stumbled, the mist thick and gelatinous around him, the sight of his sister's heartfelt sorrow still blazing in his mind's eye.

'Thaerannan!' he cried. 'I've seen enough. I beg you, lead me from this place!'

He felt her mind drift briefly against his own, but then there was nothing around him but dead, silent air. The mist broke apart and simmered away into a faint, clammy steam. Carreth stepped forward, the ground still a sucking quagmire beneath him. There was silence – but there was also something else there in front of him, a presence that sat in the gloom, brooding and malicious. He could feel it lurking beyond the edge of his vision, radiating hatred. It stoked a cold fear in his belly.

'Who's there?' he said, his voice trembling. He searched for a weapon, reaching down and picking up a slimy rock. 'Who are you?'

There was a hiss, a stench of rotting flesh that made Carreth gag. He raised his arm to shield his mouth and inched forward. And then he saw it.

It was hunched there in the dirt, crouched and ragged, fingers trailing like a husk of twigs through the slime. Lank hair dripped down its face, greasy and pale. It was clad in the remnants of tattered robes, the once white cloth stained by years of degradation into a sodden grey. It glanced up at him with yellow eyes, its face scarred and sallow, the planes of its skull visible through the translucent skin. The look in its eyes was deeper than malice, stronger than hate. The thing hissed at him, its mouth cracking open with a savage grin – a bare handful of pointed teeth, black with decay, a leering, purplish tongue that crept from the cave of its mouth like a tentacle, pitted with ulcers. Carreth, horrified, took a step back. The thing didn't move, just pierced him with that jaundiced gaze, hissing, dragging its bleeding, cankered fingers through the muck. It had been an aelf once, Carreth knew. Of course...

It was him.

The instant his mind made the connection the thing shrieked in agony, and the leering savagery of its expression melted into one of absolute despair. It shrieked again as Carreth stumbled back. It clawed at its face, ripping the skin, dragging a bubbling black blood from its rendered flesh. The stench was incredible, and as Carreth turned to vomit in the mud the creature bounded forward and leapt at him.

He barely had time to raise the rock in his hand, but he caught the creature a glancing blow against its shoulder as it tore at him with its claws. The smell of its half-dead, rotting flesh buffeted him like a wave, and beyond the stench was the electric force of its madness pushing against him, making him reel, cringing at the mute horror that this awful thing was in some way a glimpse of what he might become. A vision of a dread future, but no less deadly for that – Carreth felt its claws digging into his flesh, ripping a trail of fire across his bruised ribs. He cried out as the creature slashed at him, leaping in a frenzy to throw itself across his shoulders and drag him to the ground. Carreth crashed onto his back, his arms raised to shield his face as the thing hacked at him with its ragged nails, stinking fingers lacing through his hair and smashing his head down onto the ground. It shrieked and gibbered, spittle flying from its necrotic lips to fleck his face, the mad yellow eyes dancing like marsh lights.

He still had the rock in his hand. Carreth swung it with all his force against the creature's jaw, feeling the bone crack under the blow. The thing howled and fell to the side, and as he struggled to free himself it leapt at him again. Blood poured down its face from where the stone had cut it. Carreth got to his knees, swung out with the rock, felt it crunch against the thing's eye. It lashed out, caught its fist against Carreth's forehead and sent him sprawling. In a panic, he tried to crawl away, scurrying across the mud, lurching to his feet and limping through the mist as the creature howled with rage. He could feel it loping along behind him. He shrank into himself as he almost felt those foul claws sinking into his neck.

It is me, and I am it, he thought with disgust. *This is what I will become!*

He pictured himself in a sequence of lurching images, trapped down here in the dreadful sewer of the valley bottom, gnawing the bones of the creeping things that called this place home, the weave of magic unthreading around him and becoming an invisible thing, no longer subject to his power – his mind rotting, fragments of it peeling away even as his skin mouldered in the damp, unable to bear the weight of all the souls he had abandoned. The people he had let down – his sister, neglected, a sacrifice on the altar of his ambition, his quest for power. A distraction he had always pushed to one side.

Tuareth...

He saw her face, beseeching him in the temple before she went off to war. He saw her as a child, desperate for the attention he refused to give her. What would she say to him now, if she was here? Would she forgive him? Carreth smiled sadly. It was a question he didn't even need to ask to know the answer.

It was something he hadn't felt for months, but slowly it began to stoke a fire in his limbs. Not the pitiful self-disgust he had indulged for too long, but the simple self-respect he had given up along the way. Since Tuareth had died, he had thought only of how he could cheat her fate, how he could take on the powers of death and show them that he, Carreth Y'gethin, wielded the stronger power. Teclis himself had commanded him to act, for the good of the realm, and all Carreth had done was turn this order to his own advantage. Not to Tuareth's advantage, and certainly not to the temple's or the realm's, but to the advantage of his own pride. He truly recognised this thing that stalked him now. It was not what he would become if he stayed down here, but what he was now. It was the very worst of him.

'Pride,' he said. 'Such I name you, creature. Pride and ambition. Selfishness. Deceit. The lust for power. All that came so close to destroying this realm, once. I name you… Ocari Dara!'

He saw it lurking in the mist, hunched down, creeping on all fours like a beast. It hissed and whined, circling him, the yellow eyes blazing in the fog. It was waiting to strike again, desperate to rip his flesh apart and crack his bones to splinters. The eyes flicked to the stone in Carreth's hand. He dropped it to the ground.

'There is no light without darkness,' he whispered. He thought of Thaerannan, her eyes dark behind the veil, the sadness in her face at the lesson she had learned on the long and sorrowful path of the Cathallar. 'And there is no darkness without light.'

The creature whined long and low, like a beaten dog. Carreth stepped towards it, slowly, calmly, one foot at a time.

'I forgive you,' he said. 'As I forgive myself.'

It howled, snapped its teeth, skittered to the side, eyes madly blazing with fear. Carreth held out his arms.

'I name you one last time,' he said. 'And I name you… *Carreth Y'gethin.*'

The creature screamed, and it was like a stab of lightning, blinding, deafening. Carreth reached out, grinding his teeth, falling to his knees. He pulled the creature in, gathering it to himself. Its piercing voice enveloped him, burning through him like a spear, and as the mist began to swirl and dissipate around them, Carreth found that he was kneeling on the ground alone, and his arms were wrapped only around himself.

Blood trickled down his ribs. The cuts and scratches on his face were aching, but for the first time in months he felt serene. Tuareth was dead. He could not save her spirit – he knew that – but he could do his best to give it peace.

He stood up painfully, muscles aching. There was a thin, glassy pain in his head, and he still felt waves of nausea as they swept through his body. As he looked around the valley floor, though, it no longer seemed such a drear and forbidding place. The mist had faded, and thin beams of light now fell from high above to strike the muddy ground. He could see the path through the bog that he had followed, twisting through the marsh, passing over the rotting logs and through the spectral copses of dead trees. A vein of rock passed close by, a blade of stone that cut across the bog at hip height, smeared with dead leaves and dripping moss. Carreth stumbled over to it, cleaning the filth from the stone, laying his hands against one of the roots of the mountain and feeling its holy power suffuse him once more. He closed his eyes, and the tears he wept were ones of gratitude and faith.

'Ultharadon,' he said. 'I serve only you. Strike me down if you must, but I dedicate myself to you once more. In life, and in death.'

The mountain rumbled high above him, a shifting of its immortal bones. He gathered himself together and headed back the way he had come, battered, bruised but whole once more, and as he began the slow and difficult climb up the slopes of the valley, he heard the rumbling of the mountain gain in force and intensity around him. He felt it shudder through his body, burning through the weave of magic that grew in force and power around him. Under his hands as he climbed, the stones and pebbles began to vibrate. Higher he went, dragging himself up by root and stone, higher and higher and with increasing strength. Soon, the dirt and shale gave way to fresh grass, clean under his hands and feet, and the light broke through in waves above him, cleansing, filling him with hope and vigour – the holy light of Hysh refracted by Ulthara-don's vast bulk, the mountain looming like a continent above him. As he climbed the rumbling continued, the clashing roar of rock grinding into rock, louder and louder. When he reached the top of the slope, hauling himself up onto the grassy ridge, the temple gleaming off to his right like a shard of crystal, Carreth looked down into the shadows of the valley and laughed. Joy, pure and unadulterated, flowed through him. The noise was deafening now, an earthquake thunder that shook the very ground and sent rocks tumbling from the higher peaks.

He laughed again, his arms raised above his head and the glint of coruscating magic flickering around his fingers. Slowly, he mastered his emotions, regaining the ladder of the Teclamentari. He breathed and closed his eyes, and for the first time he allowed himself to think it.

They were going to win.

CHAPTER SEVENTEEN

WRATH OF THE LUMINETH

His found his fingers straying to it often – the skull of Kathanos, tied to his saddle by a strip of leather. Akridos tapped his fingers against the flaking pate as he watched the vast column of Mortek Guard march past, fifty abreast. The column stretched back a mile at least, the end of it invisible beneath a rising haze of dust. The Deathriders flanked the infantry on either side, in two great blocks, and behind them trundled the Harvesters and Crawlers, the Necropolis Stalkers forming a rearguard, the Immortis Guard ranked up behind Akridos as his personal retinue. The mountains of Paerthalann were far behind them now, squatting in the west, diamond shards picked out by the rising sun. Dawn broke across the plains of Ymetrica, a wash of gentle light that gilded the grass and set the faded ruins glowing in the fields. The Ossiarch army had marched all night – unlike mortal troops, there was no need for rest, no need for food or sustenance. Akridos cantered his steed and looked off towards their final target. The soft glint of Y'gethin's temple was no more than fifty miles away now, the immense bulk of the mountain rising up behind it.

To say that Ultharadon dominated the landscape would be a gross understatement, wholly inadequate to the scale and impression the mountain gave. Even in the endless pale plains of Ymetrica, the grass shimmering under the light of the risen dawn, the rolling downs flowing off towards the far silver line of the continental sea, it was a structure of sublime and almost terrifying imposition. Behind the Bonereapers lay the heights of the Paerthalann, and off to the south and north were the jagged spines of other ranges – it was a mountainous country, the plains ringed by massifs and sierras on all sides. But Ultharadon was like to these as the continent itself would be to an island off its coast. Akridos wondered at the earliest days of civilisation in this realm, and how naturally the aelves stumbling into the light would have been drawn to this place. Even fifty miles away, it was almost too big to take in. Only the sky above it, an infinite, painterly canvas of washed-out blue and cirrus white, seemed in the least bit commensurate to its scale.

'Yes,' Akridos whispered to the skull on his saddle, his fingers looping into its empty eye sockets. 'You see it, Kathanos, don't you? That mountain is what we must defile, and to range our forces against it will be the greatest test we have ever faced. But look.' He twisted the skull around, so the dead bone could see the marching troops. 'See what we bring to the battle. An army greater than any I have ever wielded before.'

He was aware then of the Immortis Guard watching him, awaiting his instruction. The bone giants strode behind him at half-pace, to maintain the proper distance. Akridos let Kathanos' head fall back and turned his attention to the plains. He cantered onwards, hand drifting once again to the soulmason's sundered skull. Rattling there on his saddle, it brought back some of his earliest memories, the impossibly distant days when he had been a man on the Stalliarch Plains and had ridden with a horde at his back, his enemies' severed heads jouncing at his side. A horde of death-dealers and killers, the finest horsemen in the realm, back when he was a king…

He had been powerful then, but as Akridos looked back on the army trailing in his wake, subject to his every command, he knew that he was several magnitudes more powerful now. The troops had been bolstered by thousands of recruits since they had first set foot on Hysh, all the scavenged dead of Ymetrica, from the Scintilla Realmgate to Paerthalann, and more besides.

'Nagash wills it,' he said to Kathanos' skull, puzzled for a moment that the skull did not reply. Akridos cackled, a crisp sound that wavered above the tread of his steed. He drummed his fingers on the skull's pate. 'You never understood, Kathanos. You could never raise your perspective higher than the task in front of your face. Nagash gives us free will not just to make us more efficient in the field, but because it pleases him to do so. It is part of his design. And to have free will is to have the opportunity to act in ways that please Nagash.' He looked again at the dry bone, the pinched, narrow teeth, the crusty brown flakes that fell whenever he passed his fingers over the skull. 'I am the pivot on which his conquest depends,' he said. 'I will kill Y'gethin, then I will destroy the Light of Eltharion, and then I will carve my empire from the lands where Nagash has placed me, in his infinite wisdom. These plains will be mine, as the Stalliarch Plains are mine, as Hysh itself will be mine in turn.'

He laughed again, tipping his head back, screaming his delight at the wide wash of the infinite sky, and all the teeming thousands of his army marched on before him.

They stood on the flat ground before the temple, a hundred yards down from the forecourt and the fountain. The grasslands rose and fell before them, stretching off towards the west, the great black shadow of Ultharadon cast down against the grass by the rising sun. The wind coursed wickedly over the plains, hurtling around the shoulder of the mountain to race across the flat ground, as if desperately sprinting away from them. That was some comfort, Alithis thought. At least it wouldn't blow the stink of the dead towards them.

Carreth stood beside her, immobile, his face strangely blank and impassive. He stood as if deep in meditation, his hands resting lightly on his staff, his robes shifting slightly in the breeze. For the first time, Alithis couldn't think of anything to say to him. She felt uncomfortable – there was something reverent and dreadful about him since he had clawed his way up from the valley beneath the mountain. She had been flooded with relief when she saw him striding across the greensward, but now... she was almost scared. He had not spoken of what he had seen there, but it had changed him, she knew, and he looked out now on the marching hordes of the Bonereapers with complete dispassion.

Alithis shivered, although with more than the cold of the breeze. She clutched her stratum hammers, her robes cascading out before her. The Stoneguard were set up in ranks on either side, their respective right and left flanks anchored on their seneschal. There were no more than a hundred of them, in two blocks of fifty.

'Small numbers only make the deeds greater,' Belfinnan said, grinning. He looked down at her from his horse, Gyfillim. The stallion ducked his head and whinnied, a gruff exclamation, as if impatient to get to battle. The breeze played about his silver mane, and his barding shone like starlight. Alithis reached up and patted the beast's mottled neck.

'Take care of him,' she said to the horse. 'You know how reckless he can be.'

'How bold, you mean, surely?' Belfinnan offered.

Alithis smiled up at the steedmaster. Their eyes met, and in the shattering pale blue of Belfinnan's gaze there was something like a well-hidden sadness. There was determination there too, though, and the same courage that Alithis felt flowing through her veins. Forlorn hope or not, they would both fight like champions.

'One more time?' Belfinnan said.

'One more time.'

'Then let's see if we can put these dead men in the ground again, once and for all.'

Belfinnan spurred his horse forward, hurtling off down the pilgrim path in a clatter of stones to meet up with his Dawnriders far over on the right flank. Alithis watched the riders form up on the grass, no more than three hundred of them strung out along the line of a slight rise. The grass was higher here and almost reached the stomachs of the horses. Alithis turned and saw the remaining wardens, grim and deadly, sprinting from the temple grounds to take up position on either side of the Stoneguard. They straddled the pilgrim road that led from the temple and stretched off like a pale river down across the plains, curving away towards the road for Scintilla and the Realmgate a thousand miles away. She looked at the temple a hundred yards behind them, cold now, the stone strangely dull, emptied of everyone who could hold a pike or wield a blade. The library staff, the minor votaries, had either picked up arms or had been sent away. Alithis smiled to see Ilmarrin standing by the fountain. She doubted even the command of Teclis himself would have elicited more than a raised eyebrow from the old retainer. Beyond the temple, so present in the landscape that it was easy to overlook it, rose the catastrophic heights of Ultharadon, the holy mountain, on which all their hopes now rested, and in whose shadow they were ready to make their stand.

Alithis looked back down the line of the pilgrim's way, where it twisted off to the south-west, towards lost Paerthalann. The plains grass rippled, a sheet of emerald and gold studded with the lost ruins of elder days. She could see the Bonereapers coming, marching with rigid precision, perhaps no more than a mile or two away now, and the sight of them despoiling the pilgrim route made her grind her teeth. A sepia haze surrounded them, the dust kicked up by their passing feet. It rose into the air like the smoke from a burning forest.

'It won't be long now,' Carreth said. He was dressed in the full robes of an Alarith Stonemage, his horned helmet like the crown of an Ymetrican longhorn. The scintillant blue skies shone above them. 'Akridos draws close, and one way or the other, this war will be won.'

'By which side?' she said, with an attempted levity that she didn't really feel.

Carreth smiled, as if thinking on a secret he was only too eager to share. His skin was glowing, she noticed, even in this clear light – a pale blue suffusion.

Standing next to him, the dark backing to the mirror of his light, Thaerannan the Desolate stepped forward. Her bare feet hardly made an impression in the grass, and the smoke that billowed from her censer, immune to the wind, pooled around them. She looked at Alithis through the veil that covered her face, shimmering in the soft light.

'There can only be victory for us here,' she said. 'For if the other side wins, it will be more than defeat. It will be… the end. Of the enlightenment of Hysh, the sacredness of Ultharadon, of everything.'

Alithis tried to meet her eye but had to look away. In many ways, the Cathallar frightened her more than the dead. She remembered the agonised hours as they waited for Carreth to return from the valley, not even sure if he had died down there. Alithis had paced the cloisters, trying to give the impression that she was deep in thought, although in truth she had felt almost paralysed with uncertainty. Belfinnan had sprawled on one of the garden benches in the shade of a weeping woe tree, idly picking the flax from its discarded seeds. Aelthuwi had been riddled with nerves and had knelt praying in the sanctuary, gazing up at the fresco of Ultharadon. Only Thaerannan had seemed unperturbed. She had walked in the gardens with the veil covering her face, her censer never out of her hand, her lips whispering hushed prayers. Wherever she walked, the grass seemed to shrivel and die. She stood there now as if this were all no more than she had foreseen, as if victory or defeat would be an equal sadness. Alithis looked away. This dread of waiting, of feeling your sweat slick on the grips of your weapons, was almost more than she could bear. She thought of Dae'annis. She thought of Tuareth. Neither helped.

'Now,' Carreth said. He took his staff from Aelthuwi, at his side. 'Take the Stoneguard out, Alithis. Meet them head-on and remember everything we discussed. This will be a sore day, I cannot deny it, but at the end of it the temple will stand. This I promise you.'

A mile from the temple, the army spread out and formed up in the spear of the mountain's shadow. The shadow fell against the rippled grass, black as a chasm carved into the earth itself. Above, the light of the orbiting spheres began to bend and refract around the mountain's northern edge, spilling like a white tide around its mottled flank. The temple sat there in its lee, a thing of perfect symmetry rendered in faintly glowing white stone, attached to the foothills of the mountain by a narrow ridge. Akridos shuddered to look at it. He glanced up, craning his skeletal neck to take in the highest peaks and pinnacles of Ultharadon, and even to his monstrous mix of souls the scale of the thing was awe-inspiring. High above, white streaks of light blended with the pale sky – the lattice of magic that crossed Hysh and cascaded its beneficent balm down onto the realm entire, and to the realms beyond. To capture that light, Akridos knew, was for the aelves a means of constructing their realmstone, the foundation of their art and culture. He sneered to look at that light, even as he felt it buzzing against his bones. When Ymetrica was his, no such light would despoil the purity of his dark, abandoned skies.

The land ahead of him was perfect for war. For the most part the ground was flat, unobstructed. There was a wide meadow of long grass on the right flank, rolling off in dips and hollows for a mile or two, but there were no trees, no outcrops of stone, no structures or ditches to prevent a sustained assault. In front of the temple, about a hundred yards from its courtyard and the glittering water of its fountain, the aelves had set up palisades and barriers of sharpened stakes. He could see their troops mustering in front of these defences, noted the gap in the centre where they would funnel back in if they needed to retreat. On the left, the ground sloped gently away for half a mile, from the temple's northern quadrangle to the edge of a valley, a place where they would certainly anchor their line. He could see a jostling wedge of the aelven cavalry forming up there, trailing back towards the ridge line.

'Miszoios,' he called. The lead hekatos marched over with a clatter of bones and armour, his spear held at arms. 'Bring up the Mortek Guard and form in depth on the left and centre – eight regiments deep.' He gazed again at the glinting progress of the Lumineth troops. There were pitifully few of them, but he was now experienced enough to know that the aelves were most dangerous when they seemed their most vulnerable. 'Ten regiments deep,' Akridos corrected himself. 'Press forward when engaged but leave enough space between each regiment so the Deathriders have room to redeploy at speed.'

'Yes, my liege,' Miszoios said.

'Spears to the front, ready to receive the charge of their horse. Receive, then advance when their cavalry breaks off. *Advance.*' Akridos hammered his fist on the pommel of his saddle. 'Always advance – we cannot give them a moment to seize the initiative.'

'It will be done.'

Miszoios saluted and marched back to the huge column of Guard, passing his orders on to his subordinates. Slowly, the great flood of infantry reformed into their respective regiments and took up position on a narrow front. Akridos spurred his steed down the central corridor between the mustering units, hauling the reins around until he faced the front.

'Strength in depth, Kathanos, do you see?' he hissed at the dead skull. Idly he stroked it, his appraising gaze sweeping out across his army as it moved into its battle formations. 'Here is where our weight of numbers will truly count.'

Takanos, the second-in-command of his Deathriders, rode up. Akridos barely needed to tell him what to do – they thought as one in these situations.

'Two thousand Deathriders to the right flank, enveloping strike,' Takanos offered.

Akridos nodded, well satisfied. 'Stop for nothing,' he said. 'Cut up their left and put pressure on the temple as quickly as possible. I will keep one thousand under my command, ready to exploit any gaps.'

'That long grass...' Takanos mused. He adjusted the strap of his helmet, loosened his sword in its scabbard.

'No doubt the aelven scum have prepared some traps for us. Take care for cavalry pits and trenches. As long as some of you get through, they will have to retire from their centre or risk losing the temple.'

'And they will not want to do that?'

Akridos unhooked Kathanos' skull from where it dangled on its strap.

'Indeed not,' he said. He stared into the hollow sockets of the skull's eyes. 'Kathanos himself informed me of their dedication to their feeble culture, didn't you, soulmason? It means everything to them, and they'll defend it to the last.'

Akridos felt the aelf soul shivering inside him, a flickering pulse of light that flared and dimmed in the heart of his soul gem. He shuddered, ground his teeth together. He looked at Takanos, holding out the soulmason's skull as if expecting it to speak. Takanos demonstrated not a shade of emotion. He finished adjusting his helmet strap and raised his arm to signal his wing of the Deathriders.

There was a rumble like breaking thunder as the dead horsemen drew up. Two thousand steeds hammering the ground, four thousand stirrups snapping against dry bone, two thousand spears jangling in dead hands. The screeched instructions from the hekatoi of each troop were like the carrion calls of scavenging birds. Akridos watched them break past the Mortek Guard, fanning out on the right, the dry grass of the meadow sloping upwards towards the rough field of tall grass. The temple caught a beam of the spreading sun as the light slipped further around the line of the mountain, sparkling like struck water. Takanos cantered up and down the line of Deathriders, issuing instructions. He drew his sword and positioned himself at the centre, at the tip of the spear. He twisted in his saddle and lifted his sword in salute. Akridos raised his hand, palm outwards, and then snapped it down. Far over on the right, Takanos nodded and pointed his sword towards the temple. His jaw moved, and a moment later Akridos could hear the shrieked command: 'Charge!'

The storm broke. The Deathriders thundered across the grass, a whirlwind of bone and steel. It was dry, well-tended ground, perfect for cavalry. Some of the riders had already couched their lances, waiting to spear their enemies the moment they appeared. The riders came in waves, in lines a hundred across, perfectly dressed to left and right. Not one was out of place. The ground shook with mad, discordant drums as their hoofbeats fell. Light caught the edge of their spear tips, the flash of polished helmets and breastplates, the thick barding of the steeds. Some of the riders were still flecked with blood from their construction, from the fresh bones harvested in the pass after their victory.

Akridos leaned forward in the saddle and signalled for his own troop of Deathriders to form up in the centre, down the narrow channels between the regiments of Mortek Guard. Once Takanos had put pressure on the Lumineth's left flank, the aelves would need to respond quickly or be overwhelmed, and that moment was rapidly approaching. He saw the Lumineth infantry scurrying into position in front of their barricades, their pikes and shields glinting as the morning began to swell beyond the mountain, breaking across its pinnacles and slopes.

'Mortek Guard!' Miszoios shrieked. 'Advance!'

The infantry began their ponderous march, unit by unit, regiment by regiment – half-steps, regular and precise, a thudding procession in contrast to the Deathriders' discordant thunder. Akridos watched the troops file past him, glanced up the field to observe the Lumineth dressing their ranks, pikes levelled, the troops in the centre wielding those vicious hammers that had caused so many casualties in the pass. Their cavalry jostled on the left, where the ground dipped into the valley, but gave no signal that they were ready to move.

He clutched Kathanos' skull, his other hand gripping the pommel of his saddle. He snapped his gaze to the lines of Deathriders as they reached the tall grass on the other side of the battlefield. The Mortek Guard continued to trudge up the sloped ground towards the temple, and his own troop of cavalry was now positioned in two great columns five abreast, the Guard funnelling by them on either side. Still the aelves did not respond. Akridos looked to the Deathriders again. He saw the beams of light bend and stab out from the flank of the mountain, felt that coruscating power as it swept across him, blinding him, blinding the Mortek Guard as they moved towards it, dazzling the Deathriders as they began their wheeling sweep to strike the temple on its southern side.

Something was wrong. He felt it. A thousand years of war, hundreds of battles, and he had never been more certain of anything.

'Kathanos,' he said, his voice hollow.

He gripped the skull. He looked at the Deathriders half a mile away now, far out on the right of the Ossiarch army. He picked out Takanos at the front as he stood up in his stirrups, sword pointed, jaw clashing soundlessly.

'It's too late... I can't call them back...'

Then, from deep in the tall grass, hundreds of aelves suddenly stood up and nocked their arrows. Even above the thunder of the charging steeds, Akridos could hear the high, piercing call of their captain giving the order – and then a thousand arrows were speeding like bolts of lightning across the grass, tearing from those deadly three-stringed bows. No more than a hundred yards separated the aelves from the Bonereapers who would ride them down, but the aelves were expert shots and not a shaft was wasted. It was as if the Ossiarch cavalry were facing the concentrated fire of a hundred bolt-throwers – with machine-like precision the aelves fired, nocked, drew, fired again. The field was alive with light, blazing from the risen sun and searing across the grass from the aelves' silver arrows.

Akridos watched the Deathriders fall in their hundreds. Steeds were blown apart in a spray of bone; riders fell, were trampled by the ones who charged behind them. Shields split and breastplates were pierced, and the whole line shuddered as if trying to pass through an invisible barrier. Those charging in the second and third lines, too close to wheel aside, crashed into the leading rank and fell in a tangle of bone. In moments, the lower half of the field was a like a charnel pit, a floundering morass of shattered bodies and broken armour. Those few Deathriders who had managed to break through the aelves' murderous fire tipped their lances and tried to charge, but whenever they came within a spear's length one of the archers would calmly turn aside and pluck them from the saddle with a well-aimed shot.

It was chaos, a disordered madness. Akridos couldn't see Takanos anywhere – he must have fallen in the first fusillade. The surviving Deathriders tried to pivot and retreat from the field, but the arrows of the aelves fell on them like a bitter rain, sweeping them from their saddles. Akridos watched in rage and incredulity as fully one half of his Deathriders were cut to pieces, not a single one spared from the aelves' vengeance. As the light poured down from the east, making the vast cathedral of Ultharadon into a monstrous black silhouette, he screamed for the legion to advance at pace.

'Forward, Mortek Guard!' he howled. 'Deathriders, on me! Strike to the left!' He chopped his sword down towards the temple, resplendent in the rising light. 'Crawlers, raze that temple to the ground!'

She remembered the moment he emerged from the valley, his robes no more than tattered rags, his face bruised and bloody. Aelthuwi had seen him first. Too fraught with nerves to stay in any one place for long, the young apprentice had walked in the gardens for a while, resolutely keeping his distance from Thaerannan, and had then paced his way out to the forecourt, where he sat by the fountain and nervously splashed his fingers in the water. Alithis had been sitting on the steps in front of the rotunda, watching him, watching the water shear and cascade from the fountain. Aelthuwi's cry had alerted all of them, and Belfinnan and Ilmarrin came running as Aelthuwi stood and pointed. Alithis had followed his direction and seen Carreth stumbling across the lawn, crossing from the slope of the valley to the forecourt. At first glance he looked like a beggar, or like one of those crazed ascetics the humans in Settler's Gain seemed to produce, maddened by their love of Sigmar. He had a calm and beatific expression on his face, and his skin was suffused with that same pale glow he'd had when he met with the Mage God in his dreams. The strain that he had carried like a burden since his sister had first visited him was gone – it had smoothed out into a look of cool, clear certainty. He looked, she realised, like the Carreth Y'gethin she had known long ago, before the trials of war had hardened him, before sorrow had carved its signature in his skin. He looked like someone who had passed beyond such concepts as sorrow and grief. It was sad, in a way. He was someone else now. Someone infinitely more powerful, and infinitely more dangerous.

Well, she thought. She looked at the tide of death unrolling towards her, the advancing Bonereapers infantry with their blazing green eyes marching on a narrow front, each one seeming to stare straight into her soul. Spears and swords glinted, armour was battered with war, shields were notched. Veterans of a hundred battles, and victors of as many. *There will be time to mourn the old Carreth when this is done. I hope...*

'Wardens!' she cried. 'Stoneguard! It seems we have guests – let's make sure to give them a warm welcome.'

Two thousand aelves bellowed and clashed their weapons together, chanting their war cries, calling on the power of Ultharadon and invoking the runes of *Senthoi, Ydriliqi, Senlui, Alaithi* – whichever they had dedicated themselves to. Alithis cut down with her right hammer and the Stoneguard smoothly ran through the gaps between the barriers, forming up in three units beyond them. She cut down with her left hammer and the wardens filled the gaps between the Stoneguard, their sunmetal pikes already glowing from the charging spells of their captains, enhanced by the aetherquartz gems each wore on breastplate or helmet. Alithis sprinted across the grass to take up her position in the centre. She felt a chill creep up the back of her neck and turned to see Thaerannan standing not a dozen feet from her, veil shifting in a diaphanous dance across her face, black robes billowing out behind her, the inverted crescent of her headdress glimmering in the light. She raised her censer and bowed her head.

'Go, aelves of the Lumineth,' she cried, in a voice like the wind howling through a lonely mountain pass. 'Fight, and fear not, for all things must die in time.'

They advanced at a steady pace, pikes levelled, the Stoneguard resting their hammers and picks on their shoulders. The Bonereapers came on, foot by foot, shields raised, swords and spears drawn back for the first blow. Arrows came sailing in from the left like meteors, streaks of white light blazing down into the Bonereapers' right flank. The sentinels were thick in the tall grass, ranked up near the ruins of the enemy cavalry.

'Keep the line,' Alithis shouted, as much for herself as for the troops. Fifty feet now, closer and closer. She could smell them as the wind shifted, the rank stench of the dead. More arrows fell, a constant percussion. Some of the Bonereapers on the left tried to form a testudo, shields raised above their heads, but with unerring precision the sentinels' arrows found the gaps and laced through them. She could hear the crackling commands as the dead captains gave their orders, the Bonereaper line shifting slightly, wheeling around on the right.

By the Mage God, though, there were thousands of them, thousands and thousands. It was absurd, she thought as they closed the gap. They were going to be overwhelmed. She girded herself. Thirty feet now. They upped the pace, moving into a light run, pikes still level, hammers drawn back from the shoulders. Alithis panted, heart pounding. Twenty feet now, faster and faster.

'Ready,' she cried. 'Get ready!'

The pulse of magic around her, the high wardens charging the sunmetal of their weapons. She risked a glance back, saw Thaerannan keeping pace with them, thin and black, like the trunk of a dead tree. Above, rolling slabs of stone wreathed in green lightning fell towards the temple, cursed stelae flung up by the Ossiarch artillery. Alithis saw a burst of blue flame, a buffeting wave of light, and then the slabs were plucked from the sky and thrown back towards the Ossiarch lines, tumbling end over end, smashing whole units to pieces.

Ten feet, pikes level. Alithis clutched her hammers, teeth bared.

'Charge!' she shouted as the shields came up, the dead men grinning, a tide of them crowding out the world, their mad green eyes like poison, their stench, the clacking jaws, their yellow teeth. 'Charge!' she screamed. 'Charge!'

The pikes came down. The hammers swung.

Carreth saw another one begin to fall and reached up to sweep the rolling slab of cursed stone from the sky with a blast of geomantic energy. He gripped it in flight, warped the pull of gravity around it and directed the stone deep into the Bonereapers' ranks. He floated on a throne of rock by the edge of the forecourt, ten feet off the ground, his staff across his lap. Aelthuwi muttered prayers somewhere beneath him, lending his power to Carreth as the Stonemage swept more artillery shot from the sky. There were too many, though – dozens were thrown off course, but for every ten he misdirected at least one got through. He watched a roiling cauldron of tormented spirits dip and fall on a strangely gentle parabola towards the temple, sailing over his head, smacking somewhere behind him as it struck the rotunda with a shriek of agony and the crash of shattered stone. He didn't turn. He felt as well as heard the gibbering agony of the trapped spirits spilling from their broken prison, sweeping across the forecourt, weaving through the falling masonry of the struck rotunda.

'Aelthuwi, if you please,' he said. He glanced down. The apprentice was struck dumb, staring back towards the temple and at the approaching tide of spirits.

'Master, I... I...'

Carreth sighed. 'It's perfectly simple,' he said. He turned on his rocky throne and grimaced. The cauldron had hit the left pillar of the rotunda, shearing it in half. A green mist that shuddered with rising skeletal faces, with spectral fingers and tendrils as sharp as blades, was rolling towards them across the forecourt. Carreth raised his hand, muttered half a dozen arcane phrases, and it dissipated like fog in the wind. Aelthuwi looked ashamed as Carreth shook his head.

'Alithis has engaged!' the apprentice said. He pointed to the Lumineth's front rank beyond the stakes and the short palisades as they struck the Bonereapers head-on. There was a blinding flash of blue light, a recoil that shuddered the ground, drifts of smoke – and when the smoke cleared, whisked off by the changing breeze, Carreth saw that the Ossiarch centre had been immolated. He saw wardens and Stoneguard stab and smash with eerie precision, lancing in with their pikes or sweeping their hammers down, splintering bone, shattering armour. The aelven troops looked insignificant in the middle of that bone tide, a blazing point of light in the middle of a blackened sheet. He knew the Ossiarch army was advancing in depth on a narrow front, but even then, they easily outstretched the width of the temple.

A hundred yards, but not close enough... not yet, not yet...

'Master, Alithis is in danger of being overwhelmed! Shall I give the order?'

'Hold,' Carreth said. He grasped his staff, felt the wind shift, smelled the change in the air. 'They must hold just a moment longer...'

He looked off to the right, pointed out Belfinnan's Dawnriders far over on the other side of the field, past the line of the pilgrim's way, as they finally sprang free and charged down the Ossiarch left. Skimming the very edge of the valley, the riders streaked in single file like the beams of aetheric light that crossed the heavens above them – the light of Hysh itself, fleet and unstoppable. The torn grass sprayed from their hooves; their polished silver armour was parade ground bright. Carreth could hear Belfinnan's wild, high war cry as he led from the front, raised up in his stirrups, sword waving above his head. On they went, tearing past the blocks of Bonereaper infantry, some of the Ossiarch troops trying to reform and pivot to take a charge that never came. The passage between the Ossiarch army and the edge of the valley was narrow, and a moment's misjudgement would have doomed the whole manoeuvre, but Belfinnan was a master at reading the moments of battle – his timing was perfect. They swept past the enemy troops, curved right like a sickle cutting grass and spread out to charge the Bonereapers' foul war machines at the rear of their force. From his position floating above the battlefield, Carreth could see the Dawnriders swarming around the ponderous catapults and those foul, beetle-like creatures with their sickle hands. Despite their numbers, for a moment it was as if the Bonereapers were being pinned between two forces, either of which they could have swatted away with ease.

Carreth watched Belfinnan signal his riders, saw the glinting specks of the warhorses break away from the wrecked war machines on the other side of the Ossiarch tide. His glance flicked back and forth across the brawling spread of troops – enemies and friends – and the moment crept closer, closer. There would be only one chance to snatch it, and once it was gone it would never come back.

'Hold…' he muttered. 'Hold, Alithis…'

He could see her on the other side of the barriers, lashing out with her hammers in the centre of her Stoneguard, never letting herself get too bogged down in the fight, aware always of the battle's ebb and flow. The Bonereaper infantry were pressing in on the left and right now, thousands of troops pivoting and reforming, jostling to fill the space where their centre had been blown to pieces by the magically charged blades of the Lumineth force. Spent bone was scattered around the field, crunched underfoot, kicked aside – bone, and bodies where aelves had fallen. Carreth's breath was shallow in his chest. He read the battle as if scanning the equations of a spell he had been practising for weeks, familiar and unfamiliar still, intricate and opaque, perfectly balanced. He felt beyond calm as he waited for the moment. Since clambering from the deep fog of the valley, hauling himself from the very depths of his self-hatred and despair, he knew he had progressed another rung on the Teclamentari. It was more than the power he felt coursing through him – now, the breadth of emotions he had tried so hard to master all his life had been smoothed away. He felt almost detached, as if the desperate fight that was playing out before him were no more than an intricate manoeuvre on a chess board. He felt neither anxiety nor excitement, only a cool certainty that everything would unfold to the design he had crafted. He reached up and touched Tuareth's aetherquartz brooch, hanging from its silver chain around his neck, the shrivelled crust of the jewel as hard as iron under his fingers. He felt nothing.

Alithis' force had been pushed back almost to the barriers. Inconceivably, they were still fighting as a coherent unit – five thousand troops holding off near ten times that number. Aelves thrust and stabbed, smashed down with their hammers, their captains chanting the incantations that would charge their weapons. Aetherquartz on breastplates and weapon hilts blazed like holy fire, burning, bright as trapped stars, channelling even greater arcane force into the high wardens' spells. Behind the Lumineth front, her bare feet planted firmly on the grass, Thaerannan the Desolate sang her sorrowful, elegiac song and drew the raw emotions from the aetherquartz, conducting it back in rippling waves of black energy towards the Bonereaper ranks. They did not feel as living things felt, but the sheer emotional weight of the energy was enough to unsettle the foul amalgam of spirits in their soul gems. Spiritually dislocated, some of the skeletal warriors stumbled and fell, and were trampled to pieces under the feet of their advancing comrades. The grass under Thaerannan's feet was a grey wasteland, spreading out to stain the pilgrim's way. But no matter how many they cut down, the Bonereapers had seemingly infinite coin to spend. The dead warriors fell, were replaced, and pressed on.

'Aelthuwi,' Carreth said. 'It is time.'

Aelthuwi swallowed, his eyes darting to the battlefield beyond the courtyard. He held his apprentice's staff in both hands, gripping it like a shield. He looked across the spread of grassland, where in happier days the long pilgrim's route had begun, and where the army had formed up only a few weeks before to begin their doomed march towards Paerthalann Pass.

'Yes, master,' he said in a small, scared voice.

Carreth watched the young apprentice sprint off across the grass, threading his way through the interlocking screen of spiked barriers. He leapt the ditches and headed towards Alithis' position, stopping just before he reached Thaerannan, who sang her dirge and was enveloped in the smoke of her censer while waves of dark energy flowed from her upraised hand. Carreth saw Aelthuwi raise his staff in his right hand, his left held palm outwards, and despite the distance he knew the words the apprentice was chanting. Carreth had taught them to him himself.

A ball of blue light materialised in the space between Aelthuwi's palm and the head of his staff. As the young aelf raised his hands the light became deeper and brighter, and at an uttered command it sped off across the battlefield like a shooting star, curving over the heads of aelves and Bonereapers alike and disappearing far down the choked path of the pilgrim's way. Aelthuwi staggered backwards, spent, but his job was done – the Lumineth forces had seen the signal, and even Carreth could hear the seneschal's bellowed command.

'Retreat!' she shouted, snapping out one of her hammers to smash a Bonereaper's skull to fragments. 'Wardens, Stoneguard! Back to the temple!'

The line had splintered in the centre. On the right, the furthermost elements were being cut down by the aelven cavalry as they swung back towards the temple from their assault on the Crawlers in the rear. The left was unengaged and still pushing on, but not fast enough – not nearly fast enough.

Akridos scanned the milling brawl at the centre, peering over the heads of his infantry as they funnelled themselves into the maelstrom – the spark and hiss of the aelves' pikes as they sheared through the Guards' armour, the answering clatter as the skeletal troops hacked down with their swords or thrust with their spears to pierce aelven flesh. So much of warfare, he knew, was just the careful logistics of moving the right pieces into the right places at the right time.

'Onwards, Mortek Guard!' he shouted, stabbing his scimitar towards the dwindling band of aelves as they were pushed back to their barriers. 'Give them no quarter!'

The Lumineth temple hung there as the backdrop to the aelves' stand. The dome shone inviolate, but he could see the listing pillar where it had been struck by the Crawlers' artillery shot, the craters in the forecourt, the debris scattered across the flagstones. Their cavalry was cantering quickly up the far right of the Ossiarch army now, skirting the edge of the field of tall grass where those damned archers had destroyed the first wave of Deathriders. Akridos saw the archers running forward to the edge of the field, shooting as they went, casting down another storm of blazing rain against the advancing Bonereapers. On the left, the ground sloped steeply down into the valley at the base of the mountain, a natural anchor for the Ossiarch flank as the army surged forward.

Akridos saw a spark of blue flame, a ball of light leaping up and searing across the battlefield from the Lumineth rear. The aelves in the centre began what he was forced to concede was the most perfect and disciplined withdrawal he had ever seen. The coordination was impeccable, the front rank disengaging and sprinting backwards while the second rank stabbed out between the gaps with their pikes, the hammer-wielding aelves on the flanks then stepping forward at the same time, unleashing a brutal, swinging assault that had the Mortek reeling. Again and again they performed this dance, and as far as Akridos could tell they lost not a single aelf while doing it. There was nothing in warfare as complicated as an organised retreat, and they had not put a foot wrong.

At least, not yet...

He saw the gap open, the pressure from the Guard forcing the aelves to pivot on their left flank when they should have closed on their right. They drew back further, half the aelven troops funnelling through the barrier of viciously sharpened stakes while the other half held off the crush of Ossiarch troops. They had seen the danger as well – some ran diagonally to take up defensive positions on the other side of the courtyard, the trenches and pits and barriers keeping them momentarily safe from the Ossiarch left flank.

They were going to abandon the temple…

The temple was a distraction, he realised. All they needed to do was hold up the Ossiarch army long enough before retreating into the foothills of Ultharadon, a fortress more impregnable than any walled city in the realm.

Arrows fell, bolts of steel and tempered wood. The Mortek Guard were being spitted all across the line, but where one warrior fell another dozen stepped up to take his place.

'Deathriders!' Akridos screamed. 'Take the left, along the line of the valley! Now, before they can reach the slopes of their cursed mountain!'

The Stonemage, Y'gethin, glowed like an afterburn from a lightning strike on the forecourt of the temple. He hovered ten feet above the ground, held aloft on some throne of rock, and he was plucking ragged lumps of stone from the earth itself and flinging them deep into the Ossiarch ranks. Handfuls of Mortek Guard were crushed and broken with every shot, splintered to pieces, bones sent sailing over the heads of their comrades. Aetheric energy crackled across the Stonemage's fingertips. Akridos sneered as their eyes met across the battlefield, and the lurch of sympathy in his soul gem turned his sneer into a snarl of pain and rage.

'Y'gethin…' he muttered. He marked the Stonemage with the point of his sword. 'Two armies lie between us, Y'gethin, but you will die on the edge of my blade before this day is through. I swear it!'

The mage saw him. His face was blank and impassive, wreathed in a bluster of magical energy. Akridos hauled his steed to break further up the left flank, his Deathriders threading between the marching regiments to form up on the very edge of the valley, where the aelven horse had earlier made its charge. A thousand skeletal cavalry were soon packed tightly on a narrow strip of ground, their riders readying their weapons, hefting their shields into position. The valley tumbled off below them, a rucked slope of grey stone and brown grass that vanished into a morass of rolling fog. The mountain loomed ahead of them, soaring up from the valley, too big to comprehend, the lower slopes dipping down in great sheets and narrowing to the broad, grassy ridge that connected them with the temple grounds. The light had fully risen now, a nimbus of white and gold that cascaded from the crown of the mountain to drown the battlefield. Akridos steadied his steed, pulled the reins, screamed for his riders to charge.

'Cut them all down!' he howled. 'Don't let even one escape!'

The riders charged, the sound of their hooves muttering through the earth. Pushing against each other, straining for space, some surging forward, some forced to fall back, the Deathriders barrelled across the grass towards the ridge line, a river of bone and metal. Shards of rock as big as their own shields spiralled out of the clean morning air, gifts from the Stonemage. A dozen Deathriders were smashed aside, the broken bodies of steeds and riders swept clean over the edge and down into the misty valley. Akridos ducked, shrinking into the saddle as a boulder hissed past him and disappeared into the valley below.

'On, my Deathriders!' he shrieked at the head of the column, his crackling voice whining high over the sound of their hooves. 'Onwards, to death, to ruin!'

The ground lurched. There was a clatter of falling stone from the higher slopes of Ultharadon, rocks and boulders tumbling down and spinning off into the mists of the valley. Akridos stumbled, his steed pitching to the side. The light trembled around him, disrupted, as if the mountain itself were shaking. The Deathriders, so close to the edge of the ridge, pulled up short as the earth beneath them violently heaved.

Akridos righted himself, casting about for the source of the disruption. An earthquake? Some self-destructive magic unleashed by the Stonemage as he realised that he was on the edge of defeat?

A low, percussive boom came up from the valley.

There was a long, troubled pause, and then another reverberating clash, like stone shattering against stone, like mountains being torn up by the roots. Mist billowed, threads of vaporous fumes that scattered in the fine, clear air. Another boom, a shudder across the ground.

'Keep moving!' Akridos bellowed to his Deathriders, trying to spur them on, but all across the battlefield it was as if the warring armies were poised to see what would happen next. He stared down into the fuming smoke of the valley, the hooves of his steed dislodging a trickle of stones down into the abyss.

And then it emerged.

It shouldered its way from the mist like the roots of the mountain itself, thrown up from the earth and spearing into the sky, trailing all the wreckage and detritus of the valley with it.

At first Akridos couldn't tell what it was. Wreathed in fog, a great slab of stone blocking out the light, it cast its massive shadow down onto the grass. He shied back, darting out of the way to avoid a huge cloven foot that thundered onto the sward. Akridos stared up at the creature, incredulous – thirty feet of stone clad in slabs of tarnished, nacreous armour, hewn rock sprouting from its massive shoulders like weird echoes of Ultharadon's own peaks and pinnacles. Twisted trees had hooked their roots into the crevices of the creature's shoulders, and its flanks were mottled with ivy and moss. As Akridos craned his neck to look up, desperately shying back to avoid its other foot as it stomped up onto the level ground, he saw that its face was like an abstract mask of some horned beast, like the longhorns they had seen near the mountains of Paerthalann. Striding up onto the grass before the temple, the Deathriders scattering out of its way, the creature hefted a massive hammer that was more than twenty feet long, its twin head a glinting flat anvil of polished rock that flashed with sparks of blue lightning. It tipped its head back, the polished jet of its curved horns sweeping out before it, and bellowed a roar that shook the very ground. Lightning crackled about its head. As it tipped its gaze back down to the milling horsemen at its feet, its cold blue eyes sparkled with rage and hatred.

'Fall back!' Akridos screamed. 'Scatter, reform in the centre!'

But it was too late for that manoeuvre now. It was too late to do anything but try to bear the brunt of the assault. Akridos watched the creature raise its huge hammer and sweep it down as if scything grass, and the hammer fell with all the relentless inertia of an avalanche.

He stabbed his heels into his steed's flanks and made a desperate leap forward. Dozens more Deathriders followed him, while others tried to haul themselves around and retreat. Down the hammer came, a pulverising blow that smashed a score of them aside as easily as if the creature had been crushing ants. It lurched forward, booming out its hollow roar, swung again, demolished another score of the Ossiarch cavalry. Splintered bone, sundered horses, shattered armour went flying across the battlefield. The creature kicked out and smashed half a regiment of Mortek Guard to pieces, then came in with its crackling hammer for another devastating assault.

It was like being in the centre of a whirlwind. Bones and broken weapons went reeling past him. Akridos tugged the reins, leapt one of the Lumineth's cavalry pits, was almost thrown from the saddle as a broken skull from the Mortek Guard came rocketing across the battlefield and struck him in the side. With the Deathriders who had followed him, he found himself far ahead of the

Ossiarch army, near the curve of the ridge as it swept along the side of the valley and turned off into the slopes of the mountain. The temple, shielded by its complex of barriers and palisades, was off to his right, the forecourt no more than twenty feet away. He could see the Lumineth troops reforming, their surviving cavalry clattering across the forecourt after having skirted the entire battlefield and routed the Mortek Guard on the right flank. Akridos could see scattered pockets of his infantry trying to assault the temple's southern quadrangle, cut down in twos and threes by the aelven archers, who were still firmly established in the long grass on the edge of the battlefield.

'Curse you, Y'gethin!' Akridos screamed, hacking at the air in his rage. 'The gods themselves will not save you from me!'

He clutched Kathanos' skull, wavering in his saddle. He could see Morfilos further back, desperately whipping the shattered bone of the wrecked Ossiarch troops into new forms and flinging them up at the stone creature's impossible armoured bulk. Spears of bone as big as tree trunks lanced up to strike it, but it batted them aside with its hammer. As Akridos watched, it stomped forward and crushed Morfilos under its cloven foot.

It was the Stonemage who had done this – he had somehow conjured this furious avatar into being, dragging it from the bones of the mountain and setting it loose with rage in its petrified heart. It was the Stonemage who had frustrated his every effort, who would deny him the victory he craved and the empire he longed to carve out in this miserable realm. It was the Stonemage, Y'gethin…

He seemed to hear the voice of Kathanos, deep in his mind or drifting across the mayhem of the battlefield.

You hate him because he is of you, and you are of him! The aelven soul inside you is part of his soul too, Liege-Kavalos. You will never defeat him. You cannot, because to defeat him would be to defeat yourself.

'Silence!' he growled.

He clutched the skull, stared at the Lumineth troops preparing themselves on the other side of their barriers. He glanced back, saw the mad rampage of the stone creature as it struck into the blocks of Mortek Guard, scattering them like so much detritus, the vast hammer rising and falling as if it were nailing each warrior into the ground. The monster's booming call rumbled across the battlefield like a thunderstorm.

You know it is true, Akridos! You have failed... You have betrayed Nagash with your insolent ambition! You have condemned your army to bitter defeat. The Light of Eltharion will live and will frustrate our master's ultimate design. You have failed, Akridos. You have failed!

'I said, silence!' he cried.

He shattered the skull in his fist and cast the fragments to the grass. He looked across the short stretch of ground to the temple forecourt. He still had near a hundred Deathriders at his back, and hundreds more Mortek Guard were scrambling away from the stone giant to join him. Half his Immortis Guard had been destroyed in the monster's first assault, but ten of them staggered now across the churned grass towards the Lumineth barriers. Battered but not broken, with such troops Akridos could conquer the Mortal Realms themselves.

He saw the Stonemage gathering his own forces, readying his fell magics, his eyes burning like the dawn. It was a meagre band, but Akridos knew they would defend their mountain to the death. So be it.

'Deathriders,' he said in a level tone. 'Follow me.'

The Spirit of Ultharadon...

It had not been seen in generations, not since Teclis himself had returned from the moon of Celennar and taught the mysteries of the aelementiri to the aelves of Hysh. Summoned out of the bones of Ultharadon, clad in plate and armed in stone, it was the soul of the mountain made manifest, a sight of awe and majesty come to wreak vengeance on the enemies of the Lumineth. Long had it slumbered in the depths of the valley, waiting, resting – until Carreth had descended to make peace with the mountain, and to cleanse his soul in utter self-abnegation.

Now it thundered over the pilgrim's way, crushing the Bonereapers underfoot, swinging that brute hammer and sundering the Ossiarch army all along the line. Carreth saw it in action and felt only awe, and it was all he could do to stop himself cowering in obeisance before it. The Spirit of Ultharadon had turned the tide at the last minute, throwing the Bonereapers into disarray, but Carreth knew that he couldn't be complacent. He hovered there above the cracked flagstones of the forecourt, the fountain behind him, scanning the battlefield. The mountain's war form was churning its way through the bulk of the Bonereapers in the centre of the field, even as skeletal troops desperately tried to stab at its armoured calves or scale its legs. The spirit brushed them off like flies. Carreth looked to the line of spiked barriers in front of him, manned by aelves who were fighting with every ounce of their strength against the Bonereapers who had decided to press on rather than deal with the immense threat behind them. Ahead of him, Thaerannan drained the dead energies of the Lumineth troops' aetherquartz and threw them back in sinuous blasts towards the ranks of the dead, immolating them, scattering them like leaves on the wind. But no matter how many they destroyed, always there seemed to be more behind.

The dead were legion, and they fought without fear.

Alithis rushed up, a bruise livid against her cheekbone.

'The bulk of the troops are through. My Stoneguard hold the line while the wardens reform towards the ridge, but we can't hold them back for much longer,' she said. 'Even with...' She looked over her shoulder at the spirit of the mountain, hammering its way through the press of Bonereaper troops. 'I know you told us this would happen,' she whispered, 'but by Teclis himself, I can't believe it's really true.'

Carreth nodded. 'You've performed miracles,' he said, 'as I knew you would.' He looked to his right, saw Belfinnan leading his troop of Dawnriders onto the forecourt after their mad dash around the perimeter of the battlefield. The steedmaster galloped over, his sword in hand, his shield notched and dented.

'The war machines are well accounted for,' he said brightly, flashing his smile at them. His armour was mired in dust, and there was a streak of blood down his breastplate from a cut on his neck. 'Didn't quite feel sporting, cutting them down like that,' he mused. 'Foul things, those Crawlers, but it felt almost like the work was too easy.'

'The hard work is yet to come,' Carreth said. He pointed his staff at the Deathriders who had scrambled out of the Spirit of Ultharadon's way when it emerged from the valley – a solid wedge of cavalry, with hundreds of troops to back them up. 'There is where we must strike.'

Akridos, he thought. *The tides of battle bring you closer than I dared to hope.*

He saw the Liege-Kavalos rallying his troops on the edge of the valley, his steed rearing up, his scimitar outstretched. Their eyes met across the field, across the heads of their troops and the lines of the sharpened stakes. So close were they now, no more than an arrow's flight away...

Carreth felt the pull of his sister's soul, smothered in that creature's disgusting form, but he pushed it to one side. There would be no saving her now. There could be only the duty he had been assigned, and the will of the Mage God made manifest.

He looked to Belfinnan, to Alithis and Aelthuwi, still stalwart at his side. He saw Thaerannan draw close, bare feet padding against the flagstones. The wardens sprinted across the forecourt to take up position by the barriers, even as the sentinels ranked up behind them, arrows nocked. All of them looked up at him, weapons ready, armoured in their courage, their trust in him. Carreth swallowed and gripped his staff, and when he spoke it was like his voice was moving through him from a plane far out of reach, high in the heavens or hidden in the void.

'Long have we held ourselves aloof from the troubles of the Mortal Realms,' he said. 'It took my sister's death to make me realise that trouble will find us all the same. It took my own failures to make me understand that we fight not for survival, or for selfish motives, or even out of a sense of vengeance or grief. We fight for each other. We fight for Hysh, and we fight against the endless drear fate that Nagash would inflict upon it. We fight for the Spirit of Ultharadon.'

'Ultharadon!' they cried.

'We are the Lumineth Realm-lords, the enlightened of Hysh, and this war will not be the end of our enlightenment. Fight with me now, my friends!' Carreth shouted. He held up his staff, basking in the clash of weapons, the roar from the Vanari wardens as they gripped the barriers, the frenzied whinnying of the Dawnriders' stallions. No more than five hundred troops all told, but Carreth had such faith in them he would have led them against any foe in the Mortal Realms. He would have charged the very gates of Shyish and cast down Nagash himself.

'Belfinnan?' he said. 'Lead the way.'

'It will be my pleasure, Stonemage!'

Belfinnan reared his horse, leaning forward in the saddle, his bright blade extended. The light struck his armour and seemed to burn the dirt and dust away. He held the moment, carved there in that light like a statue, and then, as his riders surged up behind him, he spurred Gyfillim forward and shot off across the forecourt, hooves sparking on the flagstones. At the same time, the wardens lifted and drew back the barriers, the Stoneguard unleashing one last hammer blow to send the front rank of the Bonereaper infantry reeling backwards. Carreth held up his staff and his throne of rock began to rise. He muttered incantations, peeling off the flagstones from the forecourt with geomantic force and skimming them far out across the battlefield to smash down into the Bonereaper cavalry as they began to charge. He sped forward, aware of Alithis and Aelthuwi running behind him, the wardens following the surge of Dawnriders as they cut through the gap in the barrier and smashed into the Ossiarch force like a knife stabbing into water.

'Ultharadon!' they cried – all of them, from the Dawnriders to the wardens, from the Stoneguard who smashed the outflanking Bonereaper infantry aside to the sentinels who lined up against the barriers and sped a rain of arrows far over their heads to plunge down into the ranks of the dead army far behind. There was carnage, mayhem – a tornado of violence speeding through the packed ranks of the foe, Belfinnan bellowing orders as he hacked right and left, Carreth following in the Dawnriders' wake as he cast spell and counter spell, immolating the dead with arcane blasts. They surged through the Ossiarch army, a spear tip stabbing straight for its foul heart.

Carreth saw the Spirit of Ultharadon turn to meet them, looming over the battlefield, great, mantled shoulders like the crust of the mountain itself, sweeping its vast hammer and cascading dozens of skeletal troops to either side. He saw the Bonereaper cavalry start their counter assault from the edge of the valley, stampeding over the bones of their comrades in their haste to blunt the force of Belfinnan's charge.

'Akridos!' Carreth cried. 'Face me now!'

He ripped up the ground between the two rampaging forces with a twist of geomantic energy, tearing a gouge into the earth and throwing the dead riders off course. Akridos, at the head of his troops, leapt his steed over the gap and raced onwards, sword outthrust.

'I see him!' Belfinnan called over his shoulder. 'On, my riders! Cut them down!'

It was like an immense spear piercing a shield, Dawnriders smashing into Deathriders, aelf and skeleton thrown together in a shattering collision. Horses shrieked as they were hacked down; Deathriders screeched with frustration as they were hewn to pieces, bones scattered on the churned grass. Carreth saw Belfinnan sweeping his blade out to behead three of the skeletal riders at once, but then Gyfillim, rearing, took a spear in the throat, unleashing a heart-rending scream as he fell backwards. Belfinnan tumbled from the saddle, spinning to his side and landing badly on his arm as the wounded stallion collapsed on top of him.

'Belfinnan!' Alithis cried. She leapt into the press, hammers swinging in a blur, smashing dismounted riders, dead steeds and the surviving Bonereaper infantry all around her. She planted herself by the stricken steedmaster, standing over him, a twisted snarl on her face, hammers raised.

Around her, the two cavalry forces pushed and hacked at each other, bogged down, each striving for advantage, brute force ranged against the aelves' finesse. Carreth felt a pulse in his soul, a sick, dragging sensation that had him clutching his chest. He saw Akridos launching himself forward, leaping over tangled bodies and broken horses, his sword drawn back for a killing blow at Alithis. The seneschal readied herself, leaning in as if trying to make headway against a hurricane. On the Liege-Kavalos came, with murder in his sick green eyes, his steed kicking out its hooves.

'Tuareth…' the Stonemage whispered. He saw his sister on the plains of Shyish, Akridos leering above her, the blood sheeting down her face.

Carreth, darting above the tangled ruin of the battlefield, leapt from his throne and floated to the ground in a nimbus of crackling power, his robes billowing out behind him, his staff outthrust in one hand. He landed in front of the seneschal and stabbed his staff down into the earth, sending out a rippling geomantic shockwave that threw the Deathriders back in a blast of blue light. Akridos was cast down from his steed, crashing into the ranks of skeletal infantry behind him. Into the space Carreth had carved in the Bonereapers' lines came two ranks of Vanari wardens, rushing forward, their shields locked, pikes outthrust to form a bristling barrier.

'Belfinnan!' Carreth called. 'Help him, Alithis, drag him out.'

The seneschal crouched at the stricken steedmaster's side. Belfinnan's face was grey, his eyes unfocused. Gyfillim cried no more, the stallion's noble blood pouring out into the grass. Alithis took hold of Belfinnan's shoulders and tried to pull him out from under the horse's body.

'Leave me,' he wheezed, gripping her hand. 'Keep fighting… until the battle's won… Fight, my lady. Don't… don't give up…'

'I won't,' Alithis said. Carreth could see the emotion roiling in her, the strength she needed to master it and leave him where he lay. She leaned down and kissed Belfinnan's forehead, and when she turned again with her hammers in her hands, her face was a mask of unyielding resolution.

The wardens formed a circle around Carreth as he began to cast his spell. He planted his staff in the earth and clutched it in both hands, his forehead bowed against it. He closed his eyes and stilled his breathing, tried to shut out the frenzy of the battlefield around him – the clash of weapons, the screams of the dying, the clatter of broken bone. He felt the Spirit of Ultharadon draw close, striding over the battlefield like a colossus, its stone hide pitted with scars, its armour scratched, its hammer drifting out a trail of bone dust as it bludgeoned the Ossiarch army out of its path.

None of this existed for him now. He closed his eyes and began to gather the threads of magic, plucking them from the burnished light of Hysh. There was no battle. There were no armies, no warriors pressed together in the bitter dance of combat. There was only the earth beneath him, the mountain above and the soft pulse of his sister's soul guiding him to where he needed to go. Carreth reached out to that soul – not with the grasping fingers of the death magic he had used before, but the way a brother would reach for his sister's hand before saying farewell.

His steed was a jumble of broken bones, shattered by the Stonemage's magic when he hit the ground. His Deathriders had been scattered by the enemy cavalry's charge or thrown back when Y'gethin ripped the earth apart underneath them. Mortek Guard fought in ragged bands rather than disciplined ranks, some hacking at the aelven horses as they barrelled into them or trying to spear the bristling phalanx of Lumineth warriors ahead. Behind was utter chaos, the stone colossus rampaging through the Ossiarch ranks and destroying entire units with each blow of its hammer. There were piles of dead around him, bodies of aelves and carcasses of bone, and the battle itself had degenerated into such mayhem that Akridos had no idea if they were losing or on the cusp of victory. He staggered to his feet, his sword in hand. His helmet had been cleaved in two and cast to the ground, and his cheekbone had been shattered by a pike thrust that would have blinded a mortal man. As he got up, Akridos saw another pike come spearing towards him. Deftly he sidestepped, parried with the flat of his blade and lunged forward to pierce the aelf in the throat with the point of his sword. The aelf spat blood, dropped his pike, eyes wide with shock. Akridos reached in and threw him aside, opening a gap in the line. Four Mortek Guard took advantage, pushing in with their shields, their skulls immediately shattered by a rain of hammer blows. Akridos snatched a shield from the ground and weathered the strikes as the hammer came down again and again, stabbing out with his sword to open up one aelf's face to the bone. He hacked down, chopping an arm off at the elbow. More of the Guard surged in, battering blows aside, choking the gap with their bodies. Akridos stabbed to the side and cut into an aelf's thigh, slicing the meat from hip to knee. The aelf screamed and fell, and more Guard threw themselves at her, hauling her down, short swords stabbing into her stomach. The next aelf in line dropped his pike, tried to draw his sword, but Akridos was on him too, ramming his scimitar into his ribs and pushing up until the point came lancing out of his throat. The aelf spewed blood, spattering it over Akridos' skull. He could hear an avalanche thundering over the battlefield behind him – the avatar of the mountain, demolishing what was left of the army. Akridos ignored it. There was only the ground underfoot, shaking and slippery with blood. There was only the enemy in front, the duel of blades, the gouging, shearing, biting madness of battle. This was warfare in the old style, warrior against warrior, shield to shield, and for the briefest moment Akridos almost felt that he was alive once more, that the blend of souls that roiled in his bones was but one soul entire, the one he had once carried in him with no more thought than he gave to the clothes on his back. For a moment he was a man again, a warlord on the Stalliarch Plains, a kingdom under his feet…

And then the gap in the Lumineth line widened and he saw Y'gethin, wreathed in a pale blue flame, staff planted in the earth and eyes squeezed shut with concentration. He stood there amidst the detritus of battle, the dead horses and dead aelves, the piles of bones, the mangled grass and the pools of blood. Akridos howled his name, but it was lost in the tumult. There in front of him was everything he had ever wanted to defeat – the sickening echo of the soul Kathanos had planted in him, the lord of this land and the mountain that towered above it, the king he would supplant until the kingdom was his once more. Akridos howled and drew back his sword as he staggered forward, elbowing aelves and Ossiarch troops aside, no more now than an arm's length away from the Stonemage.

'Kathanos!' he cried. 'You see? I have not failed! I am victorious at the end!'

Carreth walked the path of light and stone as the battle raged around him, sealed off from his grief, indifferent to every danger. The screams and war cries were no more than muffled thunder, and the breath of every blade as it swung past him was merely the passage of the breeze. He felt Akridos draw near, felt him envelop Tuareth's soul like a shadow, but it was the easiest thing in the world to brush that shadow aside and take hold of the light. He held it in the palm of his hand. In the aetheric plane, he looked down and gazed at the tumult of his sister's soul, flattened, stretched out, violated – but still recognisably Tuareth, her unquenchable spirit. It swirled like an eddy of cool water, like a drift of cumulus in a bright, unclouded day. It shone like a light in the darkness.

'Goodbye, my sister,' he said – and he let it go.

It was like all the dry marrow of his bones had been steeped in fire. Akridos screamed and dropped his sword, his eyes blazing in a flash of liquid green. He threw his skull back and screamed again at the raging blue sky above him, bare of cloud, washed with the piercing light of Hysh. The bones in his neck cracked and shattered. He felt the aelven soul dragged out of him, saw some drifting echo of it as it turned and dissipated on the breeze. He clutched his soul gem as it flared and sputtered. He lurched forward, fighting for every step, as if he were trying to walk through a storm. The battle was a haze around him, a blur of moving shapes and floating light. There was only the Stonemage ahead of him, and it was as if he were towering above the battlefield, as tall as Ultharadon itself – adorned with light, inviolate, something hewn from the very landscape of Hysh. He felt the Stonemage pluck the souls from him one by one, sifting them from the uneasy whole and allowing each to break apart in merciful oblivion, and as each of them was unhooked from his body they seemed to cast back an echo of their pain and suffering, a spiritual metastasis that took the residue of their agony and increased it a thousandfold in moments.

Akridos felt every atom of those agonised souls burn through him as they faded into nothing, scorching his foul unlife from his bones, bursting the soul gem on his chest plate – and if he had had eyes to weep, he would have cried for his folly in that moment, for the Stonemage had proved himself a more terrible foe than he could have possibly imagined.

He was the Light of Ultharadon, and he was invincible.

He felt blood pouring from his nose with the effort, a pain that split across his head. Black borders began to swamp his vision, but still Carreth held the web of magic tight around the Bonereaper's form, pinning him in place while the sundered souls of every mortal creature that had been pressed into his foul service were finally unshackled and allowed to drift away into a natural dissolution. The souls swirled around him, a pale mist, a glinting vapour that burned away like fog in the sunlight. Akridos stretched his jaw until it cracked and fell away, but if he made a sound in his silent scream then Carreth couldn't hear it. The battlefield was just a rumble in the background, and the clash of steel was no louder than the patter of the rain on the mountainside in spring. He felt his staff burning in his hands, and he was dimly aware of the Spirit of Ultharadon striding closer through the blundering press of troops, bludgeoning its way through the Ossiarch ranks. Akridos stood there with his arm outstretched, grasping towards the Stonemage, but any motive force in him had now been freed, and the backlash of all that spiritual torment had petrified him into no more than a motionless statue, a grotesque sculpture abandoned on the grass of the pilgrim's way.

Carreth collapsed, utterly spent, reeling to the ground and looking through black, burning eyes at the Spirit of Ultharadon as it came closer, closer, the ground beneath its feet shaking like an earthquake. The hammer rose, impossibly slow, and when it fell it was like the world ending. Down came that twin-headed anvil, a slab of rock near twice as big as Carreth himself, blocking out the light, and in one smooth motion struck the statue of Akridos, Liege-Kavalos of the Stalliarch Lords, and pulverised it into a cloud of bitter dust.

Carreth fell against the grass and rolled onto his back, aware in some faint way of the surviving Dawnriders leading the charge, the wardens rallying, the sentinels unleashing their deadly shot, the Stoneguard striking their hammers down on the shaken ranks of the Bonereapers. They were no mindless automata, though – they were warriors used to fighting on their own initiative, and they would fight to the very end. Carreth tried to get to his feet, but he felt Alithis by him, her restraining hand on his shoulder.

'Rest now,' she said, and her voice came from a thousand miles away. 'You have done enough, and then some. Aelthuwi, stay with your master. See he comes to no harm.'

He tried to speak, but the words would not come. He looked

up into the sky, a tempered wash of blue. Either in the light of Hysh or the light of his mind, he saw Teclis and Celennar striding majestically against the grim ranks of Nagash, obliterating them, the Light of Eltharion like a shining sun at their side. He reached out but his hand passed through them, and then he realised that what he had seen was not the Mage God at all but the radiant form of his sister, Tuareth, smiling down at him.

'I'm sorry,' he said, although whether he spoke the words or only thought them, he didn't know. 'For everything I didn't do, and everything I did. Forgive me.'

You are forgiven, she said. She leaned down and kissed him, and Carreth closed his eyes at last. *Find peace, my brother. You have earned it.*

EPILOGUE

SENLUI

It was a clear day, cold, with a hint of autumn threading through the air, a crisp breeze that carried with it the scent of leaf mould and woodsmoke. The grass shivered on either side of the pilgrim's way. The path itself was a trampled mess, but the field had been long cleared of the dead. The bodies had been buried, the bones had been burned, and the broken weapons had either been repaired or smelted down. The ruffled grasslands rolled away towards the Ymetrican veldt, a sparse and undulating spread of emerald and amber for a thousand miles. It was all so peaceful, Alithis thought as she gazed across it. An ocean of untroubled land, and in the distance the rising peaks of Paerthalann, the glint of silver as the veldt unfurled into a far chaparral, dusky and sere, but no less beautiful for that. It was their realm, she thought. All of it. And they had saved it.

Belfinnan sighed, leaning his weight on his right leg. The left was still weak, and his broken right arm had been carefully set and bandaged. He had a long, fiery scar against his cheek, and one eye was buried in a lurid swirl of bruises. Alithis stood by his side, her hand resting on his shoulder. Both of them were dressed in simple robes, their armour put away at last, their weapons sheathed. Together they looked down at the grave. They had buried Gyfillim where he had fallen, the stallion's final resting place marked by a simple cairn. With effort, Belfinnan knelt and laid his hand against it. A tear slid from his eye and pattered on the stone. His mouth trembled. Alithis squeezed his hand and helped him up.

'In all the years I have spent fighting,' he said quietly, 'the battles and wars I have fought in, the friends I have lost... I don't think any death has hit me as hard. I feel it in *here*.' He struck his breast. 'I raised him from a colt, you know? We found his name together as we rode the plains of Xintil, rider and steed, tracking through the wastes and plunging through the deepest forests. He was the spirit of *Senlui*, swift as the wind across the steppes... He was me, and I was him. And now some part of me is dead forever.'

Alithis leaned up and kissed his bruised cheek. She felt her own scars burning, and when she turned to leave Belfinnan by the graveside, every wound she had suffered in the battle seemed to throb at once. She grimaced as she walked back towards the temple, but behind the pain there was a note of triumph – and of relief. They had come through. Some of them had made it.

The damage to the temple hurt her almost as much as the wounds. One of the twin pillars that held up the rotunda had crashed to the ground, where it lay in three pieces on the forecourt. The dome listed dangerously to the side, although the surviving votaries were already trying to raise some scaffolding to support it. The fountain in the forecourt had been badly damaged, struck by the Bonereapers' dread artillery before the Dawnriders had silenced them. The central basin had been cracked and the sacred ox-head masks through which the water tumbled had been cast to the ground in fragments. As Alithis walked across the forecourt towards the northern quadrangle, she saw broken windows and scorch marks against the marble, places where the stone had been scarred by the passage of war. The gardens in the southern cloister had been trampled and ruined, the site of a bitter last stand by a regiment of Bonereaper infantry. They had formed a square amongst the fragrant calcimine flowers and the stargazer jasmine, and they had stood their ground to the last as they were shot down by the Vanari sentinels. That had been as far as the Bonereapers got. Ultharadon itself was inviolate, and Alithis paused to look up at it now, soaring and majestic, terrifying and comforting all at once. The soft autumn light glanced against its peaks, and the pine trees on its lower slopes quivered in the breeze. She thought of the mountain's war form, the Spirit of Ultharadon striding from the valley, stepping from legend into the brutal present. Never before had she felt such awe, such gratitude. They would have been overwhelmed without it, no matter how bravely they fought. Ultharadon had turned the tide, and nothing had been able to stand against it. Carreth had done that, she thought. He had purified himself in the darkness of the valley, and his purity and sacrifice had called out the sleeping spirit. He had saved them all.

She walked around the cloisters in the northern quadrangle and found him far over on the other side of the ornamental gardens. He was sitting on a bench by the banks of the pond, the moon bridge spanning the water above him. Like Alithis, he was dressed simply in mourning robes, although she saw that his travelling bag was on the ground at his feet and his walking staff was beside him.

'You're leaving?' Alithis said as she joined him on the bench. Carreth didn't look up. He held something in his hands, turning it over and over in his fingers. Tuareth's brooch, she saw.

'Thaerannan has returned to the Valley of Desolation,' he said. 'I'm going to join her there for a while. Pray, make penance, study.'

'What about the temple? There are so many repairs… and what about Ultharadon?' She gazed up at its dominating peaks, soaring high above the temple on the other side of the ridge. 'You would leave it now, after all it has done for us?'

Carreth smiled. 'Ilmarrin can oversee the repairs, and I know the temple will be protected while you remain to guard it.' He looked up from the brooch in his hands, staring with Alithis at the cleaving bulk of Ultharadon as it loomed over the quadrangle wall. 'The spirit of the mountain has returned to its slumbers. I have given it rest amongst the pinnacles and in the deepest valleys. In the vales and the passes and the gorges of Ultharadon, it sleeps – until we need it again.'

'Will we?' she asked. She thought of the savagery and mayhem of the last few weeks, the storm of combat and the dread of waiting for it. Surely they deserved some peace?

'Hysh has been saved,' Carreth said. 'The Light of Eltharion destroyed Arkhan the Black at the realm's edge, and Teclis himself has banished Nagash from his physical form, for the time being at least. I have fulfilled the task Teclis gave to me.'

'Then the war is won?'

'Wars are never truly won,' he said. 'If nothing else, I have learned this now. A million armies march, no matter where you look. We have tried to keep ourselves aloof, but war found us all the same. I have no doubt that in the years to come the Lumineth will need to take up a more active role in the affairs of the Mortal Realms.'

Alithis dropped her gaze. The thought should have worried her, but strangely she found a sense of resolution where the fear should have been.

'I feared the Bonereapers would be the end of enlightenment in this realm, and in a way I was right.'

Alithis started. 'I don't understand.'

'The "end" of something can also mean its purpose, its ultimate condition. Their invasion has shown us that enlightenment must have its utility as well.'

'So be it,' she said firmly. 'The Stoneguard are much depleted, but I will build them up again into a force to be reckoned with.' She looked at the brooch as he turned it over in his hand. 'Tuareth is at peace now,' she said. 'You gave her that, at the end.'

'I did. And she gave me something in return, I think.' He held up the brooch, his thumb moving over the blackened shard of the dead aetherquartz. 'She gave me truth. The courage to confront it, the humility to accept it. I had spent too long pretending to be what I was not. I played the role of Stonemage, and I played the role of her brother. In truth, I was neither.'

'I don't accept that,' Alithis said. She leaned forward, her elbows resting on her knees. She stared down at the lapping water of the pond as it wrinkled to the bank.

'I have made my penance for it,' he said. His voice was calm, measured. There was not a trace of emotion in it. 'I have moved another stage up the Teclamentari, and I am truly one with Ultharadon now. I am who I was always meant to be.'

She looked into his face, his grey eyes like a winter sky, his white hair. There truly was something of the mountain about him now, she saw. Cold and unyielding, impermeable. Like stone.

Alithis touched the back of his hand briefly and stood up from the bench.

'I will see you when you return,' she said. She bowed her head. 'Stonemage.'

She left him sitting in the gardens, clutching the brooch his sister had made. As she headed back into the temple, Alithis felt something clutching at her heart – sadness, grief or just the pain of all these necessary sacrifices. She turned and looked back at him, sitting there motionless on the bench – as solitary as the mountain, the Stonemage of Ultharadon.

She stilled her heart and went inside. There was work to be done.

The gold had been scratched and dented, and the shard of coal-black crystal was beginning to crumble under his touch. Carreth held the brooch in his open palms.

The breeze rippled across the water, a chill breath of the changing season. *Senlui*, the breath of the wind… Wherever the wind blew now, there she would be. Her soul was gone, but the memory of her would be with him, always.

When the morning had faded into the afternoon, Carreth stood with the brooch in his hand and looked out across the water. He raised the tarnished metal to his lips, and then cast it far out into the middle of the pond, where it fell like a shard of sunlight.

'Goodbye, Tuareth,' he whispered.

He shouldered his pack and took up his staff. He looked at the mountain, and the light of Ultharadon fell upon him like a blessing.

ABOUT THE AUTHOR

Richard Strachan is a writer and editor who lives with his partner and two children in Edinburgh, UK. Despite his best efforts, both children stubbornly refuse to be interested in tabletop wargaming. His first story for Black Library, 'The Widow Tide', appeared in the Warhammer Horror anthology *Maledictions*, and he has since written 'Blood of the Flayer', 'Tesserae' and the Warcry Catacombs novel *Blood of the Everchosen*.

YOUR NEXT READ

REALM-LORDS
by Dale Lucas

When disaster strikes their mountain home, a trio of Alarith Stoneguard must gather a band of heroes to stop vile Slaaneshi Hedonites from devastating the entire realm.

For these stories and more, go to blacklibrary.com, games-workshop.com, Games Workshop and Warhammer stores, all good book stores or visit one of the thousands of independent retailers worldwide, which can be found at games-workshop.com/storefinder

An extract from
Realm-Lords
by Dale Lucas

Ferendir stumbled on loose rock resting in dry soil. He first fell forward, overcompensated by shifting his weight backwards, then felt gravity – sure and inexorable – seize him. There would be no course correction – he was falling, and the steep, thinly wooded slope was about to thrust him away from its cold, sere face as though disgusted by him. In desperation, Ferendir whirled his arms, hoping to save himself from a painful impact and a merciless slide back down the steep incline. Further on, ahead and above him, he saw his master, Serath, turn back to stare.

Surely that was the worst – not the slip, not the fall, not even the impact to come, but Serath's cold, appraising glare and silent disapproval.

Then a gentle pressure upon Ferendir's back steadied him. His fall was arrested, his humiliation postponed. His other master, Desriel, had stopped his backward fall with an outstretched hand. Regaining his balance and planting his feet widely to stabilise himself, Ferendir lowered his eyes. Deep within him, buried beneath layers of physical conditioning and mental inculcation gained throughout his years as a supplicant to the mountain temple, he felt the seething, roiling forces of his emotions, like subterranean waters warmed by geothermal vents, made turbulent by a sudden underground tremor. Embarrassment, relief, fear, self-loathing – all were so close in that horrible instant, so present just beneath the mask of calm he fought to project to his mentors, that he could almost taste them.

Breathe, he ordered himself inwardly. *Just as they taught you. Regain your composure. Centre yourself. It was just a misstep… an understandable accident.*

But was it? He raised his eyes to Serath again, further up the slope.

Serath makes no such missteps, does he? That is why he looks upon me with such disdain, such disappointment. Nothing I do will ever be good enough for him.

And Desriel. Quiet, compassionate, supportive Desriel. He makes a good show of believing in me, maintaining his patience no matter how often I make mistakes, but he is probably ashamed of me on some level, as well… certain that I'm unequal to what's ahead.

The trial. My final trial.

Perhaps my final anything.

Stop, that cold, quiet voice within him said again. *Fear will destroy you. First things first, now – just get up the mountain without another fall.*

Ferendir forced himself to follow the voice's command. He continued to breathe evenly, consciously, to count slowly backwards as he did so, inhaling on the even numbers, exhaling with the odd.

Inhale. Exhale.

His heart rate slowed. The subtle tremors in his hands disappeared and the sweat upon them began to evaporate.

'Shall we continue?' Desriel asked quietly.

Ferendir opened his eyes. Looked up the steep incline of the mountainside. Saw Serath up ahead, silently impatient, still watching, radiating a vaguely disdainful air.

'Onwards,' Ferendir said, and resumed his climb.

Today, he faced his final initiation rite as a supplicant and acolyte of his Alarith temple. He could not afford to let a single misstep, a single, foolish mistake, ruin the calm and confidence he had worked so hard to cultivate within himself in preparation for this final, harrowing rite. He must be present, mindful, ready for anything yet expecting nothing.

Today, he would suborn himself to the mountain's will and beg its blessed sanction.

Today, he would be buried alive.

If the mountain accepted him, he would survive the ordeal. If, on the other hand, it found him unworthy…

'We linger too long,' Serath said from above.

Ferendir forced himself not to raise his eyes or meet Serath's disapproving gaze. From behind him, Desriel answered.

'Patience, Serath,' his master said. 'Our young supplicant was simply recomposing himself.'

Serath persisted. 'Had he stepped carefully, noted all possible impediments to his passage and skilfully avoided them, he would not have slipped, or fallen, or lost his composure.'

He could hide no longer. Trudging on, never breaking stride, Ferendir raised his eyes to meet Serath's, however difficult doing so might prove.

'I beg pardons of both of you, my masters,' the supplicant said. 'Please, let us continue.'

He lowered his eyes to the path, set one foot before the other and said no more. He leaned into the steep slope and chose his footholds swiftly but carefully.

The terrain they moved through – deep in the Ymetrican mountains of the realm of Hysh – was sparsely wooded and dreary, slate-grey knobs of cold stone and dry, subalpine soil scattered with towering sentinel trees and blanketed here and there with cushions of moss and islands of sedge. Hand- and footholds were not hard to find – there always seemed to be some jutting stone, the gnarl of a tree root or a narrow shelf of tightly packed earth awaiting his employ. Ferendir concentrated on finding the best of these, determined not to slip again simply because he had failed to closely examine where he planted his feet. As he trudged onwards, he sometimes used his small, delicate hands to assist in his ascent. He could still hear the burbling rush of the last stream they had crossed before beginning their climb, far below them, because the wind-wracked forest around them was so deathly silent, so funereally still.

Ferendir stole a glance upwards at Serath, to see if his stoic mentor yet lingered above him. To his chagrin, Serath had not moved. His master stood, bedecked in his shining white plate armour chased in gold, leaning upon his long-handled stone mallet. One of Serath's booted feet was braced upon a bleached-white tangle of deadfall wedged between two thin, sickly trees, and the stoic Stoneguard stared down at his long-time apprentice with his familiar reproachful glare. Ferendir could not tell if that expression – so subtle, so inscrutable – was a sign of complete disdain or simple pity. Serath held Ferendir's upturned eyes for only an instant, then turned his back and began to climb again.

Behind him, Ferendir heard Desriel begin to hum quietly – a slow, melancholy tune. Ferendir recognised the sombre melody at once as one of the temple's hymns, a wordless song taught to all the servants of the mountain. Its dolorous melody and slow, lilting cadence were designed to sharpen one's senses, to suppress one's conscious thoughts and widen one's consciousness – a sort of musical state of meditation, useful when undertaking laborious physical tasks such as a slow climb up a steep, wind-scoured mountainside. Ferendir was tempted to join Desriel in humming the old hymn – he had always loved the sense of plaintive peace that it stirred within him – but a part of him was reticent.

It was Serath. Though Ferendir now bore down upon his master with his senses and struggled to listen closely, he could not hear Serath humming. Serath, apparently, was centred, focused and fully present without the benefit of the hymn's quiet, hypnotic power. Therefore, Ferendir, determined to earn Serath's respect if not his affection, would do as *he* did, and remain silent, no matter how much he wanted to join Desriel in his song.

They had set off in the early hours of the morning, when the dim Hyshian twilight that constituted night was yet upon them and most of the temple Stoneguard and acolytes yet slept. His masters were each fully armoured and carried their personal weapons – an elegant diamondpick hammer for Desriel, a massive, long-hafted stone mallet for Serath – while Ferendir himself, facing a trial, wore a supplicant's tunic and had only been permitted to bring along his well-worn yew staff and a small dagger. Their path led them north-west, along one of the many narrow hiking trails that criss-crossed the rolling ridgelines and deep valleys of the mountain, taking them far from the lovely, well-hidden, tree-packed dell in which their temple resided towards the thick, shadowy forests that blanketed the mountain's western slopes. After hours of following the hill-hugging trail, they finally came to a rocky stream tumbling down out of the woods. At the stream, they left the path and followed the wending waters deeper and deeper into the shady hollows and rough-hewn gullies that formed the uneven geography of the mountain. Just as the full light of day began to bleed back into the world – Ulgu's darkness waning at last before the imminent glow of the Perimeter Inimical – they finally came to the lower edge of the thinning subalpine forest that marked the beginning of the end of the mountain's life-sustaining lower slopes. Whereas before the rolling, climbing landscape had been thick with intertwined, leafy decidua and tall, needly dreampines shading banks of shaggy verdibrush and beds of sprouting toadstools, the world above the stream suddenly exhibited signs of weariness and surrender. The spaces between the trees widened. Green turf and fronded ferns were replaced by dry soil, bald stone and isolated beds of spongy moss or obdurate sedge.

Hour by hour they climbed, the light invading the thinning woodlands growing brighter and brighter, even as the gusts blowing down from the mountain's heights grew colder and more insistent. The world stirred little, only a few lonely birds offering sad songs while from the last clinging shadows beneath the thinning trees they heard the rattle of tiny claws on stone and the soughing, subtle passage of small, fleet bodies. The moribund forest, the steepening mountainside, the air above and around them – everything, no matter how austere and faded it appeared, showed signs that it was alive, awake, hungry. This was one of the most basic lessons imparted to young supplicants of the mountain temple – or any temple, for that matter.

There is life in everything, desire in everything, will in everything. One forgets that fact at great personal peril.

Around them, the pines fell away. The only trees remaining upon the mountainside as they climbed, higher and higher, were stunted, pale and permanently bent by the hitching winds that raced down in gusting squalls from above. Those trees – spread far and wide, no hope of creating anything like a true canopy – hunched and curled against the slope, leafless and ragged as sun-bleached banners frozen forever in a wind-whipped frenzy.

Here, even that which grew slowly and stood impassively against the elements was bent into submission, subject to the implacable will of the mountain and its cold, furious winds. Seeing before him the evidence of just how merciless and unrelenting the mountain's will could prove to be, Ferendir was suddenly filled with a mingling of both awe and dread at what he was about to undergo.